BEACH

A NOVEL

LAWYER

AVERY DUFF

THOMAS & MERCER

Published by Thomas & Mercer, Seattle

www.apub.com

Amazon, the Amazon logo, and Thomas & Mercer are trademarks of Amazon.com, Inc., or its affiliates.

ISBN-13: 9781503943926
ISBN-10: 1503943925

Cover design by Faceout Studio

Printed in the United States of America

This novel is dedicated to each of my parents, Frank and Betty Duff.

PROLOGUE

He knew he didn't look like the typical person who wound up in this small room using the pay phone. But right now what he looked like didn't matter. Given the handcuffs locked onto his wrists, he was just another criminal inside, making a call and hoping for a way out.

"Bring my laptop when you come," he said into the scuffed plastic receiver. "They took my phone, that flash drive. I know it looks bad, but—no—I didn't do anything . . ."

The dark room grew even darker. He stopped talking, turned, and looked through the small Plexiglas window with SUK MY DIK etched into it. A uniformed cop blocked the light, peering in at him.

Turning away, he spoke lower into the phone this time. "I think it'll work out. Those faxes . . . oh . . . I already said that? Okay, thanks, no, really, thanks, I mean it. You're the only person I trust to do this."

He hung up and pushed open the phone-room door. As the uniform took his arm and led him down a long hall, he limped, favoring his right leg, which pained him whenever he put weight on it.

The uniform asked him, probing, "Guy like you, how'd you wind up in here?"

Knowing better than to answer, he kept quiet as the steel door from booking slammed shut behind them, and they headed along the twin bank of cells. Not many other occupants back here. Couple prisoners draped across their bunks, drunks judging by the odor of ammonia and booze reaching out to him. Still, his cell was clean. Ten by twelve, toilet in the corner, a steel bunk bed bolted into the wall.

Once uncuffed, he stepped in alone, took a seat, and told the cop, "You guys gotta talk to Venice. Seriously, they'll back me up. Where's Officer Sedgwick?"

"Told you, I don't know any *Sedgwick*, and nobody's doing nothing till morning anyhow. Doctor said you weren't dizzy or vomiting from that lick on your head, but he'll drop by to check on you in a couple hours, so . . ." He shrugged. "You're good to go."

Good to go? He was pretty sure his jailer got off on making that crack. Once the cop locked him in and left, the prisoner eased himself off the bunk, knelt down, and looked under the bed. The floor was dusty and he gently swept his hand across it, smoothing out the surface.

With his index finger, he wrote: *L@L@918-------L@L@.*

Trying to make sense of it, he said, "La, la, nine, one, eight, blank, blank, blank, la, la."

For several minutes he tried filling in those blanks on the floor and inside his head. Finally he gave up, made it to his feet, and hobbled around his cell. Six foot one, 190, athletic with dark brown hair close-cropped, he looked like a thoroughbred or like he came from people who owned them. More than that, he wasn't a person who liked his forward momentum blocked. Then again, what he looked like and what he liked didn't matter. He wasn't going anywhere except over to his cell door.

Looking back down the empty hall, he wondered when things started coming unraveled. Was it that broken glass in the picture frame, or was it the phone call at his apartment? What if he'd never answered— would he be behind bars now? Then again, maybe it all started way before either of those things, back when he was growing up on the family farm.

That puzzle was too much to solve right now, so he laid his face against the cold, painted steel and knew one thing for sure: he wouldn't be locked up on suspicion of murder if it hadn't been for one person.

He thought about the day all this began. Nothing out of the ordinary, was it? Up before dawn, rolling down the Venice boardwalk on his ten-speed beach cruiser toward the outdoor handball courts. Three concrete walls, a partial ceiling, and no back wall, just two players who would soon square off in the predawn hours.

Moist air misted his face. Nobody else roamed around the beach quite yet. That day had all the earmarks of a good one, and an hour later he was on the courts, crushing that Latino, the one with all the attitude whose name escaped him. Working the guy, about to finish him off.

He could envision his serve: a spinning blue handball compressing against the concrete front wall, and until the ball caromed away, its true direction was a mystery to his opponent. And Robert Logan Worth, attorney-at-law, age thirty-one and change, pictured that day and slowly closed his eyes . . .

CHAPTER 1

Venice, California, Ten Weeks Earlier

A bulked-up Latino in a white ribbed tank top lunged late for Robert's serve as the ball flew past him into Robert's waiting hand.

"Match point coming up," Robert said, stepping back to the service line.

The Latino didn't say anything. He was too pissed off.

"Hey, *ese*," Robert said, "you see Jacobson's cruiser? Said he had something to ask you?"

"Something about this?" The Latino grabbed his package. "Serve, *cabrón*."

Robert bounced the ball a couple more times. "Sayin' a guy looked like you was runnin' from a meter maid."

"Oh, yeah, I did her. She's wantin' more's what it was. *Vámonos pendejo*."

"What I heard was, you got off so quick, cops're hunting *El Rápido*."

The Fast One. The Latino opened his mouth to top the insult, and that's when Robert ripped his next serve down the line. Even so, the Latino got to it and underhanded a high, rising arc, forcing Robert out the back of the open court. He got to it on the run and managed a looping return toward the front wall. In play but weak, and he jammed back inside the court.

An easy shot for the other man, who let Robert's return bounce once, then *bam*! The Latino smacked it as Robert ran past. No way Robert was going to get to it in time. The ball hit low and died. Fifty-fifty it touched the wall first, not the ground, but it was still so dark, neither player could tell.

"Perfecto," the Latino said anyway. "Coulda saved you all that runnin' around, *abogado.*"

Arms raised, giving himself the point, he was posturing for the other three *cholos* in the concrete bleachers behind them. By their ink, it looked like they were Venice 13.

Reserving comment, Robert went to the front wall, knelt, and looked at the blown-in beach sand on the pavement. The initial sand mark was a good inch away from the front wall. Clearly, the shot was short and hit the ground first.

"Short. My point. My game. My match," he said, standing.

"Fuck you say?"

He closed on Robert, fronting him. But Robert wasn't someone who made a habit of backing down, and right now he wasn't even thinking about it.

"Yeah, fuck I say."

Now those bleacher *cholos* finished a shared Colt 45 quart. The one leaning back watching the beef was Raymundo Reyes, who went by Reyes. The others looked to him for a reaction, but he wasn't giving them anything.

Back on the court, the beaten Latino got in Robert's face, took it up a notch. "What? Out? All on your say-so?"

"Hey, look at the mark, you don't believe me."

He gave Robert a chest bump. Robert bumped him back harder, bracing for a fight, and said, "The mark, *cabrón*. Look at it. It was short, not even close."

"Bullshit, *ese*! Fuck, man, tell you what, I let you take it over."

"Not happenin', bro, gotta go."

Now Reyes came down from the bleachers and approached the players.

"You believe the shit you hearin', Reyes?" the Latino player said.

"Stay out of it, Reyes," Robert told him.

"Was my point. I beat this *güero* any day, any time."

"Between us," Robert said to Reyes, and he meant it.

Reyes said, "I hear you, *Roberto*, but hey." Now he spoke to the other Latino. "*Mi abogado* says ball is out, so it's way the fuck out. Feel me, *homey*?"

The guy got the picture fast and moved to the bleachers as Robert and Reyes headed for the bike rack. On the way, Robert checked his cell phone: 5:47 a.m. Saw a few incoming e-mails and sent back a couple of quick replies.

Reyes said, "Thanks for writing HSN, *hermano*. *Mi esposa* don't know how she find a stolen credit card up in my crib."

"Yeah, man, a real Home Shopping Network mystery."

Reyes pulled out a roll of cash. "How much I owe you, lawyer man?"

Robert unlocked his bike and hopped on. "Keep it, but don't say I worked for free. You'll kill my rep on the boardwalk."

"Boardwalk, shit. You destined for the big time, *hermano*." They bumped fists, then Robert rolled over to the Latino player, extended his fist, and said, "You'll take me next time, for real."

The guy bumped back and said, "*Sí*, next time, *güero*."

As Robert pedaled away, digging hard toward home, Reyes called out, "You gonna be big time, *Roberto*. ¡*Seguro!*"

"Big time," he said to himself, rolling up the mist-slicked bike path, past the dead-quiet, still-shuttered rows of knockoff-everything stalls, food nooks, and cannabis vendors.

To the west, the Pacific was still fogged in, but he could feel vibrations from waves crashing on the breakwater's granite mass. Eternal forces at work, the world's unknowable pulse beating faintly beneath his rolling wheels.

He checked several old voice mails as he cruised toward home. Several female voices: "Hey, Robert, it's me, I—" Delete. "Robert, right? Don't know if you remember me. I'm an actress, and we spoke at—" Delete. "You still live down at the beach? I was thinking about coming down this weekend, hanging out—" Delete.

Then his workday calendar showed up. It was jammed.

Pocketing his phone, he picked up his pace, dodging a drunken man pushing a boosted grocery cart. Alongside the bike path, scattered forms lay on the ground. Junkies in boxes and the walking-around crazed tucked in among young seekers, cozy in North Face bags and Schopenhauer T-shirts, a comet tail of humanity strewn along the manicured grass-scape.

Robert swerved off the bike path, crossed over the boardwalk, and pedaled a half block inland onto Speedway. Several miles long, Speedway paralleled the ocean, running north from Marina Del Rey through Venice and ending one block inside Santa Monica at Rose.

Corner of Speedway and Club, a coffee shop opened its doors, and a cop car was pulling up. Its driver chirped Robert, who waved to the cop behind the wheel. Officer Erik Jacobson, a deceptively intelligent Swede. Given his blond hair and body mass, Latinos liked calling him *El Oso Polar*, the Polar Bear. Erik hated it, ignored it, or liked it. With him, it was hard to tell.

"Bear claws on me!" Robert shouted out.

Another cruiser chirp as Robert sped past more blocked-off, car-free walk streets feeding east-west into Speedway. Past a girl in four-inch spikes and a sequined mini—wait, was that a man?—walk-of-shaming down Wavecrest Avenue. Then past Park Avenue and Paloma till he hit

Ozone, leaned hard, and cut right. He rolled up this walk street's rise till he reached a classic gray-frame bungalow with white trim.

He opened the gate, checked his mail, and walked his bike down the bungalow's side walkway to a three-car garage in back. Over it rested a framed addition, bootlegged by an owner in the seventies, when nobody cared what happened down here. Back when this part of the beach was trouble town.

Shouldering his bike, he walked up the weathered wooden stairs to his door. Grabbed his key from his pocket. Unlocking one dead bolt, then another one, he finally keyed the door handle. As he swung open his door, he checked his iPhone again: 6:05 a.m.

In the distance, someone was cranking up Ice Cube's LA rap anthem "It Was a Good Day." Like most people, Robert heard those lyrics and had to smile before he hurried inside.

And so far, Cube had it right. It was a good day.

CHAPTER 2

Inside an elegant sixth-floor foyer, an elevator light blinked green. Its polished doors glided open with a subdued chime reflecting the portal of a law firm. Robert stepped out with his laptop case in hand. Wearing a sports coat and tie now, he followed an oriental runner toward two mahogany doors laden with heavy hardware, keyed the firm's lock, and opened the door.

First, though, a ritual. He looked at a bank of names in brushed stainless steel on the wall. The top row: FANELLI & PIERCE, PC, ATTORNEYS AT LAW. Below this were the names PHILIP FANELLI and JACK PIERCE, followed underneath by five other partners' names. Most important to Robert was a thin, horizontal bar: the dividing line between partners and associates. Right below the bar, topping all other associates' names: ROBERT L. WORTH.

He stared at all twenty-two names. Then at his own. Same as he did most every morning when he was first to arrive at the firm. Ritual completed, he stepped through the door into the reception area where four Eames chairs faced one another on either side of the receptionist's desk. On each side wall hung a single painting. Both of them looked old and expensive. The one to his left belonged to Philip Fanelli. It was an elegant California landscape from the thirties: an arid windswept coastline, two cypress trees clinging to a cliff. On his right was an energetic canvas splashed with bright colors and hewn by scribbled lines. On the frame's base: *Artist Cy Twombly: From the Collection of Jack and Dorothy Pierce.*

He hardly noticed the artwork anymore but stopped here to feel the stillness and hear the faint hum of dormant office machines. As he headed past the receptionist's desk, he allowed himself a smile because he liked being first.

Once he made the hallway, the litigators' offices were to the right. So he took a left, heading into the corporate end of the firm where lawyers like Robert plied their profession. Past a handful of empty offices, he stepped into a no-frills kitchen, not so tricked out that a client would remember he's the one paying for it. After opening a bag of Peet's coffee, he got his first pot of the day going and kept moving.

Near the hallway's end, he opened the door to his office and went inside. Through his four narrow windows lay eight-inch slices of the building next door. If he angled sideways far enough, he caught a glimpse of the ocean and the Santa Monica Pier, but from any angle, it was not a partner's view.

He set down his laptop on an orderly desk dominated by a large computer screen. Behind the desk, document stacks sat on a long credenza. Post-its reminded him in red Sharpie about a closing this afternoon.

After switching on his laptop and office computer, he entered his password and logged in to the firm's workflow system. As his phone, computer, and laptop begin to sync, he grabbed a John Deere coffee cup and walked out.

An array of family photographs rested on his credenza beside the documents. Two of them stood out. The first was taken at a racetrack: a good-looking couple, early forties. His parents. Son, Robert, about twelve, wore a coat and tie like his dad. Everybody was posing, focused on a horse, its head wedged between father and son. In the second photograph: the front of a rustic, columned two-story home. Robert stood on the front porch in a tuxedo, his hair slicked back. The girl beside him wore a prom formal. Both of them were about fifteen years old and smiling those smiles most kids have on prom night.

A minute later, he returned with his coffee cup filled, noticed a swarm of incoming e-mails. All of them concerned one client: Brightwell Industries.

Once he saw what had happened to his morning, he grabbed a seat. *All right, dude, let's kill it,* he was thinking.

First, he downloaded a deal-related, redlined Sale and Purchase of Assets Agreement attached to the earliest e-mail. Brightwell was buying Palmer, Inc. back in Tennessee, and Tennessee law governed, so Brightwell, on Robert's recommendation, associated with Nashville counsel to take the lead drafting this agreement. The next hour or so he spent absorbing and editing that firm's twenty-one-page document. His changes were fairly minor until he reached Section 29: Representations and Warranties. That stopped him.

He muttered, "Gimme a break."

Working on his laptop while watching the big monitor, he opened his system file to Case File 3940 and typed a memo:

> Note: Brightwell/Palmer Contract
> Case #3940
> Re: Section 29 Reps & Warranties
> I informed our TN counsel: Client refuses to warrant that it has not committed any violation of applicable law. Client will warrant *only* that nothing has been brought to *its actual attention in writing* by proper authorities re: violation of law. Consider this point material to transaction and will so advise Client. Will also advise our TN counsel *again*, monitor.
> RLW

He saved the memo on the firm's case-management system, and as it disappeared into the ether, he entered .80 hours of billable time on his time sheet.

Next on his calendar: *Prepare Directors' Resolutions Brightwell/ Palmer.*

Still the same deal, but now he was tasked with making sure Brightwell's board of directors had properly approved the deal. Diving back into the firm's system, he found a set of Brightwell board resolutions from 2011 when it purchased a similar company. That sales agreement was very much like this one. So were the board resolutions. He knew that because he had drafted both documents.

In the body of the 2011 document, below its bold heading, appeared a series of double-indented paragraphs. Five pages of paragraphs each beginning with *whereas* or *resolved* or *further resolved.* These fact-filled resolutions, once signed, demonstrated that Brightwell's board had evaluated, and only then approved, the deal. When he reached the director's signature lines, he knew to delete one name: *Oliver Dudley.*

He took a gulp of coffee, remembering the deceased director from a lunch with Oliver and Philip, Robert's mentor. The Philip Fanelli on the firm's masthead had been Oliver's closest friend before Oliver passed away.

The pair had started the firm back in 1965. A soft-spoken man, Oliver had a knack for getting along with everyone, and in '05, he married Lionel Brightwell's only child, Dorothy. Soon after, Oliver left the firm to take on the job of Brightwell Industries' general counsel, only to die in his sleep in 2011. That was one short year after Robert came on board out of UC Hastings College of the Law.

He recalled Oliver's funeral—the entire firm showed up, partners' wives as well. Dorothy Brightwell was torn up over her dead spouse. Philip, too. Come to think of it, that was the only time Robert had seen Philip drink to excess, and he wound up driving Philip home.

While the rest of the firm gathered at Lionel Brightwell's Bel-Air estate after graveside, Robert returned to the office to work on a dog-bite case. So called because Dorian, Lionel's beloved beagle, had allegedly bitten a trespasser. The victim claimed he was lost, merely asking directions from the cook. Problem was, he asked directions from inside the gated estate's wine cellar. Rather than hand over the case to his homeowner's insurance, Lionel wanted to fight the fraud tooth and nail, believing both that Dorian was well within his rights and that caving to any shakedown got you a reputation as a pushover. As usual, Lionel Brightwell was right on the money.

Once Robert pushed back hard, the other lawyer folded. No way he wanted to fight Brightwell to the ends of the earth and recover zip, not even his own court costs. Robert had to admit, he'd been relieved. Going to trial on a dog bite or on any other case? Not his area of expertise—he'd never tried a lawsuit. But when you're the new guy, still getting your feet wet, you get going . . . or you get gone.

Robert pulled himself away from that day and quickly deleted Oliver's name—his signature line, too, because Oliver's board seat had never been filled. After reviewing his changes to the new resolutions, he e-mailed them to Brightwell's offices for directors' signatures.

That done, he was off to his next calendar entry: *Ragsdale*.

The Ragsdale deal had nothing to do with Brightwell Industries. It was a $7 million sale of a company by one of Philip's new clients, but so far Philip was MIA on this afternoon's closing. He hurried two doors down the hall to Philip's corner office and slipped through his open door.

A single Siamese fighting fish cruised the aquarium as Robert noticed a set of Ragsdale closing documents on Philip's desk. Easy to see that Philip hadn't touched them. In fact, while Robert's office was orderly, Philip's looked clean to Robert. As in unused.

Sprinkling fish meal into the water, he asked the fish, "Where's our guy, Spartacus?" Spartacus swam to the surface, gulping breakfast, as Robert made it back into his own office and banged out an e-mail.

To: Philip Fanelli
Subject: Ragsdale closing
Need your comments to closing dox.
Will see you there, right? (Fed Spartacus.)
Thx, RLW

When he finished, it was 8:06 a.m. As of that minute, Robert L. Worth, senior associate, had logged 108 minutes of solid work. That work was broken into six-minute intervals and had been entered on his time sheets. All told, one-point-nine hours of billable time. One-point-six hours of it would be billed to, and the firm would collect on it from, Brightwell Industries.

Those *billable hours* are mother's milk to the legal machine. Without those hours, law firms would eventually grind to a malnourished halt.

✢

Fanelli & Pierce's receptionist fielded calls on a busy switchboard as a male and a female client waited for their lawyers. The uneasy woman in jeans, Crocs, and a soft leather jacket was Alison Maxwell. Her vacant stare at the Cy Twombly painting was the most animation she could muster, overwhelmed as she was by whatever put her in this particular Eames chair.

A lawyer appeared from the inner sanctum. Alison started to stand, then watched the other client leaving with his own lawyer. She walked over to the receptionist, who held up a single finger—*wait*—and continued purring into a headset.

Once done, the receptionist asked Alison, "Yes?"

"Mr. Pierce? I had a ten o'clock appointment? It's been, I don't know how long . . . I have a job and—"

"I'm so sorry, but . . ." She checked the switchboard. That raised finger again. "This may be him. All right," she said into her headset.

"I'll send her right down, sir." Then the receptionist said, "Ms. Maxwell, Mr. Pierce is in Conference Room Three. Turn right, then it's straight down the hall on your right."

"I know, thanks," she said.

In the hall, unescorted by an attorney, she moved tentatively till she reached the conference room and knocked on the door. No answer, so she knocked again. Then waited, wondering if she'd made a mistake. She was turning away when she heard laughter behind the door. Then a voice said, "Come on in."

Once she opened the door, the first person visible at the conference table was Chase Fitzpatrick. Early thirties, an associate like Robert, but slick. Gym-toned with great hair, Chase was good-looking in a way that could make straight men uncomfortable.

Keeping his seat, Chase said, "Alison. Come on in. How goes it?"

"Oh," she said. "Fine."

Jack Pierce sat at the head of the table with Alison's thick legal file in front of him.

"Ms. Maxwell," Jack said, checking the Patek Philippe watch on his wrist, not bothering to stand, "grab a seat."

Alison closed the door and took a chair.

Only then did Jack see any need to rise, shrugging away his forty-two years as easily as he did the Loro Piana jacket he was wearing. Masculine and tough, at the top of his game. A man wholly confident in both who he was and what he wanted, not inclined to make excuses for either.

"Now, Ms. Maxwell," he said, "apparently we failed to connect in our previous meeting. So for the final time, here is exactly where you stand with me and with my firm . . ."

Down the hall from that conference room, Gia Marquez headed toward the corporate end. Heels, tailored slacks, and a pin-striped shirt with an open collar. Arms swinging free, the firm's office manager was on the move, peering into offices, nodding to the lawyers inside. Easy to see how walking anywhere near this woman might make a man feel more alive.

She stopped at Robert's half-open door, rapped softly, and leaned against his doorjamb. "Mr. Worth?" she said.

Robert looked up from his work, a bit dazed from concentrating, but he smiled when he saw Gia.

"Good morning, Ms. Marquez," he said, leaning back in his chair. Clearly, their *Mr. Worth and Ms. Marquez* routine cloaked an office flirtation. "No roses for me today?"

"Not yet. My Karl Lagerfelds bloom next month, right on schedule, but your time sheets are three days late. We simply cannot have that kind of . . . what's the word?"

"Sloth?" he asked.

"We will not tolerate sloth of any kind at Fanelli and Pierce. As office manager, I forbid it, not with the firm's bills going out next week."

"I'll get right on it, but only if you tell me one thing, Ms. Marquez. How totally awesome were Chase Fitzpatrick's billable hours last month?"

"That's highly confidential, Mr. Worth. I can only say Chase's hours were right near the top but, as always, not nearly as totally awesome as yours."

He liked hearing that news. He tried to stand before she took a seat, but she was too quick for him.

"Those two trial guys still doing their paddle-tennis thing?" he asked.

"Full-on bros," she said. "To hear Chase tell it, he's made a profound difference in Mr. Pierce's backhand."

Chase, they both knew, had been a tennis stud at UCLA till he blew out his ACL. While jumping the net after a humiliating loss, Robert liked to think.

"Good for Chase," he said. "We both know where his real talent lies."

"Ass-kissing?" she said. "Tops in his field, Mr. Worth, but isn't that how the game is played?"

"Beats me. I keep my head down, stay in my lane."

Gia said, "Hard work. Whatever happened to that?"

Robert gave her a three-fingered Boy Scout salute.

"You're no Boy Scout. I don't know what you are." She laid a slim pay envelope on his desk and said, "Why not let me direct-deposit your paycheck? Give me your bank info and you're good to go."

"I like walking over to the bank."

"Any particular reason?"

"Not really—stolen account numbers, wireless hacking, tossing your account into the cloud? Major banks have been breached already, and getting your money back? Can you imagine what fresh hell that would be?"

She thought about it a second. "For your balance, press one. Last deposit, press two. To find out where all your money went . . . forget it, dude."

"Yeah, get in line," he said, smiling.

"We're the only two at the firm who don't direct-deposit."

"You? Risk averse?" he asked. "Weren't you voted Most Likely to Bet the Ranch out at Santa Anita?"

Gia was about to return serve when his intercom buzzed. The receptionist's voice: "Mr. Worth. Mr. Pierce would like to see you in Conference Room Three. Right away, please."

"Got it," he said to her. He stood, grabbed his iPad, and slipped on his sports coat.

"Jack Pierce? Conference room?" Gia asked, standing, too. "Could this be your big day?"

"I don't know, could be," he said, and he wasn't joking around anymore.

She wasn't, either. "Your time sheets, please, Mr. Worth. Bills go out next week."

"Will do, Ms. Marquez," he said.

After he hurried out, she decided to check out those family pictures on his credenza. She settled in on the one of Robert and that girl. Him in his tux, her in a prom formal. Two young Brahmins, they looked like, on the front porch of that columned home.

Peering closer at the bottom of the photograph, she made out script in silver ink: *Rosalind & Robert Prom Night.*

"Rosalind," she said. "Sweet."

Leaving his office, she tossed a thought Robert's way: *Big day? Hope so . . .*

Out in the hallway, Robert headed toward the litigation end of the firm. Philip's assistant spotted him from out in reception and caught up to him.

"Robert?" she said.

He stopped, turned to look at her. "What's up, Sandra?"

"Mr. Fanelli won't be in the rest of the week."

"What about today?"

"I know, the *Ragsdale closing.* So, listen, he won't be at the closing, but he looked over your documents and said they're fine as is."

"*As is.* Good, thanks, I'll handle it," and he was on the move again.

Robert doubted Philip had read the documents. No problem; he would make a CYA memo to file, proud that Philip trusted his judgment to such a degree. At the conference room door, he knocked, opened it, and stepped into the room.

To his left, Jack headed the table, Chase to Jack's right. Alison was positioned several chairs down from them. Robert eased into a chair by the door across from her, but she kept her eyes on Jack, who was doing his thing: owning the room.

"Get over it, Ms. Maxwell. I'm telling you, you're going to take their goddamn offer."

"But—"

"The fine gentleman who just sat down is Robert Worth. He is from my corporate division. Do you know why I have summoned him here, Ms. Maxwell?"

"No," she said.

"He's here to draw up your settlement agreement. He will do so, he will do a terrific job, and then you will sign it first thing tomorrow morning."

"Ms. Maxwell," Robert said.

He handed her a business card across the table. She looked worn out to him and worn down by being in this room. She pocketed his card without seeming to notice him and stayed with Jack.

"But Brian is dead. He was only forty-one, and he got cancer from working at that warehouse."

"We'll never know what caused his death, not in a legal sense. And do you know why that is?"

She didn't answer.

"Failure to wear a dust mask. Failure to remedy same after two write-ups."

"But the company is lying about that. Why wouldn't they lie about it? Isn't that what they do?"

"Were his coworkers lying about him smoking—what brand was it, Mr. Fitzpatrick? Was it American Spirit Yellows? No wait. An e-cigarette, wasn't it?"

Chase made a production out of reading from her file. "Afraid not, Mr. Pierce. Lucky Strikes. Nonfiltered. Two packs a day, according to the depositions."

She said, "Those guys settled, so they're lying, too. He smoked a little on weekends, but he didn't even die of lung cancer. It was bladder cancer that spread to his lungs. When you took the case, you promised he'd have his day in court, like I promised my brother before he died!"

"Hey, why do you need *me*? Sounds like you have all the answers. Why don't you try proving that the guys who knew your brother are lying? Why don't you tell a Santa Monica jury—Santa Monica, where they string you up for smoking inside their houses—that your weak-willed brother chain-smoked Lucky straights for God knows how many years, and now his estate deserves a couple million bucks? You're welcome to go for it, Ms. Maxwell, because I won't!"

Robert watched Alison absorb the body shots. It was brutal, hard to watch.

"Take Mr. Pierce's advice," Chase added. "It's my experience that he's the finest trial attorney in Los Angeles."

She didn't listen to Chase. She looked at Jack when she said, "None of it's true, I think they're all lying, I . . ."

Her voice trailed, and she looked down. The room went quiet. Then she slowly raised her head and looked across the table at Robert.

"What do you think?" she asked.

The question caught him by surprise, but he didn't show it. "I've just now come on board, Ms. Maxwell. Sorry, but I haven't had time to review your file."

The truth, but it caught Jack's attention. He stood up, took the chair closest to her, a faint predatory vibe as he slid his chair even closer to her.

"Look at me," he told her.

He waited until she complied. Then he said, "Ms. Maxwell, the company is offering ten thousand dollars to settle for Brian's death. Now. You signed an agreement with my firm. In it, you agreed to be personally responsible for all costs. On the hook for costs that now exceed ten thousand dollars. Costs that you owe my firm. Now. Again. When you settle—and you will—my firm will use those ten thousand dollars to pay your costs. My firm will then graciously eat the rest instead of looking to you. Because ten thousand dollars, Ms. Maxwell?"

She looked away. She had started crying about halfway in.

"I said, 'Look at me.'"

She raised her eyes to his.

"Because ten thousand dollars is more than your brother's pathetic life will ever be worth."

Robert eyed a box of Kleenex on the credenza. Neither Jack nor Chase made a move for it. In spite of how much Jack grated on him, Robert fell in line.

Finally, Alison told Jack, "I'll think about it."

"Oh, you'll do lots more than that, Ms. Maxwell. See you in the morning. Nine a.m. sharp. That's when you sign off on your dead brother's misspent life, and we put this unpleasantness behind us."

She stood to leave. Jack kept his seat. Chase followed his lead. She walked around the conference room table. When she reached the door, Robert stood and opened it for her. With a mumbled "Thank you," she was gone.

When Robert sat down, Jack was staring at him.

"So. What do you think, Worth?"

"Once I review her file, I'll get that settlement agreement done, ready first thing."

"Not what I meant, Worth. What I meant was, do you find the litigation end of my firm's practice distasteful?"

"No, sir," he lied. "Not at all."

"This was my second go-round with her. I already froze her out in reception for an hour or so. Is that all right with you?"

"Of course, sir."

"So, tell me, why did you stand up? Why did you open that door for her when clearly I'm in the middle of breaking her down?"

"I'm not up to speed yet, Mr. Pierce. I can promise you it won't happen again."

"Make sure of it, Worth. Now look. Defendant's counsel gave me first crack at drafting her settlement and release, so what I need from you, Worth, is a release friendly to the other side. Friendly to them. One they *will* sign when I show it to them. No back and forth between the parties on this one. I want her case off my calendar, and I want that whining little bitch off my back."

"Will do, sir."

Chase said, "Tough set of facts, sir, but I've got a feeling you'd have found a way to win."

Jack eased back in his chair. "Let me share this with you, Chase. You, too, Worth. If I took it to trial, here's how it would go. I'd get those settled-out friends of Maxwell's on the stand and make them out to be liars, same with those company write-ups on his dust mask. I'd survive a motion for summary judgment, easy, and once she took the stand, spiffed up, I'd have her crying her eyes out. She's good at it, right, and I'd find enough people on the jury—all men, no doubt—who'd break off three, four hundred grand on her irrelevant sob story. Then again, how long does it take to try this case, Chase?"

"Ten days, easy."

"Or more, and for forty percent of four hundred K—my firm's cut? After the time I already spent? The numbers don't work."

"Not at your hourly rate, Mr. Pierce." It was Chase again.

Jack nodded and looked at Robert. "What do you say, Worth?"

"Cut the firm's losses, definitely. I agree," he said, even though he had no valid opinion of her case.

"Right you are," Jack said. "And right now, right this minute? Ms. Maxwell has learned my firm no longer validates her parking, and in another ten minutes, parking attendants down in the garage? Well, they'll have a devil of a time finding that beater she no doubt drove here."

"Got it," Robert said. "No friends at the firm."

"At my firm? Not a goddamn one," Jack said.

Chase asked, "Remember when she first signed on last year? She looked like primo tail, man."

Jack nodded. "She did look primo, didn't she?"

"Bet you any amount of money, that one's a tiger in the sack."

Jack rose to the occasion. "Wouldn't know about that, Chase. I'm a married man, same as you. But many years ago I heard, I forget where, 'Once you bring a woman to tears, you're halfway home.'"

"*Halfway home*, I feel you," Chase said, laughing.

Robert forced a smile, not his first, relieved he didn't have to pound it every day with these two. Even so, Jack picked up on his lackluster reaction.

"Am I right about that, Worth?"

"That's what I hear, too," Robert said.

"That release. First thing tomorrow, Worth."

"Yes, sir, Mr. Pierce," he said, already wondering how *first thing tomorrow* related to the 9:00 a.m. deadline Jack gave his client.

Jack stood, his eyes still on Robert. He hesitated, as if he might chastise Robert again, then he let it go and was out the door. Chase slid Alison's legal folder down the table to Robert and walked over to him.

"Let me give you a tip, Worth. That release better be letter-perfect or Jack will be very upset. On the other hand, your time on it will never get billed—so don't go overboard. And by all means, call me day or night if you have any questions."

"How do you do it, Chase? Your head's all the way up his ass, but your hair's still perfect."

"Go straight to hell, Worth."

"That's a stinger, Chase. Any more like that in your quiver?"

Chase's Adam's apple jumped as he swallowed, then he brushed past Robert out the door.

Let it go, Robert was thinking. *Just let it go.*

But as he picked up her file, he remembered the Fanelli & Pierce masthead out front. Philip's name came first. Then came Jack's name. So he couldn't help wondering about two words Jack kept using: *my firm.*

CHAPTER 3

"Everything okay?" Leslie DeRider asked Gia.

"Sure," Gia said.

"You sure?"

"We still on for dinner?" Gia asked, changing the subject with her friend.

Gia sat across from Leslie, a bank vice president whose desk was right off a wide-open lobby. Now both of them noticed Chase at the same time, exiting the elevator just descended from Fanelli & Pierce. Wasn't long before he started chatting up one of the female tellers.

"Chase ever hit on you?" Gia asked.

"Me and the fire hydrant out front," Leslie said, checking her lipstick. "Look at him—puts his wedding-ring hand in his pocket while he's talking. Plays with himself, I think."

"Shaves his arms and legs, too," Gia said.

"Do you go for that?" Leslie asked.

"Love it," Gia joked, "because I'm actually a gay man."

Leslie laughed, then Robert exited an elevator, so they checked him out next.

"Ever hook up with him?" Leslie asked.

"Never did," Gia said.

Both women watched him passing by.

"Why not? He's gorgeous," Leslie said.

Gia caught Robert's eye and waved. He waved back.

"Gorgeous? You think?" Gia asked.

Leslie thought about it. "No, I guess not. More like, you know, handsome."

They watched him till he walked out the glass doors, far end of the bank.

"Cool and handsome, yeah. A man," Gia said.

"Then why not?" Leslie asked.

"We work together's why not."

Leslie didn't buy it. "Got an hour till my next appointment?"

Then she stared at her friend till Gia said, "God, I don't know. I mean, we're friends."

"Meet-after-work friends or what?"

"Office friends. *Friendly.* Want me to put in a good word for you?"

"Forget it. He'd be major."

"Oh, yeah. Major-major," Gia added.

"And I've gotta get serious around here. I rolled in twenty minutes late today, and you-know-who was all bunched up about it."

"Jerome?"

Leslie nodded. "Probably have to take him out for drinks again."

"Drinks? *Drinks* is what you call it now?"

Gia looked at her until Leslie said, "I was drunk, okay?" She held her hands over her face. "Damn, I'm such a whore."

"Jerome?" Gia asked again.

"You're supposed to disagree." But Leslie was laughing now.

"I tried to, but seriously, Jerome?"

Gia picked up a canvas bag from beside her chair: the Fanelli & Pierce receipts. She stood. Leslie did, too. In her short skirt, Leslie was sexual to Gia's sensual, a couple inches shorter than Gia, the OC coastline spiraling through her DNA. They headed toward the business teller's window.

Leslie asked Gia, "Everything still . . . you know?"

"We're good, I promise. I'll give you a pass on Jerome if you promise me you're done with *Ho Daddy*."

"Don't call Dougie that. He hates it."

"Good. How about *junkie, loser, surf boy gone bad*?"

"That's harsh, Gia."

"First love, so what? I don't care how far you two go back. Guy hit you that time and you didn't press charges?"

"We still going to the track?" Leslie asked as Jerome waved from his glassed-in office. Waving back, she told Gia, "Smile at him, G, please? Act like he's got a shot with you. I'm in deep shit, please?"

Jerome was headed their way in a bold glen-plaid jacket—a pattern Johnny Carson might have worn at a Friar's Club roast.

Leslie whispered to Gia, "Think he's in love with me. Wife, two kids. Be nice to him, G, please?"

So, Gia waved at Jerome, smiled at him, too, and told Leslie, "Don't let Dougie near me, all right?" Before Leslie could answer, Gia stepped toward Jerome and made his day: "Hey, Jerome, love your jacket . . ."

CHAPTER 4

The white-marble statue of Saint Monica perched on top of the Palisades where Santa Monica Boulevard died at Ocean Avenue. In her cowl and robes, the statue resembled a luminous surfboard beneath the shivering, pencil-thin palms. Underfoot and all around, addicts got high and caught the ocean breeze from her billion-dollar view.

Across Ocean from her, Robert stepped out of a small bank, grabbing lunch on the run, and crossed Monica's namesake boulevard. As he neared his own building's lobby, a commotion caught his attention at the lip of its subterranean parking lot. A parking attendant was arguing with the driver of a beat-up LeBaron convertible. Its top was down. Alison Maxwell was behind the wheel.

He started to move on, but the driver behind Alison laid on the horn. Long and loud, its blare echoing deep into the bowels of the garage.

"Shit," he said, moving toward her now.

He checked his watch: almost an hour since she'd left the conference room. That's how long Jack's fun and games had held her up. As he drew closer, she saw him. Almost in tears, she went horizontal off zebra-striped seat covers, checking her jeans pocket for money.

When he reached her car, he asked, "What's the problem, Ms. Maxwell?"

"I don't have any . . . I didn't bring any cash, but you guys always validated, or I thought so, or I wouldn't have parked here, so I don't have—"

"Hey, hey, don't worry about it, please."

He reached for his wallet, gave the attendant forty dollars, got a few bucks' change back. In that car behind her, the driver laid on the horn again. A Love Is The Answer decal rode the front bumper.

"Happens all the time," Robert told her. "Don't worry about it."

"I'm so embarrassed. I'm . . . it's not a good day." She started crying for real, looking down.

"Better get going. That car behind you is late to save all mankind."

Alison tried to smile, but she couldn't pull it off.

"Take care," he said.

And as she pulled away, he walked into his building, disappointed in himself for reasons he couldn't quite pinpoint.

Hanalei Ragsdale stashed a letter-size envelope inside her briefcase. Inside it was her certified check. Her deal had just closed, but she kept sizing up her new lawyer, Robert Worth. He had shown opposing counsel the door and was stacking her signed documents on the conference table.

"This will take a few minutes, Ms. Ragsdale. Another cup of tea?"

"No, thank you. I'm fine now that it's over."

"That's about as smooth as it gets. We got lucky."

He was trying to stay as present as possible but closing her sale ran long. After that, Ms. Ragsdale—he smiled at her—and the buyers talked shop for another forty-five minutes. That meant starting his assignment from Jack was beginning to weigh on him.

Ms. Ragsdale told him, "What can I say, Robert? We won every point along the way, and here I sit with a certified check for my business. Certified funds for ninety-five percent of my initial asking price."

"They had the money and wanted your company. Only a matter of time before they got religion."

"I thought their lawyer was weak."

"I'd like to agree, but the truth is, he was stuck with his client. And I had you."

"Meaning?"

"Meaning you told me you were willing to walk away from the deal, so we played hardball. Those guys were playing T-ball."

She smiled.

"You were willing to walk, weren't you?" he asked.

She shrugged.

Hard for him not to like this sixty-year-old, tough as nails. "I'll messenger your executed set of documents to you. And, please, I want you to keep them in a safe place."

"There will be a set here, won't there?"

"Even so, with important documents, always keep a hard copy."

"Because?" she asked.

"Because you never know."

She liked his answer. "Impeccable logic, sir. Now . . . ," she said.

He stopped stacking papers and took a seat. "*Now*, Ms. Ragsdale?"

"I'm new to this firm, so bear with me. Six months ago, I met with another lawyer here before deciding to go with Philip Fanelli. The other lawyer's advice was to sue them to get their attention, to negotiate that way. Looking back on it, I'd say he was wrong, wouldn't you?"

Another lawyer? Sue them? She meant Jack Pierce. "Not necessarily," he said. "That's another way to go about it, Ms. Ragsdale. Philip has another philosophy, and this time we did great, but it's a judgment call." He played it right down the middle, a team player. But he agreed that Jack's tactics were wrong.

She said, "For the last three months, it's your judgment I've relied on, not Philip's. From now on, if I buy or sell anything, I plan to call you, not him."

This was a big deal to Robert. Once Philip signed off, she would be his client. That meant he would control her time sheets, get credit with the partners for her bills. A nice plus in his column whenever they got around to offering him a partnership.

"I'll check with Mr. Fanelli. I'm sure he won't mind."

"Lately, he wasn't around when I called. So if he minds?" She stood and shook his hand. "As we like to say up on Mulholland, if Philip Fanelli minds—fuck him."

Outside Robert's windows, somewhere past Point Dume, the sun dipped into the Pacific and bathed Saint Monica's face in a cotton-candy hue. "That sunset, it's Saint Monica blushing," Philip once told Robert. "Blushing from her husband's countless adulteries." Saint Monica, Robert read later, was indeed sainted for her suffering, brought on by a philandering husband.

Now the last lawyers from corporate drifted past Robert's door. He was unaware of them and of the sunset. His office door was closed, and he was buried in a file: *Estate of Brian Maxwell vs. Consolidated Construction, Inc.* Reviewing the estate's pleadings file, making notes as he read.

Even though he didn't try cases in court, he knew every lawsuit began with a *complaint* filed by a plaintiff. Basically, a beef. That was followed by the defendant's *answer*. A list of excuses: *Don't sue me here. You waited too long. I didn't do it. I did it, but it's not my fault. I did it, so what?* Together, these filings become the initial pleadings. As time passed, these pleadings grew from added facts and legal theories developed from interrogatories, which were lengthy, written Q&As.

Pleadings then swelled from depositions, which were lengthy, also, but verbal Q&As.

From what Robert knew now, Alison's brother's estate sued the construction company, Consolidated, for causing his death. It sued both for his personal loss and for punitive damages. Even though she was his estate's executor, Alison was also Brian's only living heir. That meant she, and only she, would inherit any damages that his estate collected.

The complaint Jack filed alleged Consolidated had used and processed building materials containing asbestos. That it did so maliciously, without caring if people around those materials were injured from inhaling their dust particles. As a direct result of exposure to that very asbestos, Brian Maxwell died from cancer at age forty-two.

Brian, it turned out, didn't work for the company. He was an employee of a security outfit that provided guards to Consolidated warehouses where stored insulation materials, allegedly asbestos filled, were cut to order. Brian's first problem—his own employer went belly-up and had been self-insured. That meant Brian was out of luck collecting worker's compensation from his own employer, leaving him with only Consolidated to blame.

In its defense, Consolidated claimed Brian didn't work for them, didn't wear their dust masks, lied about asbestos being stored at the warehouse, and that any asbestos product, even if cut to order on-site, had no effect on him. Besides that, Brian smoked, drank, rode a motorcycle to work, and was, in so many words, an all-around bad guy.

One thing was becoming clear to Robert. Starting out, Jack believed he had a shot at collecting punitive damages from Consolidated for using dangerous materials—asbestos—near anyone, whether that person was an employee or not. Then, the file showed, about nine months into it, a Colorado court made a finding of fact in an unrelated case: Consolidated never used these products in California. Not ever.

Even though that finding didn't get them thrown out of court—Colorado was in a different judicial circuit—it was bad news. Punitive damages—meant to punish—are a long shot even on the strongest facts. Sure, Jack could get Alison's case in front of a jury, as he'd said in the meeting. But gone was the day he could threaten punitive damages to leverage a fat pretrial settlement from Consolidated.

He got the gist of it now: the Colorado case turned the case into dead weight at the firm. A case Jack had to try in front of a jury. That meant the firm was now willing to settle for ten grand, nothing more than nuisance value.

Sorry, Jack, your firm, Robert was thinking.

His assignment was to prepare a document settling the case and releasing Consolidated from every imaginable claim Brian Maxwell's estate might have ever had against it. Almost comically, the release would cover the time period from the beginning of time to the present.

His immediate problem: find a release in the firm database for a situation similar to this one. Without that, he would be starting from scratch, facing an all-nighter and butting up against Jack's deadline.

First thing in the morning? Whatever that means.

The firm's database wasn't helping. This case was unusual. Firm lawsuits almost always involved companies suing each other and never involved personal-injury claims. This case? An individual injured in the workplace, who would normally sue under worker's compensation law, was suing a nonemployer for negligence or intentional wrongdoing.

As he stood to stretch, Philip's e-mail popped up on his screen:

Think this will help, Robert. Drafted it before you were born. Ha! See you tomorrow.

The attached release was drafted before the firm's archives were digitized. Scanning Philip's twenty-pager, Robert saw it wasn't exactly on point but had plenty of usable language. An estate. A nonemployee suing a corporation for bodily injury, and just like that, Robert gained seven or eight hours on his assignment.

Headed down the firm's empty hall, he figured he would hit the men's room and finish up at home. Maybe even get in a workout over at Gold's Gym. Past reception, he saw that the litigators had cleared out. Not unusual. They rarely stayed late unless working up oral arguments or faced with a court-imposed deadline.

He took a right into the law library, a closed-off area with multiple rows of shelves and a large reading area. Because several LexisNexis online research terminals had replaced many of the firm's law books, the reading area was largely vestigial.

Two more paneled turns would have put him at the men's-room door, but he heard an angry male voice from a narrow hallway to his left.

He stopped. That hallway led to Jack's office. The door was closed, but Jack's voice still boiled up from behind it, getting louder. Before Robert pulled back into the stacks, the door opened. Gia Marquez walked out the door, her head bowed.

He waited for what was coming, and there it was: Jack's office door slammed shut. He decided against a trip to the head. Last thing he wanted was to wind up at a urinal, side by side with a pissed-off Jack Pierce. God knows where that would lead, so he waited several minutes in the reading room before heading back the way he came.

Then he saw Carlos, a building security guard, outside Gia's door. That was the drill when you were fired: guard at the door, grab your personals, locks changed, system password changed, and out you went.

"Carlos," he said to the guard.

"Roberto," Carlos answered.

Robert peered into her office. Gia was packing her things into a trash bag. "What's up?" he asked her.

Her eye caught his—she was crying—then she went back to the task at hand, and he moved on. Headed toward his office, he glanced out into reception and saw Lionel's daughter, Dorothy, who had married Jack Pierce not long after Oliver Dudley's death. In a wheelchair sat the grand old man himself: Lionel Brightwell. Both in formal wear, father and daughter were studying that Cy Twombly painting. Robert decided to keep moving.

Back in his office, he packed his computer and asked himself, What was *that*? Gia in Jack's office. Gia fired. Then he forced her out of his mind so he could make damn sure he *ran into* the firm's bread and butter on his own way out.

By the time he hustled into reception, he wore his best game face for the powers that be.

"Good evening, Ms. Pierce, Mr. Brightwell. I'm Robert Worth."

Dorothy brightened and shook his hand. "Certainly, I remember you, Robert, from our firm parties." She leaned down, spoke into her father's ear. "Father? Do you remember Robert Worth? He's been up to the house, remember?" Lionel, pushing ninety hard, kept staring at the Cy Twombly. "Father, say hello to Mr. Worth. He works at the firm with Jack."

Before he had a chance to answer, Jack joined them. "Hello, dear," he said to Dorothy. "Lionel, sorry I kept you both waiting." He nodded to Robert without a word.

Lionel rotated his electric wheelchair to face Jack. "When did that painting leave the house?" he asked.

Dorothy stepped in. "I discussed it with you, Father. Both Jack and I discussed it with you at great length."

Lionel thought about it. "Did, huh?" he said.

"By the way, Jack, Father saw the results of his physical today, and we learned that he is in excellent health."

The elevator chimed as Jack leaned down to his father-in-law. "Glad to hear it, Lionel. That's great news for everyone concerned."

That polished elevator door opened. Jack took the wheelchair's helm and rolled Lionel inside. Dorothy nudged Robert and pointed at the California landscape.

"That painting, Robert? A much more accessible piece than the Twombly."

He nodded. "There's something about it," he told her as they stepped into the elevator.

"Something about it," she repeated. "There certainly is."

The elevator door slid closed, and Dorothy spoke first. "So, Robert, I hope you received our invitation for this year's get-together?"

"Sure did, and I'm really looking forward to it. Very much," he added.

"A house full of lawyers?" Lionel said. He asked Robert, "Tell me, Worth, what in the name of Christ could be worse than a house full of lawyers?"

"Plenty of things, sir," Robert said.

"Like what?" Lionel asked.

A beat, then: "I'll get back to you on that, Mr. Brightwell."

Hearing that, Lionel had a good laugh. "What is it you do around here to keep the lights on, Worth?"

He thought about mentioning the Palmer acquisition, then thought better of it. He doubted the chairman of the board was focused on a relatively minor deal in Tennessee.

"Whatever the firm needs, sir. Right now, I'm doing some interesting work for Mr. Pierce."

"Well, don't fuck it up or there'll be hell to pay. Ain't that right, Jack?"

"Right as rain, Lionel," Jack said, actually smiling.

The elevator door opened. Thirty feet ahead idled the Brightwell's Maybach. Rodney, their driver, headed over, smiling through his sub-par *Magnum P.I.* 'stache. Jack handed off his father-in-law to Rodney. Then he told Robert, "Remember what my father-in-law said about fucking up." He said it with a wink, but for some reason, menace laced the remark.

"Heard him loud and clear, Mr. Pierce."

"Good night, Robert," Dorothy said, shaking his hand. "It's so wonderful to see you again."

"Same here, Ms. Pierce," he replied. And he meant it.

Behind them all, a metal stairwell door squealed open. Carlos held it, and Gia exited with her garbage bag of belongings. Dorothy stared at her. Tensing, Robert thought, as she locked Jack's arm in hers. For his part, Jack looked straight ahead, not at Gia, then escorted Dorothy to the Maybach and opened the back door. Rodney loaded Lionel into the backseat beside his daughter. Jack got in front with Rodney, and the Maybach glided up the ramp into heavy fog.

Headed for his car one level lower, Robert's thoughts turned to Lionel Brightwell.

Ain't that right, Jack! Robert could still hear the West Texas hardpan and saguaro cactus in Lionel's voice. He came from the soil, same as Robert's family. Even though farmers and oilmen have little in common, if they're smart and lucky, they can sit on a lead and count their chips for decades to come. And Dorothy? A sweetheart. Maybe that had something to do with her mom working blue at Jack Ruby's Dallas strip club at the time Ruby gunned down Lee Harvey Oswald.

He heard a car coming up the ramp: Gia's roadster, a '63 Austin-Healey 3000 Mark II. Her convertible top was down. He signaled her to stop, but it looked to him like she planned to anyway.

"Hey," he said.

"Hey," Gia replied.

"Bad day?" he asked.

"Kinda," she said. "How'd it go this morning with Jack Pierce?"

"Okay."

"Just okay?"

"Not great but okay."

A moment of silence before Robert asked, "What the hell? How about you?"

She dodged the question. "Care for a piece of career advice, Mr. Worth?"

"What?"

"Always let him win."

"And you wouldn't, Ms. Marquez?"

"Let him win, Mr. Worth. *Always*," she repeated. "You work harder than anybody at that firm, harder than anyone I know in LA, and I hope things go your way."

He knelt by her window, eye to eye with her. In spite of being upset, she was trying to steer him in the right direction. That quality made him like her more than he already did.

"Let's grab a coffee sometime," he said. "Anywhere, your call, what do you say?"

She put her hand over his. "Nothing good can come of it. When a job's over, it's over. Believe I'll head to the track this weekend and figure out what comes next."

"Supposed to rain," he said.

"If you go fast enough," she replied, shifting into first gear, "you never get wet."

Then she peeled three feet of rubber onto the polished concrete floor and that was that.

CHAPTER 5

The Brightwell Maybach cruised past Bel-Air's white, arched entrance and guardhouse, past fairy-light–entwined greenery. As it eased up Bellagio Road, sprinklers sputtered on, misting the manicured lawns and ice-plant–quilted ravines. All around the cloistered canyon, the sharp smell of eucalyptus and cloying lilac mixed with the rotten smell of fertilizer.

Inside the Maybach, Dorothy mixed a vodka rocks at the minibar and chatted with her husband through the lowered partition.

"Everything was beautiful. Tony was so happy to have Father and me at his opening."

"Guess so," Jack said. "We were the best customers at his old place."

"Among the best, but still. He asked where you were, and I told him how busy you've been. Bistro Fresco, it's his dream. Small, dark, the best wine, best food, everything fresh. He's past the point where it's about money anymore."

"Ha," Lionel said. "Charged us for parking, didn't he?"

Jack smiled at his father-in-law. "Don't miss a thing, do you, Lionel?"

"Not much." After he said that, he kept looking at Jack. "Miss more than I used to, but I still see."

Dorothy said, "Oh, Jack, you'll love it. We'll go back this weekend, all right?"

"Perfect," Jack said. "Early dinner after tennis, now you're talking, darling." He reached in back and took her hand.

From out of nowhere, Lionel said, "Don't see why I can't have a nurse."

"Rodney, the glass, please," Dorothy said.

"Yes, ma'am," Rodney said. Jack pulled his arm away, and the partition rose.

Dorothy turned to Lionel. "But Rodney can lift you in and out of the car on his own, and besides that, he adores you."

"He's all right but his perfume makes my eyes itch."

"Cologne, not perfume."

"It's goddamn perfume. He showed me the bottle from Paris."

She laughed. "Well, perfume, then."

Lionel said, "All my life, sweetheart, I took the risk, hedged my bets, and raised a fine daughter, one I love so dearly."

She said, "I love you, too."

"And all I'm asking—is it askin' too much to see a nice pair of tits before I die?"

She started laughing. "We've already talked about this. You're not going to die, not for a long, long time."

"Is that another *no*?" he asked, still hoping for the right answer.

"Look, we're home," she said, peering out the window and reaching for a decanter.

At the top of Stone Canyon, the estate's gate opened. The Maybach headed up the Tudor mansion's cobblestone driveway, stopping under the porte cochere. Rodney opened Lionel's door. Jack did the same for Dorothy, who eased outside with a fresh vodka rocks.

Jack took her free hand. "Sorry about this, darling, but that call I took in the car."

"What call?" she asked.

"Something's come up back at the firm, and it requires my immediate attention."

Dorothy's face darkened. "That's not possible, we were just there."

"I know. I'm sorry as I can possibly be, but it's my name on the door."

"You're having an—Who is she, Jack? What's her goddamn name?"

"Don't talk like that. You know it's not true. I love you." Done talking, he kissed her cheek and headed for his Mercedes parked down in the drive.

Rodney pushed Lionel's chair till it stopped beside Dorothy. Her eyes never left Jack's car till it cruised past. Neither did her father's.

"Goddamn it!" she screamed and hurled her drink against the house, shattering the crystal.

"Why didn't you stay married to the other one?" Lionel asked.

He meant Oliver Dudley. Clearly, his memory was slipping a little. She turned to him, trying to calm down for his sake.

"Oliver died. Don't you remember his funeral? We both miss him but he's dead."

"Sure," he said, "I remember," but it wasn't clear he did.

Dorothy unlocked the front door, punched the alarm pad, and disappeared inside.

"Want to watch *Million Dollar Listing* with me, sir?" Rodney asked Lionel.

Lionel didn't answer. As Rodney pushed him up the ramp toward the door, Lionel said, "I don't care for him."

"Pardon, sir?" Rodney asked. "Who?"

"Bastard," Lionel said, his eyes focused and clear.

CHAPTER 6

Notes on Robert's laptop screen read:

~~Release all other Maxwell heirs, known or unknown.~~

~~Waive Section 1541~~

~~Release Consolidated affiliates, subsidiaries plus officers, directors etc.~~

No wrongful death claim brought by estate???

After showering at home four hours ago, he put Gia's firing behind him, best he could, and logged into the firm's system. Alone in his open, raftered living space, he had begun drafting the Maxwell release off Philip's e-mailed template.

Finally, he was down to dealing with the last legal issue: why didn't Jack file a wrongful death claim on Alison's behalf along with the estate's claim? Robert knew that California allowed two methods of collecting money on behalf of a wronged dead person: *wrongful death* claims and *survival* claims. But Jack's pleadings—Robert triple-checked—sued only on a survival claim.

A quick trip to the California code online reminded him of the answer. Something he knew when he passed the bar: parents and children can sue third parties for a child's or a parent's wrongful death. That claim compensates them for losing their loved one. Brothers and sisters of the same loved one, someone like Alison, cannot sue for that kind of loss.

A survival claim, like the one the estate filed, was different. That claim aims to compensate Brian's estate, not any of his relatives, for the injury done *to Brian* while he was alive. His own pain and suffering, that kind of thing. Alison would benefit because she was the sole heir to his estate, not for the emotional pain she experienced from losing her brother.

That left Robert with one question: Should he release Consolidated from wrongful death claims even though they didn't apply to Brian's estate or to Alison—and even though Jack never filed one?

Normally, he would wait for Consolidated to ask that wrongful death claims be released, too—and lawyers being lawyers, they *would* ask even though it didn't fit the facts. After some back and forth, he'd go along and get something in return. But this situation wasn't normal. Jack Pierce had been very clear: *I want a friendly document. One I can get them to sign.* That warning boiled down to this: draft the release like you're their lawyer, not hers. He decided to go along with what Jack wanted—*avoid the back and forth.* Release Consolidated from both types of claims up front.

A judgment call on his part. If Jack didn't see it his way, Robert would remove wrongful death from the release in sixty seconds and be done with it.

A few more hours of cross-checking the case file with his work and he'd be done. He was starting to breathe easy when his phone vibrated, then rang on the desk. It was from the local 310 area code. Not Philip's cell. He didn't recognize the number, so he waited for the call to go to voice mail. Could be that actress he stopped seeing months ago.

"Who'd you sue today?" she'd ask, no matter how often he told her he didn't try cases. Beautiful—that was true—but she lived for auditions. When they didn't happen, it was bad. When they happened, it was worse, and if she had been actually hired? He never found out.

No voice mail off that call. He went into his small kitchen, grabbed an apple. With the window open, he could hear the surf, and smell the salted wind blowing in over the boardwalk.

Another family picture rested on the counter: Robert and Rosalind, kids in a garlic-curing shed. Eight or nine years old in this one, horsing around beneath braided garlic strands hung from wooden beams.

That shot of the farm led him to recall the relentless, grinding work there and to recall women he'd dated in LA who never believed he often worked all weekend. And living in a down-and-dirty place near the beach? Not *on* the beach? Are you really a lawyer? They didn't grasp that his real payoff would come after years of busting his ass, and he didn't plan to get serious with a woman who didn't grasp that.

"Hard work, Rosalind, am I right?" he asked her photo.

Midthought, his cell phone vibrated and rang again. In the living area, he checked the caller: the same incoming number. Still no voice mail from the first call. Maybe a real estate agent cold-calling. No, thanks, not with former crack houses going for a million and up. Could it be Chase? Chase finding his number, calling to send him down a rabbit hole of wasted time.

His phone still rang, and he decided to pick up on the off chance Jack was on the other end.

So he answered. "Hello?"

But it wasn't Jack. It was a woman. And she was crying.

A cooling teakettle on a gas stove still leaked steam over an unlit burner. Robert found a bottle of water inside a refrigerator and closed the door. This kitchen was even smaller than his own. He took the bottle into the living room. It was small, too. Smaller still given the knocked-over bookshelf and books scattered across the floor. In the far corner, Alison

Maxwell sat on the floor in a Hurricanes sweatshirt and jeans, her knees drawn into her chest.

She wound up there after opening the door for him a minute ago. Only one minute. Seemed a lot longer than that as he knelt down and offered her the bottled water.

"I'm sure it was some kind of misunderstanding."

She rubbed her wrists with either hand, raised her eyes, and looked at him. "A . . . a . . . misunderstanding?"

"Yes, Mr. Pierce is a respected member of the bar and . . ."

She slapped the bottle away. "A misunderstanding?" her voice getting louder.

"Can you please, please, try to take it easy?"

She wasn't listening. "He said—he told me he'd try Brian's case if I had sex with him, and when I said no . . ."

"Alison."

She stopped talking, still rubbing her wrists. "What?"

He had no idea what to say or do. He prayed she could calmly revisit whatever happened and change her mind. To slow her down, he asked, "Were you here alone?"

"Yes. I was alone. Here. I told you that already."

She had not told him that, but he nodded anyway. "Right, right, you're right."

"When I said no, he went crazy. Grabbed my wrists and threw me against the wall. Pressed up against me, put his hand between my legs, pushed me down on the floor, and . . ."

She stopped. Even so, her narrative was the last thing he wanted to hear. On top of that, she was getting more agitated. Her breathing was faster, shallower.

"Did you—did you call the police?"

"He didn't rape me, all right. I didn't say he raped me. Did I ever say that?"

"No, you didn't, of course not, but please, why don't you come over here and sit on the couch? Then we can talk about it some more."

"Sure," she said. "You're right, thank you, I'm sorry."

He took her hand, helped her up. "Nothing for you to be sorry about, you're gonna be—"

But she sank back to the floor, exhaling. Seconds later, she began to hyperventilate.

"What's wrong?"

Helpless, he watched her face go white. She gasped for air. He had already hit 911 on his cell phone, even before saying, "Alison . . . please . . . don't . . ."

Too late. She passed out and rolled over limp on the floor.

The metal plates were dented on the swinging double doors at Brotman Medical Center's emergency room. That's what Robert saw right after Alison disappeared behind them on a gurney. After that, he wandered around a minute or two before taking a stained cloth seat in the waiting room.

Leaning forward, eyes squeezed shut, he dug his knuckles into his forehead and went over the surreal events of the past hour or so.

When she first called his apartment, he listened to her saying Jack had done something bad, something wrong, and he agreed to come over. Her address was in the case file. He called and texted Philip. Nada, and that time of night it was only an eight-minute drive to her building in Culver City, a two-story stucco job from the seventies with open landings and rusted railings. She lived on the ground floor, right off the uncovered, spot-patched parking lot.

That late, the complex had been quiet and dark. No action on the landings. A few locked bicycles and a dead ficus. Probably hardworking Latinos and Anglos lived here, people who went to bed early. No security cameras, either, not that he could recall. Whether that was good news or bad, he wasn't yet sure.

Not even now, pacing the parking lot outside the ER. He questioned his own actions after he took her call. What if he'd told her right then to call the police? Could have taken them an hour to get there, maybe more. Right now, she might be passed out in her apartment, and he would have failed to respond to her call for help. *A client's* call for help.

Why not carry her to his car and drive her to Brotman himself? It was only a mile up Venice Boulevard from her apartment, if that. Even so, he still believed calling the ambulance was the best move. If something happened to her on the way—in his car—he would have been responsible. Forget good intentions. Once a Good Samaritan takes charge of a situation, he owns it.

No, he was on solid footing legally. So was the firm—except for her allegations about Jack Pierce.

He was dialing Philip's cell phone again when Philip's name showed up on his screen. *About fuckin' time,* he thought as he took the call.

A swimming pool pulsed aqua light onto heliotrope bougainvillea as Sinatra sang "Summer Wind" for Philip Fanelli. At sixty-two, his gray hair thinning, Philip was only now starting to feel his age. He slipped on a terry-cloth robe in his Brentwood backyard.

Breathing hard, he said, "Sorry, Robert, I was swimming laps. What on earth couldn't have waited till morning?"

Philip listened to Robert's quick rendition of the night. "Oh, no," he said. "No need for you to come over here. Stay where you are. I'll come to you. I'm on my way."

CHAPTER 7

Rae's diner was closed. Same went for Tito's at Sepulveda and the Dunkin' Donuts by the 405. Robert and Philip wound up having a drink at the Alibi Room on Washington Boulevard.

"She had your business card, how?" Philip asked.

"From the meeting yesterday morning, first time we met."

Philip nodded. "Firm protocol to give her your card, and there was no family member to call?"

"According to her sworn affidavit when she filed suit—and according to what she said in the meeting—she's the only living member of her family."

"And that factored into your decision to respond to her call?"

"I was working on her release, a three-one-oh number came up, and I thought it might be Jack calling. Calling me a second time."

Philip nodded again. "Right, but her family situation. You knew about it from her file and from the meeting. That went into your decision to assist her, correct?"

Philip sounded like he was repeating himself, but he wasn't. Robert got it now. "Sure, yes, it did affect my decision. Once I knew who it was, I knew she had no family to call, and she sounded desperate. She was alone, so I responded by driving to her apartment. A very short drive for me, especially that time of night."

"Well, then, your only conceivable misstep was answering in the first place, and no one can fault you for that. When she passed out, you were with her?"

"Oh, yeah," he said, "it was intense. For the first few seconds, it crossed my mind she might be . . . dying."

Philip didn't respond. Robert knew they were thinking along the same lines: maybe better if she had.

Then Philip touched Robert's shoulder. "Thinking it doesn't mean we hoped for it."

Robert nodded and said, "We don't know what happened tonight, and I get that. But you weren't in the meeting with Jack and Chase."

"Ah, Mr. Fitzpatrick is in the mix, too? Tell me how that went."

"They tag-teamed her, but Jack did all the heavy lifting, roughed her up really bad. Said her deceased brother—a fairly young guy—died of cancer. Said he was weak, pathetic, that ten grand was all his life was worth. Maybe that's true, I don't know, but there was no need for it. And he kept hassling her. No parking validation, lost track of her car down in the garage. It was all way, way over the top. Cruel, almost."

"Cruel." Philip nodded.

"And after she left," Robert said, "it was just . . . *if you bring a woman to tears, you're halfway home.* Ever heard that expression?"

"No."

"Neither had I. Not until today. That's what Jack said about her after she left the room."

"And you think that cuts against him?"

"She was in tears in the meeting, and he brought her to it. Those were his words—his *exact* words. And now we're a mile from her hospital after his alleged sexual assault, having a drink after midnight."

"You're halfway home," Philip repeated. "Jack's phrase is capable of a variety of meanings, isn't it?"

"Not if you were in the room," Robert said.

"Robert, we practice corporate law, but the trial boys, the litigators? They're in the trenches every single day. We butt heads with the opposition, of course, but they often find it effective, necessary, to get down and dirty, as they say."

Robert couldn't let it go yet. "He all but said something like this would happen. Not exactly the way it turned out, but . . ."

"Let's get clear on one thing: you don't know what happened tonight. Neither do I."

"Sure. I know that."

"Now," Philip said, "if she wants to take it up with the police or file with the state bar, she's free to do so. But never forget this—Jack Pierce is a ruthless, heartless bastard. He is relentless, and yes, he is cruel. That's one reason why Jack is at the firm now."

Robert considered that comment. Everyone at the firm knew why Jack had been hired. He had pulled off a big judgment against Brightwell Industries over in Nevada. Oliver, the company's house counsel at the time, sat in on the case and watched Jack blistering Brightwell witnesses on the stand. After that, he let Philip know—only a suggestion, of course—that Jack might make a great head litigator at the firm.

Now Philip told Robert, "And never forget, not for a moment, that Jack Pierce started out in life with nothing at all. Took him years to do it, but he clawed his way to the top, and he will protect that status with everything at his disposal. Never, Robert, never will he give up what he has gained."

Late nights poolside, Philip had discussed Jack with him. How Jack graduated from Venice High, his rough-and-tumble life, broken family, the LA race riots roiling Jack's mixed-ethnic neighborhood. In spite of that, he made it to the top of the hill in Bel-Air. Life's pinnacle for some people.

But Philip calling his partner *cruel* and *ruthless, a heartless bastard?* Words like that? Not even close. No matter how many bottles of wine had been opened beside Philip's pool.

Philip had even more to say: "He isn't a man you want to cross swords with. His memory runs long, and it runs hot; his reactions can be wildly disproportionate to a perceived offense."

A warning and Robert knew it: *Back off.*

Even so, Robert asked, "I've been at the firm five years. In all that time, why did I never work with him?"

"You did, on a few research questions and on several contracts that I recall specifically."

"Not one-on-one, never directly with him. The workflow always came from you and went back to you. Always, until yesterday."

Philip nodded. "I was concerned you two might be a volatile mix, so I acted as a buffer. Then again, perhaps you aren't asking the most pertinent question about why yesterday's one-on-one occurred."

Robert felt his pulse quicken. "You mean, why yesterday? Why was I working directly with him yesterday?"

Philip smiled. "It was Jack's idea. He insisted on it before we invited you to become a partner in Fanelli and Pierce."

He could barely breathe. "Partner? I'm making partner?"

Philip raised his glass to Robert. "Next partners' meeting is in three days."

"I'm going to make partner?" It was sinking in now. "Mr. Fanelli . . . I can't . . . thank you . . ."

"You're more than welcome. High time it happened, far as I'm concerned, but I want you to listen up, to pay heed. You need to know what I'm about to tell you, but you must hold your cards close to the vest."

"Yes, sir."

Philip drained his wineglass. "One year, almost to the day, after Jack married Dorothy Brightwell, he took over Brightwell Industries. They became his client."

His client? "Didn't you and Oliver bring them into the firm?"

"True, but I couldn't fight it under the circumstances, with his marriage to Dorothy Brightwell, so I allowed it to happen for the good of the firm. Once Jack took control, all the Brightwell time sheets started going through him."

He could imagine Philip's natural disappointment in losing a client of twenty-some odd years. He knew, too, that Philip wanted no sympathy, but that didn't change what Jack's control of the Brightwell time sheets meant: Jack Pierce took the lion's share of the credit for Brightwell fees. At the partner level, that gave him real power.

Philip took it even further. "That means he controls over forty percent of the firm's gross billings. Not a good situation for the firm, being so beholden to one client, and that particular forty percent is our bread and butter. We cannot lose it. If Jack took it and went out on his own, the firm would . . . it would be quite problematic."

"Can he do that?"

"I seriously doubt Dorothy or her father would sit still for it. Even so, you can never be certain what pressures he might bring to bear. At home. In private."

In the bedroom with Dorothy, Robert was thinking, finding it difficult to quiet his mind.

"As you can imagine," Philip said, "there was considerable back and forth about bringing you in. Fortunately, the quality of your work, your billable hours, and your work ethic carried the day with a majority of partners. I gave them my word I would signal nothing to you about your impending partnership, but in light of tonight's goings-on, I think it imperative to break my word."

"Exigent circumstances," Robert said.

"Or not," Philip replied. "Again, we're in the dark as to what happened tonight, so my fervent admonition to you is this: under no circumstances mention anything to anyone, especially to Jack, about tonight's episode."

Goings-on. Episode. "Of course, but I told the nurse I'd check with her before I went home."

"Then by all means, follow through. On this one, though, I'd say the fewer bread crumbs you leave behind . . ."

"The fewer the better."

Philip checked his watch. "Well, then, I have an out-of-town guest. She'll be worried about me."

"She?" Robert asked, finally able to smile.

Philip left a hundred on the bar. They headed for the door.

"I'm older, Robert, not dead." And Philip was smiling, too.

Outside, Philip chirped the locks on his Mercedes sedan. As Robert was getting inside, Philip shared one last thought: "By the way, you did a decent thing helping the Maxwell woman, taking her to the hospital. But practicing law isn't about right and wrong. Never let yourself get emotional about clients."

After Philip dropped him off at his car, Robert picked up his laptop from home and returned to the ER. Still, he had no luck working. Whenever he came close to settling down, Jack Pierce ricocheted around his mind.

What was it Hanalei Ragsdale said? It had to be Jack recommending she use litigation as a negotiating tactic. No doubt about it: more and more activity at the firm seemed to involve litigation, and Jack was legendary at winning. With his tailored or designer-everything, it was hard to picture him in the Venice High bleachers yelling, *"Go, Gondoliers!"* After that, Jack had attended UCLA and Sandra Day O'Connor College of Law at Arizona State. Odd to Robert that Jack's law school was named after a woman, especially a Supreme Court justice. And when Jack actually practiced trial law? Tough and shrewd, even did a stint in criminal-defense work downtown, specializing in high-profile money-laundering cases.

"Mr. Worth?"

He looked up. The ER nurse walked up to him, a coffee cup miraculously balanced on her clipboard.

"How's she doing?" he asked.

"Dr. Zweig wanted me to tell you, it was good you brought her in when you did. Doctor said it looks like tachycardia secondary to acute anxiety. Her EEG confirmed it."

"Then she'll be okay?"

"Doctor said she should be. Her heart rate's getting back to an acceptable level, but doctor wants to keep her overnight for observation. Oh," the nurse said, "Dr. Zweig noted her wrists. They're bruised. Both of them. And she wanted to ask if you knew how that happened."

"I have no idea. Better ask her."

"Will do. Her family contact was left blank. Who's the family member we should contact in an emergency?"

"A brother, died last year. Other than that?" He shrugged.

"Then if you'll come to my office, sign these papers." She headed toward a door off the waiting room. But when she turned around in the doorway, Robert was already headed out the front door.

CHAPTER 8

No doubt about it. With the hospital trip behind him, Robert decided that an all-nighter lay ahead of him. That ought to give him time to go over the Maxwell release again and to handle any last-minute questions that came up around the Palmer deal. Turned out, he made the right call. At 5:15 a.m., as he printed hard copies of the Maxwell release, an e-mail rolled in from Nashville.

The Palmer deal was in the process of blowing up. Palmer warned that it couldn't come up with Brightwell's certified check due at closing, claiming an Asian bank screwed up a funds wire. Robert didn't buy in to Palmer's excuse, and after hours of back and forth, he recommended a dry closing to Nashville counsel. All parties would sign each document. Palmer then had forty-eight hours to deliver the certified check. If it wasn't there on time, the deal was off at Brightwell's election, and if that happened, Palmer would be on the hook for Brightwell's legal fees on the deal. Take it or leave it, Robert told them. And the other side took it.

Three minutes after he put out that fire, for the first time ever, Jack Pierce walked into Robert's office, unannounced.

"Finish the Maxwell release?" he asked, even before sitting down.

"It's right here, sir," Robert said, trying not to let the sudden entrance throw him while guessing that throwing him off was Jack's point.

Two hard copies lay on Robert's desk. He handed one to Jack, kept the other for himself. Jack glanced at the first page but didn't appear to be reading it.

"I had one item I wanted to run by you," Robert said.

"About the release?"

"Yes, sir. I was thinking that—"

"Wait. Is what you just threw at me finished or not finished?"

Robert knew he hadn't actually said it was finished or thrown it. He also knew it was a bad idea to argue either point. "I wanted to tell you, I made a judgment call on whether to release wrongful death claims specifically."

"And?"

"After thinking it over, I added *wrongful death* to Section One so that any claims of that nature would be released by our client, too."

"Why's that? I never sued Consolidated for wrongful death."

"I understand that, but we want Consolidated to accept this document, and I believe, as long as they are getting a release, they will likely ask us to release wrongful death claims, too."

Jack asked, "*You believe? Likely?* Really? I believe you're *likely* wrong. I believe you went too far. I'm no mind reader about what Consolidated will and will not ask for, but I won't release claims I never brought. Makes my firm look weak. It's unprofessional."

My firm again. Robert said, "Yes, sir."

He got the picture now. If he had left out wrongful death, Jack would have called that a mistake, too: *No back and forth, I told you. You should have included it.* There was no right answer: Jack planned to burn him either way.

"All right, then," Robert said, making the changes on his computer. "I'll delete *wrongful death* and the document is ready to go."

Thirty seconds later, the document started printing out. Jack said, "So, tell me, Worth, as you actually finish the release, what were you thinking yesterday in the Maxwell meeting?"

What the fuck? Robert thought. *He's coming back to that?* So he said, "My family is old-fashioned that way, sir. Always stand, always open the door for a woman. They drilled it into me, and all I can offer in my defense is that bad habits die hard."

"Bad habits die hard." Jack liked that answer. Smiled and said, "I guess so."

Robert wondered if Jack was trying to see how much shit he would take. *Does he want me to show more backbone?* Then he remembered what Gia said: *Let him win.* And Philip telling him that in three days he'd be a partner.

Jack continued. "Of course, I read your résumé before I came on board at the firm, Worth. I recall you come from south of San Francisco. Gilroy, am I right?"

"Outside Gilroy, yes, sir." Robert guessed Jack had read his résumé for the first time in the last hour. But he added, "Good memory, sir."

"Garlic capital of the world?" Jack asked, eyeing the family pictures on the credenza.

"Other places grow more garlic, but we coined the name first. The Garlic Festival is more what the town is—"

"I've been through Gilroy many times. Bet it's rough to live around the stench from that processing plant downtown. After a while, bet it seeps into your pores."

Before Robert could force a smile and tell him that you got used to the smell, Jack looked at his watch and said, "Not a word from Lady Maxwell." He dropped her release on the desk. "Toss it. She didn't stick with the game plan, and her ten-minute grace period has expired. Nothing left to do now but withdraw as counsel of record."

Without a word, Robert dropped the releases into his wastebasket. He didn't know whether Jack could withdraw so easily and he didn't care. That was Jack's problem. This whole Maxwell situation was going to blow over, even though Jack grated on him in every imaginable way. Philip was right last night: they were a volatile mix.

"Hope that my dropping her as a client passes muster with you?"

"Yes, sir, of course."

Jack stepped to the credenza and looked at Robert's diplomas on the wall behind it: University of California at Berkeley and Hastings Law. "Berkeley, then Hastings. Don't see a law review certificate on your wall." Now Jack looked at him.

"I wasn't on law review. It was offered but I turned it down."

Robert thinking: *Didn't see law review on your résumé, Jack. Where was that again? Sandra Day O'Connor College of Law?*

"Turned down law review, really? That's unusual," Jack said.

"I had obligations at home most every weekend. My family has a farming operation in the area, and that's how it worked out."

"So, you go to college and law school in the Bay Area, stick close to home. Makes sense."

"Yes, sir, but now I call LA home."

"I don't know, Monterey Peninsula, Santa Cruz, Carmel—the Bay Area's hard to beat. I get up there whenever I can."

"I spent quite a bit of time on the coast when I was younger, but it's changed. Crowds, traffic jammed up on Highway 1."

"Can't argue with you there," Jack said.

Finally, Robert thought, *we agree on traffic.*

"Fanelli tells me you might make a good lawyer—one of these days. That you might be able to go the distance."

"Go the distance? I think he's right, sir."

Jack picked up a photo from the credenza. "You mind?" he asked, after the fact.

"Not at all," Robert said, even though he minded a great deal.

It was a photograph of his whole family. His parents, his aunt and uncle, too. All of them on the front porch of the large family home.

Several Latinos were in the mix, too, and sparklers sizzled for a Fourth of July celebration.

"Even the servants got in on this one, huh?"

Meaning the Latinos. The farm's operations manager, Luis, was like family to Robert, but he found himself saying, "Sure did, couldn't keep 'em away."

"Looks like a great time." Jack kept looking at the picture. Then from out of nowhere: "Like you said to me before, your ma and your pa, they would have handled Ms. Maxwell differently from how I handled her yesterday. Is that right?"

Hearing *ma* and *pa*, Robert didn't answer. Anger pinpricked his neck.

"I guess things are different up in Gilroy. Up there at the—what is it? The Garlic Festival? All the rubes cleaned up for that one big day every year?"

Robert felt himself flush with anger. Felt it build.

"Yesterday's meeting, Worth, you blew it. Do I have to worry about you every time I turn up the heat on a client? What did you think, Worth, standing up for her? Opening the door for that high-handed bitch? Did you think, what, did you think you were her knight in shining armor?"

Robert glared at him, not sure what would come out of his mouth. What finally did: "No, sir, I didn't."

"*No, sir, I didn't?* Then why, Sir Galahad? Why? It's beyond all comprehension what you did. I couldn't sleep last night thinking about what a colossal fuckup you are. Maybe I missed it, but I didn't see Chase helping her out, did you?"

"No, sir."

"Honest to God, I've never seen anything like it. The little bitch I helped out for months. That lying little bitch doesn't even have the courtesy to show up this morning like she agreed!"

Robert looked down, nodding. She had not *agreed* to come in, but he kept nodding anyway. At this point, "Yes, sir" was all he could find to say. That is, until Jack tossed that family photo on his desk. At first, Robert didn't see what happened, he was wrapped so tight in his anger.

Then he saw his family picture on the desk. Inside the frame, the glass had cracked right down the middle. It was an accident. Even Jack looked like he knew he'd gone too far.

But Robert didn't see the look on the other man's face, or see that he was about to speak. He exploded from his chair: "Probably still in the hospital. Maybe that's why the little bitch didn't call you!"

Jack's face went hard instantly. "Wait a minute? All this time? All this time you know that piece of information and don't mention it?"

Robert didn't answer.

"She called you? You? Quick work, Worth. You already fucking her or what?"

"No, sir, not at all. I—"

"Then stop dancing around, and tell me what happened to my client."

My client again. Robert took a breath, ran it down in his mind. Jack broke the glass inside his family picture. Indefensible, totally out of line. Stop now. Ask him to leave your office, get Philip involved. No. A partner wouldn't do that. A partner would handle it himself, not run to the grown-ups for backup.

Robert said, "She had my card from the meeting yesterday. It was late. She called me at home and said she needed help. When I got there, she told me . . . she said that you came to her apartment and made improper advances." He recalled exactly what he told her: "And I told her I was sure she was mistaken. That you were a respected member of the—"

"Bet that's exactly what you told her."

"I told her that you were a respected member of the bar, that she was mistaken, and that is exactly what I told her, Mr. Pierce."

"You sure?"

"One hundred percent positive."

"Jesus Christ, I knew she was a liar. Which hospital?"

"Brotman. Culver City."

"I know where it is, Worth. After she called, why didn't you call me?"

"I considered it but didn't have your cell number. It was too late to rely on e-mail or to call your landline at home. I should have brought it up this morning, but the Palmer deal blew up back east, and I was putting out fires till a few minutes before you walked in my office."

Robert stopped, watched Jack nodding. Looked to him like he was going to defuse this on his own.

"That it?" Jack asked.

Robert was thinking about how far to go, about to answer the question, when Jack said, "Is that all of it or not? Let's hear it, Worth. Don't be such a fucking pussy."

Robert felt a white calm descend on him. "Mr. Pierce, it's better you don't call me that. I'd really appreciate it."

"*A pussy?* Okay, sorry, *Robert.* Before I call the hospital to find out about my client—is that it, *Robert? It,* as in, is that everything I should know before I make the call, *Robert?* As in, every, single, fucking thing, *Robert?*"

Robert's eyes narrowed. He swallowed hard. "The attending physician noticed bruises on her wrists. Ms. Maxwell mentioned in passing that you grabbed her wrists at her apartment."

"Hard to do that if I'm not there, isn't it?"

"It would be impossible," Robert managed to say.

"Maybe she likes it rough with her boyfriend or with strangers or with her paying clients or with who-the-fuck knows? Any of that ever cross your mind, *Robert?*"

Robert said, "I considered all of that, yes," even though he had not.

"Now, then. Have you given me every single motherfucking thing I need to know?"

Robert was about to explode, his head pulsing so hard he couldn't speak.

"Spit it out, Worth! Spit it out, you backbiting pussy. Is that all of it?"

That was all Robert was going to take. "No—she said you told her you'd drop her case unless she had sex with you."

"And I dropped her, didn't I? So you think I went to that whore's place, don't you? Sure you do, and you're wrong again. I was working with Chase last night, you worthless jackoff!"

This time, Jack swept that family photo off the desk, against the wall, and shattered the frame. That was it. Robert came from behind his desk and pushed him hard in the chest with both hands, knocking him back.

"Goddamn you. You got no right to do that!"

Jack raised his hands, all innocence and smiles. "Why not, Worth? It's my firm, and you? You're outta here."

"I busted my ass five years for this firm."

"Bust it five more, you might make partner somewhere else."

"You're the biggest fucking asshole I ever met."

Jack's smile broadened. "Already knew that's how you felt. That's why you stood up for that cunt yesterday, opened the door for her—to *show me*. But you finally got one thing right. I am an asshole and I'm paid well for it. Now pack your overalls, farm boy, and roll on outta here."

Jack headed for the door, pulled out his cell phone, and made a call: "Hey, get what's-his-name up here from security." Then he was out the door.

Jack headed down the hall. People ducked into their offices as he headed their way. After that, Robert slammed his door shut.

"Motherfucker!" he shouted, and kicked his office wall. Kicked it so hard he busted a hole through the drywall. Then he leaned on his desk with both arms and exhaled.

"Oh, man . . ."

❧

Down in the firm's litigation section, Jack calmly opened the door to Chase's office without knocking. Chase looked up from his computer screen.

"Chase," Jack said, "time we had a chat."

After that, he swung Chase's door shut.

❧

Carlos from building security waited at Robert's door. Robert jammed his diplomas and photographs into a box. Philip entered his office, nodded to Carlos, and closed the door behind him.

Robert didn't bother looking up. He knew it was Philip.

"Dorothy Brightwell. Brightwell Industries," Robert said. "I don't care who Pierce married. I don't take that kind of treatment from anybody."

"What the hell happened?"

"It doesn't matter what happened. One way or another, I was never going to make it past Pierce, not with him running the show."

"Did you mention the girl?"

"Yes. I did."

"I told you that was a mistake."

"It was impossible not to mention her," Robert said. "He kept coming back to yesterday's meeting, over and over again. He wouldn't let go of it." Now he looked at Philip. "Your partner sexually assaults a client and you let it pass? How many times has that happened?"

"We don't know what happened. Accusations like that are easy to—"

"Easy to make, hard to prove, I know the drill. By the way, Jack fired Gia yesterday. Good-looking woman like her, office manager, wonder what that was about?"

"What do you mean by that?"

Robert packed his shattered family photo, tired of dealing with it.

"Pierce didn't even work here when I started. I picked this firm because of you. I trusted you, not him. Can I have my job back? Yes or no?"

Philip looked down. "Could I have made it any clearer? For now, he's calling the shots."

"For now, for always. You caved. By the way, the Ragsdale closing went great. Hanalei wanted me to rep her because you're not around anymore. You gave him the firm without a fight. Why not go ahead and take your name off the door if that's how it is?"

Robert brushed past him, and Philip could only watch it happen, sick at heart.

Out in the hall, Carlos followed Robert to the elevators. Robert handed over his key fob accessing the computer system. Did the same with his office key.

Carlos said, "Mr. Worth, I need to have your—"

"Carlos, I told you. It's *Robert* or *Roberto*."

"*Sí, Roberto*, I need your parking pass." Carlos looked ashamed asking for it.

"Now? You kidding me?"

"No, I am not. That is what they tell me to do."

Jack Pierce again. "Tell you what, Carlos. I won't pay to park here. I'll hand my pass to the attendant on my way out. That fucker wants my pass before that, tell him where I am."

"*Roberto, por favor . . .*"

As the elevator door opened, he saw the look on Carlos's face. Reporting Robert's challenge to Jack would get him fired, too. Robert handed over his pass.

"*Gracias, Roberto, lo siento.*"

Robert nodded. Then he stepped into the elevator and rode it all the way down.

CHAPTER 9

Between sending out résumés, setting up meetings, and reconnecting with women he'd neglected, Robert fought his old habits. Like waking up before dawn, checking e-mails before his feet touched the floor, hitting the handball courts. Lying awake in the dark at 5:00 a.m., he faced long, dreary days living with the ugly truth: he'd been let go. Sent packing. He'd been fired. Shitcanned.

On his daily runs and workouts, sometimes he calculated the value to the firm of his five years as an associate. He had grossed it around $3.5 million, took home roughly a quarter of that. At bonus time, he didn't make waves because he wanted them to know he was a team player. So what if he made fewer dollars that year? Once he made partner, he'd pull down over three hundred thousand a year, minimum base salary.

Robert didn't return Philip's single phone call. That was because Philip's voice mail didn't say that he had his job back, merely that Philip was *so very sorry*. Two weeks later, Philip actually hand-delivered Robert's final paycheck. From his Ozone walk street, Robert watched Philip climb the wooden stairs to his apartment door. Watched him knock and wait for a minute or two, all of this without Robert approaching him.

Fuck him, Robert said to himself, before riding away on his bike.

His decision to ignore Philip had come easy because of the *Los Angeles Times* article that same week: Chase had been made a partner at Fanelli & Pierce. There he was: Chase's photo in the *Times*: "Fanelli & Pierce is pleased to announce that Chase Fitzpatrick . . ."

That was as far as Robert could read. That grinning no-load and those words slammed the door on any hope he had of returning to the firm.

That prick, Chase. His hair was perfect, and Robert despised him. Chase didn't do the work, made no sacrifice, worked on Jack's paddle-tennis game down at the Venice Beach courts. More than that, he beat Robert at the game.

A game. That's all it was all along. Nothing but a goddamn game. Even so, he couldn't help wondering which junior associate took his old office, the one closest to Philip. And Philip? Sure, Philip would always write him a great recommendation for prospective firms. Knowing that helped Robert's confidence at first, when he began reaching out to LA firms he'd turned down five years ago.

Turned out, those firms were eager to meet with him. Liked showing him around the offices in Century City, Westwood, or Hollywood. Liked telling him how great their firms were doing, especially over the last five years. Promising to call him back ASAP, then waiting two weeks to tell him, essentially, *forget it*. Meaning? You turned us down before, and that was a terrible call on your part, wasn't it?

It hurt his job search, too, that so much of his time had been spent on Brightwell business. Because of that, he didn't bring his own clients along to a hiring firm. His ego finally allowed him to focus on reality. Without a stable of his own clients, no top firm would pay him what he was worth.

Almost daily, he ran into his beach buddies on Speedway, at coffee shops, on Venice Pier. People he knew, people he'd helped. Erik, Reyes, lots of others, all wondering what happened to the guy they believed would make it big. The guy who didn't seem to be working anymore.

Then there was Alison. She called him once. He didn't answer and deleted her voice mail. Somehow, she found out where he lived and left birds-of-paradise at his mailbox with a note:

Called the firm to thank you, they said you didn't work there now. Sorry. I don't know what else to say. Alison Maxwell.

Her flowers he tossed to a sun-blistered Canadian couple in splitting spandex: "Birds-of-paradise, guys, have a great day!"

Even though he avoided Santa Monica, it was bound to happen one day: seeing Jack and Chase on the boardwalk near the paddletennis courts. The pair grabbing a sausage sandwich at Jody Maroni's and laughing at some inside-the-firm joke. Seeing them reminded him of Gia and that she hadn't returned either of his calls, but he wasn't surprised. What was it she'd said her last night in the firm's parking lot? *When a job's done, it's done.*

It's done. Guess so, he told himself.

Five weeks passed, and he realized he was out $20,000 and couldn't account for it. Two long weekends in Vegas with the actress, picking up her shopping-spree tab. New interview suits, rent, gym, restaurants, tips, parking, fuck. Finally, he realized he could spend twice that much and it wouldn't make a dent in his pain. In the anger boiling up in traffic, or with tourists walking on the bike path: *It's a bike path, douche bag!* Or yesterday at 6:10 a.m., going off on that freestyle skateboarder two blocks over from his apartment. The one who made the mistake of cranking up "It Was a Good Day."

He was drinking too much, scored hashish at a medical-marijuana store on Abbot Kinney, and smoked it to calm down. Chilling out on the beach, running the Santa Monica stairs, hitting Gold's midmorning, working on his tan, hiking the Santa Monica Mountains, living the life, hanging out. Sure, a great for a lot of people, but he wasn't geared to hang out.

His business calls to firms he knew around town became cold calls to ones he didn't. Résumés now went over the digital transom based on areas where he was willing to work, then later to locales within a ten-mile radius of Ozone. And ten miles from home meant he would consider working in downtown LA.

So what? He knew what he had to do. Get a job. Any job. So when that downtown firm reached out, one he never would have considered a month ago, he picked up on the first ring, knowing he shouldn't have. And when they told him they wanted to talk, to discuss terms of employment, he let them know he felt confident he could work them into his schedule.

CHAPTER 10

All three lawyers who sat across from him in the conference room had dandruff flecking their suit shoulders. No, he corrected himself. The two male lawyers had dandruff-flecked suits. Not the woman. She wasn't wearing a suit.

He first met them downtown on the forty-fifth floor of the tallest building west of the Mississippi River. The US Bank Tower, formerly Library Tower, was a terrorist magnet for that reason, he learned from a security guard, while cooling it for twenty minutes in the lobby for his elevator pass.

"Sorry about the mix-up," one of these lawyers told him.

"No problem," Robert said, mentally adding that twenty-minute lobby wait to the fifty minutes it took him to drive here, not counting the ten-minute walk from underground public parking at Pershing Square. Walking from there to the tower because this firm didn't validate parking.

Strolling with the interviewers through their firm's barren halls, he urged himself to stay positive. *These guys are okay. They have families. They do a ton of banking transactions, and they're building a mergers-and-acquisitions department.*

Later, sitting in his interview, he was recounting to them how the Palmer closing blew up back at the firm and his solution, letting them know he was a problem solver when one of them raised a hand, midsentence.

"We have no doubt you are well qualified. No doubt at all."

"None," said the woman, checking her file. "You had an excellent recommendation from a *Philip Fanelli*."

"Great," he said, but something was wrong. Had they picked up on his thinly masked desperation? Had he laid it on too thick about what a mack-daddy go-getter he was?

The woman said, "Having said that, we would consider starting you first of the month if we can come to terms."

"Where there's a will," he said, smiling and wishing he hadn't.

"But we don't need a deal maker or a closer. We thought we were clear about that in the ad."

"The ad?"

"In *California Lawyer*. The ad."

"Right," he said, clueless. "Of course."

"So, even though we are aware of your qualifications, we see you more as a . . ."

The shorter of the two short men slid a black binder across the table. "We see you sinking your teeth into these new pension regulations. Our clients are overwhelmed right now with all the new rules coming out of Washington."

Robert couldn't bring himself to touch the book: *Pension Protection Act of 1996*. Best guess, it ran a thousand pages with page headings like *Reg.1009.4 (g)(i)-(ix) et. seq.*

"Pretty intricate material, we know, but we're prepared to pay competitively."

Robert decided to be polite, to see if he could get out of here with an offer. Maybe he could still beat traffic home on the I-10.

"I'm right here," he said.

"Sixty," the woman said.

"Sixty?" Robert thought about countering at one twenty.

"Only part-time," she said then. "Sixty dollars an hour."

"Sixty dollars," he said. "An hour. Part-time." He swallowed. "You're hiring me as what?"

"As a junior associate. You'd be considered for partnership in, I'd say, roughly five years."

"Provided you measure up," someone added. "Who knows, before that, you could drop in on our M-and-A guys down on forty-three, see if you could lend a hand."

Right then, Robert saw something he hadn't noticed in any interview so far. They were getting off lowballing him because they were cheap like those plastic birds-of-paradise in the vase behind them. Cheap was in their smug DNA. Sure, they could send someone six blocks to the flower district, have fresh flowers wholesale for two hundred bucks a week, but why do that when you can jam that money into the unlined pockets of a three-for-one Men's Wearhouse ensemble?

"Mr. Worth?" one of them said, not the woman this time.

He didn't answer because something else was dawning on him. Something he missed because of his ring rust from smoking dope and drinking whiskey. He looked at the woman who told him about Philip Fanelli's favorable recommendation. "Jack Pierce—did he also write me a recommendation?"

"We're not at liberty to discuss that."

She didn't have much of a poker face. She already revealed what *Philip Fanelli* had to say about him. Now she wouldn't tell him whether or not Pierce even wrote a recommendation. But Robert knew: Jack Pierce had definitely kicked in his two cents on the subject of *him*.

Their last insult brought Robert to his feet. At the window, he stared at the smog-choked city, where farther out his line of sight, syruping traffic oozed past a burning mattress on I-10.

"That view, the best money can buy," someone chirped behind him.

Jack's recommendation had torpedoed him. And not just here. All over town. It killed him anywhere he might've had a shot.

"But we need your answer, Mr. Worth, and please, we expect you to be precise."

Precise. He thought over his situation, then turned back to them. Tried not to hate them and failed.

"Thirty-eight minutes," he said.

"Excuse me?" the thin-lipped one in the middle asked.

"I see it like this. You three are the firm's hiring committee, and that tells me, with you three, this fifty-person firm is putting its best foot forward."

The crew nodded in appreciation.

"So I'm quite confident saying there's gotta be forty-seven bigger losers backing you up, back in your Motel Six rabbit warren, and my first day sinking my teeth into those pension regs? I'd jump through that window—that one right there." He pointed it out. "And I'd count my blessings on the way down because I'd never have to see your pale, sad faces again."

They were all standing in varying states of outrage when he grabbed his briefcase.

"Oh," he added, opening the door, "and I'd jump after working here *precisely* thirty-eight minutes. Head and Shoulders, fellas, have a good one."

Once Robert exited the tower, he walked straight down West Fifth toward Café Pinot, never noticing the '06 lift-back Celica parked up the hill. Or the lean, fit man inside watching him. A one-year, glow-in-the-dark Narcotics Anonymous bracelet dangled from Stanley Tifton's mirror. Jack's occasional go-to guy, Stanley cracked open a fresh pack of Larks, caught their familiar aroma, and made a call on one of three burner phones in his console.

When Jack Pierce answered without a word, Stanley brought him up to speed.

"He looks pissed off, that's for sure. Had to drive all the way downtown for the interview, and it didn't go well. As we speak, he's walking into a bar, middle of the day. I give him six months before I run into him at a meeting."

"What about the other?" Jack asked.

"Grunion still aren't running," Stanley said, coding his words. "Between following your farm boy around and trying to pin down my guy—he's got some kinda bronchitis, fuck if I know—but anyhow, my guy says grunion ought to be running wild by next week. Give me a call when you . . ."

He stopped talking. Jack had switched off midsentence. That wasn't unusual. Stanley remembered the grunion running at Cabrillo Beach, way back when. A group of Venice High students watched hundreds and hundreds of those small fish beaching themselves, mating under the fading moon. Everyone else in their group was yelling about the grunion running and jumping around like madmen, but Jack never said a word.

Same thing, even today. Long as Stanley had known him, he never knew what Jack would do next or what he was really thinking.

It was cool and quiet inside Pinot: concrete and glass with polished aggregate floors. Back at the bar, Robert ordered a glass of red wine—whatever was open—and tried coming to grips with how his life was shaping up. Or down. He knew the stunt he'd pulled inside that firm had been ill advised. Okay, stupid, but he'd reached the point where he didn't care. Not quite fuck it, but fuck it's angry next-door neighbor.

And there they were on the bar: birds-of-paradise. Real ones in a clear glass vase, grounded in round, gray rocks, and soaking up vivid, filtered water.

He was thinking about Alison Maxwell as he stepped through the bank of rear glass doors.

Outside on a dining terrace, skyscrapers towered around him, but it was somehow intimate. And Alison stayed on his mind. So did the birds-of-paradise she left at his mailbox, the ones he tossed to spandexed strangers. Sure, maybe she paid five bucks for them to an illegal vendor on a traffic median, but she didn't have two nickels to rub together. Jack dropped her brother's case, no friends in LA, no family anywhere. She still called him, bought flowers, wrote him a note. Even so, he never called back.

As opposed to Jack Pierce. *Relentless and cruel,* Philip said of him. No doubt about that as he paraphrased to himself Jack's likely Robert Worth recommendation: "In spite of my repeated efforts to work with him, Mr. Worth showed poor judgment, had questionable legal skills, and vandalized his office upon his abrupt departure."

So he swallowed some wine and reviewed his dwindling options: returning to the Bay Area for some kind of government work, starting his own practice in LA from scratch, without funds. Or . . . his mind began slowly turning toward a third option. An option still inchoate.

"Have you decided what you want?"

This came from a waitress standing beside him. He didn't answer because that third option was still taking shape.

"Sir?" she said.

An option that quickened his pulse in a good way.

"Would you like to be seated?" she asked.

"No, thanks," he said, handing her his empty glass. "But I think I know what I want . . ."

Free weights lay on Robert's apartment floor underneath his TRX work-out straps on the bedroom doorjamb. Family pictures sat on his coffee table, a couple more on the mantel over the bootlegged fireplace. Robert sat at his desk typing into his laptop, squeezing the life out of a gel ball, and feeling better than he had since the day Jack fired him.

With his new business cards ordered and on the way, he opened a software application: Plaintiffs and Defendants, Los Angeles County. Once he entered *Alison Maxwell*, the app began to search the county court's database for other cases involving her.

That photo of Rosalind and him in the garlic shed rested on his kitchen windowsill. No need to actually look at it before asking: "Talk to me, Rosalind, what do you think? Think I should burn his ass? Show Bel-Air Boy who he's dealing with?"

On his way home from Pinot, he'd detoured to Bel-Air and found the Brightwell estate, top of Stone Canyon Road. The home where he attended all those firm parties, years gone by. Standing at the mansion's tall iron gates, his hands grasped two cold bars. Their strength reminded him of the power Jack must feel living like this. People who lived up here had made it. All they had to do now was hang on to what they had.

Now on his computer screen, the county-court results showed up: *Alison Maxwell/No Case(s) Found.* The same result had been served up by his earlier *Alison Maxwell* searches of Orange, Riverside, and San Bernardino Counties. Alison was clean. So he started typing again.

"Let's do it, Rosalind," he whispered. "Let's burn Jack Pierce's little house down."

He opened one of his desktop folders. Its title: *Worth Work Product.* Twenty Word files appeared inside it. From among them, he selected a document called *MCP-PNA, July 12, 2012.*

Once he clicked on that document, he wondered: *Alison Maxwell was clean. Jack Cross Pierce, how clean are you, bro?*

CHAPTER 11

A logjam of local business cards and flyers with tear-off phone numbers littered a bookstore bulletin board: *Rentals Needed! Lesbian Roommate Wanted! Yoga With Sonya! My Cat: Murdered! Lost Dog: Answers to Trey or Tree!*

Standing beside the bulletin board, Robert slid off his shades and spotted Alison kneeling on the floor back in the mystery section. She was sorting and stacking incoming novels, and as he headed her way, she looked up and saw him. She looked down again.

"Hey, Alison," he said.

"Hi," she said.

"Your flowers, your note. My apologies, I never got around to thanking you."

Still looking away, she said, "I called the firm to thank you. For calling the ambulance, riding to the hospital, and all they said was, you were no longer with the firm."

"Right. I was fired."

"No." Looking at him now. "Oh, no, did I have anything . . . was it my fault?"

"No," he said. "It was mine."

She didn't know what to say. Neither did he. A few awkward moments passed as she shelved a few more books.

"Looks like you're doing better," he said.

"Much better, thanks to you."

"Scary thing to see up close," he said.

"Was it, really?"

"Yes. Really."

"I never passed out like that before," she said.

"First time," he nodded. "What do you remember about it?"

"Not a lot. I was looking at you, and then it was . . . kinda . . . lights out."

"I mean, before that."

"Before that? My luck. Everything!"

She tried to find a smile, couldn't quite catch one. "I'll never forget what you did."

"Neither will I," he said, and he meant it.

She went to her thermos, sitting on a bookshelf, and refilled her cup with green tea. "Want some? Package said it will help me live a carefree life."

"What's it called? Fluffy Bunny?"

"Opium, I think," she said.

He caught a first flicker of her postlawsuit personality.

"I'm sure you landed somewhere great," she said. "Where are you now?"

"Actually, that's why I'm here. If you don't mind my asking, whatever happened to your brother's case?"

She shrugged. "I tried some other lawyers, but they all turned me down after they heard he withdrew. I wouldn't be surprised if they talked to him, too."

"Count on it," he said.

She moved to another shelf. "This new mystery by Michael—"

"No, thanks, not today. But look," he said, "I was always curious. That night. The night Jack Pierce assaulted you. Did you tell the ER doctor what he did?"

He could see her anger simmering. "I thought about it, then I wondered, why would I want to do that? So I could talk to all his buddies at the police station about it? So I could hear that arrogant prick call me a liar again and run down my brother? I'm done with it, with him, done with all of it. He humiliated me enough already."

"Me, too."

"You?"

"Last time I ever talked to him, he mentioned he was working late with Chase Fitzpatrick that night."

"Him? All he ever did was get coffee and kiss butt."

"Face it, he has a gift. A few weeks ago, he became a partner at the firm. Funny, huh?"

"Him?"

"I'm fired, then *bam*. Chase makes partner."

She was thinking about it, and he wondered if she would reach the right conclusion.

"Oh," she said. "Like he was getting a payoff?"

"Bribe, payoff, that's how I see it, but I'm biased where those two are concerned."

"So, Chase would go along with his story? Oh," she said again.

"If you don't mind, I'd like to talk to you about another case. Are you doing anything for lunch?"

"What other case?" she asked.

"Yours," he said. "Your case."

Robert bought them each a smoothie and walked with Alison toward the skate park entombing the Venice Z-Boys' old hangout underneath tons of concrete ramps. They sat down at one of the picnic tables, also concrete, where addicts shot up at night, a stone's throw from LAPD's Venice substation.

Earlier, he'd suggested the Sidewalk Cafe but she'd brought her own lunch. A homemade lunch every day was his guess. He wasn't strapped for money yet, but Alison was.

At the picnic tables, she finally spoke to him. Her first words about his proposal since he put it to her on the boardwalk: "You want me to sue the firm? Sue it for malpractice?"

"No, no," he said. "I want you to sue *him* for malpractice. Not the firm. *Only him.* He'll try your case if you have sex with him? Drops it if you won't, then sexually assaults you? That behavior reeks of malpractice."

She took her sandwich out of a baggie and said, "Look, I lived and breathed Brian's case for a year, and the thought of doing it again? I can't do it."

"I know it's a lot to take in, me showing up out of the blue, but if you'll hear me out, it's not Brian's case anymore. It's yours—your case—and I'll take it on contingency. You only pay me if I—if we win."

"Really, I can't, I'm sorry, I want my life back again. The way it was before."

"How was it before?"

"It was . . . I didn't have *some* things, but I was fine with it."

"Money?"

"Sure, there's that, but I didn't need much." He didn't say anything, let her think about it some more. She said, "But I guess after Jack Pierce started talking those big numbers for Brian's case, sure, to be honest, my expectations changed a little."

"How much you owe the hospital?"

"A ton. They keep calling."

He leaned forward, intense. "Let me handle the case. *Your case.* I promise, it'll be short, and after we're done with him, it'll be sweet for you."

"But they said in the meeting you're not even a trial guy. Are you?"

"You're right, I'm not. But he won't let it go to trial. You'll win, Alison. You'll win because he's got too much to lose."

She saw his conviction, how important it was to him.

"I guess I owe you that. No. I do. I do owe you that. All right, I guess so." She reached over and shook his hand.

"Deal," he said, turning on his iPad. "Let's do it."

"What—now?" she asked.

"Got time?"

"Right now?" she asked again.

"If you have time, why not get started?"

"I guess—I mean—what all do you need to know?"

After he opened a file on his iPad, his list of prepared questions appeared. "I know this is hard . . . but for starters, did anyone else happen to see him at your place?"

"Really? Now?"

"Two things about me. I'm always on time, and I'm always prepared."

"Okay," she said. She looked down, like she was conjuring up a bad memory. It was about twenty seconds before she answered him. "Not that I know of. Nobody saw him. I should never have opened the door. I—"

"Hey, you didn't do anything wrong. We take it slow, get started, no need to finish today."

She nodded.

"So, nobody in your building saw him and said anything to you about it?"

"No, nobody. Lots of tenants get up and go to bed early. Construction workers, people like that."

"After he showed up, did he force his way in?"

"No, not at all. He showed up with a bottle of Chateau something-or-other, some big-deal bottle, and said it was a peace offering for yelling at me."

"In the meeting?"

"Right. Where I met you."

"Exactly what happened once you let him inside? Take me through it, would you?"

"So, I was sitting in . . . no, wait. I was making tea in the kitchen when he got there, and I heard something, so I went to the window, and he was standing outside the door, big as life."

Robert recalled: there was no peephole in her door.

"Then I let him in, and there was some chitchat about my great apartment. I think he went to the kitchen for wineglasses, but I didn't have any, so he used whatever I had. Oh, I did have a corkscrew, and he opened the wine and said it had to breathe, you know, making a production out of it."

"Sure," he said. "I hear you."

"And then he looked around the living room, wanted to see what kind of books I read. Then, oh, yeah, and he used the bathroom, and when he came out, he said the wine was ready. After that, he got down to it pretty fast . . ."

"It?" he asked.

"His sales pitch," she said. "Whatever you want to call it."

As she talked, her story unfolded in his mind like this:

In the living room, Jack offers her a water glass of wine and she takes it, tentative. He takes a drink. So does she.

"You know, my firm has a tremendous amount of time invested in your case."

"I know."

"But it's to be expected. Lawsuits have a way of getting out of hand. Are you sure you choose to go forward with it after all that happened today?"

"Yes," she said. "That's what I want."

"Well, then, your choice requires a commitment—from both of us."

"But I told you today, I want to take them to trial."

"*Sure, you do, but why should I not petition the judge to let me with-draw? I mean, what's in it for me?*"

"*Our fee agreement. You get a percentage if we win. That's our deal, right?*"

Back on the beach, Alison stopped talking. She looked at Robert and said, "*Requires a commitment? What's in it for me?* I knew that second he wasn't there to talk business. I kept hoping I was wrong, thinking I could handle anything he might try."

"Go on," he said. "I understand."

"So, anyway," she said, "he put down his glass on the kitchen counter . . ."

As she spoke, Robert let himself go to her apartment again:

Jack puts his glass on the counter. Takes hers; puts it down, too. He caresses her arm, moving closer.

"*Fee arrangement? Try again, Alison. You're a very bright girl, so think about my question this time, and use your God-given imagination.*"

She twists away from him and heads for the door, tells him, "You're gonna leave now."

He follows her. "All right, but remember, if I drop your case, I'll tell any lawyer who considers it and asks my opinion that it's a dog."

She stops. "Why . . . why would you do that?"

"*Because it is a dog. And because I can.*"

Her eyes flash, her voice rising, "You fucking jerk, get out of here!"

He likes seeing her anger, gets off on it. He pulls her away from the door and bears down on her, throws her against the wall. She struggles, kicks over a lamp, but he presses his weight against her. Holds her against the wall, grabs both her wrists, pins them to the wall over her head.

"*Stop it!*" *she screams.*

He forces his mouth over hers. But she twists away.

One of his hands goes between her legs, inside her sweats, his other to his zipper. She struggles hard, trying to break free.

"*Get away from me!*"

He throws her to the floor. Going for her, he knocks over a bookshelf, his chest heaving. He jumps onto her, puts his body weight on top of her. She tries to knee him in the groin, but he blocks it. Puts his knee on her thigh and pins her leg down.

She tries to hit him, but he grabs her wrists again. Rolls her over onto her stomach and pulls down her sweatpants, her panties, too, both around her knees. She tries to scramble away and sees him, wild-eyed behind her, in a cheap mirror resting on the floor.

Alison and Robert, sitting at the concrete table:

"And then he stopped," she told him.

"Any idea why?" he asked.

"Sure. In the kitchen, on my stove, my teakettle started whistling, and it got louder and louder."

"Loud enough for neighbors to hear?"

"Maybe. Anyway, he just . . . kind of . . . stopped. Then he stood up, pulled on his pants, and told me, 'Too bad, you'd be a hall-of-fame fuck.'"

Robert finished taking notes.

Standing, she gazed out at the ocean, still reliving the night. "He didn't rape me," she said.

"But he sexually assaulted you. For your malpractice case, it's close to the same thing. Mind telling me what happened next?"

"Well, he went in the kitchen, turned off the stove. Wait, no, he used his shirt to twist the knob. He took the wine bottle and our glasses and my corkscrew. I screamed at him to get out, and he said, 'How can I get out? I was never here.'"

"I was never here," Robert repeated, typing those words.

"He left, closed the door, cleaned the door handle off, too. Then I locked it, put a chair against it."

She rubbed her wrist absently as he finished taking notes on his iPad. He recalled the simmering teapot on her stove and her chair jammed against the door when he arrived.

"And after that, you called me?" he asked.

"Yes," she said.

"Okay, so . . ."

"No, wait, not exactly. Not at first. I was fine at first, I thought, went in the bathroom, washed my face, thinking I was lucky almost. But anyway, afterward, I started getting more freaked out, hearing things outside, checking the door. I felt so weird. Then I remembered your card."

"My card, sure. So, you called me."

"Twice, I think?"

"That's right, two times. One thing I need to ask—because we both know what he'll try saying about you—did you ever have sexual relations with him?"

She took a deep breath. "No. Never."

"Alison, it won't change anything if you did. It changes nothing but I need to know."

She stood up, looked at him, and said, "That never happened. Not ever." She checked her watch and stood up. "I better get going."

As they headed back to the bookstore, he said, "I really appreciate what you—"

"Thing is," she said, "he always seemed like he was on the prowl when I first met him, always coming on to me."

"Where was that?" he asked.

"The bookstore, after he and Skippy played paddle tennis at the beach. Lots of times they'd get lunch at the Sidewalk Cafe or at Jody Maroni's and come in the store after. Just the way he talked to me. Asking what kind of men I dated, did I like girls, did I go for sex toys. He thought it was cool, but he gave me the creeps."

He made a mental note of this add-on and handed her his new business card. ROBERT WORTH, ATTORNEY AT LAW. No address. His name and phone number.

"Thank you," she said.

"You're my only client, so thank *you*."

He watched her walk past the Sidewalk Cafe into the bookstore. He made it fifty yards up the boardwalk when she caught up with him. She'd remembered something else:

"When he had me down on the floor, he took something out of his pocket or from somewhere, but then the kettle thing happened, and he dropped it on the carpet. It was glass, like a capsule, and it bounced around. One of those party drugs, I think."

"Amyl nitrite?" he asked.

"Maybe, I don't know," she said.

"The capsule. Any chance you have it?"

"No, it was gone, guess he took it with him. Does that help?"

"It can't hurt," he said.

Even without knowing California criminal law well, he believed that Jack's drug possession would help her case. Maybe help it a bundle.

CHAPTER 12

Around eleven that night, Robert drove over to Alison's building on Venice Boulevard, trying to put himself in Jack's shoes the night of the assault. Right off, he decided Jack wouldn't park on Venice, believing as he did that Jack went there to have sex with Alison whether she wanted to go along or not. Not a man with a plan, a former criminal lawyer with a plan.

From the street, Jack would have seen her well-lit parking lot, the **MANAGER** sign on the building. Even with no security cameras visible, he wouldn't have parked in the lot or on Venice. Any of his high-profile cars would be remembered at her building or possibly get boosted if left on the street.

So Robert parked on the first residential street past her building. No streetlights, no restricted-parking signs, plenty of spaces. He got out of his car and waited. No lights came on, no dogs barked, and her building's chain-link fence and gate gave onto this street. Turned out the gate was unlocked, and a short, direct stroll took him to Alison's ground-floor unit.

Makes sense, he thought. *Quick and easy, quiet and dark.*

Next morning, he arranged to meet Alison again for lunch and asked her to bring her legal file to work.

By noon, the Santa Anas blew hot off the Mojave Desert, throwing a thin yellow blanket over the city. The beach started hot and went from there, so they took a table under the Sidewalk Cafe's candy-cane awning, where she signed an engagement letter with him.

After that, she showed him an unopened letter from Fanelli & Pierce. It had been sent certified mail one week after her hospital stay. Inside it, he found Judge Cleary's order approving Jack's motion to withdraw as counsel of record.

By now, Robert's own research told him that to withdraw, Jack could request an *in camera* session with Judge Cleary. An *ex parte* hearing without Alison present. No doubt, the hearing was congenial. Both Jack and Judge Cleary were members of the Bel-Air Country Club, Robert had learned. Very wealthy members, very exclusive, very old money, and even though Jack wasn't old money by club standards, the Brightwells were.

Looking over at Alison, he could tell that actually seeing the withdrawal motion irritated her.

He told her, "Better for you that he withdrew. That's consistent with our theory: you won't go along with him, so he withdraws. If he had let your situation slide? That's not as good for the good guys."

"Good guys? That's us, right?"

"Yep," he said. "All day long."

After that, he learned more about her. A native of Florida. Nuclear family: mom, dad, and older brother, Brian. Dad had been a contractor— not a general contractor, but he did okay for a while. Then he took out a bank loan and opened a kitchen showroom. "We had installation crews and were doing great till 2008," she said.

"You worked with him?"

She nodded. "It was fun. I liked it." She stood and fanned her face. "I'm burning up, could we take a swim?" she asked.

"Sure," he said.

After she changed in the bookstore bathroom, they headed for the ocean. "What happened after '08?" he asked.

"Florida real estate in '08, '09?" she asked. "People stopped paying, but everybody still expected Dad to pay them. Late 2010, he dropped dead of a heart attack with seventeen lawsuits against the business."

"God, sorry," he said. "What about you, coming west?"

First she'd landed in the Valley because of cheaper rent. Took a few temp jobs, saw her brother up in Topanga every so often. Topanga was too isolated and expensive for her, but six months in, Brian was diagnosed with cancer, and she moved in with him.

"Rough couple years," he said.

"A lot worse for them. What about your family?" she asked.

"Lucky. Both my parents are still alive. They live on a family farm up in Gilroy. You know, the simple life."

They reached the waterline north of the Venice Breakwater. She dropped her towel from her waist. He shucked down to his short pants and tried not to check out his client's body. But, he noticed, she had one. Shore break was closing out fast, so they hit the water on the run and dove under the slamming waves, fighting the undertow till they made it past the break line.

Out there, the water was calmer with welcome cold pockets. They held their position against the ebb and flow of the surf, still blowing a little from their effort. Then she lay on her back, floating, staring into the cloudless sky.

She looked over at him. He edged closer to her and said, "I'll do everything I can to make him pay for what he did."

"I believe you," she told him.

Then he told her about another firm employee who had been fired the day before him. Without saying Gia's name or job description, he told Alison he planned to talk to this woman. Even though Gia hadn't returned his calls, Robert was pretty sure he knew where to find her.

CHAPTER 13

"Here for the Seabiscuit Tour, Mr. Worth?"

That's what Gia first asked when he caught up with her that weekend at Turf Terrace at Santa Anita Park. Gia and her banker pal, Leslie, both on their feet screaming and clapping as racehorses thundered down the homestretch. Leslie's jeans skinny, Gia's loose, both in heels and blazers, a couple of killers. Gia must have won because she hugged Leslie as the horses crossed the finish line.

Then Gia headed to the cashier's window with her winner. That's when she saw Robert and made the crack about Seabiscuit.

"Biscuit?" he asked her. "Maybe, Ms. Marquez. Want to go?"

"Dead-horse tour?" she asked. "Not really."

She kissed his cheek, then asked, "How's life treating you, Mr. Worth?"

"Not as good as it's treating you," he said, eyeing the hundreds the cashier counted out for her. "Not returning my calls, Ms. Marquez?"

"Good seeing you, anyway," she said.

They walked back to the table. A bottle of champagne arrived, and Leslie waved thanks to a group of men a few tables over. They waved back. Robert watched the men talking among themselves, wondering who the fuck he was, this guy sitting down with their women.

"So, Robert," Leslie said, right off the bat, "you about ready to buy a house?" Before he could answer, she opened her blazer to reveal *I Heart Banking* printed boldly at chest level on her T-shirt.

"Not really. Not right now," he said, looking at Gia when he said it.

Leslie said, "Beach property is on fire, right, and we've got superlow rates now, right? We're super, supercompetitive."

"Leslie works at a bank," Gia told him. "Can you tell?"

He smiled. Reached for their champagne.

"Venice, right?" Gia asked him.

"Santa Monica," he said, popping the cork. "A block north of the Venice–Santa Monica line."

"Venice used to be cool and hip," Gia said. "Until Google decided it was cool and hip. Now I'm not so sure."

"Stay away from the coffee shops, you'll miss ninety percent of 'em," he said.

She smiled, watched Robert pour champagne into two flutes.

"Haven't seen you in a while. Been on vacation?" Leslie asked him.

"Kind of," Robert said, looking at Gia again.

Then Leslie waved to a man down in the cheap seats. He waved back. About thirty, he wore a short-sleeve shirt, unbuttoned to show off a wifebeater featuring Che Guevara's silk-screened face and raised fist.

"*Viva la revolución,*" Gia said about the shirt. "Dougie. What a douche bag."

"No, he's not," Leslie said. "He's a little—"

"A little douche bag." Then to Robert about the guy. "Dougie wants to meet us here. I finally say okay, but he runs out of gas."

"His gauge is broken," Leslie offered.

"Gets towed, leaves his wallet in the car, and walks here," Gia said.

"Let him sit with us, please? I'll pay for him."

"See this guy right here, Les," Gia said, talking about Robert. "That's how a man dresses, not wearing a mass-murderer guinea T. You're not, are you, Mr. Worth?"

"Not today, Ms. Marquez," he said, finding that no matter what, it was hard for him not to dig Gia.

"Shows up with his very own wallet," Gia said. "Pours our drinks without being asked, doesn't spill a drop. Good-looking, too, if you go for the garlic-farmer-turned-lawyer type."

"Gia hates Doug," Leslie added, taking no offense to Gia dogging him so hard.

Gia nodded at the other table of men. "One of those guys buying the champagne comes over. Dougie's sitting here, know what he does? Gets in his face and says, 'You blind, dude? They're with me, dude! But thanks, anyhow, for the bubbly, biatch!'" Telling it, she's throwing gang signs like Dougie would. "But our boy here?"—meaning Robert—"He keeps his seat and tells the guy, 'Listen, man, the girls really appreciate the champagne.' And Mr. Worth, he'd look at us, see if we were interested in him; we'd shake our heads no, so he'd tell the guy, 'Hard to believe it myself—they're both with me.' Then everybody shakes hands and that's that."

Leslie loved Gia's rap, turned to Robert. "That what you'd do, Mr. Farmer Man?"

"Almost," he said. "But I'd stand up first."

"Why?" Gia asked.

"Show the guy a little respect—he bought champagne, right? Smile at him like I mean it," he said. "Same time, standing up, I'm sayin', 'This is as close as you get to the girls, Horace. Any closer, you need to get around me.'"

Leslie whispered something to Gia. Gia smiled at whatever it was. Then they looked at him so he'd know their secret was about him.

Finally, Gia asked, "We need to talk?"

"I'd appreciate it," he said.

Leslie stood up. "Gotta go anyway." She held out her hand. "C'mon, I love your Healey. I have a real date tonight."

Gia dug into her purse, handed Leslie a set of car keys. "Don't let Dougie drive. Don't let Dougie stop for a tattoo and make you pay for it, and don't let Dougie shoot up in the car."

"I won't! I swear."

They were both laughing. Robert wasn't sure where the kidding ended and the truth began with these two. Even though they were the same age, he could tell Gia was protective of Leslie. He heard Leslie ask, "Call you later?" and Gia saying, "Maybe. Careful with my car."

He noticed a betting slip on the table. When Gia sat down, he handed it to her. "Hers?" he asked.

Gia tore it up. "She always bets the superfecta, wants to win big."

"Bankers? Who knew?"

Her eyes stayed on the horses at the starting gate when she asked, "Thought you might be in the market for a house."

"Not for the foreseeable future," he said.

"Something happen?"

"Same as you," he said.

Looking at him now. "Fired?" she asked.

"And they're off!" the loudspeaker screamed.

In the parking lot, Leslie opened the driver's door of Gia's roadster. Dougie took shotgun but didn't like doing it.

"You gonna let me drive or what?" he asked once they were inside.

"Told you *no* twice, didn't I?"

"C'mon, Les." He tried to snag the keys, and she slapped his hand away.

"Stop. She's probably looking at us."

He stuck his feet out the car window and lay down, his head in her lap.

"Dude, stop fucking around, okay?"

Undoing her belt buckle, he said, *"Oops"* and tried reaching inside her pants.

She grabbed one of his earrings, started pulling on it.

"Fuck. Okay, okay, leggo, leggo."

He was upright now, but she was still holding on.

"Be a good boy, and west of Lincoln, I might let you drive."

"Dig," he said. "I'm jonesin' for Fatburger, babe."

"Fuck Fatburger. Buckle up, Che."

"What's *Che*?" he asked as she mashed the accelerator and flew across the parking lot.

Back inside the racetrack, the last horses streamed across the finish line. Gia tore up her ticket. "You changing my luck, Mr. Worth?"

"Hope not," he said. "I still have a horse in the race."

He gave her the bare minimum about Alison's situation without using her name. Only that a former firm client might have some kind of claim against Jack. That it would be helpful if Gia told him what happened when Jack fired her.

"Who says he fired me?" she asked.

"I saw you that night in your office. You were in tears."

"There's nothing I can say. Too bad about your client—whatever that's about—but I can't help."

"Come on, you were office manager, paid the bills. You knew everything going on at that firm. What's the problem, us talking?"

She went quiet at the question.

"That night in the building's garage," he said, "I was standing beside Dorothy Pierce when you came out of the stairwell. You were office manager for years. You've been to the mansion for how many firm parties? Eight? Nine? More than me, for sure, and she almost put Jack in an arm bar when she saw you."

Gia dropped a hundred-dollar tip on the table, signaled her waiter.

"Something happened between you and Jack. His wife knows about it, right?"

"A simple parting of the ways, Mr. Worth."

"Really? Then why's he yelling at you in his office that night?"

Hearing that item from Robert surprised her. Still, she didn't respond.

"Yeah, I was on that end of the firm, and I heard his voice through his office door. What was that all about?"

"I don't like being yelled at, so I quit. That work for you?"

"Look, the guy pops amyl nitrites and freaks out on women. You know about that, too, don't you?"

"Gimme a break. You're saying your client told you that?"

Evading her question, he said, "That's what he was up to, later the same night he fired you. C'mon, all those years at the firm, you gotta know what he's like."

"No, I don't," she said, standing. "In this town, you never know anybody."

❧

Not much happened on their drive from Santa Anita back to the Westside. Robert found a fifteen-minute oldie set of Tom Petty and The Heartbreakers on the Bronco's radio. Gia rolled down the window and eased back in her seat, kicking it on the 101 to "Refugee." They wound up taking Sunset off the 405, and she pointed lefts and rights for him after they reached Brentwood.

On the way, he looked at her a couple of times. Hard not to. Beautiful, exotic—Asian and Hispanic—but there was *something* dancing around behind those dark eyes. Something telling him: *Stay away if you're smart.* Still, she was so much fun, so easy and intelligent, it was hard to believe her *something* was anything serious.

"Funny, after working together," she said, "how it's not the same afterward."

"Not exactly the same."

"Before, everybody walks through the same office doors, sees those two paintings on the walls, and then there's all the work things in common. All the gossip, who's killing it, who's not."

He thought about it, too. "The big case, the big merger, payday." He switched gears. "What'd Leslie whisper to you back there?"

"Girl stuff."

"C'mon," he said.

"Said if I don't sleep with you tonight, she was gonna kill me. Not her exact words."

He smiled. "Think she's gonna kill you?"

"Definitely," she said. "Stop here."

He pulled to the curb. They were north of Montana in front of a ten-unit condo, a high wall around all of it. Not far from where O.J. Simpson didn't murder Nicole and her friend, Ron Goldman. The neighborhood was exclusive, dark and deserted this time of night, same as witnesses said at O.J.'s trial.

"What's the deal with you and Leslie?" he asked.

"Oh, she puts up with me playing hard-ass. I put up with her playing dumb, and every once in a while, we get lonely."

She came right at him with it. He tried to look like he was taking it in stride as he went around the car and opened her door. She liked him doing that, making the effort, he could tell. Then she got out.

"Really need an answer, don't you?" she asked.

"More than you know, Ms. Marquez."

"So, here you go," she said. "I had an affair with Jack Pierce. Years ago, a serious affair, before he married Dorothy Brightwell. Guess she figured it out, huh?"

"An affair?"

"Grown-ups doing what grown-ups do, Mr. Worth. And sometimes women cry in their offices about stupid things."

"What about his office? Door's closed, he's screaming at you?"

"You mean losing my job, right? '*Throw in a dozen toner cartridges, Ace, and you got yourself a deal. Get those time sheets in, Mr. Worth.*' Hey, I got sloppy at work and he chewed me out. Made him so mad, he fired me. Now I draw unemployment, but I put in for head groundskeeper at the track." Holding up crossed fingers, kidding around. "Wish me luck."

Before he could speak, she moved closer to him. "Look, Jack makes people crazy, so do yourself a favor. Put him away. Put him way behind you, and move on."

"And do what? Wait five more years to hear I'm not partnership material somewhere else?"

She didn't answer. Instead, she surprised him with a kiss. Slow at first, then wrapping both her arms around his neck, getting the feel of his body with hers before pulling away.

"I'd invite you in for a drink, Mr. Worth, but you deserve better."

Cryptic as she often was, she turned away. No point in trying to discuss it anymore. When he drove past her, she stood in the condo unit's dark, gated entrance, keys in hand, reading her mail. Around the next corner, he pulled to the curb. Sat there in the dark and thought about what she'd told him. That Jack didn't harass her. Bored with her job, she messed up. Her onetime boyfriend yelled at her, fired her, and now she was drawing unemployment and chilling out.

Still, something bothered him. Something else. *Her roses.*

He opened his door, jogging back the way he came.

Ten minutes later. Six long Brentwood blocks away from Robert's parked car, Gia strolled up the walk of a Craftsman bungalow. She crossed to a large bed of roses in her front yard. After deadheading a few bushes, she clipped off several lavender Karl Lagerfelds. From the shadows across the street, Robert watched her unlock the door and walk inside the bungalow.

Ten minutes earlier. He figured out why her roses bothered him. For years, he knew Gia grew roses at home. Not a few bushes, a ton of roses, and she brought them to work. He seriously doubted any condo owner's association would let her *fertilize* roses in its small common area.

When he first made it to the condos from his car, Gia was already two blocks away from where she'd been reading junk mail, pretending it was her personal mail. So he followed her four more blocks.

Now, he watched the lights come on inside her Brentwood home. A nice place. The small Brentwood home she'd just lied to him about.

CHAPTER 14

An hour later, those Karl Lagerfelds soaked in a vase on Gia's living room coffee table. Her iPhone rested beside a second, cheap mobile phone. When her iPhone started ringing, she hurried out of the bedroom in a T-shirt and checked the caller. Seeing Leslie's photo on the screen, Gia answered.

Right off, Leslie said: "You better not be alone."

"He dropped me off and split, sorry to bum you out. What's up?"

"I think Dougie's using again," Leslie said. "I dropped him off in trouble town, some sketchy guy he knows over there."

"Using again, yay . . . You owe me a hundred bucks."

"That's so mean," Leslie said. "He wants to go to rehab in Mexico."

"Yeah, right. Bet's a bet, and once a junkie always a junkie," Gia said. "How was your date?"

"Fast and furious. Yours?"

"Wasn't a date, I told you," Gia said.

"What'd he want to talk about?"

"Nothing much. Got fired, same as me, and wanted to compare notes."

"Fired? You kidding? *Him?*"

"It happens," Gia said.

"Tell me about it—I lost a corporate client Friday. A big one and they complained directly to Jerome—said they didn't feel like I was *there for them* like our ads are always saying."

"Were you?"

"Kinda," Leslie said. Then she asked, "Is everything still, you know, okay?"

"Want to get together?" Gia said, changing gears.

"Not tonight, but yeah."

After hanging up, Gia went over to an alcove with built-in drawers. The alcove had been turned into a wet bar with framed photographs and memorabilia hanging on its walls. There was an old photo of her maternal grandparents: Chinese immigrants, the men in black suits standing on a black Ford's running board in the desert. Another old one: a Latino sailor in US Navy dress whites, her father. Then one of her Asian mother in a waitress uniform, posing with young Tony Bennett at the Beverly Hills Hotel coffee shop.

She poured a glass of water, stared at a framed Hollywood Park betting slip from December 22, 2013. The day Hollywood Park shut down. Last race ever, she picked Depreciable to win and lost by a nose to Woodman's Luck. And she made it with Leslie the first time at a run-down motel outside the track.

A framed postcard hung beside that old betting slip. That one she took back to the couch. Lying down, she lit a pinner joint. On the postcard: rustic cabins by the sea. Across its face in red script: *Seahorse Inn, Capitola, CA, Come Back And Sea Us!*

She stared at the cabins, grabbed a serious hit off that joint, and sleeved a tear from her cheek.

CHAPTER 15

Late the next day, Robert sat in a white Escort rental up the street from Gia's house. In daylight, he could see her bungalow, an outlier in a neighborhood of large, newer homes. The dirt alone in this neighborhood went for close to a million five. That much he knew. But not Gia's lot. Between a title report, Google maps, Zillow, and cruising her neighborhood, he learned quite a bit about her house and her finances.

Her home, she inherited from her parents, who bought back in the seventies. The lot had been carved out from large, deep lots on either side. No garage or alley access in back. That made street parking Gia's only option. Even if she wanted to petition for a driveway variance in front, her neighbors would surely fight that kind of nonconforming use.

To Robert, all this mattered because Gia owed $750,000 on the house and was delinquent on her property taxes. A real estate agent told him her property was worth about what Gia owed on it.

Big mortgage, no job, Gia still managed to hit the track and live a chill life. That's what Robert was thinking about when Gia walked down to her roadster and took off, heading away from him. He pulled out in the Escort and followed, laying a few cars back as she made Bundy, headed south.

Ten minutes later, Gia valeted her Healey and went inside Water Grill. Then she and Leslie appeared inside at the open window. He lucked into meter parking and watched them from across the street in Palisades Park.

Thinking about Gia's property again, he agreed with that agent and believed the property's highest and best use was resale to a next-door neighbor as a teardown for a pool or tennis court. Her house, then, wasn't the reason Gia had so much financial breathing room.

Gia didn't appear to have a care in the world. That made him even more curious why she'd lied to him about where she lived. That lie reinforced his belief she was hiding something from him and that her secret was tied to Jack Pierce.

Every few days, he'd met up with Alison to buy a book, have a cup of coffee, take a swim, and he had to admit that he liked hanging out with her. Quick, clever, and it seemed to him that every day she put between herself and Jack Pierce was a better day. To her credit, she hardly ever asked about her case. The only time she did, she asked how long before it was over.

"I believe we'll have results by the twenty-sixth of this month."

"Two weeks from now?" she asked.

"Give or take. That's the big day," he said.

"What happens on the twenty-sixth?" she asked.

"Can't tell you."

"Oh," she said. "You a member of a secret government organization?"

"That is correct. Undercover."

"That explains the Escort," she said.

Other than that, she wasn't interested. That was good for now, but her lack of interest worried him. Clients could change their minds, turn on a dime, leave town, so if and when she did, he had already prepared for it.

As far as Gia was concerned? Following her around the Westside and Beverly Hills, he found that his questions about her remained unanswered. Unemployed, she still managed to drop $500 a day. Shopping, lunches, spa visits, dropping by her bank. The only person with a more boring life?

Me, he decided. *A boring guy following a beautiful woman with a boring life.*

That changed about one week in. One night he was about to call it quits when a guy showed up at Gia's in a Lamborghini. Got out, engine idling, posing. Slick hair, Ryan Seacrest–cut jacket, he didn't bother opening her door when she got in. No way his Escort could keep up with Lambo Boy, so Robert dozed off until a slamming car door woke him.

It was Leslie, getting out of her car, taking a seat on Gia's front steps. Three minutes later, Gia rolled up in an Uber SUV, got out, laughing. Leslie stood up, laughing, too, reading a text—from Gia, no doubt.

A loser date for Gia, he guessed. The women had drinks on the porch, then took it inside. Two hours later, the lights went off. When he left at 11:00 p.m., Leslie was still there.

"Boring," he said, driving away. But now, it was down to just him.

The next day at noon, the man at the counter of the rental-car lot told Robert it would be two hours before his blue Focus was ready. That Focus was his stealth replacement for the white Escort. He decided to walk to the bookstore, but by the time he made it there, Alison was gone.

As he was about to text her, the owner said, "She might be there," pointing at that jammed bulletin board. "Yoga," she added.

A *Yoga With Sonya* flyer was posted in the clutter, so he jogged over to the given address on Amoroso, five blocks inland from the beach. Lululemoned yogistas streamed from one end of Amoroso like butterflies. Couple of guys, mostly women. He followed their trail back to Sonya's vine-covered, rambling wooden house halfway up the block.

Looked like Alison was the last to leave, standing in the yard with a fifty-year-old woman—Sonya, he guessed, lean and otherworldly with a dazzling mane of silver hair. The women embraced, and as Sonya headed inside, Robert opened her front gate for Alison. Unlike the others, she wore a sweated-through, faded 'Canes sweatshirt and tight stretch shorts.

She was surprised to see him. "Thought you were picking up your Tesla rental?"

"Ejector seat wasn't ready. Boss lady said you might be over here. You look . . . relaxed." He meant *beautiful,* because she was. She toweled off as they walked down the street toward her car. "Didn't know you did yoga."

"*Practice* yoga," she said. "I'm still a novice. It's my escape. I'd never get by without it. You know, every time I come here, get into it, start to really relax, it always makes me think about what we're doing."

"How so?" he asked, hoping he guessed wrong about where this was headed.

"Some nights I still dream about what happened. Don't get me wrong, not bad dreams, but it makes me remember Brian, and my mom and dad, and pretty soon, I'm in a place I don't want to be. To live. A place where I don't want to live. And you're following this woman around, spying on her? And it's all really . . . I don't know."

Robert didn't want to tell her about Gia lying to him. It was too hard to explain. When he got right down to it, he wasn't sure he could explain it to himself.

"I hear you," he said. "But I know she's hiding something."

"But is she hiding stuff about him?"

"Yes," he said. "She definitely is," but he knew he couldn't prove it even as he said it. "Would you drop by my apartment after work?"

They stopped beside her LeBaron—top down, those zebra seat covers. "Sure," she said.

"Great, use the back gate," he said, already jogging down the street before she changed her mind.

❧

Late that afternoon, Alison knocked on his door. When he let her in, she said, "There's a man parked in back of your house."

"It's all right, I know him," he said. "Come in, have a seat."

She looked around at his Spartan surroundings, took a seat on the couch. A closed legal folder and a pen rested on the coffee table in front of her.

"Water?" he asked.

"Sure."

He went into the kitchen, out of sight. On the mantel was the prom-night photo of Rosalind and him, among others. It caught her eye.

"Apple? Orange?" she heard him ask.

"Orange, thanks," she said.

She went to the mantel, picked up the photograph, and took a closer look. "This your girlfriend?" she asked.

He came to the door, peeling her orange. "Rosalind. My sister," he told her and went back into the kitchen.

"Loser takes sister to the prom?" she asked, smiling.

"Right after Dad took that, I drove her to her boyfriend's house."

"Pretty. Does she still live up north?"

He came back in. He sat down on the couch, put her bottled water and sectioned orange plate on the coffee table.

"No," he told her. "She died."

She put the picture back on the mantel and sat beside him. "She's so young. What happened? Sorry, it's not my—"

"That's okay," he said. "People ask."

He gathered himself then. "She was assaulted, raped, same night that picture was taken."

"God, you're kidding."

"Her boyfriend drank too much, pulled off the road, didn't want to drive drunk. But they got in a fight. She started walking home and on the way . . . They never found the guy. A deviant passing through town was what the cops said. After that, she got deep into drugs in college, overdosed her sophomore year and . . . all the rest."

"I'm sorry. What about her boyfriend?"

"At first, I wanted to kill him, but it wasn't his fault. He was never the same, either. Went to San Francisco and after that, who knows?"

"Is that why you went to law school?" she asked.

"No, I'm a lawyer because I didn't want to farm. And I'm not a crusader, but I talk to Rosalind sometimes, ask her advice. Stupid stuff like that."

"It's not stupid," she said. "Show me," pointing to the folder.

He opened it and showed her the document inside. "This power of attorney, if you sign it, lets me take care of whatever needs to be done in your case. Anything and everything, all the way down to settling the case for you."

She started to speak. He stopped her, pointed to a clause in the document. "See this section right here?"

"Sure. *Termination*," she said.

"Read it, would you mind? I made sure it was very clear."

After she finished, she looked up. "I can end it anytime I want, right?"

"Anytime you want for any reason or for no reason at all. All you have to do is let me know in writing. An e-mail to me will do the trick."

She was nodding.

"If you sign this, you can put the lawsuit out of your mind. There's nothing for you to do. *At all.* But it's up to you."

She stared at the mantel. At his prom-night photo. She reached for the pen.

"Not yet, hang on," he said and stood up. "Guy in the alley's a mobile notary, needs to witness your signature." He walked to the window, called down the notary, then told her, "You won't regret this, Alison."

"Nail Jack Pierce to the wall, all right?"

"Nail him," he said. "Will do."

They heard the notary's footfall on his wooden stairs.

CHAPTER 16

Robert imagined Gia's red-lacquered fingernails clutching a gearshift as she grabbed second gear ahead of him in her Austin-Healey roadster. She roared north on Pacific Coast Highway past Malibu Country Mart, and before Pepperdine U, she whipped a right turn. A minute later, she cruised up Malibu Canyon Road, a two-lane blacktop throwback to the fifties.

Trailing behind her, Robert muscled his blue Focus to keep up. Lucky he hadn't missed her altogether back in Brentwood. Just as he'd approached her house, she flew past him in the Healey. He'd turned around, spotted her on San Vicente, caught up with her on Entrada heading north on PCH toward Malibu, so he lagged her up the coast.

PCH. Where Frankie and Annette and Gidget hung out; what Dinah Shore meant when she invited the world to *see the USA in a Chevrolet*; and where Thelma Todd died in a hail of gangland bullets outside her own after-hours joint.

After turning onto Malibu Canyon Road, the Healey and the Focus were the only two cars headed inland, so he had to hang even farther back on the two-lane. So far back that a truck pulling a horse trailer got between them. That worked for a mile or two, but she was getting too far ahead, and on the next straightaway, he made his move. Bad news for him. It was a Focus move, and halfway past the truck, he glimpsed the Healey roaring right, down a side road.

A quarter mile later, he turned around and floored it back toward PCH. And there was that turn she took: Piuma Road. He took it but had lost a lot of ground. On his navigation map: twists and turns ahead for ten miles. As he was starting to think she was out for a spin, putting her roadster through its paces, he caught a car in his rearview. Coming up fast.

As it sped past, Robert caught a glimpse of the driver: Jack Pierce.

"Oh, yeah," he said, slamming his steering wheel.

Five hundred yards farther down Piuma, Jack banged a left onto Cold Canyon Road. Robert slowed down and caught sight of a sign up ahead: **Saddle Peak Lodge 200 Yards.** Jack's brake lights flashed at the lodge itself. Robert slammed to a stop, parked on Piuma's shoulder, and started running back toward Cold Canyon.

By the time he reached Saddle Peak Lodge, the valet had already parked Jack's Mercedes. Two cars away from it: Gia's red Healey.

Not a lodge at all, this brown-clapboard roadhouse was cradled by the Santa Monica Mountains with a big-money canyon view to its west. He eased through the front door: animals with antlers on hewn-wood walls, exposed beams overhead, a working stone fireplace, and wooden vines woven into chairs.

Then he saw Jack and Gia, escorted through the far dining area to an empty outside patio.

I get it, he thought. *Still early, not many customers yet.*

Rustic, romantic, out of the way. Easy enough to write copy for a place like this. He took a seat at the end of the bar and leaned back on his stool. When he did, he could see Jack and Gia seated outside, thirty yards away. The two of them sitting there, he could tell, like a bad first date.

The maître d' walked up and offered to seat him.

He passed on her offer and ordered a beer from the bartender. Rugged, handsome, forty, he looked like an out-of-work actor to Robert, so after a couple of minutes shooting the breeze, Robert gave it a shot: "Excuse me, didn't I see you on . . . what was it . . . I know I saw you in . . . help me out?"

"*CSI.*" The bartender smiled.

"Knew it. *Miami,* right?" Robert guessed.

"Right on."

"Lotta industry people come out here?"

"Some. Not enough. Too far from the studios except for Sony."

Robert could tell the bartender was past bullshitting himself: up for this part, up for that one. Once actors gave up acting, the ones he'd met were pretty decent guys.

"Man sitting outside looks Hollywood," Robert asked, meaning Jack. "Agent or what?"

"*Charles?* I don't know what he does."

Jack's waiter came up to the bar-service area, set down his pad.

"One O'Bannion Single Malt for the gentleman, Pellegrino for the lady."

The bartender cracked open a Pellegrino for Gia. Set a half-full bottle of whiskey on the bar. "Tell Charles that Gary said we're out of his O'Bannion. Then tell him Gary thinks there's a bottle in the storeroom, and Gary will run get it special, just for him."

"Will do, Gary," the waiter said.

"She *The Famous?*" the bartender asked the waiter.

"No. She hasn't performed since that day."

Both of them laughed. The waiter took off with Gia's Pellegrino.

"Do you know *Charles?*" Robert asked, meaning Jack.

"Comes here quite a bit, but no. One of those guys likes a fuss made over him."

Robert nodded. Made sense to him. "*The Famous?* I gotta ask . . ."

"I wasn't here that day, but that's her nickname. Short for *The Famous Tattoo Girl.*"

Robert said, "Sorry I missed seeing that. Who is she?"

The bartender said, "Well, I was never in *CSI: Miami,* so that depends."

Robert slid a hundred-dollar bill across the bar as Jack's waiter came back. Gary poured whiskey into a highball glass, told the waiter, "Tell Charles his pal, Gary, cracked the seal on his O'Bannion, the very last bottle in stock." He winked at Robert.

"As you wish," the waiter said.

The bartender snapped that hundred at the waiter like they'd share it.

"You have any idea who *The Famous* was?" the bartender asked.

"Not really. Younger, though, a lot younger than Charles. Had on shades, ball cap, short skirt, but, dude, was she hot for him or what?" the waiter said.

"Upstairs, right?" the bartender asked, meaning for the waiter to share with Robert, not him.

"At first," the waiter told Robert, "I thought she was goin' down on him at the table. Then they took it upstairs, one of the private dining rooms. And get this: you could still hear 'em goin' at it from down here."

"And you have no idea who she was?"

"One-shot deal far, as I know. A pro, maybe? But after their show, she came down the stairs, took it right out the front door. Oh. And the way Charles always does it, he pays cash, or the girl does. No credit cards."

"So he's always just *Charles*," Robert said, and both guys nodded.

The waiter headed away with Jack's whiskey, and Robert followed him into the first dining room.

"What about her tattoo?" he asked the waiter. "Where was it?"

"Got a customer here, boss."

Robert stuffed a twenty in his pocket. That stopped him.

"Upper calf, right below the knee," the waiter said.

"What'd it say, you remember?"

"It was small. A word, maybe, more like a personal motto or a creed, not a big dragon or wolf. Hey, boss, I was trying not to look."

He turned to leave. Robert stopped him.

"Right leg or left?" Robert asked.

"Seriously, boss?"

The waiter headed though the door, out to Jack's table. Through a paned window, Robert watched them. Watched the waiter serve Jack his drink, take out his pad to write down their food order. There was no touching or kidding around between Jack and Gia, not that he could see. To him, Gia looked like she was sad.

As the waiter headed back inside, Robert turned to leave. That was when he saw Jack slide a thick white envelope across the table to Gia. And in the next heartbeat, she reached out, and the envelope disappeared into her purse.

The lobby of Gia's Brentwood bank was busy. It was almost 6:00 p.m. Robert waited in an out-of-the-way chair, facing a desk with a shiny nameplate: CHRISTIAN DUMAR. A banker in a striped suit tapped him on the shoulder.

"Are you sure Christian said your meeting was today?" he asked. "It's his day off."

"Yes, today. We were very clear about it."

"We close in ten minutes. Are you sure someone else can't help you?"

From the corner of his eye, he caught Gia walking in the door. Once she made it to the marble table, she filled out a deposit slip and pulled out that white envelope from the Saddle Peak. Counted the wrapped stacks of cash from inside Jack's envelope on the table.

"Tell you what, I'll catch him tomorrow." Robert stood and shook the banker's hand. "My bad," Robert said and slipped out the doors behind Gia.

Ten minutes later, he fished her receipt from the trash barrel outside, where she'd tossed it. Then he went back to his Focus and unwadded it.

$20,000.00, her receipt read. All cash.

CHAPTER 17

A cue ball smashed a diamond-shaped eight-ball rack, scattering balls all around the table. Alison was shooting, sank two stripes on her break, and kept her turn.

"Think I'll go with . . . mmm, let me think . . . stripes?" she asked him.

"Your call," Robert said, chalking his cue.

She made her next shot.

He'd already told her on the phone about Gia's envelope of cash, and she suggested meeting here, at the Tattle Tale Room. Ever since, she hadn't mentioned Gia's envelope. That surprised him.

She made another shot. He chalked his cue again. "Next time I pick the game, okay?"

"Like what?"

"Bowling?"

"I'll get my ball out of storage." She made her next shot, too, looked up from the table. "So, you think Jack's paying that woman to keep quiet about something?"

"Sure you want to know more?"

"A little more," she said. "I don't get it. He fired her, didn't he?"

"I'm not quite there yet, but I gotta believe Jack's been a very bad boy."

"No surprise there."

She settled down, missed a hard bank shot but left him buried behind the eight. He circled the table, looking for a shot.

"Nice leave," he said.

"Brian had a table in his living room. He said eight-ball is half strategy."

He settled down to his shot. She leaned her jeans' button-fly into his target pocket, innocently chalking her cue. More strategy.

"Now what?" she asked. "You'll call him at the law firm?"

"Nope." She was definitely distracting him with that button-fly. "Would you mind?" He motioned her away from the pocket.

"Oh, sorry." She moved. But not much. It didn't matter. He had no shot.

"You'll go see him at the firm?" she asked.

"Nope. I'm trying to shoot, Alison."

"You're running out of time, you know? Tomorrow's the twenty-sixth—that big deadline you keep talking about."

"I'm about to run the table," he said. "If you want to concede, I'll let you save face."

"Please, take your time."

"Do me a favor while I'm thinking. Get that envelope out of my jacket, please."

She went to his jacket, found the envelope. Ivory card stock, heavy like it might be a wedding announcement. She brought it to him. "This?" she asked.

"Mind opening it?" he asked.

She opened it and pulled out an engraved invitation.

"Do me another favor and read it."

So she did: *Dorothy and Jack Pierce request the pleasure of your company at their Bel-Air home on Stone Canyon Road. Catering by Bistro Fresco of Beverly Hills.*

"You gotta be . . . what?" she said.

"Your game," he said. He set his cue on the table. "I kept my invitation to the firm party. Read the date."

She read it and looked up. "The twenty-sixth? You're going?"

"My best suit's already laid out on the bed. You want maximum leverage, don't you?"

"I guess so . . ."

"Me, too. If you can handle it, I want you to come with me."

"What, to his . . . to their home?"

"Sure," he said.

She thought about it. "God. I don't know if . . . I don't know . . ."

He said, "Last time he dealt with you at the firm, it wasn't your best day, was it? Same thing goes for me, and it left a bad taste in my mouth."

She nodded. "Both those guys."

"Oh, Chase, he'll be there, too. I want to take it to Pierce, right at him, right on his home court."

"You think it will help if I go, too?"

"Seeing you? My date? Behind his big gates, inside his house? The law, it's half strategy, too. What do you say? You want to nail him, right?"

She thought about it some more. Then she looked right at him and said, "I'm in." Then without Robert asking, she said the same thing again.

CHAPTER 18

Expensive breasts were treated to a last-minute fluff inside a skimpy cocktail mini. Chase and his braless wife stepped from their Range Rover, handing it over to the valet in the Brightwell mansion's porte cochere.

The couple walked toward the open front door, where Dorothy greeted them. "Good evening, Mrs. Pierce. Chase Fitzpatrick," he said.

"Of course, Chase. You're my husband's favorite."

"And my wife, Meridian," Chase beamed.

"*Meridian*? Do come in, Meridian, and hurry," she said, eyeing the younger woman's cleavage. "I can see that you're chilly."

"Should've worn a sweater, right?" Meridian said.

"Oh, no, dear, that would spoil the whole effect."

Dorothy handed them off to a server with *hors d'oeuvres*. Looking outside with a brittle smile, she softened when Philip stepped from his BMW sedan. Once he reached the door, he handed her a bouquet. It was nothing showy.

"Ah, Philip, my favorite Fanelli in the world. Are these for my husband?"

He smiled back at her. "They say bringing flowers to a party distracts the hostess from her duties, but these were so lovely, Dorothy, I hoped you would grant me an exemption."

"They are lovely, Philip. And it's lovely to see you, too."

Philip looked outside. No other cars were pulling up, so he closed the front door. He shook her hand, and she whispered, "If you'd just shoot me, I could miss all the fun."

"It will be fine. You're among friends."

The Bronco's windows were open, its air conditioner blowing full out. Robert had parked fifty yards down Stone Canyon from the Brightwell gate. Alison sat beside him in a black shift. Tanned now, she was athletic and slender, a brunette with long, sun-streaked hair. Every bit of five ten in heels, she fanned herself with a Johnny's Pizza menu and asked, "Why can't we go in now?"

"Not yet. It's all right to be a little late."

"Who is this guy who's supposed to call you?"

"Rolando. He works for Bistro Fresco."

"For the caterer? You know him?"

"Not well. I met Rolando yesterday, paid him two hundred bucks."

"To do what?" she asked.

"To keep tabs on the man of the house."

No time for a more elaborate answer—a head-miked security guard started closing the gate. Robert dropped the car in gear and drove up to the driveway.

"Afternoon," Robert said. "Running a little late. Robert Worth and a guest."

Robert showed his invite to the guard, who checked him against the guest list and peered inside at her.

"Sure thing. Robert Worth and guest. They'll take your car up top."

"Thanks," he said.

Driving in, Robert was relieved. His educated guess proved right. Showing up. Him? It never crossed Jack's mind, and his name was still on Dorothy's list.

Halfway up the drive, his cell phone rang. He stopped. Checked the screen: *Rolando.*

"*¿Roberto?*"

"*¿Sí?*"

"*¿El Macho? Está en la cocina.*"

"*¿Con su mujer?*"

"*No, con otra chica. Ayy . . .*"

"*¿Que pasó?*"

"*Su Mujer. Aquí. Shit.*"

"*Gracias, mi chico.*"

He clicked off, turned to Alison. "We're going in through the kitchen. You mind?"

In the kitchen, caterers scurried around, assembling dinner. It was a large room, larger than four of Robert's apartments. Near the pantry doorway, Jack huddled with Meridian, standing a little too close to be talking sports. Across the room, unaware of them, Dorothy opened and closed custom cabinets, searching for the best vase for Philip's flowers.

Once she found a small one, she slid them in, arranged them, and went to one of four custom sinks to add water. Right then, she spotted her husband and Meridian. Jack didn't see her. Not until she was ten feet away.

"Excuse me?" Dorothy said.

His expression gave nothing away when he turned to her and said, "Ah, dear, you know—"

She cut him off. "May I borrow my husband—*Meredith?*"

Chase's wife didn't have the sense to leave and said, "Lots of people make that mistake—it's *Meridian*."

"No, it's not. Meridian isn't a name. It's goddamn geography."

"Oh, of course, Mrs. Pierce," she said, her pumps clattering away on one-of-a-kind floor tiles.

Dorothy told him, "If I ever catch you with another woman, Jack—"

"Don't act that way, Dorothy. She's my partner's wife, my go-to guy. I introduced them, remember?"

"Certainly, I remember. What I don't recall is how you met such a lovely young woman in the first place."

"Please, this is crazy, darling, and we have a house full of guests."

He kissed her cheek, gave her a hug, and left. She set down the flowers and picked up a vodka bottle from a serving table, then poured four fingers over ice and splashed a breath of tonic on top.

"Lemon or lime, Ms. Pierce?"

She looked over at a nearby prep table. It was Robert, standing with Alison, and holding a paring knife.

"Lime, please. What in the world are you doing back here?"

"I was late," Robert said. "Hoped we could slip in without anyone noticing, but . . . this is Alison Maxwell, a friend."

"Hello, Alison."

Robert handed Dorothy a slice of lime on a cocktail napkin. She dropped it into her drink.

"Mrs. Pierce," Alison said, "you have a beautiful kitchen."

"Oh, thank you. I'd planned to use it more myself, but Jack and I, we're both so busy that entertaining winds up being a great challenge."

"Your counters, are they Carrera?" Alison asked.

"No, Thassos, but the two are similar."

Alison paced around the clean, white counters and cabinets. Stainless-steel accents everywhere, Miele appliances, two gleaming commercial refrigerators with glass doors, double ovens, Gaggenau serving tables, and heat lamps.

"I've never seen anything like this. The level of finish, the workflow . . ."

Dorothy joined her, and they took a walking tour. "It was a mess when Father bought it, the kitchen, that is. The rest of the house, we didn't need to change it structurally, except for the heating and air conditioning."

Alison stopped at the range. Eight feet long, red enamel with stainless trim, it looked like a work of art. "La Cornue?" Alison asked.

"Yes, you're familiar with it?

"Only from magazines. I had a client who ordered one, but his check bounced when he was arrested."

"Arrested?"

"I'm from Florida. He was a drug dealer, I think."

Dorothy smiled. "Are you an interior designer?"

"No, no, my family installed kitchens back east. We had a showroom, but nothing—I mean, nothing at all like what you did here."

"Thank you so much, dear." She took a swallow of her drink and turned to Robert. "I make it a point not to follow firm business, but I couldn't help but notice that Mr. Fitzpatrick became a partner. That cannot have been good news for you, and I'm so very sorry."

"That's kind of you to say, Ms. Pierce."

"*Dorothy*, please, each of you."

Robert said, "Thanks, Dorothy."

Then he gauged this woman. Intelligent, talented, pretty without any outside help. Drinking too much because . . . He could only guess what she went through married to Jack and recalled her tight reaction when she saw Gia in the firm garage. All of it made him decide to take a chance.

"Actually, I haven't been truthful. The firm let me go a while back, and I need to speak to your husband about some loose ends. I still had my invitation, and this was the only way I knew to reach out to him."

"Oh, that law business is so brutal. Capable as you are, I'm certain you've already landed on your feet."

"Very close to it. Any way we could surprise your husband now?"

"Well, Robert, Alison, I can only say this." She set down her drink, finally having fun at her own party. "If Jack isn't expecting you, we mustn't keep him waiting."

≈

The Brightwell living room went dead. And it went dead fast. Jack's face hardened when he saw Dorothy walk into the room, arm in arm with Robert and Alison. Harder still when his wife said, "Jack, we have a special guest. He desperately needs to have a word with you, so I obliged him."

From a quilted couch, Chase bolted upright when he saw Robert and Alison. One of his suede loafers swiped a glass of Bordeaux off the coffee table, and as wine cascaded onto a Persian carpet, Meridian gave him a hard elbow shot. In a nearby wingback chair, Philip settled in to watch as Robert and Alison approached Jack.

"S'up, Jack," Robert said. "Believe you've met Ms. Maxwell, haven't you?"

"Hi, Jack," she said.

He hated the *Jack* thing. Somehow he kept his cool. "In my study, Worth. Right now."

Robert ignored him. Looked around till he found Chase on his hands and knees, blotting that wine stain with cocktail napkins.

"Chase," Robert said, walking over to him, "read all about you in the *Times*. Congratulations, man. You earned it."

Chase was mumbling something. Robert could barely make it out: "Was that: *Go fuck yourself, Worth?* Great material, another winner." He looked at Meridian. "Must be a ton of laughs living with Chase." Looked to Robert like she was about to toss her wine in his face. "Go

120

ahead, do it," he said, patting Chase on the back. "Make it even worse for your boy."

She backed down.

Across the room, Mr. Brightwell had whirred up to Alison in his wheelchair. "What's your name, sweetheart?" he asked.

"Alison Maxwell."

He shook her hand, then held on to it.

"Lionel Brightwell. Call me *Lionel*, makes me feel eighty again."

"Sure, Lionel, I'd like that."

Now Jack moved in on Robert and gripped his forearm. "Let's go, sport, outta here." Rolling his arm into Jack's thumb, Robert broke the hold and returned to Alison's side.

"Alison, will you be all right out here for a little while?"

Lionel butted in and growled, "Hell, yeah, Worth, she's all right. She's with me."

She gave him a good-luck wink, and he gave her one back.

"Okay, Jack," he said, "let's do it, bro."

They walked past Philip. He nodded to his protégé, but Robert ignored him and left the room with Jack.

Lionel was digging Alison and motioned her down, whispering to her, "All of 'em are vultures, waiting for me to die so they can pick over my bones."

"Young stud like you?" she whispered back. "They're dreaming."

He roared at that and beckoned a roving server, who came right over. Lionel took a glass of wine. Alison noticed the server's name tag: *Rolando.*

"Well, then, Alison, you're driving. It's nursie's night off. Over there."

He pointed at Chase and Meridian. She was spritzing the carpet with soda, too, almost in tears. Chase desperately blotted wine with a bar towel.

As the wheelchair pulled up, Chase told Lionel, "The stain, it's definitely coming up, sir. I don't think it will be a problem at all."

"Brought this rug back from Italy after the war. After my beloved Forty-Fifth took Salerno and Anzio. Know what that carpet's worth, son?"

"No, sir, I don't."

"Appraiser didn't, either. Must be why he said it was priceless. Know what *priceless* means, boy?"

"It's coming out, sir. See?"

"It comes out, *podnah*, or you're cuttin' my lawn the next two hundred years."

Alison knelt down, tapped Chase on the shoulder, and pointed at another stain.

"What?" he said, seething.

"Missed a spot. Right under your nose, you ass-kissing, a-hole . . ."

CHAPTER 19

It wasn't the study's twenty-foot ceilings, walls of bound books, or paneled gun cases Robert noticed first. It was photographs of Jack—scuba diving, mountain climbing, sparring with a trainer. Several more framed shots showed him in the LA Marathon or last leg of the LA Ironman, digging deep to finish.

The moment Jack closed the door, he took off his jacket and said, "Rodney?"

"Sir?"

The Maybach driver rose from one of two facing couches centered on the fireplace. But Jack kept his eyes on Robert while he spoke: "Out, Rodney. Check on Dad."

"I'm not dressed for—"

"Check on Dad, thank you."

Twenty seconds later, Rodney was out another door, far end of the room. The entire time, Jack stayed focused on Robert.

Once the other door closed. "One-shot deal, Worth. Grab the tart, get her out of my house, and we call it day."

"Checked the records, Jack. It's not your house—it's Dorothy's."

"Dorothy's," Jack repeated.

Then he feinted a left jab and threw a hard right cross into Robert's face. Caught him on the cheekbone and sent him over a couch, breaking the coffee table as he crashed to the floor.

Robert lay there, trying to clear his head.

"C'mon, Worth, let's see what you got. That's what you wanted when I fired you, wasn't it?"

Robert struggled to his knees, knowing now he had guessed right gaming this out—good chance he'd have to take one for the team today. Guy hit harder than he figured, but there was one thing he knew when he made it to his feet. He wasn't throwing a punch in Bel-Air. Not inside this house, Jack's or not, where technically he was a trespasser. With Bel-Air security involved, he could go to jail, and with the right Beverly Hills judge, he could be worrying about making bail, not working this case.

"No, thanks, Jack. Enough flexing for today."

"What I figured," Jack said, making a call on his cell phone. "Benny, it's Jack Pierce. A trespasser refuses to leave my residence. No, nothing I can't handle. Send a car, I'll be waiting."

Trespasser. Robert heard it and was meant to. Jack wasn't using the private head-miked guys outside, going instead through formal channels that would jail him on Jack's say-so.

"Have it your way, but remember—I tried to settle before we filed suit."

"Settle what? Her brother's case is shit. If you had really reviewed his file, you'd already know that."

Robert thought about it: talking about Brian Maxwell's case was a detour, but it might be a nice avenue to the main event.

"*Estate of Brian Maxwell vs. Consolidated Construction?* The case you told Chase and me was worth three, four hundred thousand? The case you told your client was worth ten grand? That case?"

"You're gonna second-guess me? Based on casual remarks, speculation about the size of her brother's verdict?"

"Dunno, you were pretty clear about it."

"Wonder how Chase remembers that conversation? Seriously, Worth, all this wasted motion, that's it? You're coming up here, coming at me with *that*?"

"Wrong case, Jack."

"There is no other case, Worth."

"Sure, there is. My case involves hospital records. It involves tachycardia, secondary to acute anxiety. And it involves bruised wrists. All of it caused by sexual assault by my client's lawyer. Her lawyer, the one who told her he'd drop her case if she didn't have sex with him. And guess what? He dropped her case. It's her claim against you, Jack. And it's for malpractice."

Robert was amazed Jack kept his cool.

"Malpractice, against my firm?"

"Not against the firm. Against you, personally."

"Either way, a corporate drudge like you? You couldn't find the right courthouse."

Actually, Robert had looked into that issue and knew two things: Alison's actual ZIP code was Culver City, and Culver City residents sue Bel-Air residents in Santa Monica.

"I can find it, and when I do, I'm suing you for a million eight. For malpractice. Suing you personally."

Malpractice and *a million eight* hung there as blue lights flashed outside. A Bel-Air security officer stepped from his car. Jack hesitated, then cranked open a casement window and called out to the guy. "My bad, Benny, he was on the guest list. Dorothy sends her apologies. She never tells me anything. Wives, right?"

The security officer waved, got back in his car. Jack turned back to Robert.

"Let me see your cell phone." Robert showed it to him. "Let me see you turn it off."

Robert powered off his phone and put it on the table. "Now you," he said.

Jack powered down and put his phone by Robert's. "Let's be clear. If you have a backup device, you don't have my permission to record what we are about to say."

"Same goes for me," Robert said.

Jack took the lead. "Sounds great sitting here, doesn't it? Malpractice, a million-eight verdict, piece of cake. But you're no trial lawyer, just a bitter ex-employee who couldn't play hardball with the big boys. End of the day, it's still your trailer-trash client's word against mine, and good luck with that."

"You're right about one thing—only one thing. I am bitter. But it's not only Ms. Maxwell's word I'm counting on. There's another ex-employee. Her name is Gia Marquez."

"Gia Marquez has nothing but good things to say about me and always will."

"Sure about that?" Robert said.

"Quite sure," Jack replied.

"I'd say good things, too, if someone were paying me to keep quiet. Paying me lots of cash, helping me out with living expenses, while I cruise the Westside, chilling out."

"You're speaking in tongues, Worth. You can't ever prove—"

"I can show her twenty-thousand-dollar cash deposit made at Bank of Brentwood, then I'll let Ms. Marquez explain her deposit in her deposition. Or any other of her deposits for large amounts of cash that I might find in pretrial discovery."

He left out what he saw and heard at the Saddle Peak Lodge. He didn't want Jack spreading money around up there, clouding memories.

"Depositions? Discovery?" Jack asked. "My trial calendar's full, unlike yours. We'd get around to her deposition, when? A year from now? Two years? And a trial? A verdict? Appeals? You might be who-knows-what by then."

Robert saw it: Jack was threatening to drag out the legal process with tactical delays. A weak position to be in. He knew he had Jack backpedaling now, so he went in for the kill.

"Trials, verdicts, appeals—so what, Jack? I'm filing suit in two days. In two days, Ms. Maxwell's public complaint will allege what you did to her: physical threats, sexual assault, threats to drop her case if she didn't go along. I'll couple that with your cash payments to a former office manager, payments made so that she could keep her Brentwood home. And that the hush money was paid to keep her quiet about your affair with her."

"Allege whatever you want. I'll deny every allegation, have the case dismissed, and before it's over, I'll have your law license."

"Not before I call the *Times*. Not before I tell them about a lawsuit involving a certain Bel-Air power couple. About an innocent wife and her deviant husband. You know, *TMZ* might even want an exclusive; Harvey Levin works out at my gym. Hard not to wonder, isn't it? How will all this play around the Brightwell dinner table?"

"Don't you get it, Worth? Even now? Your client is using you."

Ignoring the questions, Robert said, "You know, I did do some legal work for you at the firm. That was a long, long time before you summoned me to the Maxwell meeting."

"So Fanelli told me. Who cares?"

"You do. You care a lot because Fanelli never told you I drafted your prenuptial agreement. Did he happen to mention that?"

"What?"

"It was so long ago, Fanelli probably forgot the specifics, but I did a hell of a job and I was proud of my work. So proud that I kept a copy of it in my files at home. It's real simple and real clear: *Dorothy pays you zero in a divorce if she can show infidelity.* Tell me now, Jack, who's using who?"

This time, Jack didn't move or say a word.

Robert had figured out the prenup was Jack and Dorothy's, even though Philip left both parties' names blank. Once Robert found out the firm represented the wife, and the husband repped himself, he knew the contract was between the engaged lovebirds.

Finally, Jack said quietly, "Your client's a liar. A goddamn liar."

"Yeah? Then where were you were that night? Prove to me you weren't in Culver City—assaulting my client—and this whole thing will go away."

"I already told you—"

"Working late with Chase? When I get him under oath, facing perjury with his law license at stake, he'll fold, and you know it. So, where were you? It's a simple question. Same question your wife and her father are gonna be asked in their depositions."

"I've got no problem proving where I was. None at all, but take a seat."

Jack sat down. Robert stayed where he was until Jack said, "Worth. Please."

Please? He took a seat facing Jack on the other couch.

"Coming here tonight, bringing the game to me, you finally showed me something. Something I didn't think you had. You showed me you're prepared to go the distance."

Go the distance? He hadn't heard that chestnut since the day Jack fired him. Those finish-line photos Robert noticed earlier backed up Jack's metaphor.

"Finally something we can agree on, right?" Jack asked.

"Could be," Robert said.

"And given what's happened, I think it only fair that I—that we reconsider your partnership. Fanelli, as you might guess, will have no problem doing so."

Robert closed his eyes and let those words wash over him.

"I'd be lying to say I haven't pictured this moment," Robert said.

"Well, nobody wants to make a liar out of you," Jack said, smiling at him.

First time for everything, he was thinking. And he said, "How do you see it working, Mr. Pierce?" He could tell Jack liked being *Mr. Pierce* again.

"I'd start you at two hundred twenty-five thousand, Robert."

Robert? That was a first, too. "I don't know," he said. "Kind of disappointing under the circumstances."

"Then I'll go two-seventy-five," Jack countered.

Robert said, "We'll end up at three hundred base salary, but let's put a pin in that number for now. One reason I chose the firm in the first place was the prospect of a view. Is there a corner office available with an ocean view?"

"A corner's not possible now, but there is a large office on the front of the building. Full ocean view, and I'll leapfrog you on the list for a corner. In all candor, that might be a while."

Robert leaned back and gave it some thought.

"I'll make it happen."

"There's one more thing, Mr. Pierce."

"Three hundred thousand base salary? I agree, so let's put this thing to bed."

"So, all I need now is that you fire Chase. I can't work with him," Robert said. "Something about him rubs me the wrong way. And that needs to happen today. Now. Right here in the other room."

That demand brought Jack up short.

"What's the problem? He's a litigation partner, and I'll see to it you never work with him."

"No, he's not a litigation partner . . ."

"Last time I looked he was a—"

"He's your bought-and-paid-for alibi. There's no conceivable way you can fire him, is there?" Robert stood up. "Besides, I won't take your job offer. I don't sell out my clients like you do, because we both know that would be blatant malpractice."

A calm descended on Jack. He stood up, too, and told Robert, "Do you think I'd ever give all this up?"

"Pay up. One million, eight hundred thousand dollars—not a cent less—and nobody ever knows. A small price to pay for silence. That's part of the deal—nobody ever finds out from my client what a scumbag you are."

"Call me next week at the firm. Now get out of here." Jack turned his back on Robert, dismissing him.

Robert said, "Here's how it's going to work. I need your answer on Monday morning. By 11:00 a.m. *sharp*. That's when I file this at the Santa Monica courthouse." Robert handed him a folded document from his jacket and said, "Read it. See if you have any questions."

Jack started reading Alison's four-pager against him. Her beef. Sure, Robert could have gotten away with checking boxes on Santa Monica's Civil Case Cover Sheet: *Legal Malpractice, Unlimited Amount; Jury Trial.* Could have alleged minimal facts, too, and let Jack's imagination run wild about things Robert wasn't yet divulging.

But Robert didn't have that luxury. Jack needed to know how bad his life was going to get, so he was reading a full-blown, bare-knuckle version. Four pages that painted a picture of his conduct toward Alison: her brother's death, Jack's promises of success, her abusive meeting with him at the firm, then a double shot of sexual assault, chased with withdrawing from her case in a judicial hearing behind closed doors. Four pages that his wife and her father would see. The only thing he left out was an allegation about amyl nitrites. That piece of business, he held back.

He didn't wait for Jack to finish.

"You're not on the front steps of the courthouse by eleven sharp, start packing up your go-the-distance Ironman selfies, and get ready to kiss all this good-bye."

Without waiting for an answer or looking back, Robert left the way he came in. Once the door closed, Jack sank onto the couch, the complaint dangling from his hand.

"Goddamn, Gia," he said. "Goddamn it, what have you done?"

❧

"You're kidding me. Your breasts?" Robert asked Alison.

"I swear, he wanted to look at them. Wanted to admire them, he said."

"Jesus," he said, laughing and lowering a baggie of ice from his face.

They were walking along the boardwalk not far from his apartment.

She said, "Lionel had a glass or two of wine, really feeling it, but what a great guy. Then Nurse Rodney showed up, and I got the picture: Dorothy can't have other women around. I feel sorry for her father—her, too. All that money, and look at the mess they're in."

"You saved me big-time back in her kitchen. Dorothy really liked you."

"I was so nervous at first, then . . . Oh, I saw your man, *Rolando*. What was that all about?"

"Rolando, two other waiters at Bistro Fresco. I paid them to tell me when they saw Jack hitting on anybody. I thought it would give us an edge if we caught him doing his thing."

"His thing? You were that sure?"

"Not like it happened, but he hit on my dates the last two years. Nothing serious, *let me show you around the house*, that kind of thing. I didn't think too much about it back then."

"I don't believe it. You had dates?"

"It happens," he said, rolling his jaw from Jack's punch.

She took his baggie of ice and said, "Hold on." She went into a corner market closing for the night. Its eclectic sign: EGG ROLLS, KABOBS, PIZZA, TACOS.

Waiting for her, he looked around. Shop lights were shutting off, the night crowd starting to take over. Rougher, a harder edge, and in the shadows, hooded addicts with pipes began to materialize. A ragged girl with knotted hair and sun-scabbed lips hit him up for smack change. He remembered her: fresh-faced a year ago in her creased khakis and Tommy Bahama shirt. His money wouldn't help, just the opposite. After the flywheel came off lives down here, the only thing that worked was serious rehab and a new vector.

The boardwalk, he was thinking after the girl moved on. One of those SoCal places you had to visit. Nobody said it was a good idea to stay.

Alison came out of the market and tossed him a new ice-filled baggie. He held it to his face as the lights inside that shop dimmed, too, throwing them into the shadows. Out there in the dark world, he heard the shore break smack the sand, and right here, he knew lawyer and client were standing too close, looking at each other with the fresh taste of winning running wild inside them.

Alison pulled out of the moment first and started walking again. "I loved going up there," she told him, "but I don't want anyone getting hurt."

"C'mon, he's all talk," he said.

"What do you call that, Ali?" she said, pointing at his eye.

"Sure you want to know?" he asked.

"Maybe a little," she said. "A little more than I do."

"I call it backing him into a corner. He's got no decent alibi for that night."

"That's gotta be bad." She thought about it. "Chase, right? That's the best he could come up with?"

"He was too cocky. He committed to that story early on, and that was a big mistake. Should've kept his mouth shut, the same advice he'd give any client."

They turned inland onto Brooks, walked toward Speedway. Then she asked, "Do you know anybody out here? I mean, really know them?"

"One person, I think," meaning Philip. "Other than that . . ." He shrugged.

"I meet lots of people at the bookstore, and they all talk shit. Everybody's got something big, no, something major going on. I don't believe any of them anymore."

"Sometimes I think there's not enough to go around in LA, so people lie to make up the difference."

She looked at him. "Do you think people come to LA to forget who they are?"

"To forget, to reinvent themselves, sure. I've seen lots of that," he said.

"All your family pictures, you're still connected. You know exactly where you're from. You're so lucky to still have them, to have a family, a home."

"I know," he told her. "I am."

Inches from each other this time. A definite sexual vibe, and Robert knew it was a bad idea.

Again, she eased away first. "I'm gonna go to my car and head home. Alone, okay?"

He nodded. "Alone. Definitely, alone."

"I don't expect miracles, but thanks for trying. For believing me."

"It's a winner. I'll call you when I know something."

She was halfway to her car when he called out: "Tell me again about Chase cutting Lionel's grass."

"I already told you!" she said, turning around and walking backward.

"Meridian was crying? C'mon, tell me again!"

"When I see you!" she laughed, waving to him.

He watched her get in her car, turn on the lights, and disappear into Sunset Court. Too jacked up to go home, he walked south toward

Venice Pier. While he walked, what Alison said about having a home stuck with him.

Home. A week before he took on her case, he'd driven up to Gilroy, four hours north on the I-5. He turned off CA 152 before Gilroy proper, then north through the familiar, fertile farmland nestled beneath the Diablo Range. Game plan was to show up at the farm, surprise his parents, tell them what happened, and hit the road. The whole visit, two hours tops.

Just as he'd reached Worth Avenue—the family driveway, really—he stopped and looked down the eucalyptus-lined drive to the gate. *Rancho Rosalinda* was emblazoned over the gated entrance. That stopped his forward momentum even after being away, more than at home, the last fifteen years.

Worth Avenue. The family called it *Big Worth Avenue* in honor of his grandfather. Philip had been impressed with this mailing address: "It's not every day I meet a person with a street named after his family."

"It's a small town," Robert told him not long after he and Philip first met.

"Even so, Robert. *Worth Avenue?*"

Sitting there in the driveway's eucalyptus shade, he realized Philip had been a big piece of his professional puzzle. In most ways, the biggest piece.

That he happened to meet Philip at all was because he caught fire in high school his sophomore year. The year Robert got serious at Harkins School in nearby San Jose. The year he saw the uphill road for mediocre students and started going all out in sports and academics. His burst of excellence through senior year was enough, in state, to land him in Berkeley, and from there to work his way into Hastings College of Law in San Francisco.

He started backing out of the driveway. He knew he couldn't bring himself to take his sad tale home. Headed back to LA via Gilroy, he pulled in at one of his family's roadside produce stands. Wooden support beams, a real roof, and roll-up polyurethane flaps. He hadn't recognized either of the Latinas on duty, so he went inside.

Rustic by design: garlic-pepper jellies, garlic oil, wooden bins of squash and pears, melons and cherries, even a dried-chili Christmas wreath. Garlic strands hung everywhere. Red garlic and artichoke garlic, the reds in long, thin, mesh weaves, the artichokes woven into strands with their long, supple stems.

Scratching a single clove of red garlic, he raised it to his face, and smelled the juice. Memories flowed from its powerful scent, making him happy and sad at the same time. He wondered if he was old enough to feel nostalgia.

"The reds, some people call them *Italians*," one of the Latinas said of the red garlic.

"I know," he told her.

Close by the Venice Pier, Robert headed into a bistro, corner of Speedway and Washington. At the bar, he ordered a glass of wine, caught the garlic from a pasta primavera being served. Again, his mind turned to that produce stand and his drive to LA from Gilroy. Most of the way, Philip Fanelli had dominated his thoughts.

Some people call them Italians, that Latina told him. Philip Fanelli and bread crumbs and garlic: that was Robert's path out of law school and down to LA. Not slugging it out against Stanford grads and the rest of the civilized world, who all clamored to practice in the City by the Bay.

Philip had been teaching a Hastings Law corporate seminar at the request of an old friend. More about actual practice than recent cases, the lecture was called *Bread Crumbs*. Philip's analogy to Hansel and Gretel emphasized the importance of leaving a paper trail based on correspondence, documenting client positions, and correcting inaccuracies to all disputed facts so they weren't so easily held against the client later on.

"Assuming, of course, there has been no wrongdoing," Philip told the seminar. "Should wrongdoing occur, corporate counsel will likely be last to know, and if corporate counsel is first to know? Anyone?" he'd asked.

After a couple of preachy answers about good client communication, Philip said, "No. If you're first to know about wrongdoing, you were probably in on it and likely headed to jail."

At lunch break, Hastings Law students crowded around Philip, letting him know how sharp they were. Each one had researched Philip's firm. A killer LA outfit: Brightwell Industries in the bag, a solid backup client base, a boutique gem at the beach in Santa Monica.

Knowing all of that, too, Robert bailed on the seminar and sped down to the farm. Once inside a storage shed with Luis, they selected the best Italian reds on hand. After that, they stapled them inside a mesh sleeve. Normally, *Rancho Rosalinda* would print in the paper panel, but this time Luis and Robert and a few workers did the panel up right.

The seminar was over when he got back, but Philip was still there in a meet and greet. Still rehearsing his pitch, Robert waited till the suck-ups—other suck-ups, actually—had gone. Philip was alone but had made dinner plans with the competition.

"Mr. Fanelli?" he said.

"Ah, our mystery guest." Philip didn't seem insulted he'd ditched the seminar, merely letting Robert know he'd noticed.

"One question, if I may," Robert said.

"Why not? Let's hear it."

"Do you like garlic, Mr. Fanelli?"

Philip stopped packing his briefcase. "I'm part Sicilian, part French. I'd better."

"I just drove down to my family's place south of here. I believe my time was well spent."

"Better spent than listening to years and years of my accumulated wisdom?"

"I hope so. From my family's farm," he said, handing the garlic sleeve to Philip, who read the panel's inscription: *Italian Red Garlic Selected for Philip Fanelli.* Signed by Robert, Luis, and Luis' guys.

Philip pointed to the sleeve. "You're *that* Robert?"

"Yes, sir. Robert Worth and those men who signed, they harvested and cured that sleeve."

Philip shook his hand. "Pleasure to meet you, Robert. Leaving my talk like you did, do you consider yourself a risk taker?"

"Not really, sir. Like you said, it's garlic. Your last name's Italian."

Philip laughed.

"All the students talking to you on break are smart. So am I. But I wanted you to know: I'm the only one willing to go the extra mile."

"So you are," Philip said. "Where are the two of us going to dinner?"

That Christmas, Robert drove to LA with a group of other students and called Philip from Shutters on the Beach Hotel in Santa Monica. Philip's wife was up in Santa Barbara, recuperating from her latest chemo, and Robert found himself grilling salmon with Philip in his Brentwood backyard. Poolside, one of many such dinners that lay ahead once he moved to LA.

It was during one of those meals gone late that Philip confided in him: his firm had never been sued for malpractice. Not once, not even by a shakedown artist. Philip, Robert could tell, was proud of that record.

Now, in the bistro by the pier, Robert finished his wine and paid his tab. As he walked home on the boardwalk, his thoughts returned to the firm's malpractice history. Technically, he believed, the firm's clean record was still unbroken. His client was suing Jack, not the firm.

"At least that's something," he said as he opened the door to his apartment.

Once he showered that night, Alison's observation on the boardwalk kept coming back to him: *so lucky to have a home.* Instead of kicking back, he opened his laptop and selected a desktop folder: *RLW STUFF.* He opened it. It was encrypted, calling for his password. He typed: Z-A-C-K-M-A-Y-O and stopped. Then he closed the *RLW STUFF* file.

Thinking: *Go ahead, man. Go ahead and do it. Now. Go.*

Pulling out his cell phone, taking a breath, he hit a button on his iPhone. *Calling Home* showed up on his screen.

Inside the home where Robert was born, his father answered.

"Robert? Well, well, how are you, son?"

"Fine, Dad, great. How about you?"

His father said, "Pretty fair, no complaints."

"Not too late to call, is it?"

"No, son, not at all. Good to hear your voice. I'm in here with the bills. No end of 'em running a farm, but you know all about that."

"Oh, you're in the study?" Robert asked.

"Uh-huh. House is kind of empty right now."

Robert didn't need to close his eyes to picture the house where he grew up, its Will Rogers Ranch design, even the prom-night photo on the study wall alongside other family memories. His fifty-five-year-old father—people said Robert favored him—would be sorting mail at the huge wooden desk dominating the long, rectangular room.

"Where is everybody?" Robert asked.

"Gone over to Pleasanton for a horse race. Mom, too. Not sure they'll make it back tonight. They might head into the city, kick up their heels. Why don't you get up here, or is your blood too thin from being down south for so long?"

Robert sucked in a big breath. "I called . . . I wanted to tell you that—there was a big shake-up at the firm. And I lost my job."

"But you worked so hard for them all those years."

"I know."

"What about that big partner, Phil? I thought he'd taken you under his wing?"

"They made some bad business decisions, had to thin the herd. Know what I mean?"

"All too well. I'm so sorry. I'll do anything I can to help if you'll let me."

"No, thanks, Dad. With any luck, I already have something else in the works."

"Well, you've done it all on your own." His father choked up a little. "You know how proud I am of you, no matter what. But I'm serious. Why not come home, spend some time till you get squared away?"

"I have résumés to work on, job interviews and all that, but as soon as I have a free weekend, I promise."

"When I tell Mom you called, she's gonna ask me—you seeing anyone special?"

"Could be. Give Mom . . . just make sure you tell her I said hi, okay?"

"Will do. Better get back to what I was doing before I lose track."

Later that night, after he went to bed and turned off all the lights, he lay alone in the dark.

Finally, he whispered, "Dad. Jesus . . ."

CHAPTER 20

By Monday at 1:00 a.m., Robert had finished redrafting several critical parts of Alison's complaint and grabbed four hours of sleep. Then he got up and rechecked her legal file against every assertion he made in her complaint.

At 8:45 a.m., he pulled near the Santa Monica courthouse and fed a two-hour meter on Olympic. By 9:05, he'd passed through security and was standing in line to see a filing clerk. At this stage of the game, he didn't want a clerk telling him, "Sorry, sir, the court's website is out of date. Filing fees have changed." Or "Sorry, sir, you will need to use our new civil summons form. Wasn't that posted on our website?"

No need to be a litigator to know things go wrong, and even though he had no intention or desire of filing these papers, he didn't need Jack to be right: "Told you, Worth. You couldn't find the right courthouse."

That was not an image he wanted lurking anywhere in his mind.

The filing clerk let him know that his check was made out properly and the forms he'd used and the boxes checked were in order. Then, before the clerk stamped the first page of his complaint, he pulled it and walked back outside. Knowing for sure, if forced to file the complaint, it would be accepted.

He fed his meter, then strolled to the end of Santa Monica Pier and back. Down at Urth Caffé on Main, he ate a bowl of granola and drank a decaf. No caffeine today—he was as jacked up as he could ever remember. By the time he made it back to the courthouse, it was 10:45. Unlocking his car, he took out his notebook and papers—make-work— and strolled back to the front stairs.

At 10:50, he pictured the Brightwell study and saw himself telling Jack: *Front steps. Santa Monica courthouse. Eleven a.m. sharp.*

At 11:00 a.m. sharp, he looked around. Food trucks had pulled up on Main Street. Civil servants trickled out for sustenance. He walked back to his car and made a show of feeding the meter, all the while looking for a sign that Jack was driving up. Or getting a ticket. Or lying dead in a crosswalk. But he was nowhere to be seen.

Fuck him, he said to himself and walked back inside the courthouse. Back through security, delaying the process as long as possible. Once his keys were snug in his pocket, his belt rebuckled, it was 11:06. The Filing Clerk door, thirty feet away. No choice now—he could not back down. He eased toward the door, but this wasn't what he wanted. Pierce calling him out. Pierce a no-show. He eyed the front door. No one was coming through it. He was out of options, but as he cleared the Filing Clerk's wooden threshold, he heard Jack's voice.

"Hold up, Worth."

Robert turned around and looked down the long hallway. Jack was sitting on a bench. Beside him was an attractive woman in her forties, and because she wore a black robe, he knew she was a circuit court judge. Jack had been inside the courthouse all along.

"Want you to meet someone, Worth," Jack said, waving him over. "Come on, I want you to meet Judge Rosen."

More of Jack's fun and games. His every instinct as a lawyer told him to speak to this Judge Rosen. To any judge, for that matter. It was never a choice—it was disrespectful not to do it. But walking over to

Jack, who didn't show up by the deadline? Who was still playing games? He couldn't let that happen.

"Can't do it," Robert said, not sure if Jack heard him or not.

He walked into the clerk's office and stood in line. It was all he could do to keep his breathing under control.

Cocky asshole, fuck him. That's what Robert was thinking when Jack walked up to him.

"I had an early trial conference with her. What was I supposed to do?"

Robert didn't answer. Jack said, "Let's go outside, talk this over."

"If I walk through security again, we're done talking for good."

Without another word, Robert headed outside. Jack followed him onto the lawn. They each held up their iPhones and powered down.

"Look," Jack told him, "I thought about what you said this weekend and had a thought."

Robert gave him nothing in return.

"For right now, and for purposes of settlement only, how's this sound? You kept coming back to that meeting at the firm with Chase, your client, me, right?"

Robert shrugged. "I mentioned it once."

"After she left the room, a four-hundred-thousand-dollar jury verdict might have been kicked around. That is, if the case had even gotten to a jury, so I was thinking . . ."

He knew what came next. Jack offering $400,000 for Alison to go away, offering to call a few colleagues, set him up with a job. Right then, he saw the wisdom in holding back Alison's strongest allegation against Jack.

"Hold on, I'm confused," Robert said.

"Well, what I'm saying is—"

"No, no, I hear your four hundred thousand, all right, but when you add that to my nonnegotiable one million eight, that's more than two million. Even more than I'm asking for?"

"You're out of your fucking mind. You think I'm paying her a million eight over that dirtbag brother?"

"You trial boys call this bluffing, right?"

"No, Worth, we call it take it or leave it." Jack was in his face now.

But Robert kept his cool and shoveled Jack what he'd been holding back. "Three more things you should know about her complaint. One: I'm serving the lawsuit on you at Stone Canyon Road—not at Fanelli and Pierce. Two: I've added *use of amyl nitrite* to my complaint, as in *use of a dangerous drug during commission of felony assault.* That item might even get the DA's attention. Who knows? Maybe your pal Judge Rosen can get involved. And a big number three: I don't care if Brian Maxwell was snorting asbestos flakes off a hooker's ass on his deathbed—this is *her* case, *not his*—and she won't take a million seven point nine nine nine nine nine. She won't take one penny less than one million, eight hundred thousand dollars."

Jack definitely reacted, hearing about his use of amyls for the first time. Looked to Robert like someone just put a blowtorch to Jack's Ferrari. Robert headed back inside the courthouse, made it to the steps, but already knew what was coming next.

"All right," Jack said.

Robert turned around. "All right, what?"

"One point eight."

Jack looked different to him now. Not defeated, but something was missing from his shoulders and arms. Not beat forever, he knew that, but beat for the moment, and seeing that felt good. Robert held up his phone and turned it on. So did Jack. Once he gave Jack his cell number, he said, "Text our deal to me."

Jack texted him: I accept offer of 1.8 million to settle our case.

Robert could have insisted on more detail, but for now this would do. They had only one case between them, so *our case* could mean only one thing. And he understood why Jack was vague. It was a text. Phones get lost, misplaced, and phones get picked up by spouses.

At that point, they took it out to Robert's car, where they covered the details with an economy two lawyers can bring to the table if they want to.

First, Jack didn't want to meet him in public again. Everything would happen outside the firm. Robert could e-mail Jack at his personal e-mail account, which Jack furnished. They agreed Robert was to draft the document and that two things mattered most: the money to Robert and to Jack, secrecy in the nondisclosure.

"No games," Robert said. "You pick up a typo, I make a mistake, fine. We'll initial the change right there. Short of that, it'll be ready for your signature."

Jack nodded.

"The release will cover all of her claims against you and—"

"And the firm."

"And the firm," Robert said. "And my client's release to you will be very broad."

"Better be. Talk to me about how you see nondisclosure working."

"Well, I have my client's power of attorney to dispose of any and all—"

"No good. I want *her* signature on the nondisclose. Not your signature *for her*."

He'd already thought about this. Jack had the winning argument. Why should it be left to Jack to check Robert's power of attorney to make sure no loopholes favored Alison?

"Agreed," Robert said, taking notes on his laptop. "It will bind her. It will be all-inclusive. She has, of course, discussed the underlying facts of the case with me."

This was the heart of the matter for Jack. Robert knew he had to make sure there was no wiggle room permitting Jack's behavior to leak out without a severe penalty. Jack would reject any such proposal and be justified doing so.

"The nondisclosure, it will also bind *you*," Jack said.

Robert knew that this point would be a deal breaker for Jack. No way Jack would allow Robert to dine out on his big win like lawyers tend to do. No—always do. Robert got it. In Jack's shoes, he would ask for the same protection.

"All right, I'll sign the nondisclosure agreement, too," he said.

There was one other deal point Jack might bump on. Robert decided to bring it up now: "You should know I already discussed the underlying facts of your case with a nonparty."

Jack closed his eyes. "Who?"

"Fanelli. *That night.*"

Jack looked at him for the first time since they'd sat down in the car. He looked almost sad.

"Exactly what did you tell Fanelli?"

"Everything my client told me to that point. That you berated her in the meeting. That you were in her apartment and assaulted her. That you threatened to withdraw from her case unless she had sexual relations with you. You hadn't withdrawn yet, so your actual withdrawal didn't come up."

"And the drug-use allegation?" Jack asked.

"At that point, I was unaware of the allegation, so I never discussed it with Fanelli. I haven't spoken to him since I left the firm."

"And Fanelli's reaction to what you told him that night?"

"He told me it was impossible to know what had happened. And that I should keep quiet about it, leave it up to her to take legal action, if any."

Robert omitted learning from Philip that he was on the brink of partnership. It had no bearing on this case and might cause friction later between Philip and Jack.

Easy for Robert to guess what Jack was thinking: counting in his mind the times he'd seen Philip at the office, in partners' meetings, at the firm party. Philip had even seen Robert *with* Alison, and Jack had to realize that Philip would have already mentioned her accusations if he planned to do so. Jack would conclude what Robert had already concluded: get this thing done, and get it done fast.

Jack said, "Write it up like that, and not one more word with Fanelli. Disclose to me in writing exactly what you told him. Put that in an exhibit to your release, and I'll agree to it. As long as you and your client both sign off."

"I agree," Robert said. "Unless either of us is compelled on the underlying facts."

More shorthand. Were he *compelled to testify* about Jack's behavior by any governmental agency, that part of the deal was off for one simple reason: no court would accept a private agreement as an excuse not to testify about a crime. The party *compelled* could be jailed for contempt until he saw the error of his ways.

"And one more thing," Jack said. "If either of you repeats this slander, I want five million in liquidated damages. Joint and several liability, and you and your client pay my attorney's fees to collect from you."

Robert hadn't gotten quite this far gaming this conversation but knew what Jack was driving at. Owing *liquidated damages* meant Robert and Alison agreed in advance that if they violated the nondisclosure agreement, Jack had been damaged to the tune of $5 million. No dollar amount of actual damage to Jack needed to be proved in a trial.

Joint and several liability, attorney's fees to collect? If he agreed to this, and Alison talked about what Jack did, the entire five million could come out of her pocket, their pocket—*or his pocket alone*—as Jack saw fit. Not to mention the added expense of paying Jack's attorney's fees.

"No," Robert said. "The amount of damages is excessive."

"Why? If you two keep quiet, it will never come up. And if you talk about the underlying allegations, it could cost me far more than that."

Robert gave it some thought. She didn't allege actual rape. Liquidated damages for disclosing rape would be unenforceable. No court would make a rape victim pay damages for revealing the crime of rape. But this situation was a relatively minor sexual assault. It was contested by

Jack, and no police or medical report existed. Off the top of his head, he believed Jack would have an easy time collecting the $5 million in damages. He also knew he would never breathe a word about the case, but what if Alison violated the nondisclose, and Jack decided to sue only him?

Screw it. Let Jack take a judgment against him. He'd file for bankruptcy, not too far away from what he was facing now.

End of the day, both men were taking a risk. But end of the same day, the exchange of money for secrecy trumped those risks.

Even so, Robert said, "Need to talk to my client. I'll get back to you tomorrow at the latest."

"Tonight, if you can."

"All right."

Both men were calm. Robert started his car. Jack opened his door and got out. Robert drove away, his head pounding from the immense effort of staying cool. Once he made it off Fourth onto Bay Street, he pulled to a painted-red curb, jumped out of his car, and circled it several times. Then he fist-slammed the hood of his car and yelled, "Gotcha!"

"What if I asked if you wanted to be financially secure for the foreseeable future?"

"Trick question, right?"

During her lunch break, Alison and Robert walked out along the Venice Pier.

"Humor me," he said.

"I don't know. I've never thought about that before. But sure, yeah."

"There's only one catch," he said.

"Knew it. So I'm not gonna be a royal?"

He stopped, turned to her. "You can be a royal if you can keep a secret about what happened between you and Pierce. Not the queen, more like a duchess."

She saw how serious he looked. "My answer, it's that important?"

So far, he'd told her only that he'd met Jack that morning, not that they'd reached a number. He was comfortable keeping it from her because he had her power of attorney.

"Think about it," he said. "Did you talk to anyone besides me about what actually happened between you and Jack?"

"No, I didn't," she said.

"Anybody back east, anyone in Florida you might have called, anybody in your building, at work, at the hospital? Anyone you e-mailed or texted?"

She agreed to go over her records and her phone history since that night to see if she had forgotten someone.

"Because if you forget someone," he said, "you won't be a duchess anymore."

"How many times have I called you about the case?" she asked. He was still thinking about it when she said, "When I call you tonight, that will be the first time. I don't like talking about it—I start getting mad at myself and at him, and what good does that do?"

"Got it," he said.

They reached the end of the pier, way past where the surf broke. Out where the concrete deck turned into a hundred-foot-wide gladiator's circle.

"Here's the deal," he said. "When we're done with this lawsuit, we'll come out here and jump off the pier."

"Only if we sneak out after it's closed," she added.

Hard for him not to like her. The two of them bumped fists on their future pier jump. *Cool girl,* he was thinking, retro in leopard flip-flops, madras Bermuda shorts, and a Sidewalk Cafe 100 percent cotton T-shirt.

He was thinking, too, about how private it was way out here. How it might be a good place to meet someone late, hush-hush, on the sly.

CHAPTER 21

No tricks, gimmicks, or legal games—he and Jack each wanted this over and done. That night he was deep into drafting the release when Alison touched base. She was positive she hadn't told anyone about what had happened to her. Far as he was concerned, that made her a dream client.

Next morning, he worked till about noon, then put on his sweats and jogged over to Gold's. After working out, he grabbed a smoked-brisket sandwich to go from Gjusta on Sunset Avenue and headed home. But even after working out, he had trouble staying focused on Alison's agreement. Lack of focus, a rarity for him.

Apparently, from the phone calls he'd been getting, he was still in light rotation with a few women he'd dated. At first, he thought his lack of interest had to do with the pressure of this situation. Or spending $500 on a date, ending up with a hangover and third-degree sheet burns, questioning why he'd bothered in the first place. Back of his mind, though, he knew what it was really about. His client. The woman. Alison Maxwell.

On his way home, thoughts of her were interrupted by a text rolling in from Gia's number:

Mr. Worth. Bel-Air Hotel. Suite 207.

Gia? Must've saved my number, he thought. *Maybe she changed her mind about inviting me inside?* Didn't matter. Right now, he didn't have time for a detour, even for her. Then Gia's second text showed up. This one stopped him in his tracks:

Don't embarrass yourself w/your client, Mr. Worth.

Your client? What was she talking about? He'd been intentionally vague about his client when he met her at Santa Anita.

Embarrass yourself? he wondered. *About what?*

At home, he polished off the brisket and kept thinking about her texts. Wondered if a prior text had been dropped in transmission. It happened sometimes. Too many Westsiders with multiple cell phones hated cell-phone towers. He muted his phone.

Ten minutes passed. He fidgeted at his computer, trying to reengage with Alison's paperwork. It wasn't working. He grabbed his cell phone—no new texts—and called Gia's number. On her voice mail, he asked her to give him a call.

A half hour later, he broke down again, texting her when her next text came in:

Mr. Worth. Risk Never Sleeps by Seymour Watkins. Suite 207

What?

Driving to the Bel-Air five minutes later, he caught a break going north on Twenty-Sixth. A half hour after that, he made a left off Sunset Boulevard onto Stone Canyon Road. Once he'd valeted his car at the hotel and passed drunken newlyweds groping each other by the swan pool, he took an exterior, trellised corridor that ran sidelong through the grounds. Spanish tile underfoot, bougainvillea overhead, ultraromantic, if that's why you happened to be here.

Then he reached Suite 207, knocked softly.

Seconds later, Gia opened the door. "My man," she said. "How you been?"

"Great," he said, stepping inside the suite. Its sleek, muted tones looked more *W* now than like its old-Hollywood roots.

She was casual in loose-fitting jeans again and a white oxford-cloth shirt. Looked like a man's clothes, but Gia didn't look like a man in them.

"You look great, too, Mr. Worth, but appearances are always deceiving in this town."

When he didn't answer, she said, "Drink?" and walked over to the bar.

He sat down on the couch, put his cell phone on the coffee table, and turned on *Record*. "I'm keeping track of what we talk about, Gia."

She put her phone on the table, too. Hers was turned off. "Fair enough. I'm not. Not yet."

"And if you have another device recording this, you don't have my consent to use it, right?"

"Sure, but it's no fun teasing you if you record me."

"Do your best."

No matter what, he could not discuss Alison's case. Otherwise, he and Jack would be arguing about disclosure of *this* third-party conversation, too. "You texted me, said some things I don't get. What did you mean by *embarrass myself*?"

"Right," she said. "*With your client.* Scotch and water?"

"Without the Scotch. Let's hear it."

She brought over their drinks. "Well, there's quite a bit you don't know about Jack Pierce," she said, sitting down across from him.

It dawned on him, she could well be on Jack's team. What was it Jack told him? *Gia Marquez has nothing but good things to say about me and always will.* And there it was: Gia bringing him up right off the bat.

"I know enough," was all he told Gia.

"Did you know we met here Saturday night? Me and Jack?"

Saturday night. That meant after the firm party. He didn't answer but couldn't help thinking: *The Bel-Air is a five-minute drive down the hill from the Brightwell estate.*

She kept going: "Met here for a long, long time. He accused me of conspiring with you. He thinks the two of us are trying to blackmail him."

"So what? He was wrong. It won't be the last time."

"Hard to blame him for thinking that, Mr. Worth. *Twenty thousand cash?* You knew how much he gave me, to the dollar, so it didn't matter how many times I denied it."

"Like I said, won't be the last time."

"How long were you following me?" she asked.

He didn't answer.

"You must've seen my receipt. No way you waited around for days inside my bank, so you saw me where? Saddle Peak?" Nothing from Robert. "Earlier? Later?" she asked. Still nothing from him. "Boy, did he underestimate you or what?"

"*He* or *we?*"

"I never did. You'll see what I mean, I swear."

He only nodded.

She took a drink and said, "What have you done to Mr. Worth? When's he gonna come out and play?"

"Your texts. *Embarrass yourself,* Ms. Marquez? *With your client?*"

"Oh, that," she said. "Guess you could say, once Dorothy washes down a couple of bedtime Xanax with vodka, school's out for Jack. Did you know this suite is where he brings his women? Not 208 or 206. Always 207. He's predictable once you know him, very predictable once you know where to look. Did you know he likes doing girls two at a time? Right here, whenever he can swing it?"

He had no idea where she was taking this.

She said, "And sometimes it gets a little rough—not *hard* hard-core—but the boy has an aggressive kink. Whips. Handcuffs, those amyl nitrites you mentioned to him, toys large and small, that kind of thing."

"Where does he score the amyls?"

"Don't know the guy or the girl, even. They talk in code on a burner, talking something about *the grunion*."

"Top secret. I'll cuff him up and piss on him if he's into that," he offered.

"He's back!" She reached out for a fist bump.

He bumped her and stood. "Pierce is kinky, I get it, but I'm not embarrassed, and I don't need help. As far as risk never sleeps? It's catchy and it's true, but Seymour Watkins? I never heard of the guy."

She stood, too. "Well. I'm kind of embarrassed about what comes next, so . . ."

Gia, embarrassed? Hard to imagine.

At the bar, she made another drink, not smiling anymore. She didn't drink at the track or at firm parties that he could recall. This was her second drink since he'd gotten here, and he'd never seen her nervous about anything.

"We kid around a lot, but I do like you," she said. "And I respect you. So, anyway . . ."

Stalling, he could tell. She headed into the bedroom. He followed her. Being here couldn't be about having sex. He didn't see her being nervous about that. Him, maybe, not her.

In the bedroom, her bikini already lay on the bed: black fabric on top of white bedcovers. So small he might have missed it if he wasn't paying attention.

She picked it up and said, "All those kinks and whips and cuffs and stuff, it's funny. Because when you think about it, the girls aren't prisoners. Jack is."

"Prisoner? You mean, Dorothy?"

"Worse than that. *Lionel.* Give me your phone, I don't want you to miss anything."

Once he handed it over, she slipped into the bathroom, set his phone on the counter. "Don't look," she said, leaving the door open.

He lay down on the bed, stared at the ceiling till he heard her say: "How can I still get zits?" Rolling over, he looked in the bathroom. She was eyeballing her forehead in the mirror, and she was naked.

"C'mon, talk to me," he said, still looking at her in spite of his good intentions.

She gave him a little smile, like she was telling him, "Nice body, huh?" not making a big deal out of it. Long legs, *moca* skin from her Latino father, jet-black hair from both parents. Toned but never set foot in a gym, he bet. She stepped into the bikini bottom and pulled it up. Then the top. That took a little longer. After that, he stopped looking at her like she'd asked in the first place.

"How much do you know about the firm?" she asked. "The real firm?"

He knew there was what firms revealed in *Martindale-Hubbell*, the who's who of law firms. Then there was what really made a law firm tick, down in its dark basement. There was a time Robert believed he had a handle on both ends, learned at Philip's feet, until Jack blindsided him. Now, he wasn't so sure.

"Why not tell me about the real firm?" he asked. "Am I still recording this?"

She checked his phone. "Yep," she said. "So here goes. Once upon a time, a good man named Oliver Dudley married a sweet Texas girl who lived in Bel-Air. Dorothy Brightwell was her name. Oliver worked as a lawyer for her daddy at his big oil company—"

"Worked as house counsel," he corrected.

"Right, but when all that bad stuff went down and the price of oil and gas tanked, even though it wasn't his fault, Oliver took it real hard.

So hard that one night, in that beautiful house where he lived with his beautiful wife and her father, he stroked out in bed."

Robert was thinking, *Oliver took it hard because he was, as Philip often said, a good man.* A big reason why he'd been Philip's best friend.

She asked, "You drove Philip to Oliver's funeral, didn't you?"

He nodded, felt her weight as she sat down at the end of the bed. Day of that funeral back in 2011, he remembered it. He'd been at the firm less than a year and had Lionel's bite-happy beagle on his mind.

She laid his phone on his belly. He opened another voice file and hit Record. "Yeah. I drove Philip to Forest Lawn. He was really torn up."

"An old-school gent. I like Mr. Fanelli. Do you? Still?"

Still like Philip Fanelli? He shrugged. At one time, he loved Philip like a father.

"Let's see how much you like him after hearing this," she said, getting back to the funeral. "There we were at the cemetery, a death in the firm family, and we all turned out. You, me, Pierce, Fanelli, Chase, all the others. A command performance, right?"

He nodded.

"Lots of sad people, and boy, Dorothy was torn up and messed up, too. And Jack and I, we were still hot and heavy, but on the sly."

Jack again, he was thinking. *Careful, Robert.*

"After the casket was lowered, Dorothy wheeled Lionel to the limo, and Jack helped her inside. Oh, wait. First, he took her hand. Then he hugged her. Then he helped her inside. All the girls from the office noticed, all of us going, *Are you kidding*? I mean, Oliver's casket wasn't all the way to the bottom of the grave, or maybe it was, but you get it, right?"

Another nod. He had to take her word for it. He'd been focused on Philip. Worried he might take a header on that bunched-up artificial turf underfoot.

"And Lionel," she asked, "remember how bad he looked?"

"I do." Philip had commented on it in Robert's car afterward. *On death's doorstep* was how Philip had put it.

"So now," Gia said, "we're all up at the big house, and everybody's having drinks and sucking up to Lionel. Jack and I snuck upstairs."

"Upstairs where?"

"Lionel's bedroom, I'm pretty sure. There was an oxygen tank."

He looked at her, cross-legged in that mesh bikini. "Really?"

She hid her face in her hands. "I know, just fooling around, but still. And so, anyway, ten minutes later, downstairs—boom. He asked Dorothy to show him around."

Balls on that guy, he thought.

"That night, I waited for him here in 207 like we planned—but he never showed. Thing is," she said, "before I left the estate—and this is what I want you to know—I went into the living room to tell Lionel I was sorry, polite like my parents taught me. He was sitting in his wheelchair, and I thought he was so sad, looking off in the distance. Gazing like old people do sometimes."

Robert knew what she meant. He'd seen his father gazing off across the farm. Lost in thought, and his father wasn't considered old.

"He wasn't gazing, though," Gia said. "He was staring at his front door. At Jack, standing there with his daughter. A wolf inside the door." She leaned closer to Robert. "He couldn't take his eyes off them, didn't even know I was there. *That's* what Jack didn't count on. Lionel was eighty-four then, eighty-nine now, and Jack gave him a reason to live. That's why the old boy got well. Why he keeps hanging on—so he can grind poor Jack down."

Grind Jack down? How?

He started a third recording file. "I'm curious," he asked. "Did you and Jack discuss any current litigation he might be involved in?"

"Sure, litigation between you two. You're asking a million eight for malpractice, and good luck with that. How long has he put you off so far?"

Not once so far, he thought, but he couldn't answer her without discussing his case. Jack, on the other hand? He could talk to anyone. Shout it from the rooftops if he wanted. The lawsuit was his secret, and sharing it was up to him.

"What are you driving at?" he asked her instead.

"Well, unlike you, Jack direct-deposited his paycheck. So I know what he earns, and I'm saying he doesn't have a million-eight cash. Not even close to that much."

That brought him to his feet. "What?" he asked.

"He pays all his and Dorothy's living expenses. He insisted on that when they got married, and he pulls down, what? Two million a year?"

Two million. That's the number Robert used when he was deciding to sue him for the million eight. He figured Jack could handle that much without upending the matrimonial applecart.

"Half his salary goes to the tax man," Gia said. "Thousand a night for this place. That's a hundred grand a year at the rate he fucks around on Dorothy. Tailored clothes—what's he call them? *Bespoke?* Travel with Dorothy, best restaurants, big man grabbing checks all over town, European sports cars, top cabin everywhere, year in, year out."

"Loans. That's what banks are for," he said.

"Sure, if he asked Dorothy to cosign, and that I kinda doubt."

He doubted it, too, and tried to stay calm as he went over what this might mean. Dorothy owned the house. That Cy Twombly in the lobby wasn't Jack's, either, was it? All he owned was his name on the frame. Even so, the idea he might be strapped never dawned on Robert, especially after Jack's text to him confirming their million-eight settlement.

Listening to Gia, he started to worry.

She said, "Look, Mr. Worth, I know him better than you ever will. Better than Dorothy, too. So believe these two things: he burns what he earns, and he'd rather die than admit it to you."

"Yeah?"

"Oh, yeah," she said. "He hates you as much as you hate him."

That's a start, he decided.

"Besides," she said, "I don't see myself testifying against Jack under oath. Under penalty of perjury. You were in my shoes, would you?"

Before he could answer, she was out the patio door. He followed her outside, and as she eased herself into a steaming Jacuzzi, he set down his phone on the deck to pick up their voices.

"Why?" he asked. "Why even think about protecting a guy like that?"

"Thinking about what's best for me. Either I'm willing to incriminate myself—under oath—or I'm not."

"Wait a goddamn minute. *Incriminate yourself?* He's the one who . . ." He stopped before *committed a crime* slipped out. He hadn't given up yet on his current deal with Jack. "Tell me what you're talking about."

"I won't incriminate myself. Once Jack finds out that I won't, that's gotta be bad for your team."

Very bad. Forget actually going to court. It was *the threat* of litigation that carried weight for Robert. Without his threat of Gia testifying—the very heart of his claim—Alison would be facing her word against Jack's—again. Yeah, very bad news for Alison—and for him.

"What are you saying?" he asked.

"Risk Never Sleeps," she told him. "That's on Seymour Watkins's business card."

Seymour Watkins. He wondered where he'd heard that name.

Gia turned on the Jacuzzi jets, told him to quit recording her. Then she told him what really happened when she was fired from the firm.

Turned out, Seymour worked for the firm's insurance broker, calling on the firm several times a year to make sure it was satisfied with its coverage. RISK NEVER SLEEPS, his card read, but Seymour, fifty-five, did, sometimes even dozing off in the firm lobby.

Because the insurance company never moved off its quote, anyway, it fell to Gia as office manager to entertain him on the firm's nickel. They'd always end up at Chez Jay's. Peanut shells on the floor, Sinatra and Tony Bennett on the box, right down Ocean Avenue from Santa Monica Pier.

There Seymour would sit, slouched across from Gia in a dim booth, plowing into a rib eye, positive that this drunken year he would finally bed Gia Marquez.

"Face looked like it might explode any minute," she told him. "Finally, it did. Well, not his face. His heart."

Insurance, he kept thinking. What had the ex-office manager done with the firm's insurance to incriminate herself?

Quite a bit, he learned. Gia knew, same as Robert, that the firm had never been sued for malpractice. Still, it was paying well over $100,000 a year for malpractice coverage. "Insurance it never used," was how she put it to him. So one day, she walked the firm's quarterly malpractice insurance premium check down to Jack's office, along with a batch of other checks. As managing partner now, Jack signed it. After that, she walked the signed check—for $25,000 and change—downstairs to Leslie's desk.

Gia had scribbled her signature on the back of it. Then Leslie, a bank officer, made the deposit into her good friend's personal account.

Before she went that far, Gia called Seymour and broke the bad news: the firm went another way on their malpractice insurance, but they'd still use Seymour for everything else.

"No hard feelings," she told him. "Drop by whenever you're in town."

After that, she altered the firm's certificate of insurance that proved it was currently covered. A simple one-page printed form. All she did was change the dates of coverage on the old one, typing *x*'s in boxes for Limits of Liability, Type of Coverage, and Deductible.

"Stupid easy for something so important," she told him, and when she circulated the one-pager to the partners, nobody said a word.

Gia wouldn't have risked it when Philip ran the show, but with Jack in charge, office procedure had gone a little slack. Gia made the firm deposits *and* picked up its bank statement, which included the firm's actual check with her forged endorsement on back.

Year one, she sweated out the firm audit, but they signed off on the books and took their big fee like good boys. After that, she got used to living with the risk, slipped Leslie five grand each quarter, cashed premium checks, and lived large. That is, until Seymour's heart exploded chuffing a Pall Mall straight outside Hustler Casino in Gardena.

Seymour's replacement, she told him, was an actual professional who did what any pro would do. Call on the managing partner of the firm: Jack Cross Pierce. Ask Jack what he could do to recommission the firm's malpractice coverage.

Hearing that, Jack knew Gia was the only person with access to pull it off, so he laid hands on the firm's bank statements, almost a formality, and nailed it down quick. All Gia had needed was an insider at the bank, and that meant her friend downstairs: Leslie DeRider.

"He fired me the night you heard him screaming," she told Robert beside the Jacuzzi. "But Lionel doesn't know a thing about this. Not one word. And he never can know. But come rain or come shine, there he sits, Lionel Brightwell, still hanging on to life. Delaying the day Dorothy inherits the whole shooting match, and grinding poor . . . well, you know, right?"

Yeah, he knew. Sitting on a chaise, his face buried in his hands: *grinding poor Jack down.* She turned off the jets, floated in the water. It was quiet and still in the canyon, but there was plenty of noise inside his head. He tried coming to grips with things he knew for sure, making educated guesses about others.

First of all, he believed her story. Jack must have met her here and filled her in on Alison's lawsuit. No other way she could know about it. And Robert already knew the firm paid about $100,000 a year for insurance it never filed a claim on. Gia liked to gamble. She must have liked her odds cashing those checks.

And admitting multiple felonies to him? That made her whole story even more credible. Until now, she had protected Jack, lied to Robert after Santa Anita about why Jack had fired her. But now? Access to her loyalty was up for grabs.

She stood up, slid from the water, and sat beside him, her body wet and hot, radiating onto his.

"The cash he paid you?" he asked. "That was to keep you quiet, right? Keep you in line?"

She nodded. "Until you showed up with all your talk about suing for malpractice." A bell chimed inside, and she excused herself to check on it.

Alone now. The more Robert thought about her story, the more sense it made. All of it had the ring of truth. After Jack fired Gia, he must've cooled off and made nice in spite of what she'd done. He needed her to stay quiet about *his mistakes* conducting firm business. In the Brightwell study, Jack must have flipped out when he heard about Gia's hush money. No doubt, Jack believed Gia had broken her word and already revealed the truth to Robert.

Grinding poor Jack down, he thought.

Now, he recalled his last night in the firm lobby. There was Dorothy, telling her husband that Lionel's physical's results came back. That Lionel was in excellent health. And there was Jack reacting: "So glad to hear it, Lionel," he'd said. "That's great news for everybody."

Overreacting, Robert thought. *Great news for everybody except you, Jack.*

It was no secret at the firm that Lionel would hold his financial reins till the very last minute of life, longer if he could. That was when Dorothy would slip out of the top one percent and into the upper echelons of the very wealthy. Less than a billion after estate taxes, but not much less. No doubt, Jack had already imagined ways to lay his hands on as much of it as he could. If that meant only 10 percent of the fortune, a hundred million was a payday Jack could surely live with. Forget the prenup. If Jack wanted, he could stay married and live even larger than ever.

Gia came outside, sat beside him in a thick hotel robe over . . . he wasn't sure over what.

She said, "In my defense, I lie a lot. But it's usually to myself."

"Gia," he said.

"You know where all this is headed?"

Catching up, he saw what was already clear to her. He had stepped into a situation bigger than anything he could have scripted. Bigger and better for his client.

If Gia was right about Jack's finances, suing him personally wasn't going to cut it. He sells a few cars quick, picks up a half million, and maybe he bullshits a bank on a signature loan for another quarter million.

But a million eight, cash on hand? If Gia was right, no way he had it. That meant Alison's case was now aimed at a new target.

The firm.

Basic partnership law stated—and he paraphrased it to himself: *If one partner fucks up, they all fuck up.*

To him, that meant this: Jack Pierce allowed the firm to go uninsured at the time he assaulted Alison Maxwell; had an affair with the office manager, the same woman who lapsed the firm's malpractice insurance; and he paid hush money to keep his partners from finding out about it.

Under partnership law, each of the partners were responsible for his behavior. Like Jack, the firm would never want an internal situation like this one going public. Rumors alone would kill them. He thought about how the exaggerated gossip might unfold among Westside legal wags: *What? They let their malpractice insurance lapse? The managing partner raped a client while he was tripping out on PCP? Screwing the office manager? Raped her, too? So, Brightwell's business is up for grabs, right?*

And on and on. Some two-bit firm could survive it. Not Fanelli & Pierce. Same difference as O.J. Simpson murdering his wife versus O.J. Smith doing the same thing. This firm could not withstand an assault on its own business judgment—what it was often paid fees to possess—and stay on its feet. Once public, this news was a fierce liver shot to the firm's body. The firm would pay up, possibly faster than Jack paid, because each partner had so much to lose.

The firm. All the partners and each of them. The deeper pocket. If Jack wasn't flush, that's where the money was.

As Alison's lawyer, he had an obligation to go against the firm if need be. To sue them all and make them all pay. Fair's fair. They let Jack Pierce get out of hand, gave him the firm's reins. Not him. They let Jack bully a firm client, assault her, and withdraw from her case. Not him. And Philip and the others let him get fired without lifting a finger.

"The firm," he told Gia.

"What I thought, too," she replied. "I told Leslie to wait over at the pool. Be nice, and maybe she won't ask for too big a slice of our pie."

"What are you talking about, our pie?"

"Hey, I'm out five hundred cash money on the room, and if I sleep over, I'll want snacks," she said, kidding around with him. "Did you think ahead, Boy Scout? Bring a swimsuit?"

Our pie. As they headed over to the pool, he tried sounding indignant about Gia wanting a cut. According to her own version of things, she'd committed bank fraud, for Christ's sake. Even so, he'd already figured she would want compensation for filling him in, tilting his way against Jack. And why not? Why not go ahead and make her *a consultant* for his side, long as he could keep a lid on what it cost his client?

It turned out, Gia wanted enough to pay off her mortgage and back taxes, even gave him an accurate number on her loan balance. Once he backed her down to a $500,000 consultant's fee, the heated pool opened up in front of them, its sky-tinted water turquoise and pink in the darkening canyon.

The only swimmer was Leslie, her banker suit folded on a deck chair. One lap, crawl, the next, underwater. Strong swimmer, an OC girl doing her thing.

Far end of the pool, a waiter set up guacamole, chips, and beer. Leslie worked a sidestroke now and talked to Robert and Gia. "Hey guys, s'up?"

"Not much," Robert said.

"You sure? This place is kind of romantic."

Gia took his arm. "Easy, Les, he's got a lot on his mind."

"Just sayin'," Leslie said. "You two look baller together."

Gia walked him down to the far end, signed the drinks ticket, and the waiter took off. Leslie swam over to them. In one motion, she swept out of the water, straight to her feet like a competitive swimmer.

"Hola, Roberto," she said. She sat beside Gia, slid Gia's robe off her shoulder, and kissed her bare skin.

Friendly neighborhood banker, he couldn't help thinking. *Jesus, these two.*

"So," he said. "Hi, Leslie."

"Is this place cool or what?" Leslie asked. "How'd you find it, G?"

"It's been around for a while," Gia said.

"No, I mean, it's so hard to find. My GPS is fried. I drove around forever. Finally, a Bel-Air cop showed me the way."

Lights flashing, he'd bet.

Gia stood, dropped the robe. "You two talk. She's diabetic, Mr. Worth," she said before knifing in the water.

Diabetic? He wondered what that had to do with anything.

"You're from the artichoke capital?" Leslie asked him.

"No, that's Castroville. I'm from the garlic capital, Gilroy."

"Oh, right, right, but both of them are close to the bay."

"Monterey Bay is over the hill, not too far as the crow flies."

"Did you ever surf Four Mile?"

"Never had time to surf growing up," he said. "Farm boy, I had lots of chores."

But he had surfed Four Mile when he was younger. Before he got serious his tenth-grade year. Four miles from Mission Street in downtown Santa Cruz, a secluded beach, cliffs on the point, walk-in access only, an epic break when it was going off.

"Yeah," she said. "I heard it was undeveloped all around there. I want to try it out but no time these days, not since becoming a grown-up. As you already know"—she pointed to her chest, nipples straining the sheer material—"I *heart* banking."

He recalled her T-shirt from Santa Anita. "That's the word on the street," he said.

"What about Mavericks?" she asked.

Another surf spot up north of Santa Cruz, real monsters up there. "Why don't we get back to banking, Leslie?"

He could tell she didn't want go there. She stood up, that one-piece clinging to her. No need to worry about hidden recording devices. Through the gap in her thighs, he saw Gia swim up behind her, lay her arms on the coping, and wink at him.

He told Leslie, "Gia said we should talk about something."

Leslie touched her toes, came back up. "Well, yeah. So." Another breath. "I was wondering, if you had a bunch of client money, what would you do with it?"

"I don't know. Why?" he asked, letting her do the talking.

"Well, like, if you had a client, say, and if you both put your money with me? A lot of money? I'd keep my job, keep it for sure. That way, I don't lose my benefits, my medical and, you know, like that."

Her medical. He peered around Leslie's body at Gia.

"Diabetic," Gia said again.

"I could never promise you that, Leslie," he said.

Leslie wasn't much of a listener. "After that, I would make sure I earned your business. Seriously, Robert."

"I can't do it," he said. "Sorry."

He wondered if she had lost touch with reality. Guilty of bank fraud, and she's pitching him like a Better Banking Bureau rep.

He told her, "If I ever had a client with money to place, I could recommend, but I couldn't tell them where their money should go."

"Really?" she asked, looking to Gia for help.

"I'm right here, Leslie," he told her. She turned back to him. "I can't promise that, but I'll do what I can."

"You do it, G," Leslie said. "You're better at this stuff."

Leslie dove in the pool, swam underwater to the other end. Gia eased out of the pool, took his arm again, and started walking him out. "She could grow a conscience one day, Mr. Worth, burn me down at her bank. And that would be bad for you, too. You thought all of it through yet?"

"Not quite," he said.

But he'd thought about it on the fly. He'd go along with what they were asking, but there was no point in them knowing he had Alison's power of attorney.

"My cut of a settlement, I could put with her. My client's share? All I can do is ask."

"Sue the firm, Mr. Worth. We each go down to her bank, you and your client open new accounts with my girl, Leslie, and keep our money there for a month. All of us. For *one month.* She gets credit for bringing in new business, keeps her job, her benefits, and there you go."

Or, he was thinking, *Gia tells Jack she won't help me, and my client gets next to nothing. If that.* An easy call for him—his obligation to his client controlled the situation.

"See what I can do," he said as they reached the stairs. "Who knows? Maybe Leslie will kill it and earn my banking business."

"You never know," Gia said.

"I hear you. But sometimes you do," he said.

She smiled at that, then hugged him and whispered, "I care about the bad things I did, Mr. Worth, but after a while, I got used to it."

That sad look on her face again. Behind her who-gives-a-fuck front, he believed there was something normal about her she was trying to hide.

Now he heard Leslie saying, "Me 'n' Gia still need to finish our deal, you mind?" Leslie was near them now, talking from the water.

Gia smiled. "You know, Mr. Worth. Girl talk?"

Walking away into the exotic landscape, he heard a giggle behind him. Only human, he looked back. Gia sat on the pool's edge now, legs dangling down, gazing down at Leslie's face moving slowly through the water till it came to rest between Gia's thighs.

CHAPTER 22

An Amber Alert for a missing child was in effect on the jammed-up 405, everyone slowing down, on the lookout for a kidnapper's beige Toyota pickup. Easing ahead in crawling traffic, Robert had time to think over what had just happened.

Back at the hotel, going after the firm sounded easy. Clinical, almost, like civilian casualties. If Jack was too strapped to pay the freight alone, suing the firm was the only way to go. Suing Philip, too. Doing it for his client. He had no other viable choice.

Suing Philip Fanelli. He was suing Philip Fanelli.

He said it to himself several times, inching forward in the jam. If he didn't go that route and Jack was strapped? Maybe Alison pocketed a few hundred thousand, a hundred grand or so still coming his way. After that: no job and no prospects. No point lying to himself about it anymore. *Retribution, revenge*—that's what he wanted for his client and for himself. Pierce—berating him in the meeting, in his own office, insulting him every way he could think of. Pierce—upending his life and giving him a bullshit recommendation. All of it unnecessary, driven by whatever wanton need burned inside that man.

Traffic opened a bit, and as he jumped over to the I-10 West exit, he realized there was no one he could talk to about his own situation.

About his anger. Not his parents, not really. Not Philip—that ship was getting ready to sail. Erik? He would get it, but he had real problems—don't-get-killed-at-work-Daddy problems.

That left Alison. Opening up to her was crazy-wrong. That didn't stop him from thinking about her. Not as a client. He wanted to talk *to her* about his bizarre day at the Bel-Air.

Instead, when he got home, he grabbed his fourteen-ounce Cleto Reyes gloves, jogged to the gym, and beat the heavy bag till he couldn't raise his arms anymore. That squared him away, cleared his brain.

At home that night, he calmly stepped back from it all, tried to make sure he took the right approach. Lawyers, he knew, typically negotiated a settlement by starting with a big number and negotiating against the prospect of expensive, protracted litigation. *You don't like my last offer? Okay, see you in court.* But serious litigation was an idle threat coming from him, and everyone on the other side knew it. Sure, if they rejected his number, told him to get lost, he could hire real litigators to try the case. But that firm would wind up with half the money after taking huge litigation costs right off the top. And once all of Philip's partners found their dirty laundry exposed in open court? They would have no choice but to deny everything—deny, deny, deny—and fight Alison Maxwell's case for years.

Given all that, better that he came up with a reasonable settlement number now, then promise secrecy forever to all of them. Better that he stick hard on his reasonable number and put a short fuse on the negotiation. Bring them to heel, and do it fast. And as he drifted off to sleep that night, a settlement number floated into his mind. A number that came from an impeccable source: Jack Pierce himself.

CHAPTER 23

VENICE PIER CLOSES AT MIDNIGHT. The next night, Robert passed that sign with his iPad folder at 11:15 p.m., headed to the end of it to meet Jack.

As he moved farther out into the ocean, a few fishermen drifted back his way, Latinos and Asians, mostly. A rising tide sent good-size waves rolling beneath him. Pier pilings shook underfoot, mollusk-crusted concrete pulsing that raw energy up to him.

End of the pier, he took a seat on a bench. From here, it was a straight shot to shore, a 722-foot runway. At 11:25 p.m. Jack walked onto it, headed his way.

His mind turned to trial lawyers and their hand in this pier's past. Before he moved here, Venice Pier had been shut down indefinitely. A 150-pound chunk of concrete fell off Manhattan Beach Pier, twenty miles south, and paralyzed a jogger. Same kind of thing had happened once before, and that jogger deserved every nickel he'd recovered. Afterward, piers up and down the coast, including this one, closed to avoid the trial-lawyer feeding frenzy. All that, when the only thing each pier really needed was a big sign: **DANGER! YOU COULD DIE WALKING UNDER PIER!**

And there was trial-lawyer Jack, playing games. Stopping to read that Pablo Neruda poem posted on the railing, something about the peaceful sea and the sky, sealed under Plexiglas for its own protection.

Robert walked behind the bench and leaned over the railing. The water was dark and smelled like stale brine, dead fish, and crankcase oil.

Could be Jack had a check for a million-eight on him—Robert seriously doubted it—but ready-to-sign hard copies of a $1.8 million settlement agreement rested in his iPad folder. E-mails to Jack about a new deal were also ready to fly if need be. Either way Jack played it, Robert was good to go, confident that wireless reception way out here was good because he'd checked coverage again, three hours ago.

When he turned around, Jack stepped into the concrete circle, facing him. Gladiatorial at night, the circle was illuminated by lights atop four sets of concrete poles, each pole capped by aluminum coolie hats and tagged by somebody called *El Tigre*.

Robert stayed at the railing. Jack stopped fifteen feet away.

"Let's see your money," Robert said.

"Your check. The one-eight. I don't have it. Why I wanted to talk tonight, face-to-face."

"Sure," Robert said. "Man-to-man."

Putting him off. Right then, he knew Gia's version of Jack's finances was true. Dealing with only Jack was a thing of the past. Still, he wanted to hear Jack's explanation. Why not? It cost nothing to hear it.

"I need till middle of next week," Jack told him.

"Why's that? Today was your deadline, and it's pushing midnight."

"I'm liquidating funds in an overseas account, a hedge fund that allows only quarterly withdrawals, so you'll have to bear with me."

"A hedge fund?" was all Robert said. But he was thinking, *Hedge funds are for rich guys like you. No dinero, and Pierce is still talking down to me.*

"Sorry to hear that," Robert said. At the same time, he hit Send on his iPad and let that e-mail go flying.

"Check your e-mails, your personal account," he told Jack.

"Why? I just checked in my car."

Robert didn't answer. He looked at Jack until Jack checked his phone and found an e-mail that said:

> I reject your offer of $1,800,000 to settle our lawsuit.

"That was your last extension," Robert said.

"What extension?"

"Oh, that's right. I didn't give you one." He sent the next e-mail to the same address. Watched his screen till it was *delivered*.

"But I'm telling you—" Jack started to say.

"Forget it, new ball game. Read what I just sent."

"Read what? We have a deal. We agreed on every deal point, every word of it!"

"Read it," Robert said. "Hey, maybe you'll like it."

Jack started reading. Wasn't long before he looked up. Clearly, he *didn't* like it.

"You're suing my firm? For five million dollars?"

"Five million was your number. How much you said you'd be damaged if this got out. And that was for you, solo. For the whole firm? Way I see it, they're getting a deal."

"You and me—we had a deal. The firm stays out of it."

"No can do. This is the direction my client decided to go."

"Fuck you. This is where you want to go."

"Work it out with Fanelli or I file suit against the firm in one week. You don't, it'll be the top news item of the day. Bet anything it plays way bigger than your story would have played."

"Don't you fucking deny it—it's you doing this. You and that black-mailing piece of garbage, Gia."

Again, Robert kept his cool. "It's me and whoever makes you pay, Jack."

"Goddamn you! You and your whore client both."

"You know, Jack, you called her *whore* and *trailer trash* and *bitch* and *cunt*. That stops now, got it?"

"Got it, Worth. You and that Maxwell slag can go fuck yourselves."

Jack kept talking. Robert heard more insults flying at him, set down his iPad on the bench, already knowing Jack wanted to get it on. Even as he spoke, Jack's fists were rising, his knees bending, weight shifting onto the balls of his feet. Same thing Robert was doing, a beat behind Jack, but this time, a beat behind on purpose. That delay let Jack get off first with the same move that worked for him before. Feinting his left jab— all set to throw his big right cross and put Robert on the ground again.

Before Jack could get off his money shot, Robert cut loose with his own right lead, fast and powerful, catching what he wanted to catch: Jack's unguarded chin. Turning his fist over, he followed through till he was past the plane of the other man's body, his own body halfway to the ground and out of harm's way. Same punch Juan Manuel Márquez threw putting out Manny Pacquiao's lights. To be fair, Manny walked into it and Jack didn't, but either way, he caught Jack on the button, even as Robert rose and pivoted right on his left foot, getting his guard back up.

Turned out, there was no need for the guard. Jack went down in the pigeon shit. Onto the fish guts and spit-covered ground, and he stayed there. Robert knelt beside him and could tell from Jack's eyes that he was shook up, trying to get his bearings. More than that, he looked humiliated.

Robert said, "You're the whore, Jack, not her. Got it? And you fucked the wrong people this time. Five million dollars. Five million from *your firm*. And I'm done talking to you. From now on, I deal only with Fanelli."

Robert walked away. Behind him, Jack struggled to one knee. "What goes around comes around!" he shouted.

Robert stopped inside the lit circle. "Tell you what. If it ever comes around, I'll give you a call. Meantime, pull up your pantyhose, Jack. Pier closes at midnight."

Then Robert headed for shore. Jack stood and steadied himself on the nearest bench, staring at his adversary. If Robert had decided to stick around another sixty seconds, he would have had a question. It would have been this: after all that just went down, why was Jack Pierce smiling?

CHAPTER 24

Six days after Robert decked Jack on the pier, the Cy Twombly painting was gone from firm reception. So was Philip's California landscape. Gia noticed their absence before Robert did, because he was still thinking about the firm foyer: the name *Jack Pierce* no longer appeared beside the door.

Robert and Gia sat in reception with Leslie, each of them here to settle with the firm.

The day after Robert decked Jack, Philip promptly called him, asked him to send over whatever was already drafted for Jack. Robert agreed to it.

Fortunately, Philip told him, the firm did no business with Leslie's bank. If it did, all bets were off because the firm must disclose *possible banking irregularities*, as Philip called them, to its client. Robert hated to admit it—that thought never crossed his own mind.

His conversations with Philip bordered on surreal. Philip didn't bring up why they were talking or their recent past. Same thing during the days that followed as they went back and forth on deal points. Civilized, productive, and surreal.

Two days ago, the only remaining issue material to Robert came up. He had asked for certified funds from the firm at closing. That way, the firm's total payment was good the day the certified check was deposited. But Philip asked Robert to accept a firm check. That way, they could still close on Robert's deadline. Philip explained that in the hurry to closing, the firm had trouble coming up with $5 million. Two partners were actually considering fighting the lawsuit, but Philip had kept them in line.

"In line so far," Philip told him.

Robert knew that six lawyers agreeing on anything was a freak of nature. Knew, too, that Jack was strapped for his share. And Chase? He was a brand-new partner but still on the hook for his own share. Chase couldn't shoulder that load. Not with dual Range Rovers, a house in Brentwood, and bespoke suits like his idol, Jack. And the other partners? Fat mortgages, kids in the best schools, Bel-Air and Riviera Country Clubs, high-maintenance, top-drawer everything. No doubt about it to Robert: Philip had real-world problems coming up with that much cash so quick.

Thinking it through, he also knew that once Philip signed the agreement, he bound the firm. If its check was bad, the firm had to pay Alison's attorney's fees to collect. And that meant Robert would collect *on the check* by hiring real trial lawyers, no longer using a one-man band: himself. Serious legal firepower suing on a simple bounced firm check, not suing on the intricacies of a settlement agreement. More than that, all bets would be off keeping the scandal confidential because the firm was in breach of contract. That, plus the firm still had to pay the bounced check.

"Yes to noncertified funds," he told Philip, comfortable with his enormous leverage.

So there they were. Robert, Leslie, and Gia in the firm's lobby. Leslie leaned over and asked him, "You worked here?" almost prim in her business suit. He nodded.

"Wow," she said. "Where is she?" meaning Alison.

Gia nudged Leslie and said, "Hey, Les, c'mon."

Robert was impressed with Gia. She handled the contracts for Leslie and herself. Not him. He knew she'd been around the firm long enough to know that hiring a new lawyer could unravel any deal. Another lawyer trying to show her what a hotshot he was. All she wanted from Robert had been his Word file for his own final agreement. The dollar amount and party names, he'd left blank, so she typed in the blanks consistent with Leslie's and her situation. As long as Robert was willing to sign it, Gia told him, she and Leslie were, too.

Smart woman, he thought in the lobby, eyeing a high-end suede folder in her lap.

On his end, Robert needed Alison's witnessed signature on the settlement agreement, so he met Erik and her that morning at Rae's on Pico. He opened two hard copies of the settlement agreement to the signature page, folding the rest of it under. The only part of the contract visible to her was a paragraph about California law governing the agreement. He told her the bare-bones truth: she needed to sign to move forward with her case. So she signed two sets of documents at Rae's. So did he, right below her name.

Erik witnessed both signatures and started in on how Rae's was where Tony Scott shot the breakfast scene in *True Romance*, as if Rae's were really in Detroit for the movie. Next, Erik told Alison about his novelty item, Natural Gas, a handheld elastomeric cylinder with the uncanny ability to mimic a wide variety of human flatulence. About that time, Erik waved to his Thai wife and two kids, rumbling through the door for pancakes. That's when Robert excused himself, hugged Erik's wife, and headed over to the firm.

In the firm's lobby, Philip's assistant appeared and escorted Robert, Gia, and Leslie down the hall to a conference room. No game playing with Philip, no cooling their heels. Within ten minutes of arriving, they were seated in a conference room on the corporate end of the firm.

When Philip came in, Robert stood and shook his hand. The handshake was firm, Philip's hand dry, and Robert could see Philip was energized. A new man, as they say, the two of them speaking in person for the first time since he'd been fired.

"Everything in order?" he asked Robert.

He placed all the signed papers opened to their signature pages on the conference room table. "Far as I know, Mr. Fanelli. You are aware that Ms. Marquez and Ms. DeRider represent themselves?"

"I am aware," Philip said. He looked at Leslie, who chewed gum nervously. "You, I don't know." Then he looked at Gia. "Ms. Marquez. All of this business? I was disappointed."

Gia didn't answer him, kept looking out the window. Leslie said, "I never did anything bad like this before, Mr. *Panelli*."

Philip let her mistake slide, examined the signatures. "Oh, I won't tell anyone about it, Ms. DeRider. I promise. And you can speak freely about it to anyone who signed these documents. That includes me, by the way."

"Oh, thank you so much."

"But—if you two ladies, either of you, were to talk about it, dear? Talk about it to anyone else? A third party it's called in the agreement you signed? Were you two to speak of this situation to any such living soul, Ms. DeRider, it will be my life's work to have you imprisoned for a very long time."

"Oh, well, then . . ."

"Leslie. Enough," Gia said. She looked at Philip. "She gets it. Me, too. Keep quiet or else. Fair's fair, right?"

"Not in this instance," Philip told her. He handed Robert two envelopes, Gia one, and they all stood.

Robert asked, "Any chance I could I have a word with you, Mr. Fanelli?"

"Of course. I was about to suggest it myself."

Philip went to the house phone, spoke into the intercom. "Carlos? Come to the conference room now, please. Thank you." He turned to

Gia and Leslie. "Now, you two consultants try not to touch anything valuable on your way out."

A minute later, he opened the conference room door. Carlos stood there. The two women walked out. Robert could see them walking down the hall with Carlos, Gia looking straight ahead, as if drawn into herself.

✑

As the women reached the lobby, Leslie imitated Robert in the meeting, saying, "'Any chance I could have a word with you, sir?' I mean, I knew Robert was hot, but he's, like, one of the big boys, right?"

"He is," Gia said. "One of the big boys."

"I'm still sketchin'. I mean, what's his angle in all this?"

"I don't know," Gia said. "Maybe he doesn't have one."

"Everybody has an angle, you told me, right?"

"I know that's what I said. Him?"

Gia kept mulling it over when they reached the elevator doors.

"How you been, Carlos?" Gia asked.

Carlos said, "Pretty fair, Gia. You?"

"Not bad," Gia said.

But she was still thinking about Leslie's question. Wondering whether Robert had an angle as the elevator door opened in front of them.

✑

Philip's desk was cluttered with work, not unused like it had been before.

"Have a seat, Robert," Philip told him.

As he took a seat in front of the desk, Robert's eye caught Spartacus cruising past an upright diver figure. That diver was new, wasn't it?

179

Philip took a commanding seat behind his desk. "Well," he said.

"I'm glad you wanted to talk so I could say, I know you gave me a good recommendation. I didn't start out planning to sue you, either you or the firm, and I . . ."

Philip raised a hand to stop him. Chase appeared at the door. Ignoring Robert, Chase said, "Excuse me, sir?"

"Yes, Mr. Fitzpatrick?"

"I'm heading over to Santa Monica courthouse. Anything you want me to check on while I'm there?"

"No, thank you, Mr. Fitzpatrick, but I'm delighted you came down to the corporate end and checked with me."

"Of course, sir," Chase said and left.

"Go on, Robert, ask me whatever questions you have."

Robert started with, "Sure. Fitzpatrick? Still a partner?"

"Yes, but at my pleasure, and every day when he steps off the elevator, Mr. Fitzpatrick's chest fills with dread as he wonders whether this day will be his last."

Robert didn't reply. Philip said, "Go ahead, ask me."

"For the night in question, Chase Fitzpatrick lied to cover for Jack Pierce."

"Mr. Fitzpatrick would have eventually covered for Jack, but it never got that far," Philip said. "So he never lied to me. That would have been a mortal sin. Still, venal liars like him should suffer, too, and having him genuflect to me will suffice for now. Unlike you. You have been straightforward and aboveboard, and I understand why you took the action you did. But," he added, "had I been in your shoes while you still worked here? I would have shown more patience dealing with Jack. A bit more. Then again, you and I are different people."

He listened closely. Philip was always a good read, especially between the lines. "Yes, sir. We are different, but in the long run, very much alike, I hope."

"Thank you. That said, my former partner's behavior toward you was unspeakable, and I believe you have every right to know what happened to him."

"I'd appreciate it," Robert said.

Philip crossed to the aquarium, sprinkled fish meal into the water. "Once I learned from Jack what was afoot, I called a special partners' meeting. He showed up and did not look at all well, which, as you know, is quite unusual. From the looks of his bruised face, he had been in an altercation with someone who shall"—he paused for effect—"remain unnamed."

Philip kept telling the story, recounting it so vividly, Robert could see the partners' meeting in his mind's eye:

Jack stood in front of Philip, Chase, and the five other partners. Head down, he was humbled, disheveled.

Philip told Jack, "How could you let something like this happen, Jack? How in God's name could you do such a thing?"

"Ms. Marquez and I had an affair. I was careless with the firm's business."

The other partners piled on then. "Careless? Try gross negligence. The firm had a spotless record until you took over. Fuck anybody but the office manager, you idiot!"

Jack said, "I understand that, and I failed you all."

Now it was Chase's turn. He stood up and said, "Screw you, Jack, I'm not paying. I just made partner, and I haven't got that kind of money."

"Chase, I—" Jack started.

Philip cut them off. "From what I hear, Mr. Fitzgerald, you may have had a part in the initial encounter with Ms. Maxwell, so I ask you: Should the firm look into your whereabouts, thoroughly, on the night in question? Once the firm did so internally, perhaps we might divine from your time sheets and your phone records and from a serious interview with your wife that you shouldn't be seated at this table at all?"

That put Chase back in his seat.

"You will find your share of the money, Mr. Fitzgerald, as will each of us, or you will lose your partnership as well as your ability to find work elsewhere. Am I being perfectly clear with you?"

"Yes, sir," Chase said. "Very clear."

Jack said, "I'm resigning from the firm, effective immediately."

"Incorrect, Jack." Philip again. "Your partnership is terminated— for cause—and you will forfeit any and all interest you may have had in the firm. The Cy Twombly in our lobby belongs to the Brightwell family, certainly not to you. I'm quite certain that the Brightwells will want it returned, so I will see to it."

"All right," Jack said.

"Further," Philip said, "because Dorothy Brightwell has been a valued client of this firm, the firm has agreed. We will settle only after your infidelity has been disclosed to her and to her alone. Now go."

And Jack walked out the door . . .

In Philip's office, Robert came down to earth. Jack's extramarital history was going to be disclosed to Dorothy. He looked at the man who'd engineered that piece of good news. The man who now said, "The upstart prince is banished from the realm, and the natural order is restored."

"Sounds about right. And the Brightwells?"

"The Brightwell business, I will fight for and keep. And Dorothy Brightwell? Surely, she will divorce him knowing of his infidelity. I believe you know where that particular allegation leaves the profligate Jack Pierce?"

He nodded: no payment was due Jack under his prenup with Dorothy.

"You drew blood, son. You destroyed him."

"He had it coming," Robert said.

"He did. In full. Anything else?"

He was curious about the missing California landscape but didn't ask about it for two reasons. Philip likely sold the painting to come up with his share. Second, it was none of his business. Philip came closer to him. "You know, I gave up buying friends for Spartacus because he always killed them. Sometimes, he even attacks his own reflection in the mirror. Do you follow me?"

"Like . . . Jack?" he asked, reaching for Philip's metaphor.

"Like Jack, certainly. Like you as well. You two are not at all the same person, but you are similar in one respect. You hate to lose. And Jack, he needs to win. At the end of the day, for your sake, I hope the two traits don't amount to the same thing."

Philip walked him to the door, shook his hand, and said, "Fact is, both of you are trying to prove something to the world. Him, I don't care about. You, I do. So don't wind up being the last fish in the tank."

CHAPTER 25

Candles flickered inside red-and-white holders around a Bel-Air Hotel suite. Bedcovers lay on the floor, and a shower was running in the bathroom, all of it the aftermath of a serious lovemaking session. By the bar, Jack poured himself a neat O'Bannion single malt from his personal stash.

On the bar: twenty wrapped stacks of hundreds, ten hundreds per wrap, $20,000 in all. Next to the money lay a ziplock baggie filled with white powder, and it was the baggie that had Jack's attention at the moment. Wearing plastic gloves, he held the baggie up to lamplight, and when he turned it, that powder inside sifted and sparkled.

From his briefcase, he removed a folded sheet of white wrapping paper, slick on one side, the kind used to wrap fish at supermarkets. After that, he laid the baggie inside a long, narrow jewelry box, like one from Tiffany's for a gifted bracelet. He scissored enough paper to wrap the box, then did the same for the wrapped stacks of hundreds.

"Yo, Stanley," he said, joking around with himself, "what's up, my man? Grunion running today?"

He snapped off the plastic gloves, took a swallow of single malt, and opened the bathroom door. Steam billowed into the bedroom. He turned on the bathroom fan and stepped over to the shower, tapped on the fogged-up shower glass.

"Need your help out here, my love. There's work to be done."

A female figure behind the glass turned off the water.

"Couldn't hear you. What's up?" the woman asked from the swelling mist.

"I have no clue how to gift wrap our friend's packages." He handed her a thick towel over top of the glass. "Do you?"

CHAPTER 26

The evening after his meeting at the firm, Robert put Philip's cryptic *last fish in the tank* warning behind him and valeted his car at Shutters in Santa Monica. With his briefcase in hand, he made his way into the broad low-ceiling lobby dotted by couches and chairs, encouraging people to talk, drink, and get to know one another. He didn't see Alison at first even though they were on for 7:00 p.m., then he caught sight of her on his right.

A waitress was taking her order, but as he closed on the pair, the waitress abruptly backed away from Alison, then hurried to the service bar.

Robert took a seat, far end of the couch where Alison was seated. "Hey," he said.

"Hey," she said, smiling at him. "And thanks for leaving me at Rae's today with your buddy."

"Erik? What did he do?"

"Natural Gas. Ring a bell?"

"I suggested you might not be into it."

"A handheld fart machine? What girl wouldn't be?"

"Natural Gas," he said. "Get it?"

"Comes with a how-to booklet and everything," she remembered.

Erik's pathway to millions, as he put it, when Robert had applied for the trademark. The waitress came back and set down Alison's sparkling water.

Looking only at him, the waitress said, "Care for a drink, sir?"

"Same as she's having," he said.

"A lime, please," Alison said.

"Sure thing," the waitress replied, still avoiding eye contact with Alison. The waitress left, and he turned to Alison. "You two are . . . what?"

"Do I look like a dyke magnet to you?" she asked.

Short skirt, sandals, and a white jean jacket over a black T-shirt. *Hair in a ponytail. Keeping it simple,* he thought. To him, she looked like a magnet, period.

"Not sure what one looks like," he said.

"Know what she said to me?" Without waiting: "'I get off at eleven. Let's get together, and I promise, you'll get off, too.'"

"Whoa, sounds like a guy's line."

"I know, right? A cheesy guy line."

"She looked kind of upset?"

"I told her, 'Eleven? That can't be right. That's when you can go fuck *yourself*.'"

He smiled at that one. Then the waitress came back, set down his drink. "Enjoy," she said only to him and left, still frosted.

"I had to quit yoga class because of Sonya," Alison told him.

He remembered Sonya: the silver-haired woman, hugging Alison outside her house on Amoroso. "The silver fox?"

She nodded. "Sonya got more and more friendly, lots of touching. What's up with that?" she asked.

"Beats me," he said. "Mind if we leave your girlfriend's wait zone and check the view?"

"Great idea," she said, looking at his briefcase. "What's going on?"

"Show you outside," he said.

He opened the door for her onto a small deck. Six empty tables, a heavy mist hanging in the air, space heaters roaring. Lights from the Santa Monica Pier offered a melting rainbow as they grabbed a table. He opened his briefcase, pulled out two copies of a document.

"So," he said, "those papers you signed today had to do with a big settlement conference. Could have gone a lot of ways, but the way it went, you're done."

"Done?"

"Done," he said. "It's over."

"What are these, then?" she asked, pointing at the new documents.

"I'm withdrawing as your attorney of record, and I need you to sign these. One set for me, one for you."

"I don't get it. I . . ."

"I need you to sign. You'll be fine with it, I'm sure. If not, tear them up after we talk."

She signed both pages, filled in the date line.

"If you'd write down the time of day, too, that would be great," he said.

"The time?"

"The time right now. What time do you have?"

"Seven twenty-eight," she said.

"Seven twenty-eight p.m. Pacific Standard Time. Write PST, that'll be okay."

She wrote down what he wanted. Then he signed and dated them, too, adding *7:29 p.m. PST* beside his name.

"You're being weird. You know that, right?"

"I know," he said. He pulled a thin envelope from his briefcase and handed it to her. "The settlement conference today went well."

"What?"

"Open it now if you want," he said.

She opened the envelope, removed a check, looked at it, and let out a shriek. "Get outta here! It's for—it's for—we won? Are you? Are you?"

For a second, she looked like she might pass out. Then she sat there a long time. Then she said, "I . . ."

That's as far as she got. After that, she started crying, and he sat with her. When she stopped, he took her hand. The first time he'd ever touched her that way.

"You all right?"

"Yes, I'm great, thank you, so much, I . . . whew," she said. "Excuse me."

She walked over to the balcony, looked out at the ocean. Then she looked down for a while. He made a quick phone call to the front desk while she gathered herself, and when she came back to the table, tears filled her eyes. She put her hand on top of his and squeezed it, and behind her tears, he saw hunger like his own. She raised his hand to her lips and kissed it. "I can't believe you did this," she said.

He put his hand over hers. "No, *we* did it, and Jack Pierce? Fired from the firm. Now he's just another out-of-work lawyer."

"That guy," she said, shaking her head. Then she moved closer. He felt the current arcing between them.

"Know what would have been really weird?" he asked.

She wiped her eyes and whispered, "What?"

"Your lawyer kissing you. That's why I resigned at 7:29 p.m. PST."

"Kissing me now? That wouldn't be weird at all, would it?"

It wasn't a question. So he said, "Come here."

Without hesitating, she slid into his lap, slipped an arm around his shoulder. He could feel her trembling when he kissed her on the mouth. After that, they made out till he said, "I made a dinner reservation."

"What do you think about . . . room service?" she asked.

"Already checked with the front desk. They're booked solid."

"Cocky," she said, smiling.

"No, hopeful."

Then she stood up and asked him, "Mind if we go to your place and say, 'Fuck dinner?'"

♨

Robert didn't mind. Out in the Bronco, she tugged out his shirt, unbuttoned it, and bit his neck. Once he squeezed over to the passenger side, she climbed astride him.

He kissed her deep, lifted her skirt, and she unzipped his fly. She pulled her panties aside and moaned, taking him inside her, ready for him. He pulled her T-shirt up, taking first one nipple in his mouth, then the other.

She whispered, "I wanted you for so long . . ."

His hand snaked around her neck, grabbed her hair to pull her mouth onto his. As they kissed, hungry, she threw back her head and started moving on him. Slow at first. Then she started moving faster.

♨

Oh, he'll love hearing about that, Stanley was thinking, meaning Jack.

Stanley had been street parked in his Celica watching Shutters' valet stand. He spotted the lovebirds coming outside, playing grab-ass with each other till one of the valets brought the lawyer's car around.

The Bronco drove past him, but before Stanley could follow, the Bronco stopped on a side street.

Stanley thought, *Man, oh, man. Bet they're going at it right there,* and cut his engine.

He got out with his burner phone, lit a Lark, headed their way. Walked past them and heard them fucking like minks inside. *Probably a screamer,* he guessed, and crossed the road fifty yards ahead of them. Acting like he was on a phone call, he came back their way, far side of the street. There she was, on top of him, really going to town.

Oh, yeah, Stanley was thinking.

Maybe he'd bullshit Jack a little, give him his money's worth, and tell him he batted off the Bronco's side mirror in Shutters' parking garage. Jack would start in on him about surveillance, but he'd tell boss man, "It's Stanley, Jack. I always check."

Tonight, Stanley wondered how this pair had crossed Jack. Didn't they know Jack always got even? No, not even. He always wound up on top, same as at Venice High all those years ago.

Good-looking as Jack was, it took the cool high school crowd a while to figure out how tough and vindictive the new kid was. Not too long, though. Not the way Jack punched, fast and hard with bad intention, like the boxers say.

Getting back in his car, Stanley wondered if Jack had nailed the lawyer's girl. Who knows? He'd laid everything with a pulse since they were kids, Jackie had. Like the hairdresser in that old *Shampoo* movie.

No one really knew Jack, but Stanley felt like he came as close as anyone, going back as far they did. When he got caught breaking and entering those times, it was lawyer-friend Jack who got him into diversion, twice. Third time, Jack let him do eighteen months in County, but even then he hadn't quit shooting up.

Couple times, with Jack's wife out of town, Stanley had driven up to the mansion on Stone Canyon. Sitting around the kitchen bullshitting with Jack, him drinking carrot juice and Jack with that single malt he liked drinking now. Like old times, except Jack's slut of a mom wasn't asking her ten-year-old son to zip up her dress and tell her how young and pretty she looked before leaving on another sleepover. And up on Stone Canyon, Jack's mom didn't leave behind his beat-down dad, sunk into the living room sofa, hacking Viceroys on disability, and mainlining whatever vodka quarts had been cheapest down at Mercado Diego.

Stanley knew Jack hadn't forgotten all that early life mess, either. Once, old man Brightwell starting barking phlegm upstairs, and the sound carried down to them in the kitchen. Hearing it, Jack had raised his glass to Stanley.

"Cheers, Stanley. To old times."

And Stanley was thinking, *My pal made it all the way up the hill to the big leagues. Effin' Jack Cross Pierce.*

He flicked that NA bracelet on his car's mirror. Going on two years sober. Before that, he'd slipped up, started running that shit again. He knew he could keep it on the straight and narrow if he did one simple thing: Stay away from smack. Don't get anywhere near smack. No way could he handle smack. No way could he do *just a little* smack. Not ever. Not even a little skin pop, or he could OD again.

"I am a junkie," he said in his car. And like he told Jack last week: "The thought of it, the idea of running smack, starts me fiending for it."

Like he was fiending this very second, Jesus. He already knew what those horndogs in the Bronco were up to, rest of the night and then some. So instead of following them, he drove over to his regular meeting, a church up on Colorado, and sat himself down for some bitter coffee and fellowship.

CHAPTER 27

Alison lay across Robert's bed, blissed out, wearing nothing but a distant smile. Stretched out across from her, he was naked, too, and immobile. On their way home from Shutters, between more gropes and probes, he brought her up to speed about keeping quiet about the case—keeping mum forever. About how they were obligated to meet Leslie at her bank on Monday, keep their money there for at least one month. How the cash payout would be delayed for a little while. But she had no real questions or problems with the scenario—she got it.

Now, in his apartment, he tried summoning the energy to grab a champagne bottle on the bedside table. A bridge too far at the moment as a loud series of knocks landed on his front door. Neither of them moved.

"Food's here," he said.

"Can't get up," she said. "But food . . ."

They both lay there.

"All right, I'm going," she said. "Like this." She started to get up. He pulled her back down, giving her the point. He grabbed a towel, wrapped it, and walked out.

As he paid the delivery guy at the front door, he heard her call out, "Which one is it?"

"Sushi," he called back, closing the door.

She joined him in panties and one of his Hastings Law hoodies. "We can't eat sushi in bed, right?"

"Bad idea," he agreed.

So they mixed the wasabi and soy sauce and sat at his dining-room-table-slash-desk, feasting on brown-rice sushi—salmon and yellowtail—and soft-shell-crab hand rolls.

"You're incredible, you know that?" she said.

"C'mon, who's counting?"

She jabbed him in the arm with a chopstick. "Not *that*. I mean, I never thought we'd beat him. That we'd win."

He reminded her about Jack's weak alibi, his overall weak position, and she said, "Not the case so much. It's more the way I think, the way Brian thought, too. We were the little guys, and my dad used to say little guys always lose. *Get hosed* is how he put it, and he said it all the time, even before his business went belly-up."

"Little guys, they lose a lot. He's right."

"I thought about my dad lately—before today, even—and I decided all that losing was his fault."

"How so?" he asked.

"He took out a loan on our land and put it all back into the kitchen showroom, then he doubled down again. Three years later, too late, our land was worth real money—again. Developers were all over it, paying top dollar—again."

"But you did win today. You have the check. It's for you. You won."

"I know I did, but . . . wait."

She went back in the bedroom and came back with one of his bedside photographs. In it, Robert's mother and father sat tandem on a racehorse in a corral. Mom proudly held a blown-up check, beaming for the camera.

"Look at your mom and dad. Is it just me, or do they look like movie stars? They look like sky's-the-limit people. See what I mean?"

He nodded. "I took the picture, and I see how it looks, but it wasn't like that. That filly was Sweet Lorraine. She placed in the money that week."

"Meaning?"

"She finished third—*finally* in the money. And that check on steroids Mom's grinning about? It barely covered the feed bill that year. Then there's the trainer, the vet bills, and all the rest. If you're really, really rich, and we weren't, it's cool and it's glamorous. But what horse racing is mainly? It's expensive. And it's risky, and the farm lost lots of money doing it before we quit."

"You're saying everybody fucks up?"

"No. I'm saying people who have money? Especially them."

"Come on," she said.

"Seriously. People with money can afford to make bigger mistakes, and they make 'em all the time." He told her about the family vineyard. "End of the day, that was a bust, too."

"What are your parents like, besides being craps-shooting maniacs?"

Smiling, he said, "When you get past that big farmhouse, I guess they're like anyone else."

"Anyone else? I don't know about that. I . . ."

Another knock on the door. He grabbed some cash off the table to pay the next delivery guy.

"Pizza and sushi? What were we thinking?"

"We weren't," he said.

After he paid for the pizza, he asked her, "Bedroom?"

"Pizza? Definitely bedroom."

Back on his bed, between slices of cheese, pepperoni, and mushrooms, they kept talking. Seemed like the words flowed easier with the lawsuit behind them.

"You like it over in Culver City?" he asked.

"At night, when I open my windows, if the wind's blowing right, I can hear big-rig blowouts on the 405. Urban, cool—I'm sick of it."

"Lot of things in storage?"

"Some, over in the Valley. It's probably been on *Storage Wars Tarzana* by now."

"On what?"

"*Storage Wars*, that cable show."

"Show about what?"

She told him how they auctioned off unpaid storage lockers to a cast of regular bidders. "You missed a lot of epic TV working so hard," she said, kidding around.

"Got some catching up to do," he said. "You know, I'm thinking about getting a new place. Something bigger."

"Me, too, now. A lot bigger."

Silence as they kept eating.

"Listen," he said, "we don't know each other as well as . . . as well as some people who . . . you know, decide to . . ."

For once, he was lost for words. She didn't help him out.

"What I mean is, the last five years I worked hard, worked too much, especially the last two years, and I put off making any commitment for a long time except for work, and what I'm thinking . . ."

She finally let him off the hook. "Hey, I know, let's get a place together."

"Yeah," he said. "Like I was saying."

He told her about a builder down on the Peninsula that was in over his head. Once he had his certificate of occupancy from the city, he found termite damage in his *treated* floor joists and was wrestling with vendors over who was responsible for repairs.

"What's it look like?" she asked.

"Like this," he said, pulling a brochure from a bedside-table drawer. "Right on the beach."

"Love it," she said, reading. "I'm in if you are."

"Let's check it out first thing," he said, and leaned over to kiss her.

She slid an arm around his neck and didn't let him go. "When you first walked in that conference room, I could tell you weren't like those guys."

"Not an asshole?"

"No, really. You didn't like what was going on, but they were into it. Then later you helped me out in the garage. And what'd I do? I got you in trouble, but you still made it all work out, and honestly, I don't know anybody else like you."

Before he could thank her, she pushed him down and got on top of him. He swept the pizza box onto the floor.

"Staying over tonight, right?" he asked.

"Let's get something going," she said. "That's what I want."

He leaned up and kissed her. "Yeah, let's do that."

"And by the way," she whispered, as he went inside her, "you *are* incredible . . ."

At 12:15 a.m. Robert bolted up in his bed, disoriented. Across his bedroom, he caught a female form in the darkness. It was Alison, getting dressed.

"What's wrong?" he asked. "You leaving?"

"Get dressed," she said. "We won. Move your ass."

A half hour later, after sneaking over the locked gate of the Venice Pier, they leaped from its railing, holding hands, and hit the dark Pacific Ocean, screaming.

CHAPTER 28

Present Day

"Need you to drop your pants, Mr. Worth."

Robert had been dozing off and on in his jail cell when the doctor spoke from his cell door. Now the doctor was coming in, along with the same cop who'd locked him up—what was it, two, three hours ago? He rolled himself over and up into sitting position, slid his legs off the bunk, and put his feet on the floor.

Standing stiffly, he unbuttoned his jeans, dropped them to his ankles. His right thigh was wrapped in surgical gauze, his dried blood dark where it had seeped through.

"How's it feeling?" the doctor asked, unwrapping the gauze.

"Hurts."

"Hurts or throbs?" the doctor asked.

"More hurts."

When the gauze came off, Robert saw the wound: about four inches deep, one inch wide.

"You mighta gotten lucky," the doctor said.

In jail? Stabbed? Lucky? Looking back on it, he thought, *Yeah, maybe I was lucky. So far, anyway.*

"Want you to take all these," the doctor said. He handed Robert a white pill packet and a small bottle of Arrowhead water. "Two more Augmentin, three extra-strength Tylenol with codeine for pain. That makes six Augmentin taken so far, and I'm leaving you two of each if you need them. I'm not seeing any redness, nothing out of the ordinary, anyway."

"Thanks," Robert said, and gulped down all five pills.

The doctor handed him another packet and said, "If you get an increase in pain or swelling, either one—and I mean if it hurts like hell—take the other two Augmentin and Tylenol right then and get somebody in here, ASAP."

"What's wrong?" Robert asked.

"Knife was clean, that's not my concern, but a sewer drain empties seven, eight hundred yards up the beach from where you were. Never know what kind of bacteria's floating around. Surfers pick up hep C, but MRSA's my primary concern."

The badass bacteria that put you in intensive care on an IV? No, thanks, Robert thought.

"Any word from Officer Sedgwick?" he asked the cop.

"Told you before, don't know him."

Seltzer? Segway? Schwartz? Robert wondered if he had the name wrong. But Sedgwick had been ready to shoot him on the dark beach, and that made him all the more memorable.

"What about the body?" Robert asked. "At the coroner's, right, Doc?"

"Yep. They're telling me the wounds to—"

"Hey!" somebody shouted.

A man in a suit leaned on the cell door, looking in. His left eyelid drooped under scar tissue, and his cheeks bore old pockmarks. "Plenty of time for that coming up," he told the other two, but he was looking at Robert.

The cop said, "I hear you, Detective."

"In the morning, then." And this time the detective was talking to Robert, without the pretense of a smile.

After the detective left, Robert couldn't pry anything else from the pair in his cell, other than the detective's last name: *DeGrasso*.

Once the doctor cleaned Robert's wound and rewrapped his leg, he left his patient on that cold metal bunk, his features drained. The heavy metal door slammed shut at the end of the hall, echoing. A bad sound, even when you're getting top-shelf treatment.

Made sense they'd treat him like a VIP. Innocent man lands in jail, loses a leg? No, wait—innocent *lawyer* lands in jail, loses a leg. Sounded like a lawyer joke: *Hey, you hear the one about the innocent lawyer losing a leg in jail?*

A little too close to home. He threw an arm over his face, tried to forget about DeGrasso's hard look, and tried to fill in the blanks in that number sequence he'd traced in the dust under his bunk.

"La, la . . . nine, eighteen . . . da, da, da, da, da . . . La, la . . . shit."

That's as far as he could take it. Same result as earlier, but now the codeine mercifully buzzed his brain.

Looking back, he wondered, *What if none of it had happened?* Maybe he'd be sitting in the conference room with his law partners, offering to take the lead in firing Chase for padding his time sheets. Then again, here in the real world, Chase wasn't the one in jail.

He considered his options. Hire a criminal lawyer to tell him his Miranda rights? To tell him not to speak to anyone about anything, then hold out his hand for a fat retainer? Call his father, his mother, his uncle, middle of the night? God knows what that would stir up at the farm. If he needed anybody from there, it would be Luis, the farm manager, but about all Luis could do is find a criminal lawyer in Gilroy.

Doesn't matter, he convinced himself. He didn't need help.

So far at least, nobody had said a word to him about the gun. Had Sedgwick—whatever his name was—seen it last night? He didn't mention it if he had. With everything that had been going on, it was hard to know exactly where it might have landed below those cliffs.

He remembered the pay-phone call he'd made earlier that night: she said she would come for him, didn't she? And he asked her to bring his laptop, didn't he? And he'd been careful along the way, right?

Have I left enough bread crumbs? he finally wondered as that codeine took a firm hold and breezed him away . . .

CHAPTER 29

Thirteen Days Earlier, Santa Monica, California

Robert's and Alison's dealings at the bank had been straightforward so far: opening their new accounts with Leslie and endorsing the law firm's settlement checks for deposit only.

With Alison beside him at Leslie's desk, Robert now watched Leslie inside the manager's glass cubicle across the lobby. *Jerome*, she said his name was, and from over in the cubicle, Leslie was waving at them. So was Jerome. Robert nudged Alison and they waved back.

According to Leslie, the standard bank drill was this: it would put a bank hold on their funds for ten days. Their debit cards would be available in fifteen days—no exceptions. Until the ten-day holding period passed, there would be no funds available. Hearing that from Leslie, Robert balked at 100 percent of their funds being held up—especially on the law firm's local check. Leslie agreed with him and was still talking to Jerome about cutting them some slack.

That was the beauty of a certified check, he was thinking: the whole amount available today. But had he insisted on it with Philip, who knows? The whole deal with the other partners could have come unraveled for no reason, or for any reason at all.

"This whole thing blows my mind." Alison squeezed his hand.

"I know," he said, staying cool but thinking, *Yes!*

Leslie walked back across the lobby and took a seat at her desk. "Sorry that took so long, bank stuff, but I have good news. I told Jerome exactly how you and I feel about the one hundred percent hold on your funds."

She waved at Jerome, mouthed, "Thank you." He waved back.

"He said we can go ahead and transfer twenty-five thousand dollars into each of your new accounts. With checks this large and with them being local, he couldn't see the bank holding up all of your funds for ten days. Like I told you before, I want your business."

"I can live with it," Robert said. "Alison?"

"I'll make it work," she said, squeezing his hand again.

Leslie handed them new-account counter checks.

Robert said, "Alison? Any questions?"

She shook her head, and Leslie handed Robert their two receipts.

Robert looked them over. Each had been initialed by Leslie and by Jerome at his request. Each had been debited by the bank to show $25,000 cash in each checking account. He tried to hand Alison her receipt.

She said, "You keep it. I'm too nervous."

"All right, then," he said, standing.

Leslie gave each of them her business card. "I'm so glad for the opportunity to work for you. If either of you have questions, you can reach me at that number," she said, pointing to the card. "And I wrote down my personal number, too. Call me day or night, at home, whatever, I'm serious."

Robert was a little surprised by how professional Leslie came across when she wasn't stealing things or going down on Gia. "That's it, then," he said.

"Thanks for everything, Robert."

"Don't mention it, Leslie," he said, looking at her till she nodded.

"Got it," Leslie replied. "I definitely won't."

As Robert and Alison started to leave, Gia strolled in wearing white jeans and a dark blue blazer behind classic black Ray-Bans. An hour ago, Robert had made sure Gia finished her business with Leslie before he and Alison approached Leslie's desk. He wondered why she'd come back.

Straightaway, Gia walked up to Robert and said, "Missed you earlier, Mr. Worth." Then she looked at Alison without speaking.

Now he understood. Robert introduced the two women. "Gia Marquez, I don't think you've met Alison Maxwell."

"No, I haven't," Gia said, without bothering to remove those Ray-Bans. "Alison."

"Gia," Alison said, her expression flat.

The women almost shook hands, then didn't.

Gia asked Alison, "You two together now?"

Without answering, Alison took Robert's arm. "We better get going, Robert. When are the movers coming?"

Before he could answer, Gia told Alison, "Guess you already know, you're with a really, *really* great guy."

"The best," Alison said.

As Robert and Alison left the lobby, Leslie noticed Jerome standing up behind his desk, waving at them. Leslie steered Gia toward the exit nearest her desk.

"Let's book," she told Gia, "before Jerome starts drooling on you again."

❧

Out on Ocean Avenue, Alison stopped Robert beside his car. "Not even with you a week and I'm already being a bitch."

"Gia worked at the firm," he said. "She's the one I told you about way back. Jack fired her."

"Oh, okay," she said, getting it. "Did you two ever . . . you know?"

"If I did, I wouldn't tell you. But we didn't."

"That's helpful," she said, smiling now. "They're both so beautiful, that's all."

"Leslie, I don't know that well, but Gia, she's a little troubled, I think. I don't know if you'd call us friends or what."

"Hot *and* troubled. Much better."

"No, no, I think the two of them are with each other, off and on," he said.

"Hot, troubled lesbians? Keep digging, lawyer man," she said, but she was laughing now.

She asked, "The lawsuit—do I need to know more about what happened?"

"Your call, but here's how I see it. The less you know, the less you can reveal, and the less risk you run of disclosing anything about it to a third party. Then again, I'm not your lawyer anymore."

"What are you exactly?"

"The guy who wants to get you back in bed. Kidding aside, do you want to know more about it?"

"Not really." They started to get inside his car and she told him, "I trust you."

In Palisades Park, quivering Mexican palms kissed the sky as Gia and Leslie took a seat on a green metal bench. "Can you believe it?" Leslie told her. "Jerome said they're gonna enroll me in executive training at UCLA."

"Give yourself some credit, baller. It's not every day new clients drop four-point-five million on your desk."

"Hells, no! Today I'm the LeBron James of banking."

"Where's your headband, bitch?"

"Swear to God, I'll buy one at lunch and wear it all day."

They leaned back, gazed out at the ocean.

Gia asked, "What about Alison Maxwell? Learn anything about her?"

Leslie gave her a serious look. That didn't often happen. "I can't say anything about a client. My new banking leaf, it's turned over for real."

"Right, I shouldn't ask."

"Why do you want to know about her?"

Gia shrugged.

"You *do* have a thing for him. Why didn't you go for it before, G? He was wide open."

"I told you, it wasn't like that with him."

"You know her or what?"

Gia shook her head.

"What's the deal, then?" Leslie was getting confused.

"I don't trust her," Gia said.

"But if you don't know her—you messing with me or what?"

"Listen, this past year, hanging out all the time, hooking up, that was great, right?"

"It's still great." Gia looked away, and Leslie said, "Oh, I thought we were, you know, getting somewhere."

"We were having fun, okay, so do something for me, would you?"

"Sure, I guess."

Gia lowered her voice. "I talked you into cashing the firm's checks, all right? So it's great you're putting that part of your life behind you. Do yourself a favor, Leslie, and find a decent person to hang out with. And to be with."

"But I was gonna throw us a party and everything."

"Anybody but me. I mean it, and Dougie, he's bad news. You gotta stay clear of him."

Before Leslie could say anything, Gia handed Leslie her Healey keys and registration. "I signed the roadster over to you. No liens, and I know how much you love it, so keep it, sell it, it's yours."

Leslie looked at the Healey keys, her eyes brimming. "Thanks, G. I'm gonna miss hanging with you." Then she added, "We both know I'm not the smartest guy around. Not smart like you, but if I lost this job, I'd wind up getting dialysis down at County. My promotion, now the car? It's all killer and you made it happen. You'll always be the shit to me, G."

They stood and shook hands, then Leslie watched Gia strolling away, across the burned-out grass.

CHAPTER 30

"Can we do something besides engage in all this sexual intercourse?" Alison asked Robert. It was their first night in the beachfront condo. He was pretty sure she was joking, but just in case, he rolled her body off him.

Their three-story corner unit was on the sand, one of four in an otherwise-unoccupied building. Downstairs, the movers had stacked their boxed belongings in the living room, along with his filing cabinet and their furniture. Exactly where all of it still lay. An enormous glass slider led from there onto a front deck, and eight feet below that was the beach.

Both of them had seen *Last Tango in Paris* and remembered the pad where Marlon Brando's character and his lover got down and dirty and occasionally talked. They quickly nicknamed the new place *Last Condo in Paris*.

They got away with paying the owner $6,000 cash for two months, no deposit. Rent was usually three times that and called for a one-year lease with a two-month deposit. But the owner's contractor issues brought this sweet deal their way.

It was quieter down on the Peninsula than up in Venice. The board-walk foot traffic stopped twenty blocks north at Venice Pier, so at night they slid open the windows, listening to the ocean pounding and letting the breeze flow over their bodies.

Finally, they had time to hang out, get to know each other. Real time without the eight-hundred-pound lawsuit in the room. Turned out, each of them had been alone, pretty much, the last few years. Him because of work and her because of family turmoil, especially Brian.

Straightaway, she wanted to pay off the hospital. By paying cash now with a counter check, they worked her bill down to $3,000 from twice that.

"I have the money," she told him. "They helped me, and I owe them."

Robert had been surprised she'd been unattached when they met, and she told him, "Problem is, the guys were all alike. All obvious. I mean, we'd go somewhere, and they'd throw money around and wink at me like, *Hey, baby, check that out. Ready for sex yet?* I'm not a prude or anything . . ."

"No," he said, "you're not."

"But it was always the same—the guy, I mean. Didn't matter if they were agents or actors or businessmen or what. They were all boring—to me, anyway."

"No bikers?" he asked, teasing, but it turned out she knew about bikers from living up in Topanga with Brian.

"Bikers, they're mainly two groups. Druggies—anything you ever thought you wanted—and posers. Brian usually hung with guys in a small third group: *real men*, but they were married with kids. Brian, he wasn't a saint, but you'd have liked him. He smoked a cigarette every once in a while, and he'd take a drink, sure, and rode a Harley that was always in the shop. Played guitar, too, whenever he got a chance. Good at it," she told him, "but nowhere near LA good."

Most days, Robert and Alison hung out. One day they noticed a five-story billboard on a boardwalk building: **Dos Equis' Most Interesting Man in the World.** That inspired a game: *Most Interesting*

Day in the World, inspired, too, by the half brownie each they'd eaten, courtesy of a nearby marijuana hospital.

Rules were simple. Each of them would pick four storefronts in a row and make that into a hypothetical interesting day. Loser had to wear a boardwalk T-shirt of the winner's choosing.

After a half hour of research, they met up at Breeze Avenue. Her day: buying a monogrammed glass crack pipe, learning her Egyptian name, checking into Phoenix House for crack addiction, and eating an entire funnel cake, whatever that was. He countered with: buying two pairs of genuine Ray-Bans for nine dollars and ninety-nine cents, eating two dozen fried Oreos, getting his nipples pierced, and putting a henna, garlic-clove tattoo on his ass. It was close until she showed him her real Egyptian name on a genuine papyrus scroll. Rest of the day, he wore the *I'm Her Bitch* T-shirt she picked out for him.

Those days were good ones. Hitting the beach; a few movies; hiking the Santa Monica Mountains; walking, sometimes running, the Santa Monica stairs; drives up the coast; breakfast at the farmer's market in town, at Mercedes Grill by the pier; jazz brunches on Abbot Kinney; lunches at Gjusta and Tacos Por Favor; dinners at Gjelina and Joe's, Chaya Venice, and Komodo on Main.

These were the days they just wandered and talked. He recalled the first time they made love in the Bronco, how she told him she'd wanted him *for so long*.

"For how long?" he asked.

"Ever since you told me about Rosalind," she told him. "At your apartment," she added. "The day I signed that power of attorney."

She wondered the same thing about him. Joking around, he told her he had no impure thoughts until withdrawing as her attorney. Then: "Truth is, it was earlier that same day. When you came out of Sonya's yoga class."

"Why then?" she asked.

"I could tell you were over it. You were strong. For the first time, I could see you." Then again, there were those shorts she was wearing.

"Sure you're not gay?" she asked, smiling about what he'd just revealed. For the next few hours, he did his best in bed to answer any questions about his sexuality.

As the days passed, he learned how Alison felt trapped the last three years. First, there was her mother's automobile accident back in Florida. It was partly her mother's fault, and the settlement was small. What killed her mom, though, wasn't the accident but the infection she picked up, Alison believed, in the hospital. After dropping out of the University of Miami to take care of her, and a year after watching her die, she still couldn't find a lawyer.

"Hard to blame them," she told him. "Who wants to spend the next five years going after a big hospital on contingency?" She was ready then to split the Florida Panhandle, when her father's store went belly-up. "So I helped my dad until he worried himself to death."

Finally, she moved out to LA, into the San Fernando Valley for the cheap rent.

"Then it was Brian's turn?" he asked.

"My family died fast," she said, "like rock-and-roll drummers."

He couldn't help laughing. She did, too.

"I loved them. I miss them, but c'mon. All of them in three years, seriously?"

She asked about his family, too, and he told her about his grandfather, Big Worth, who settled a big spread in Gilroy, and his grandmother, who wanted to be a movie star until she met Big Worth. They had two boys who were expected to stay and work the farm, and each son had one kid apiece.

"One of Big Worth's grandchildren was a boy," he told her. "He was strapping, smart, well hung, and handsome."

"Wait—you had a brother?" she asked.

"Pay attention. He was named *Robert Logan Worth*," he told her.

"Was it hard, the work?" she asked.

"It started at dawn, chores, helping Luis and the guys load irrigation pipes on trucks, shovel fertilizer. When I was a kid, back before machines made a lot of sense, we planted and harvested by hand. So from elementary school till I went away to high school, I'd help out. So did Rosalind," he told her. "Just how it was."

"You picked garlic?"

"Why I'm so strong," he said. "Really glad I did it and glad I don't do it anymore."

"Me, too," she told him.

With a seventy-inch flat-screen hanging on the master-bedroom wall, she helped him catch up on pop culture. He'd never seen *Game of Thrones* or *House of Cards* and had pretty much dropped out of cable after the last *Sopranos* reruns. He admitted to seeing the last episode of *Sex and the City*, didn't know about *Modern Family*, was unaware of *Black Mirror*, and thought he remembered the *Mad Men* pilot.

One night they caught HBO Boxing. When he was a kid, he told her, lots of times he hung out after work with Luis and the largely Latino workers. Their favorite fighter, and so his, was Julio César Chávez, *El César De Boxeo*. In the boxing ring set up in Luis's backyard, all the Latino kids, Robert among them, would try to imitate Chávez's style when they fought one another.

"The greatest fighter of all time, *huevos* like basketballs, fists of granite, the heart of ten lions."

Relentless aggression, thudding body shots that dropped opponents to the canvas in agony. To this day, he loved Chávez and had always booed Oscar De La Hoya replays because Oscar was born in America, not in Mexico.

"That makes no sense," she said. "You're American."

"Not when it comes to boxing."

"Okay, *Roberto*," she said, "put on some clothes."

They hit the Brig over on Abbot Kinney, and they danced and sweated and made out and slammed shots. Even ran into Leslie outside with her wasted friend, Dougie, the dude Robert remembered from the racetrack bleachers. Leslie was drinking soda water, gave each of them another business card, and promised to call them again—like she'd done twice already.

If Robert and Alison hadn't been making out as they left the Brig in their Uber Prius, they might have noticed Stanley. On a stoop across the street, drinking a fruit smoothie, he watched them split the bar. But neither of them was paying attention then or the next morning, nursing hangovers at Mercedes Grill, squinting behind shades at the human parade flowing past.

"Did Strand Security call back yet?" he asked, staring at his cold coffee. Strand, their condo-security providers.

She checked her phone. "Not yet. Think I might throw up."

"I beat you to it," he said. "Go for it."

As Alison stood up for the bathroom, Stanley cruised past in a wide-brimmed straw hat, wearing a backpack and looking like John Q. Citizen, he thought. Right after that, he ducked into the Korean market, hoping to score a box of Larks before getting back to condo surveillance down on the Peninsula.

CHAPTER 31

People are easy to figure when you're not using, Stanley was thinking after he refused to settle for Parliaments with the Koreans. After that, he'd driven south on the Peninsula and meter-parked at the cut, where leisure craft exited the thousand-slot marina before making open water.

Not in a hurry as he strolled up Speedway. The lovebirds were still eating, and he knew where they lived. He'd been onto them way before they moved into their new condo.

At first, he figured their move to the Peninsula from Venice was a bad development for him. Up on Ozone, the boardwalk was a huge tourist draw, right behind Disneyland. That gave him a built-in excuse to be anywhere he wanted near the lawyer's place: lost, hanging out, whatever lie came to mind. But the boardwalk ended where the Peninsula started. Only one mile long, the Peninsula was three, four hundred yards wide, and its walk streets and beach were typically near-deserted. That made hanging in a car or wandering around on foot bad news. Before too long, someone was bound to ask if you needed help. As in: *State your business.*

But that Peninsula condo actually wound up making his life easier. A week earlier, Stanley watched *the subjects* meet a guy who drove up in a white Navigator and keyed them into a corner unit using its Speedway door. An hour later, the garage door onto Speedway rolled open, and all three stepped outside. As the garage door came down, a condo key changed hands.

Then they all split. So Stanley split, too.

Same night, he came back. The beach was deserted. He walked fifty yards out onto the sand to get comfortable with the situation. It was totally dark out here, so dark it gave him the creeps. Even so, he made himself sit in the sand for more than an hour.

Waiting. This part was much easier when he wasn't using. When he was? After five minutes, he'd be making a move for the building. Worried, mostly—not about occupants returning—but about whether Alonzo would wait with that *chiva* balloon like he said he would over in Oakwood.

Waiting wasn't a problem for his friend Jackie Boy. Jack never had a problem with it. Watching and waiting and staying three steps ahead. That was his strong suit—that and being a class-A cocksman. Even when they were kids, Jack was like that, and even when Jack messed up, he always landed on his feet.

But him? He remembered breaking his arm, same summer Jack's leg was in a cast. First time Stanley picked up a surfboard was at POP Venice, a surf spot a mile from where he sat now. As he paddled out through the break, a wave turned the board broadside, and when the board pinned itself into the hard-sand bottom, his body kept going. *Snap* went his arm—he could still hear that sound. Kids on shore saw it, too, saw him crying after his arm broke and called him a dumb-ass douche.

But Jack's broken leg? Jack told everybody he was skateboarding, skitching a metro bus, when a dog ran out in front of him. So he dumped his board, broke his leg, and saved Benji's life, he told all the girls.

"Aww," the girls would say, hearing about the dog. Same time, Jack was winking at the guys, guys knowing the story was BS, and Jack scoring points both ways.

Over the years, Stanley thought about their two casts and decided Jack would have made out great with the same surfboard accident Stanley had at POP.

"Aww, does it hurt?" the girls would have asked Jack.

Anything for Jackie Boy. But Jack's family life was shit. Way worse than Stanley's own, and Stanley came to believe that somehow, everything evened out in the end.

Sitting on the dark beach, he checked his watch. Ninety minutes he'd been waiting out here. *Fuckin' A.*

The lovebirds' corner condo unit was still dark. In fact, every unit in their building was dark. All dark this time of night? To its left and right, the other buildings were lit up, occupied. But nobody was inside this one. He got the picture now. Empty with no broker's sign? For some reason, this was a problem building for Mr. White Navigator.

Stanley stood, dusted off his jeans, and focused. The time was right. To hide his footprints, he walked a hundred yards up the beach before angling inland again. Once he reached the concrete beach sidewalk, he walked back to that corner unit.

Telling himself all the while: *You are a man coming home late from work, Stanley. That is exactly who you are. Do it like you own it, motherfucker.*

Slinging his knapsack seven feet up onto the patio, he grabbed the railing, pushed aside miniature palm fronds, dug his shoes into the building, and pulled himself up. Easy as pie, sliding now into the darkest patio corner. For five minutes, he listened. Just in case. Then he was sure. The lovebirds hadn't moved in after talking to the Navigator. Movers would come tomorrow, next day—who knows?—but not yet.

Standing, pick set in hand, he saw the patio door was halfway open. *Makes sense,* he was thinking as he slid it, took off his shoes, and eased inside. Nothing to steal yet, so the owner was airing it out for his new bootleg tenants.

Nice pad, even in the dark. Narrow but a good-size living room and a pass-through from the kitchen. A full bath on this level off the hallway to downstairs. A mezzanine office. A master bed and bath upstairs with a master balcony overlooking half the living room. Past the master level, the stairway rose another half level to a roof deck.

Three alarm pads in all. One was inside the garage by the interior door. Another at the top of the stairs on the second floor, and a third inside the door to the master bedroom. No red lights blinked anywhere. Not yet activated, but he bet that would change. Empty building, a little spooky, the girl sometimes alone? But even if they activated the system, the builder hadn't bothered arming the roof-deck door, thirty-five feet above the sand.

Good place to grab a smoke, he was already thinking.

It took him another five minutes to decide how to go with surveillance. Too bad there was no DVR or alarm clock. Those would have been the easiest places to set up three pinhole cams and voice-activated recorders, the ones he carried in his knapsack.

That same night, after rigging the corner unit, he climbed onto Unit 3's balcony from the beach, using his pick set on that unit's slider. And he was in.

Once the lovers moved in, Stanley started listening in on them from his unit. Recorded them fucking and talking and eating and talking and fucking, making notes for Jack. Reception in the living room, kitchen, and master suite was good. The garage and roof deck, he hadn't bothered with. Too much concrete echo in the garage, and too much wind up top.

Once, he remembered, Jack called him on his burner and told him, "Don't call me for a couple days. I'll be unreachable."

"Cool," Stanley told him. Wondering at the same time if Jack made that one up like he did the Benji story. *Unreachable,* like he was some kind of international man of mystery.

Lighten up, Stanley, he told himself. So what if he made it up? Scoring this gig was great. Jack could have paid a high-profile pro to handle it. Then again, maybe Jack was thinking about top-gun PI Anthony Pellicano: popped by the Feds, and all the celebs who hired him had been running scared. Knowing that, Jack could have figured using a small fish was better than getting rolled up in a large scandal with a real player.

Far as these two in the condo went? Jack hadn't told him what intel he wanted, and Stanley knew why. After all, Jack could never be 100 percent sure Stanley wouldn't start using again. And if he did slip up, the less he knew about Jack's motives, the better for Jack.

In fact, Stanley wasn't sure he could show any concrete link at all between Jack and himself, even if he wanted to.

My man Jack, he decided. *He's even three steps ahead of me.*

And the lovebirds, they seemed nice enough. Somehow they'd crossed the big man, and that's not something you wanted to do. Whenever the time came, Stanley knew one of them, maybe both, would take a hard fall.

He dug out his last Lark on Unit 3's roof deck, lit one up, thinking about his verbal report tomorrow. He'd tell Jack how great this job was, finally getting to live at the beach, that kind of breezy rap.

Only a couple new things to report, anyway. The lawyer and his girl still fucked a lot, talked about their families, binge-watched TV in the master. And outside the Brig last night, they ran into that banker girl they did business with the week before.

Leslie DeRider. The business card he grabbed off her desk said so. At the Brig, the young guy with Leslie had gone back inside the bar. Ten minutes later, the muscle hauled him out. Either got himself dosed with *la rocha,* or he shot up in the bathroom and got a little carried away. Stanley's money was on the junk.

When Stanley crossed Abbot Kinney for a closer look, this pair was getting in her car. He heard the banker chick ask that loser, "Why do I love you so much, you fucking asshole?"

"Because I'm lovable," he heard the loser tell her.

He had a feeling Jack might get a kick out of the exchange. Maybe he'd even spice up the story a little, be self-aware telling it, say something like: "One thing we can agree on, Jackie Boy. The whole world loves a junkie—am I right?"

CHAPTER 32

How much longer till their funds cleared? Three days?

Robert was doing that mental math when his beach bike's rear tire blew out on Speedway, and he skidded to a halt north of Washington. Saw the nail stuck in his tire and wondered if he should lock his bike to the stop sign and jog over to Gold's, or call Alison for a lift home?

He went with the Alison option and called her on his cell. His call went to voice mail. Then he texted her about his flat, hoisted his bike on his shoulder, and headed back to the condo, a fifteen-minute walk with this clunker biting into his shoulder. He hoped she would catch his text and swing by in her car, but she never did.

As he reached their condo, he realized he'd left his keys inside. He rang their unit's voice box on Speedway. No response from her. That started to bother him. When he'd left for the gym, she planned to hang out, clean the dishes, maybe go through her moving boxes still piled, like his, in the living room.

He went around the ocean side of the building, lay his bike against it behind a row of newly planted palms. He didn't spot her on the beach, so he pulled himself up onto the patio. The sliding door was open, same as when he left. He stepped inside the living room.

"Alison?" he called out.

Still no reply. All her boxes were where the movers left them, a slight obstacle course to weave through. He called her again and heard her phone vibrating on top of her nearby desk.

Then his own phone rang: Strand Security Systems. This small, local outfit had taken longer than expected with the alarm setup given that they were a new account in new construction.

He picked up her phone and answered. "Hello?"

"Who's this, please?" Strand asked him.

Once he verified his ID to their satisfaction, they started to give him the new alarm code.

"Hold up," he said.

He opened Alison's desk drawer, reached in, and found a Sharpie. Alongside it: a revolver and a pair of handcuffs. Loose bullets rattled around the drawer beside them.

"Go ahead," he told Strand, staring at that handgun while they told him the initial password, a random string of numbers and symbols, reminding him to personalize it ASAP.

After he hung up, he headed upstairs to the master. She wasn't there, either. Then he thought about the roof deck they never used, so he took those five stairs up to its door. It was unlocked, and he swung it open. There she was.

Wearing her 'Canes sweatshirt and shorts, she sat sweat-drenched on a beach towel, facing the ocean. Eyes closed, her index finger covered one nostril. Her diaphragm fluttered as she forced oxygen in and out of the free nostril into her lungs. As he came closer, he saw her belly rise and fall with her internal flow.

"Alison," he said softly.

She didn't reply. He repeated her name, but she was in another zone. He sat down and watched her, his back against the stairwell wall.

A minute later, she emerged from that other place, and her eyes opened.

"Whoa," she said when she saw him.

"Hi."

"Back?" she asked, inhaling deep. "Back already?" Now exhaling.

"Picked up a nail. I called, texted, got a little worried."

"About what? *Me?*"

"A little," he said.

"Come on, me?" She stretched her neck, cleared her head.

"You all right?"

"Think so, spaced out, probably not doing it right."

"What is it?" he asked.

"*Kundalini* breathing. Supposed to be great once you're good at it. While you're doing it, you're supposed to think about . . . visualize . . . a coiled snake at the base of your spine, spreading its energy into your body."

"Does it work?" he asked.

"I don't know yet, a little, I think. I want to work on my breathing, work on staying calm. You know, *calm?*"

"*Calm*, sure, I know," remembering their ambulance ride to the hospital.

He crawled over beside her and kissed her cheek. Her face was warm, salted with sweat. He let her know about Strand Security calling, and after a few minutes, they decided to make their alarm code: *A+R+lastcondonp* in memory of Marlon Brando.

Then he told her why he looked inside her desk and asked her, as casually as he could, why there was a handgun, bullets, and a pair of handcuffs inside it.

"Oh, shit, I forgot," she said. "I should have told you, I'm sorry. All that stuff was Brian's, for his job. The gun was his already from Florida. He was a pretty good shot at the range, that's what he said, anyway."

"Did he ever cut loose on anybody?"

"No, but that warehouse where he worked, it was pretty scary at night. I went there once, out in the middle of nowhere."

She stood, stretching, back straight, reaching for the sky with both hands, inhaling. Leaning forward, exhaling till her palms went flat on the deck. "A Sun Salutation," she told him.

And there in the bright sunlight, he saw it: *a light scar on her leg.* Right near the top of the calf.

He couldn't help staring at it, remembering the day he'd followed Gia to Saddle Peak Lodge. That day came rushing back to him. Gary, the bartender, and the waiter joking about Tattoo Girl. *"Was Tattoo Girl hot for him or what? . . . All over his ass . . . thought she was gonna go down on him at the table."*

Jack's waiter telling him that the unknown girl's tattoo had been small, personal—located at the top of her calf.

He reached out, touched her scar. "Thought I knew every inch of you?"

She moved her body into an inverted *v*, butt in the air, her hands flat, facing her heels. "Downward-Facing Dog," she said, almost losing her balance.

"Freak yoga accident?" he asked, sticking with the scar.

"No," she said.

Trying to hand-walk back to her feet, she lost her balance this time, toppled onto the deck, and rolled over next to him.

"Dizzy, whew," she said and told him about the scar. "It's from canyon cruising on Brian's Harley. Calabasas, maybe, somewhere way out in the mountains, and I burned it on his tailpipe."

"Calabasas? Are you the lost Kardashian?" he asked.

"Hope not." Then she asked, "Were you smoking just now?"

"Weed?" he said.

"I keep smelling cigarette smoke."

He stood up, walked over to the rail, and looked onto the beach side. A few sunbathers sat a hundred yards out on the sand. A few buildings over, workmen checked out a rooftop HVAC unit. One of them was grabbing a smoke.

He pointed. "Must be them."

Now she saw them, too. "Guess so," she said.

He gave her a hand up, and she slipped underneath his arm. "When we talk about Brian being a security guard, it brings up all the bad stuff. That's behind us, right?"

"Old news," he said.

"Let's not talk about it anymore, don't you think?"

"It's over; we won."

At the same time, he tried to remember something important from Brian Maxwell's case file, stored in his filing cabinet. Something he wasn't quite clear on: deposition testimony about *a handgun*.

And as she moved ahead of him and opened the door, his eyes locked on her scar, staying on it until she stepped into the dark stairwell.

Two units down, Stanley leaned into the five-foot parapet wall separating his unit's roof deck from Unit 2. The girl had almost nailed him a half hour ago when she came onto her own deck. First time he knew of that either of the lovebirds had used it. Lucky for him, he heard her opening the door. That gave him a few seconds to drop down against this wall and hide.

Waiting till the pair went inside, he wondered if he should tell Jack what he heard. That the girl used to ride motorcycles with her brother. Why not? But would it even matter to Jack? Stanley didn't know. Because he still didn't know why he was spying on them in the first place.

It was almost midnight when Robert reached for his filing-cabinet key taped to the back of the cabinet in the living room. With it, he unlocked his case-file drawer.

One minute earlier, upstairs, Alison reminded him that tomorrow she was picking up her final paycheck from the bookstore. As she stepped into the shower, he told her that his bike was still outside on the beach. That he'd be right back.

In his case-file drawer, right behind their bank-receipts folder, rested a thick accordion folder: Alison's legal file. The shower was still running upstairs when he opened the file and flipped through it. Several minutes later, he found what he wanted: the sixty-five-page deposition of a Consolidated employee, a guy who claimed to know Brian Maxwell.

He started scanning pages, moving fast until—there it was. The employee stating for the record: *Brian brought his own gun and handcuffs with him to work. A gun was a job requirement for security guards, I think.*

After slipping her file back in the top drawer, relieved, he ran down the interior stairs and through the door onto Speedway. Under a full moon, he rounded his building to the concrete beach walk and found his bike still resting against the building.

As he was about to shoulder it, he noticed something behind those newly planted dwarf palms. Leaning down, moving the fronds aside, he saw scuff marks marring the building's fresh paint job. Facing the beach now and looking for activity, he found it impossible to penetrate the darkness out there. The light was better along the line of beach units, but the beachfront was deserted in both directions.

Still curious, he ditched his bike, headed up the concrete walk toward the other end of his own building. As he was passing Unit 3, the next-to-last condo, he stopped, leaned in, and saw scuff marks on that wall, too. Even more marks here than down at his unit.

Stepping off the concrete onto the beach, he looked up. Unit 3 appeared totally dark, its slatted shades drawn, upstairs and down. Even so, he took a running jump, grabbed the balcony railing, and pulled himself onto its deck. Ten seconds later, his face pressed against its living room window. Nothing to see, even up close, due to those closed shades.

Now he leaped over the railing, landed on the walk, and took off running, leaving his bike behind. Inside his unit, he quietly ran upstairs to the living room level. Thought about the gun in Alison's desk, decided against getting it, and kept running upstairs till he reached the roof-deck door. He opened it, stepped outside, eased the door closed, and took off again. Up and over Unit 2's shared parapet wall, then up and over the next wall till he was on top of Unit 3. Easing over to its roof-deck door, he pushed down the door handle. No go—it was locked from inside.

Turning back for their unit, he noticed a Styrofoam cup on the deck. He picked it up. It brimmed with cigarette butts. He pulled one out, read its brand label in the moonlight.

Larks? he wondered. *Somebody still makes Larks?*

Then he noticed two burned-out butts on the deck itself. Each one stood straight up like a soldier. He wondered how long they'd been standing up that way, blocked from the breeze. Wondered, too, whether what he'd heard was true. Straight up: that's how convicts let cigarettes burn out in prison.

Whoever had been on the deck could still be inside Unit 3, he decided, and well after midnight, he texted the owner about what he'd seen. After that, he slipped into bed with Alison and lay there without touching her.

Doubt had crept into his thinking, no point denying it. He was concerned about . . . his problem was . . . he didn't quite know what. No point in worrying Alison, too, he decided, reaching for her.

"Hey," he said.

Her back was to him, her eyes already open. "Hey," she said.

"I was thinking," he said, "once our checks clear, why don't we get out of LA for a while?"

"Get out?" she asked. "We're still moving in?"

"When's the last time you left town?"

"Forever ago."

They were both quiet for a minute.

"Like, with a camper?" she asked, turning toward him.

"Or a Winnebago."

"You're a bigger hick than I am," she said.

"Mexico? Cabo?" he asked.

"Not in a Winnie," she said. "We'd wind up in an open grave."

"How about cross-country?" he asked. "We could see the Washington Monument, Statue of Liberty?"

She said, "Or go straight up Highway 1, all the way to Canada. There's that highway all the way across. Maybe?"

"Canada? Canada, *eh*?"

"They have great travel books at the bookstore. We could check it out tomorrow, if you promise you'll never do that accent again."

"*Eh?*" he asked.

"Stop it," she said, moving on top of him.

He said it once more. But once he was inside her, he decided to drop the accent and do whatever she wanted to do.

CHAPTER 33

Standing on the street outside Tito's Tacos in Culver City, Stanley expected Jack to pick him up any minute. Still waiting, he thought about what had happened with lawyer man the night before.

From Unit 3's roof deck, he watched the lawyer picking up his bike. Something must have dawned on the guy, and by the time he stopped down below him, Stanley knew it was time to split. He was cool with that; he'd gamed it since day one. There were only two ways in—the beach and Speedway. Somebody came at him from the beach, he'd hit the unit stairs down to Speedway. Coming at him from Speedway? He'd hit the slider out to the beach.

So last night was simple. By the time the lawyer was on his front deck, he had already made the living room from the roof. Ten seconds later, he slipped down the stairs to Speedway. After that, he was vapor. What he left behind was only the homeless-man crap he wanted to be found.

And here came Jack, cruising up Washington in some bullshit rental. Stanley got in, and as they started driving down Sepulveda, Jack asked, "Grunion running, Stanley?"

"Like crazy, Jackie Boy," he said, handing over six amyl nitrite caps.

Right after that, he let Jack know his cover had probably been blown the night before.

All Jack said about that development was: "Let's see if it matters."

They drove around a few hours, Stanley reading aloud all his written surveillance reports, with Jack occasionally listening to actual recorded conversations. Even pulling over and watching videos of the pair when it suited him. It impressed Stanley, how Jack's expression never showed if he saw or heard anything that interested him.

It wasn't too long after the lovebirds started talking about RVing to Canada or Mexico or wherever that Jack told him, "Think we're good. Here's what you're going to do next."

Jack told him exactly where to set up his new safe-deposit box and exactly how he wanted Stanley to handle the key. Then they went into how much time Stanley would need inside Unit 1 alone, and when he would need it.

Stanley told Jack, "Better you get them out of the place for at least an hour, guaranteed," but he believed fifteen minutes inside, tops, would do the trick.

"I'll make it work. Day after tomorrow. It's set for then," Jack told him.

After fifteen, twenty more minutes nailing down the details, they rolled up to Tito's again. When he started to get out, Jack told Stanley to leave behind his written reports and his computer.

"After you get out, go inside Tito's. Then turn around and wave at me."

"You got it, Jackie."

As he headed toward Tito's, Stanley knew what was up. Jack didn't want him to grab the rental's plate numbers or see the rental agency on the tag holder. Always keeping their one-on-one's difficult for Stanley to verify.

So he knew what he would see when he turned around to wave: Jack was gone. That didn't matter. He ordered a beef-and-bean burrito with cheese and thought about the twenty-grand cash payday headed his way. Knowing that was going to happen, he planned on two AA meetings every single day for six months after he scored the money.

"Who knows, maybe three a day," he said to himself, then asked the counter man for a twelve-dollar Tito's ball cap and extra tomatillo on that burrito.

CHAPTER 34

"I'm buying," Robert said.

"Hell, yeah, you're buying," Erik told him.

They were grabbing a cup of coffee at Groundworks not far from the Venice police substation. Robert was bringing his buddy up to speed, and Erik was writing up a police report.

"And you talked to those workmen on the other roof?" Erik asked.

"Yeah, this morning. They saw my guy over on Unit 3, smoking, wearing a painter's cap."

Robert told him what else the workmen said: that the guy was good-size, tall, Anglo, and tanned. "Middle-aged and he smokes Larks," Robert added.

"They still sell those?"

"Must," Robert said, and told him, "I did a walk-through of Unit 3 with the owner. We found an old sleeping bag, canned food with the labels ripped off, empty bottles of cheap wine, and chips."

Erik said, "Sure, we get squatters at the beach all the time."

"Even on the Peninsula?"

"Not like up in Venice, but they cruise the Peninsula on bicycles, checking out mailboxes, stale flyers, parked cars staying parked, interior light patterns. Hey, free rent, ocean view, no five-0 riffraff hassling 'em. What's not to like?"

Robert saw the logic: his building was a primo squatter candidate.

"Guy takes a middle unit, too, not the far-end unit, so you gotta walk in front of it to see inside. Lot of 'em are ex-cons and they're not stupid. Dumb," he said, "not stupid."

He finished writing the report, and Robert signed it.

"I'll file this, but I still don't get it. Other than the building, is there a connection between you and Lark Boy?"

"Lark Man," Robert corrected. "A guy I know, I'm pretty sure he hates me."

"Help me out here. *Who* hates you enough *for what?*" Erik asked.

It was the right question, but Robert couldn't answer it. He paid for their coffee, acutely aware of his nondisclosure agreement with Philip and the firm. To tell him about Jack, Robert would need to discuss the settlement agreement with Erik—a nonparty. That would put Robert in clear violation and jeopardize both his and his client's payday.

"Guess you're right," Robert said. "It's probably nothing."

From out of nowhere, Erik said, "Jack Pierce."

That floored Robert. He didn't breathe a word until Erik asked, "Fanelli and Pierce. You used to work for Pierce, right?"

"Right," he said and left it at that.

"Get along?" Erik asked.

Robert decided not to touch that one.

"You told me a guy you know, you're pretty sure he hates you. And you sure as hell left your firm in a hurry, so I'm running Pierce's name by you, that's all."

"You know him?" Robert asked.

"I put in five years downtown before I made it to Westside, so let's just say Pierce was known."

Erik told him a story about a cop he heard about back then. A straight shooter who rolled out of Los Feliz. He got papered to testify against one of Jack's money-laundering clients but held up solid under Jack's cross. The client went down off the cop's testimony, and Jack's loss played big in the *Times*. After that, seemed like the cop's life went haywire. Wife started seeing somebody, the cop thought, and every time he turned around, criminals were filing paper on him.

"Complaints?"

"Excessive force, abusive language, till one day his brothers in blue showed up with a warrant off a corroborated anonymous tip, found a bag of blow in his garage. A big one. No prints, though, and the union fought it. Cop swore it was planted, but he wound up losing his wife and was lucky to grab his pension."

"What happened to him?"

"Dunno, wandered off like old lions do. What I'm sayin', there was a lot of inside baseball about Pierce being the one who made it happen."

"All this time, why didn't you ever tell me?"

"Why do that? You were killin' it at work, man, and never mentioned the guy's name once all those years. Why rock your boat?"

Robert tried coming to grips with this new story. Remembered that Philip warned him about crossing Jack. That Jack's reactions could be *wildly disproportionate to the offense.*

Then Erik pointed out: "And all that cop did back then? He was under oath, telling the truth on the stand. Just a cop doing his job . . ."

Robert left the coffee shop without telling Erik about meeting Reyes right before that. And without mentioning Reyes's take on those two Lark butts standing upright on Unit 3's deck.

Reyes told him, "Guy's a convict, *carnal.*"

So, he offered Reyes $500 to ID the smoker. "Maybe he bought Larks somewhere at the beach, or near here, or something," Robert said.

"Seguro, es posible," Reyes said, then Robert offered five hundred more for a decent photo of Lark Man.

"Thousand's great," Reyes said. "That'll pay for my new head shots."

Turned out, Reyes was up for a speaking part in *Street Cred 6*.

Robert fist-bumped Reyes and told him, "Break a leg."

❧

By the time Robert found Alison at the bookstore, she was at a table in back with stacks of travel books around her: Northern California, the coastlines of Oregon and Washington, Canadian Rockies, the Statue of Liberty, Lincoln Memorial.

Once he joined her, she showed him the Winnebago website on her iPad: The Brave. "That model's got our name on it," she said.

"Sleeps four," he noticed. "We could start a band, go on tour."

She elbowed him, but it was definitely baller. He still liked the thought: getting out of LA like they discussed last night.

As she showed him The Brave's compact yet spacious bathroom, his eyes drifted to the scar on her calf. Other parts of his conversation with Reyes intruded on him. He had looked at Reyes's ink and asked him, "Did you ever change your mind, have one of 'em removed?"

"Sí," Reyes told him. He pulled up his shirt and revealed a blank spot. *"Era mi favorito."*

His tat of the Blessed Virgin Mary on a Harley had been his favorite. His grandmother made him burn it off.

Robert had checked the light scarring on Reyes's stomach. Its texture looked the same as the scar on Alison's calf.

"¿El láser?" Robert asked.

"Sí, chico."

Depending on the ink and the colors, Reyes told him, it took about six weeks to heal.

"Six weeks?" Robert wondered. Tattoo Girl was at Saddle Peak Lodge months ago.

"So, how's your new crib, *y tu novia*?" Reyes asked him.

His new girlfriend? Robert didn't answer Reyes's question, and here in the bookstore, Alison asked him, "What do you think?" He was a little lost in space, wrapped up in his own questions, and she must have picked up on it.

"I mean, about crossing Canada. Do you think we could put the Winnie on a train if we got bored or tired of driving?"

"Looks beautiful up there," he said. "You think any more about going through Vegas, seeing Hoover Dam, the Grand Canyon, Graceland?"

"I saw the Grand Canyon twice, Graceland a bunch. I'm a Florida girl, remember?"

They talked over the trip, going back and forth on the route, and he was relaxing even more into the road-trip idea. Until he stood up, looked out the row of big front windows, and there they were: Jack Pierce and Chase Fitzpatrick, taking a table at the Sidewalk Cafe. Directly outside the bookstore door. Each wore shorts, and each one set a racket bag beside their two-top.

"You know," Alison was telling him, "if we went north, we could stop in San Francisco. Maybe see your farm on the way? That would be cool, huh?"

"We could do that," he said absently, staring at the two men.

She stood up. "Maybe it's too soon for that, but if . . ."

He was nodding, still ignoring her.

"Look, if you're embarrassed about my meeting them, just say so."

That got his attention. "*Embarrassed*, what? The farm? You kidding me? Sure. They might be out of town, let me check."

Once they'd paid for a few travel books, he said, "Look, Jack and Chase are eating lunch outside."

She looked over and saw the two men. "Those two assholes?"

"No matter what they say, keep going. See you back at the car, okay?

"Back at—What about you?" she asked.

"I don't know. It depends."

"On what?"

"I don't know," he said. "I'll tell you after."

They walked out of the store into the narrow walkway between the store's entrance and the restaurant. Alison went first. Ignoring the two men, she made it to the boardwalk and kept going.

Robert stopped at their table, and told Jack, "I want a private word with you."

Before Jack could answer, Chase said, "Hey, Worth, saw your client walk by. Is she really a tiger in the sack?"

Robert leaned down, like he was going to whisper to Chase. Instead, he gave Chase a quick love tap, short and hard into his nose.

"Fuck!" Chase screamed.

He jumped up, rocked the table, spilled their water, and leaned forward. Too late. Blood was already dripping onto his white V-neck.

"You pisswad!" he screamed.

"Ice it down," Jack said. "My old colleague needs a word with me."

Jack watched Chase rush away. For some reason, it looked like Jack got a kick out of Chase shedding blood.

"Stay away from me, all right? I mean it," he told Jack.

"Stay away from you? Since when is that a problem, Worth? We always ran in different social circles."

He leaned closer to Jack. Close enough to whisper: "We both know what the fuck I'm talking about."

"I don't have a clue what you mean, Worth. You were always two steps ahead of me. Isn't it enough I don't have a job? That my marriage is on its last legs? What more could you possibly take from me?"

"Nothing. And if I get more than nothing back from you, we have a problem."

"We can do *nothing*, I guess, or—do you remember Judge Rosen?"

Sure, he remembered her: at the Santa Monica courthouse, sitting on the bench with Jack.

Jack told him, "I tried introducing you, but you had bigger fish to fry that day. Tell you what. Why don't you drop by her courtroom tomorrow, first thing. Nine a.m. sharp?"

"Why would I do that?"

"Check Rosen's website. I'm on her docket—the only item on her docket—and you're so far behind me now, that I—oh, wait, almost forgot—a very good friend of yours will be there, too. Bet anything you'll be glad you came."

A very good friend? Jack was rocking him, big-time, and he tried to hide it.

"One last time," Robert said. "Stay away from me, or I swear to God, I'll—"

"You'll do what? Say it, Worth. You'll kill me? *Kill me*, Worth? Popping Chase is one thing, but I'd be careful who hears you making threats like that against me."

"Stay the fuck away from me! Hear that?"

He looked up. Everyone nearby was staring at him. He'd been going at Jack louder than he thought.

"Stay away *from you*? Don't you mean stay away *from us*?" Jack asked. "Let me see how this works for you. I promise I'll never venture down onto the Marina Peninsula again. And you have my word on that."

Us? Marina Peninsula? Only one way Jack knew that: from the guy in Unit 3.

"You heard right, Worth. Exactly what are you prepared to do about it?"

That was the last thing Jack said to Robert that day. But it was enough. Five seconds later, once Robert made it onto the crowded boardwalk, he hated Jack Pierce enough to kill him.

CHAPTER 35

"That insane prick. You knew he'd be there, didn't you?" Chase asked Jack.

"Cool down. How the devil would I know that?"

They were walking up the boardwalk, a half mile from where they'd almost eaten lunch. Chase held a wet towel against his swollen nose.

"If I sued him for assault and battery," Chase said, "I'd pick up a quick fifty grand, easy."

"Why? You had it coming. You insulted his girl and he popped you. Somebody talked that way about Meridian, what would you do?"

Chase didn't answer. Jack looked at him. "How's it going at the firm?"

"Fanelli's gonna shitcan me. Every day that goes by, I can feel it."

"Wouldn't worry about it too much."

"Easy for you to say," Chase said.

"No, no, listen up. Firing you, that's not how the firm works."

"How then, *maestro?*"

"More like, Fanelli will start drying up the workflow coming your way, redirect it to his guys or other guys in litigation. End of the fiscal year, the *senior* partners will get together—you won't even know about it. Everybody will talk about your pathetic billable hours, how they have no choice but to cut your share of profits. A few years of that . . ."

"Meridian will leave me if that happens. What would I do without her?"

"I don't know. What would you do?" Jack asked.

Chase glared at him. "What's that supposed to mean?"

"Means losing her wouldn't be a problem—not if you had the stones Worth has."

"The fuck is it with you today? You call me from out of the blue to play paddles and grab lunch, then you cut the set short, and ever since Worth showed up, you're in my grill."

Jack didn't bother answering. Ahead of them, the boardwalk ended at a row of high-end, two-story, concrete town houses.

"Where'd you fuckin' park, Malibu?" Chase asked.

"Almost there," Jack said. "Seeing Worth reminded me of something. How Worth always said you would cave as my alibi. Matter of fact, that's what he used during his negotiations with me. My biggest problem was, I always knew he was right."

"Hey, the whole firm was breathing down my neck. Fanelli thought you were lying—no way I was going to commit perjury over it."

"Fanelli didn't *know*. Like you said, he *thought* you were lying. All you had to do was get Meridian to back you up, to say, 'Yes, Mr. Fanelli, my husband was working with Jack that night. I picked Chase up at the firm. I saw Mr. Pierce with him.' After all I did for you, Chase, guess that was too much to ask."

"Meridian's not cut out for that kind of pressure. You giving me a lift to my car or what?"

"Sure," Jack said, "I'll take you all the way."

They made it around the end of those town houses. Jack's car was parked on a guest pad. Chase walked to the passenger side to get in. "They're gonna tow you, parking here," Chase said.

Jack stayed beside Chase. "Friend of mine lets me use the place when he's out of town." Then Jack added, "Fifteen hundred dollars a night, Fitz. Guess Meridian's cut out for something, right?"

"Fifteen hundred—what?"

"Meridian? Worked at Caesar's in executive training? Believe that if you want, but that's not what I remember. What I remember is: *Flip me over, baby. Flip me over and do me.*" He's laughing now. "Pretty good line for a whore—she still use it?"

"Fuck you, motherfucker."

Chase took a swing at Jack, but it was a tennis-player punch, telegraphed from out in Pacoima. Jack rolled it off with his left shoulder, slid in close, and sank a vicious right uppercut deep into Chase's solar plexus. When Chase's face came down, Jack drove a knee into his groin and pushed him into a landscaped pod, where Chase doubled up in pain.

Chase squeezed out: "You burned every bridge in town. Nobody'll hire you. Nobody'll work with you. Keep driving that piece of shit, Pierce, you're an out-of-work loser."

Jack strolled to the town house door, rang the doorbell, and told Chase, "All these years working side by side, you still don't know who I am." He headed to the driver's door of his rental car and opened it.

"Then again, Chase, nobody does."

Chase lay in the bushes, crying, and heard Jack's car drive away. The town house door opened behind him. Then he heard Meridian asking: "Jack, that you, babe? Where'd you go, doll?"

CHAPTER 36

In the fading beach sunlight, Stanley's needle-tracked arms glowed golden beneath his sprayed-on tan. From his car idling on Speedway down from Robert's building, he eyed the Bronco as Robert drove it into Unit 1's garage, then raised his camera's telephoto lens.

In his viewfinder: Alison stepped from the car, and Robert grabbed a couple bags of groceries. She punched their alarm code into the garage's pad, and Stanley captured, the third time this week, rapid shots of her hand.

The garage door began to close, and Stanley drove past the condo, up Speedway. Wind gusts from the west rocked his car. At Driftwood, he stopped, looking seaward into the sinking sun. A charcoal storm front gathered out there, taking its time moving in. He rolled up his window against wind-shot sand and checked his photos. Looked like he caught ten out of eleven numbers the girl just punched. He cross-checked them with numbers from earlier shots and saw no last-minute changes to their nonsensical password: *A+R+lastcondonp*.

"Good to go," he said, and headed home to get ready for Freddy.

CHAPTER 37

That night, howling storm winds blew sideways off the Pacific, shaking the condo's plate-glass slider. Outside, greedy raindrops sucked up dry sand and smacked their windows with it like tiny bullets.

Robert and Alison were making their first homemade dinner since moving in. A Whole Foods chicken stuffed with garlic and lemons roasted in the oven. Rosemary potatoes, too, drenched in olive oil and cooked with garlic cloves.

"The garlic," she told him, "is in your honor."

"An homage," he said.

Alison was reading an online recipe for Caesar-salad dressing—even more garlic. At the counter, he poured his third stiff whiskey of the night.

Their lights dimmed for a moment, then came up again.

He slip-stepped through their boxes over to the window and looked out, mulling over what he'd learned from Judge Rosen's website. Her docket tomorrow: *In re: Jack and Dorothy Pierce.* That was it, the only item on her docket. Same thing Jack told him when he challenged Robert to drop by the courthouse.

"Want anchovies?" she asked.

"Do you?" he asked.

"If you do," she said.

"Whatever you think," he said. "Damn, this rain is—whoa, there they go!"

Two cheap beach chairs flew off their deck into the night.

She saw it, too. "Damn, those were heirlooms." She tore romaine lettuce into pieces and dropped it into a salad bowl. They didn't speak for a while. Until she asked, "What did you think he would be doing now?"

"Who?"

"Guy you're thinking about all day. Did you think he'd be panhandling for spare change?"

"Man can dream, can't he?"

"Seriously. You've been acting weird ever since we ran into him."

He walked over to her and sat at the kitchen counter on their one bar stool.

"*Ran into him?* You think we ran into him?"

"Well, yeah. They used to eat there all the time after playing paddle tennis."

"Oh, right," he said.

She'd mentioned that to him a while back. He wondered if he should tell her more about her case. For the most part, he'd done a decent job steering her clear of it, but for him, the case was filling up the room.

So he explained more about the nondisclosure agreement and why it was okay for them—as parties to it—to talk about the case.

Then he explained more: that they'd sued the entire firm, not only Jack. That's why they got such a big settlement. And once the firm was involved, Chase had to pony up his share, too. A smaller share because he was new coming on board, but a big chunk of change for a new partner.

"Poor Chase," she said, smiling.

"I know, but look: I understand every deal I ever made, know the deal inside out, but when I settled your case with the firm? Chase had just made partner. One month later—boom. He's out, what? Two years of salary because Jack screwed up."

"Screwed up? What he did to me?"

"That, yes, and more," he said, meaning Jack's malpractice insurance screwup. "Now, say you're Chase, and Jack's not at the firm anymore. He's gone, *adiós*. Can't help you, can't hurt you, but he cost you real money. Do you ever speak to Jack again?"

"I don't know . . ."

"Sure, you know. You wouldn't speak to him, and you wouldn't hang out with him, either."

She pulled the roasted chicken from the oven, set it on the counter. "Well, then . . . what? What does it mean?"

"That's my problem—I don't know what it means. But there they were today, played paddles, grabbing lunch like nothing ever happened."

"Maybe they moved on . . . Maybe we should, too?"

Frustrated, he downed a swallow of whiskey. "You don't move on from that. It was a big deal. We hurt them, and they were pissed off about it—*really pissed off*. Each one of 'em, same as I would be and same as you."

"Is that all that's bothering you?"

"Christ, isn't that enough?"

"Our checks clear when?"

"Tomorrow, end of the day. Next morning at the latest."

"Winnebago or not, we'll leave town, and life is good, right?"

He didn't answer. "Chicken smells great," he said. "Need any help?"

"No." She looked at him, cutting the chicken with a large, sharp knife. "My Caesar salad's a disaster area."

"Potatoes are vegetables, right?" he asked.

"Think I'll have a drink, too," she said.

"What'll it be?"

"Same as you. On the rocks," she said without looking at him.

Ten minutes later, they started dinner at their dining table, his desk from Ozone. If anything, the wind and rain outside had built up since they sat down. This was a major storm, rain lashing the front windows, sheeting down, and their deck already pooled six inches of water.

At the table, he was online, checking weather reports. "Storm advisory says another hour at least."

"Wow," she said.

The condo lights dimmed again. Robert and Alison went quiet, their clinking cutlery swallowed by the elements.

Finally, she said, "Last night . . ." She stopped talking until he looked at her. "Last night, when you went outside to get your bike, I came out to the balcony." She pointed upstairs. "And I saw you going through my legal stuff. Through my legal file."

"I did. I'm sorry," he said.

"Why?"

"I found a gun in your desk, bullets. You never told me about it."

"Then I told you why I had it. Didn't you believe me?"

"Yeah, I did."

"But?"

"I wanted to double-check. Guess it's too many years being a lawyer. And I'm sorry, really."

"A revolver, it's not a big deal where I'm from," she said. "We lived in the boonies. There were alligators in the yard sometimes, rabid raccoons. And if I remembered I had it when that douche bag came to my apartment, who knows?"

"Cheers," he said, raising his glass.

She drained the rest of her drink without toasting. "You told me what happened to your sister, then I signed that power of attorney and turned my life over to you. I trusted you with all of it. *Trusted* you, Robert."

"I know," he said.

He hoped he was wrong about where all this trust talk was headed, but he had no idea how to stop it. Ever since he'd seen that scar on her calf, he had wrestled with texting Alison's picture to the Saddle Peak bartender. Have Gary ask around about Tattoo Girl on the off chance someone remembered seeing Alison. *Why go there?* he kept telling himself, but now that's exactly where he was. *There.*

Alison spoke again. "This whole time, I never once second-guessed you about what you were doing."

"You were great about it," he said. "The best. And I came through, right?"

"Do you trust me?" she asked.

Trust. There it was again. Before he could answer, she went for another whiskey. From the kitchen counter, she asked, "Do you think I had sex with Jack Pierce?"

Right there, laid out on the table. Blood rushed to his head from whiskey and from emotions. Exactly which emotions, he wasn't sure, but they all ran hot.

He said, "I lost my job over what you told me."

"You're a lawyer," she said, turning on him now. "Taking my case doesn't mean you believed me. It doesn't mean anything. I told you day one, outside the bookstore, the very first time we talked—the guy hit on me. He hit on me a lot, but he was this heavy-duty lawyer, and he was going to take Brian's case. Jesus, if you were me, what would you do?"

He nodded, agreeing, but couldn't shake the image of Alison as Tattoo Girl. Of Alison *all over Jack* at Saddle Peak, like the waiter said.

"How'd that happen again?" he asked. "I don't think you told me exactly *where* you were when Jack took your case."

"So fucking sorry for messing up like that. Here you go. That day? The day you're so interested in? The big day? He called me and told me it was a good idea to get together face-to-face and sign that retainer thing."

"At the firm, right? Because that's where my first-time clients always met me."

"No, not the firm." She tried to remember. "Where was it . . ."

"See if this helps—Saddle Peak Lodge?"

"Right, Saddle . . . how did you know?"

His stomach tightened. "Jack's kind of predictable once you get to know him. Very predictable. That's what I heard, anyway." *From Gia,* he didn't say.

Now he got up, made another drink, and wondered what happened to roasted chicken, rosemary potatoes, and watching the storm from their bed in the dark.

She said, "We ate lunch. I signed some papers. He ordered wine. I drank water."

"Where'd you sit?" he asked. "Nice patio outside?" But he was thinking, *How about upstairs? In the private dining room? You and Jack banging away?*

"I don't remember where we sat," she said.

"You don't remember?"

"I went there twenty times at least. So I can't remember where I sat, okay?"

"Nobody eats way out there twenty times in what? Two years you've been in town? Nobody. Ever."

"Really? Not with Brian and the guys he rode with, you asshole? It's fifteen minutes from Topanga—on his bike. A great drive on a bike. Twenty times—maybe more. What the fuck is wrong with you?"

"Tell me, then. What about the Bel-Air Hotel?"

"Tell you *what* about it?"

"That's his drill: Saddle Peak, the Bel-Air, two girls, a little rough stuff."

"Wait, wait, let me get this straight. Now you think I get tied up, fucked by my lawyer at some hotel? With another girl? That I lied to you about Sonya, about that lesbian waitress? About doing girls? That I'm one of his little *whatevers*? Is that who I am to you?"

Their voices rising now.

"I said that's what Jack's into. That's his drill, and that's all I said."

"How do you know what he's into? One of those sluts at the bank tell you? That Gia, maybe? That one? For all I know, you were fucking her. And you were fucking Jack and her! Were you?"

"No. I wasn't. You know that."

"Do I? Fine, then, I'll take your word for it, but you? Take my word? Trust me? Fuck, no!"

Hard to tell which one of them had up a fuller head of steam. Now Alison opened her desk drawer and grabbed the handcuffs.

"You think I like rough sex? That it?"

"Since you're asking?"

She threw the cuffs at him. "Go ahead. Cuff me. See how much I like it. C'mon, we did it every other way. Let's go. Let's see if I like it that way!"

He tried to pull back, standing. "Alison, c'mon, let's just . . ."

A huge blast of wind outside rattled their sliding door, and *boom*. Lights went out in the building. They stood in silence. Outside, it was power-outage dark. Dark the way only the beach and ocean can get. His eyes hadn't adjusted. He couldn't see her. Then a handcuff clicked in the dark.

"Go ahead!" she screamed. Her hands shoved him hard in his chest. He fell back, hit a stack of boxes, and tumbled onto the floor.

"You fucking lunatic!" he screamed back.

"Do it. Cuff me up. Go ahead. Let's see how much I like it. Go ahead!"

He jumped up, moved toward her voice. She pushed him again in the dark. Furious, he groped till he found her. When he did, he grabbed her shoulder, fumbled with her till he found the hand she'd already cuffed. Then he turned her body and pushed her facedown onto the dinner table, plates and glasses flying off it.

"You asshole," she said.

"That's what you wanted, right?"

He didn't stop. She had pushed every one of his buttons. Some of them twice. Pulling her arms behind her, he snapped the other cuff closed. He reached around the front of her jeans, fumbling for her zipper.

"What you asked for, right? Right?"

No answer came back in the dark. Her zipper was moving.

"Right, goddamn it?"

As her zipper slid down, he felt her body shaking. Even worked up as he was, that stopped him. Chest heaving, he reached for her face, felt her tears soaking it, and pulled away from her. He sank to his knees at her feet, his adrenaline still ramped with booze and anger, testosterone and suspicion, the wind still howling in the darkness.

"Where's the key?" he asked.

"Drawer," she choked out, crying.

At least he could see better now, but as he reached in her drawer for the keys, a noise came from upstairs. Even in all the wind, he could hear: *thump*. She heard it, too. Her crying stopped.

"What . . . what's that?" she asked.

Another *thump*. He found her, unlocked her cuffs.

"Stay here," he said. "Call 911."

Fumbling in the dark, he found the revolver in her desk drawer.

"What're you . . . What's going on?"

He started loading bullets into the gun. "Call Erik Jacobson in my Contacts." He found her hand, slipped his phone into it.

"Who's up on the roof in all this?" she asked.

"Gonna find out," he said. "Stay here."

He dashed away with the gun, and she dialed 911.

"Hello," she said, "we have an intruder . . ."

Upstairs, water poured through a skylight, down the walls, and the wind created a vacuum in the stairwell. No matter how hard Robert pushed, the deck door wouldn't open. Finally, he laid a shoulder against it, held down the door lever, and pushed into it off the far wall, hard as he could.

With a big sucking sound, the door flew away from him, banging against the exterior stairwell. He fell out onto the deck, pulled back into the open doorway with the revolver. The exterior stairwell structure: six feet wide, twelve feet long, eight feet high. Its mass sheltered him from the incoming storm.

Lights were off all over the Peninsula. There was that sound again. Three in a row this time: *Bam! Bam! Bam!* From the other side of the stairwell. He eased to his feet, moved around the stairwell corner, into the wind and rain. Revolver leading, heart pounding.

Wham! he heard. He pinned himself against the stairwell wall. Edging closer to its far corner, sweeping water from his eyes. Peering over at Unit 3 but unable to pierce the darkness.

"Got a gun!" he screamed. "It's loaded!"

His voice, lost in the wind. Ten, twenty seconds, waiting, and right when he's making his move around the corner—something heavy whistled around that corner and struck his temple. His gun flew from his hand and he dropped to the deck. Out cold.

Minutes later, Alison peered around the stairwell corner, gripping a baseball bat. Saw him lying on the deck, blood streaking his face.

"Robert! Robert! Oh, no!" she cried out.

She stepped out into the wind, crawled out to him. And just then—*bam!*

Over her head, the object struck again. She saw what hit him: a one-pound buoy, tied to a twenty-foot, quarter-inch sailboat line. The line had tangled on the front-balcony railing. Every so often, the wind caught the line just right and whipped the buoy around the stairwell, slamming it against the wall.

She grabbed him by the shoulders. Slipping and sliding, she pulled him back into the sheltered doorway.

"Robert, please . . . c'mon . . ."

Ten more seconds passed before he came to. When he did, he looked up at her, dazed.

"You're okay?" she kept asking.

She was crying, stroking his blood-soaked face. He asked what happened. She told him. Once he understood what she was telling him, he asked, "A buoy?"

"Want to file a report on that buoy?" Erik asked Robert. "Assault with no intent whatsoever?"

Erik's squad car idled in the Speedway, lights strobing. He was talking to Robert, writing up the mishap on the roof and what had happened earlier that day.

Robert was adding as much flavor as he could from his last conversation with Jack: "Just put down that I suspect someone is trying to do me harm based on threats that were made earlier today."

"This makes two reports so far. You into something over your head?"

"Hope not," Robert said, and reached for a stuffed Shamu toy he was sitting on. "Yours?" he asked and laughed. It had been a while since he'd done that.

Checking his cell phone's Thai translation app, Erik said, "Taking my *miia* and two *luuk chaay* to SeaWorld." His wife and kids.

Then Erik got down to it. "I know there's things you can't tell me, I get that, but seriously, man. I know you from the beach, the handball courts, from you helping me out, and you're a stand-up guy for sure.

But you never back off. Me? I like that about you. Still, every once in a while, think about taking a step back."

"Even when you know you're right?" Robert said, signing the report.

"Especially then. If I hadn't, years ago LAPD's bagpiper would have been squeezing 'Amazing Grace' over my dead ass."

Robert saw that his friend was serious. "I hear you, man. I do. Thanks."

"By the way, my trademark went through today. Natural Gas, baby. I'll get your sweetheart a first-run unit. After you left Rae's the other day, she was seriously into it."

"A handheld gizmo that makes fart noises. You surprised?"

"Women," Erik said, "the last true mystery. I'm around. *Sawatdee khrap*, dude."

࿂

Fifteen minutes later, Robert lay across his bed in the condo's master. Alison held a towel filled with ice against his head and lay down beside him. For a while, they didn't speak, each of them tired of apologizing to the other. Then he tried telling her more about what he knew.

"I didn't want you to worry, thought I could handle it all myself, but Jack . . . I'm starting to think he wants us out of the way."

"You mean, what? Wants to kill us?"

He had her full attention now. "I don't know, not really, but . . ."

"He's just a top-tier ambulance chaser, isn't he?"

"More than that. He started out practicing criminal defense, was damn good at it. Got a lot of bad people off—drug dealers, money launderers, who knows what kind of scumbags he knows who owe him favors."

He told her what Jack had told him earlier today: Jack knew they lived on the Peninsula. "I never said a word about where we lived. Any way he'd know that?" he asked.

Not from her. She hadn't told anyone.

He told her, "I think someone was watching us from Unit 3."

As he told her his suspicions, other worries surfaced, and he told her about them. "Mr. Fanelli, my boss at the firm, he was my friend. He told me Jack was destroyed by our lawsuit, but that's not how he acted today. He acted like he . . . like he was in on a big secret, and once I found out what it was, it would be too late. Too late for us."

"I don't know what happened with you two today," she said. "I went to the car. But cocky? Walking by him, yeah, I can see that. Cocky, definitely."

"So goddamn cocky," he said. "And if I put you in danger—the last thing you need is another trip to the ER."

"Too much excitement is bad." She nodded and kissed his forehead. "The wrong kind of excitement. Guess you're right; he's up to something. But I know this. He's trying to poison your life—*our lives*—and that won't work if we trust each other."

"Pretty smart, aren't you?"

"Working on it," she said.

"Look, I want to go to the Santa Monica courthouse tomorrow morning. Would you come with me? It's important, and I don't want you here alone."

"Is this about Rosalind?"

"What?"

"Your sister. Protecting me because of what happened to her?"

"I promise. It's not because of that."

"Why are we going, then?" she asked.

He told her what he knew about Jack's divorce hearing in front of Judge Rosen.

She said, "This one last thing *about him*, I'll do it for you. But look. I know I needed help when you met me. Not anymore. I'm a big girl and I don't need you to protect me. We'll go to the courthouse because we're partners."

He nodded. "And after we meet Leslie at the bank, we get outta town."

"Leslie? The hot banker you swear you didn't sleep with and I believe you? That Leslie?"

Smiling, he said, "That one. Did you find my key?"

"Taped behind your filing cabinet? Nobody would ever look there." She reached in her shirt pocket, handed it to him. "You worried about your filing cabinet?"

He slipped his filing-cabinet key onto his key ring.

"Not really," he said. "I don't know . . ."

CHAPTER 38

Jack and Dorothy Pierce sat together at the table in front of Judge Rosen's art-deco courtroom. Not exactly *together* but at the same table. That was the first thing Robert noticed, watching from the back row with Alison. The second thing: between Jack and Dorothy sat a single attorney, Roxanne Paris.

Robert had seen her in the news. High-profile, she worked out of a Century City firm that ate up several floors of high-end commercial space.

Back of his mind, he'd hoped Philip would be here with the Brightwells. That Philip was the *good friend of yours* Jack taunted him with.

Judge Rosen spoke into her mike: "Our next, and only order of business, is the matter of *Pierce versus Pierce*. Ms. Paris, do you wish to address the court?"

Roxanne stood up, speaking with confidence bred of storied courtroom wins. "Your Honor, I represent both parties, and I am delighted to report, my clients have reached an amicable settlement in this matter."

"Excellent news from where I sit," Judge Rosen said.

Roxanne asked, "Have you had an opportunity to review our proposed final order, Your Honor?"

"Certainly, Ms. Paris. Do both parties understand that each has thirty days to appeal this order should either have a change of heart?"

"Not likely." It was Dorothy talking.

A hearty courtroom laugh followed. Even Jack was laughing. In fact, everyone in the room was laughing except Robert, Alison, and Lionel Brightwell. He had nodded off in the aisle in his wheelchair.

Roxanne said, "One additional matter, Your Honor. If it please the court, both parties would ask that the court consider one final item."

Judge Rosen checked her watch. "Very well, proceed."

"We would ask the court's indulgence in assuring my clients that the property settlement between them will be sealed and withheld from public view."

"*Sealed?* Is that weird?" Alison whispered to Robert.

"Unusual." Maybe weird, too, for such a high-profile couple.

Judge Rosen said, "I'd like everyone to approach the bench. And if possible, let's make it quick."

"Tee time at Bel-Air, Your Honor?" Jack asked.

"Good guess, Counselor," Judge Rosen replied. "Anybody see Harvey's *TMZ* villains out front?"

Everyone laughed again. Lionel perked up in his wheelchair and looked around. But Robert had his eye on Jack, Dorothy, and Roxanne. Judge Rosen held her hand over the mike, and everybody up front was kidding around, like they all planned to go clubbing tonight.

Right then, Mr. Brightwell whirred over to Robert and Alison. Robert stood up and said, "Good morning, Mr. Brightwell. Robert Worth."

He shook Robert's hand, but his eyes stayed on Alison. His grin offered a glimpse of a youngster still residing inside his eighty-nine-year-old frame.

"Alison Maxwell," he said, with no coaching needed with her name. "You never came back up the hill to see me?"

She took his offered hand. "This guy right here might not like it if I did that. Otherwise, I would have."

"Give an old man a minute, would you, honey? Just the two of us?"

"Robert?" she asked.

"Sure, I'll be out in the hall."

He headed for the closer of two exits and glanced up front. Jack was looking right at him. Then Jack winked at him, and Robert pushed hard through the door.

Out in the hallway, a few lawyers and litigants trickled up and down the hall. Robert sank to a wooden bench, frustrated and confused.

Philip's image came to mind first. When they'd last spoken at the firm, Philip planned to keep Brightwell as a client. Had he been too optimistic? Had Brightwell jumped ship to Roxanne's firm? Looked that way, and he hoped he was wrong.

Sitting in the hall, he pictured Jack and Judge Rosen together on this very bench. Not only sitting, he decided. *Sitting together.*

On a hunch, he Googled Judge Rosen on his iPad. Rosen, it turned out, attended Sandra Day O'Connor College of Law, same as Jack. After that, she'd been a prosecutor, working out of downtown LA.

Rosen a prosecutor, Jack doing criminal-defense work. The same age, classmates, then courtroom adversaries. Pals from way back and, knowing Jack, more than pals at one time or another.

He wondered what Jack's point had been, taunting him yesterday. Getting him into Rosen's courtroom?

Did he want Robert to see his power? To see that he was in a bracket beyond what Robert could fathom? Or was there more behind it? Was Jack signaling he had planned his exit from the firm and from his marriage before Robert ever sued him? Was it possible Alison's lawsuit was something Pierce welcomed? Or, at least, that he used?

That wasn't possible, he decided. Jack had been fired, his name taken off the firm masthead. He saw it with his own eyes. Together, Robert and Alison had taken more than $4 million of his firm's money.

Gia broke off another half million for good measure, and Jack, the primary wrongdoer, paid his share. That money was real. Leslie had called both Alison and him, confirming their meeting tomorrow. That was a lock.

And Dorothy? She had her prenup and knew Jack had engaged in infidelity.

Infidelity, he thought. Bland contract lingo for blatant, brazen, serial womanizing, and right behind him, in Rosen's courtroom, Dorothy owed Jack nothing. Exactly zero dollars.

He emerged from where these ideas lurked and collided, glancing to his left. Ten feet away, Gia Marquez sat on his bench. His heart rate ramped.

"Penny for your thoughts," she said. Then she saw how he was staring at her. "Maybe not."

Now he knew the identity of *his good friend.* "Why?" he asked Gia.

"You first, Mr. Worth."

"You and Jack are together?" he asked.

"Looks that way. He moved in with me, let's see, about a week ago?"

"Jesus. You helped me, ruined him, so you could get him back?"

"Told you, didn't I? It was never about money for me. Nobody in your life you never got over?"

He didn't answer.

"All these years, I never got over him. Two bad apples, huh?"

"You're nothing like him. You like thinking you are, but you're not. Guys like that never change; they get worse. Don't you know that?"

"You've changed, Mr. Worth. I told you he makes people crazy, remember? And look at you now, sitting outside his divorce waiting for . . . waiting for what?"

He stood, heat rising. "But I'm not the one living with him, am I?"

She didn't meet his eyes. "No, you're not. So back off, all right?"

But he didn't. "Smartest woman I know, doing this to herself. Why?" No answer. "He's screwed everything that moves ever since you met him, and he always will. He's a sociopath."

She shrugged. "I know everything about him. *Everything*, okay? And we love each other."

"That right? Like your big date at the Saddle Peak? Maybe you can go there again, hand each other envelopes of cash under the table. Hey, I know—maybe *The Famous Tattoo Girl* can come along for a threesome. You, him, and Tattoo Girl. Might be a nice change of pace for him. Oh, wait—that's no change of pace at all, is it?"

For some reason, hearing what he said, she came alive. She stood, fronting him. "What are you talking about?"

"Forget it," he said, getting a grip on his anger. "None of my business. I was out of line. I'm sorry, I—"

"No—you said *Saddle Peak*. Then something about what? A *tattooed girl?*"

Before he could answer, from behind him Alison said, "Fuck you, Gia."

He wondered, among other things, how long Alison had been listening. "Alison?" he asked, turning around. That's all he got out before she rushed for the courthouse door. Before he could follow, Jack emerged from Rosen's courtroom and took Gia's hand.

Robert stopped, looked at them.

"We're done in there," Jack told Gia. "Home free, babe."

Gia didn't say a word. Her eyes were still on Robert. Then Jack turned to him, "Glad you decided to show, but you saw what happened. The damn settlement's sealed. Must be hard for you, seeing the two of us so happy. But hey, odds are good that Chase is getting divorced, so that's working for you."

"Cool it, Jack," Gia said.

Robert headed for the door again. Jack caught up with him and took his arm.

"Wait up, my man."

Robert looked beaten as Jack told him, "Want you to remember this, Worth. Remember this as you count the endless hours of your new life dragging by. Remember that nobody ever fucked you over like I did."

Endless hours? Dragging by? Robert was out of words. Nothing left to say as Jack returned to Gia. Robert could see her standing in the shadows. She looked small. Hurt and embarrassed.

And Robert was certain he'd never see her again as he ran out of the courthouse.

CHAPTER 39

Lucky for Robert, the LeBaron's convertible top was down because Alison wouldn't brake to let him inside. After chasing her down two levels of courthouse parking, he managed to leap into her moving car.

Headed down Main Street, he wanted to ask what Lionel had said to her earlier. Judging by her Don't-say-a-fucking-word-to-me look, he decided that could wait.

She'd driven ten fast blocks down Main when she brought it up herself.

"Know Nurse Rodney?" she asked.

"You mean—" That was all he got out.

"Rodney ran off to Palm Springs with his boyfriend, so Lionel offered me a job taking care of him. Great, huh? Isn't that awesome."

"Well," he said.

As she ran a yellow light at Venice and Pacific, he braced himself against her dash. "I had no idea Gia was going to be there."

"Who cares about Gia! Fuck Gia Whoever, fuck Jack, and fuck you."

He wondered how much she'd heard in the courthouse between Gia and him. Then he found out.

"This tattooed girl. The one who goes to Saddle Peak with Pierce? Who is she?"

"I don't know," he said.

"Jack Pierce, Saddle Peak, and a tattooed girl—you think it's me, right?"

"Can we please—Jesus!" Screaming because she ran a red light at Washington, headed onto the Peninsula. He waited a full minute before speaking again. "Can we just talk, please?"

He reached for her. She slapped his hand away. "No, shit, don't touch me. Do not. I can't be around you anymore. I have no idea who you are. Who the fuck are you?"

It wasn't really a question, so he didn't answer. She pushed the garage-door opener on her visor. The door started rising ahead. She squealed inside—almost clipped the rising door—and slammed to a stop.

"It's over, okay? I'm done with it," he told her.

"You're so full of shit. I told you, I'm not your dead sister. I'm not your fucking tattooed lady, and I don't need you to save me. Everything we need, we'll have it tomorrow. But you think some other lawyer got one up on you, and—"

"It's done. I'm over it," he said.

"No, you're not. You'll never get over it. You think there's something wrong? Who cares what's wrong? Who gives a shit?"

She jumped out, hurried toward the alarm pad. He opened his door, sat in the car.

"I'm over it, seriously. Please, c'mon."

He watched her start to punch in their alarm code. It wasn't armed. She turned to him, crying.

"This whole thing, you and me, it was never about us. I knew it last night, but I kept hoping I was wrong. It was always about him. Day one, *we* were always all about *him*. I am so outta here."

She disappeared into the stairwell.

He didn't move. *Way to go, bro,* he told himself.

Once he slid out of her car, he heard her banging up the stairs. He walked to the stairwell door. Then he remembered. The alarm. He'd set the alarm before they left.

"Alison!" he shouted. "Alison, stop! Come back!"

No answer.

Upstairs, she rushed down the hall toward the living room. She heard him calling and wasn't about to stop. Ahead of her: their beatbox and TV were stacked by the slider onto the patio. That stopped her cold at the hall's kitchen entrance.

"What . . ."

She peered in the kitchen. Drawers had been pulled open, the floor covered with trash-can debris.

"Are you . . . ," she said.

Then she heard his voice, louder: "Alison, stop, wait!"

She turned around. Looked back the way she came. Robert was halfway down the hall when a man in a ski mask swung out from the utility closet behind him.

"Behind you!" she screamed.

The attacker raised a metal pipe. Robert started to turn around, but he was a split second too late. The attacker let fly with a vicious blow, and even though Robert managed to block part of it with his shoulder, the attacker's shot caught him, side of the head. The force of it knocked him to the floor, and he lay there, perfectly still.

That left the attacker good to go. He ran down the narrow hall toward Alison. She dashed into the kitchen, grabbed a big knife out of the sink. Too late. He grabbed her hair, twisted it in his fingers, and jerked her body back into his.

"Don't think so, doll!" he screamed.

Her knife clattered onto the floor. She tried reaching behind her head, to get at him, to gouge his eyes, but the attacker was strong, and his grip gave him more leverage than he needed. Pushing her body over the counter, he grabbed her hair with both hands now.

"Lights out, bitch!" he screamed.

She could barely breathe. Nothing she could do about what was about to happen. He pulled her head up by her hair, ready to bash her face into the granite counter when he caught a flash of motion to his right.

Robert jumped him without a sound.

The attacker's fingers snagged in her hair. That worked against him now as Robert got an arm around the attacker's neck from behind, choking him out, hard as he could. The attacker got both hands free of Alison, pulling at Robert's choking forearm. He was about to lose it when he twisted his body, snaked a hand between his neck and Robert's arm, and stole a breath of air. Then he grabbed Robert's forearm with both hands and torqued his body, hard as he could. That powerful motion broke Robert's grip on his neck and slung him over the counter into the living room.

In the kitchen, Alison was scouring the trash-covered floor for that knife when the attacker booted her in the ribs. She doubled up, and he dropped to the floor, looking for the knife, too.

Moments earlier, Robert crashed onto the living room floor. In a second, he was up. Tearing open Alison's desk drawer, he grabbed her empty revolver. Hands shaking, he started to fumble a bullet into the chamber.

Before he could load that first one, he heard Alison whispering: "Please . . . don't . . ."

He whirled with the empty gun. The attacker—a knife held against her throat—edged from the kitchen into the hallway.

"How 'bout I slit her throat, dude?"

"You touch her, I'll blow your fucking brains out."

"Robert . . . ," she pleaded.

"Gun's empty! I saw it!" But the attacker wasn't sure.

"That's why I loaded it. Let her go, and get the fuck outta here!"

"You didn't load nothing." He wasn't sure about that, either.

"Wanna bet, motherfucker?" Robert cocked the revolver, bluffing. "Let her go, and get out of here. I won't follow you."

Off their stalemate, the attacker suddenly tripped Alison and pushed her toward Robert. She fell, tumbling into him, and they went down together. That gave the attacker time to race back down the hall. Taking the stairs three at time, he burst out the door onto Speedway.

Robert knelt, held Alison's shoulders, looked in her eyes. "You all right?"

"Think so," she said. "I can't believe . . ."

He picked up her revolver, went to the desk, and tried to load it. But bullets fell from his shaking hand and bounced around on the carpet.

He gave up loading the gun and took her hand.

"You were right. He wants to kill us."

"Not gonna happen," he said. "Call 911."

"All right, I will. I'm sorry," she said.

She watched him take off, running down the hall. She lay back down on the floor, trembling. Heard their Speedway door slamming behind him.

"He was right," she said.

Then she tried to breathe.

Robert hauled ass on foot down Speedway. He had the attacker in sight, seventy-five yards ahead. Looked like the attacker had pulled up that ski mask as he jammed left onto a walk street.

His head pounded from that pipe shot. He ducked left off Speedway, scrambling down a street parallel to the attacker's. He made it to Pacific where Grand Canal blocked the way.

Looking right, there was the attacker again, who ripped down that mask before Robert got a look at him and reversed course into the street he'd just exited.

Once Robert made the corner of the attacker's street, the man was halfway down it, topping a chain-link fence and dropping into a home-construction site.

Robert jammed down the street to the eight-foot fence. No visibility inside—a green-mesh fence cover blocked his view. So he grabbed the fence top, pulled himself over, and fell hard on the other side, half expecting the attacker to jump him.

When he didn't, Robert got to his knees and made out the attacker booking toward the rear fence. Robert ran toward him as the guy slipped through the fence. Latino workmen on the second floor of the house started yelling at Robert. All he could make out was *pendejo* and kept going.

At the back fence, green-meshed, too, he found a slot between fence sections. Squeezed through it like the attacker did into the rear alley. Right then, a two-by-four came flying at his head. He ducked, turned, and raised his arm, but a four-inch nail sticking out of the end of the board spiked into his deltoid.

He scrambled to his feet.

"Like it?" the attacker screamed through his mask. "Here's more!"

Swinging the board in tight arcs, he backed Robert up till he was pinned against a workman's vintage pickup. The attacker raised the board overhead, but Robert rolled away—just as the board smashed the windshield, setting off the alarm.

More *pendejos* rained down from the second story as Robert snapped off the truck's antenna and lashed the attacker, backing him up. The attacker dropped his board and covered his face, so Robert struck at his arms, whipping them, too, found his face again, slashing at that mask. Getting results, judging by the pained noises the attacker was making, and now it was the attacker backed against that fence.

With nowhere to run, the attacker bounced off the chain link and booted Robert square in the chest, knocking him back. Robert tripped over a pile of scrap lumber and went down. That was the attacker's chance—he took off down the alley to a sagging wooden fence and pulled himself over all seven feet of it.

Robert followed, sluggish, clambered over the fence, too, but crashed onto a row of garbage cans, spilling onto the ground of a backyard. A paint-peeled beach house ahead, looked like a place that time forgot, and there went the attacker, clearing the side of the ramshackle structure.

Robert staggered to his feet, gassed, when a shotgun blast rocked the yard.

"Stop right there!" a male voice shouted.

He froze—his attacker was long gone. A crazed elderly man in a bathrobe leveled a shotgun at him from the back porch. "On the ground now, or I take both of 'em off at the knee!"

Robert went belly-down fast. Guy took his time walking over, got the gun barrel right down in his face.

"You kids getting drunk up in the bars, coming down here at 2:00 a.m., throwing shit in my yard, pissing on my fence."

Robert didn't risk telling him it was noon, or worse, that he was a lawyer. "I had a break-in. I'm your neighbor. Five blocks up the beach."

"You're what?"

He said it all again, gave his address. The man finally pointed his shotgun skyward.

"Neighbor?" he asked. "Then you get what I'm saying."

CHAPTER 40

Stanley thought his face looked badass in his Celica's mirror, all those lashes lawyer man dealt him with that antenna. With a fresh carton of Larks on the seat, he had just now driven over to Mailbox United and parked in its rear lot. It was on Lincoln. He wanted to, he could grab a hand job next door for forty-five bucks, plus a tip if he ever planned on coming back.

This mailbox outfit had what Jack demanded: no cameras inside or out and sparse foot traffic. Two days ago, Stanley stepped to the counter, gave them two sets of fake IDs, and filled out forms for a three-month bit, the minimum. They handed back one key to his box.

As he tried to Purell more construction-site paint off his hands, Jack backed in beside him. Now they faced each other. Stanley handed him the key through his window, and Jack went inside, holding a package. That left Stanley with his thoughts about what had happened with the lunatic lawyer.

At least he had the right alarm code. That was about the only thing that went according to plan. After meter parking at the jetty cut, he'd headed up Speedway with his day pack. Just a guy going to the beach, wandering around till he saw the pair drive to the courthouse in her car.

Good to go, he thought, but when he reached their Speedway alarm pad, the Navigator pulled up, parked on the corner. Navigator got out of it, and Stanley started moving again. Two minutes later, the Navigator's work crew pulled up in a truck, and they all piled into Unit 3. Maybe to fix up after him, maybe for rain damage last night, it didn't matter. For the time being, he was screwed trying to breach Unit 1 undetected.

No point trying to reach Jack about this hiccup. Each of them had a burner with no texting capacity. Besides, now was the time. It needed to go down now.

"Today, no matter what," Jack had told him.

So he hit the beach, stayed in character, kicking it with his backpack. From there, he could see the Navigator *jefe* and his crew on the roof, Navigator making notes, pointing out this and that to his crew.

Watching them, his stomach churned, his nerves monkeyed, and his greatest prison fear surged up out of the dark. Fear of being cornered. Better part of an hour he watched, Navigator taking his sweet time, till they all split. That put him outside Unit 1, fronting the alarm pad, one hour and change after the lawyer split.

In a huge rush, panic building. Not the excitement he'd feel on a hot prowl. That was almost sexual. The pressure he fought now was This-is-gonna-end-bad pressure, that trapped-inside feeling he felt every single hour of every day he was doing time.

And there it was, the next wrong thing: the front slider swollen shut from that storm, blocking his out via the beach. Even with the slider stuck, he stacked a few of their things in front of it. Made it clear to anyone with a brain: this was nothing but a low-level burglary. Obviously, this crime could be—had to be—related to that squatter in Unit 3, and that would be a dead end for everybody. *Ha!*

Then the situation inside the condo compressed more. His thinking: *Forget grabbing your cameras. First things first. Do what you're here to do.*

After that decision, time melted. Seemed like seconds later, he heard the garage door open downstairs. The car driving in. Voices in the garage, the lovebirds fighting, and he spotted that utility closet down the hall, and he ran into it, hiding in total darkness and losing his shit—

"Looks right to me, Stanley. Now you. I'll wait here."

It was Jack, coming from the mailbox outfit, handing over the one and only key. Stanley put on his painter's cap and went inside. Keyed open the box and saw what Jack had left him: a square object wrapped in slick, white fish-wrapping paper. Then he tooled over to the counter with it and with his papers filled out in advance, he canceled his box, forfeited his deposit. They didn't want his key—they'd need to make a new one—so he headed back out to his car.

Once he was behind the wheel, Jack said, "Toss me your key." Stanley handed it over. "Why's there paint on your hands?"

"Did some work around my house last night," Stanley said. "Calms the nerves."

"What the hell happened to your face?"

"Little dustup with your lawyer."

"Dustup? Did he see your face? Yes or no, talk to me."

"Nope, had it covered. Don't worry, you're good."

Jack eyed him from his car. "Oh, I always worry, but I worry especially hard when I give a junkie a chance to change his life."

What Jack said was true. Stanley didn't like hearing any of it, but the white package on his seat took some of the sting from Jack's words. Listening and nodding, he cracked open the Larks carton, opened a fresh pack, and fired up a smoke. That helped some. Not much.

"How's it possible?" Jack asked. "They were gone, what? A good hour and a half?"

"We used decent phones. I coulda texted you, vice versa."

"Texting's never an option, Stanley. I held up my end, same as always, same as when we were kids, but you?"

There it was. Jack never letting anything go. Stanley wanted to tell his friend about the Navigator showing up, how careful he'd been waiting on the beach, how he wound up fighting the lawyer, kicking his ass, but he knew Jack didn't want to hear that. No matter what he said, Jack would accuse him of making excuses, and sure enough, here came the twenty motherfucking questions:

"Did you cancel the box?"

"Yes."

"Do I need to double-check, make sure you did it right?"

"No. I did it right."

"You sure this was the only key?" Jack asked, holding it up for him to look at.

"Yes. The only one."

"I'm not gonna find out there's another key. A key tying us together, am I?"

"No. You're not."

"Even though you're a convicted felon, I don't mind being tied to you. We went to high school together. I was once your attorney of record. What I don't want is being tied to you this week. *Especially today.*"

"Got it," Stanley said.

"Suspicion, I can handle," Jack told him, not letting up. "But proof? That's another matter entirely, isn't it?"

Stanley stared down at his white package while Jack reamed him, humiliated him. Package or no package, he decided, he didn't need this shit from anybody.

"Why don't you cool it, Jack? You said he was some farm-boy lawyer outta the Bay Area. John Deere tried to take me out today, okay? All the way out. Lucky for you, I can take care of business."

"*Take care of* . . . twenty grand for a few days' work and you're complaining? Twenty K's what I used to make every other day, week in, week out."

Stanley watched Jack smiling like he did sometimes. He'd seen that smile over the years, always meaning it for someone else. But this time, Jack was giving him that smile.

Now Jack was starting up that cheese-eating rental he was still driving. Jack's parting words to him: "What I know about hard-core junkies like you. No matter what you do for them, no matter how hard you try helping them, it never fails. They always find a way to let you down."

Once Jack took off, Stanley sat there another half hour, trying to process his anger and shame. What should he do? Call his sponsor? Go to a meeting? Hoist free weights? Take a run?

Go home, he decided. *Take a run, hoist some iron, make a protein shake, take my vitamins, go to a meeting. No, make the shake first. And have a good, sober life.*

Digging deep after what just happened, he made himself say: "Jack Pierce. You are my friend. And I mean it. Jack Pierce, I want you to have a good life, too."

CHAPTER 41

Robert couldn't believe it, winding up at Brotman a second time. This go-round, he was checked into the ER, too, a couple of Vicodin already under his belt. His nurse had given him a tetanus shot and was dressing the nail puncture in his shoulder. He poked his own ribs. They hurt, bruised from crash-landing on those garbage cans. Not as bad as Alison, though. Once again, she'd been admitted for overnight observation.

Now he looked back on what had happened, once his gun-toting neighbor let him go. Headed up Speedway, he spotted an ambulance in front of his building. Two paramedics loaded Alison inside, an oxygen mask over her face. The garage door was open, her car halfway into Speedway.

The paramedics told him. "She had some kind of seizure, looks like, called 911."

Once he gave his ID, he jumped in with her. As they took off, he figured she'd tried to drive herself to the hospital and couldn't handle it.

In his ER cubicle, his phone vibrated. He picked up. It was Erik, second time they'd talked in the last hour. The cops were dusting Unit 1, Erik was saying. Turned out, Alison's keys were still in her ignition, so Erik pulled her car back in the garage, left her keys on the kitchen counter.

"Do I need to drag my tired ass to the ER?" Erik asked.

"I'm all right."

"Hold still," the nurse told Robert.

"What?" Erik asked.

"Nurse's saying she's never seen a man strong as I am."

The nurse blushed. "I mean it. Don't move," she said, not meaning it anymore. She finished with him and began cleaning up. The hospital wall phone rang, and she answered, talking to a doctor.

"Tell me what went down today?" Erik asked.

Robert told him the intruder was wearing a ski mask, knocked him down with a pipe, and put a knife to Alison's throat. Robert told him about the standoff inside the condo, too.

"He was pretty big, about my size. Think I marked his face up when I caught up with him."

"*Caught up with him?* Whatever happened to taking a step back? You outta your fuckin' mind?"

The nurse tapped his good shoulder. Whispered that Doctor Zweig would like to speak to him about Alison, and asked if he minded.

"I don't mind at all," he told her.

After the nurse relayed his message into the wall phone, she walked out.

"Well, are you?" Erik asked.

"Am I what?"

"Out of your fucking mind?"

"Hear me out," he told Erik. "It wasn't burglary. I think the guy wanted to kill me, kill both of us. I don't know."

"Hey, your stuff's stacked up, ready to go. Patio door's stuck from the storm. You two walked in and surprised him—that's not it?"

"I don't buy it. Guy knew I had a pistol, but he didn't—"

"Hold up—now you've got a pistol?" Erik asked.

"Alison's. Well, it belonged to her brother, but my point is, he knew there was a pistol and didn't take it."

"He tell you that, or you have a sixth sense?"

He explained how the attacker called his bluff with the unloaded pistol, the guy yelling how he knew it wasn't loaded. "Meaning," Robert told him, "he already saw it and didn't steal it."

Erik mulled it over. "Burglary down on the Peninsula? Simple to conceal; a pistol's first thing he'd go for. Might be the only thing he grabs. So, you think the whole thing was staged?"

Robert knew to stay mindful of his nondisclosure agreement. If Jack's prior bad behavior or the firm's insurance missteps made it into a police report—*a public document*—Robert was done. His settlement money—all of it—would be gone and then some. Even so, why Jack wanted to hurt him *now* was based on what happened *then*.

But Robert needed to get what he believed into the record, so feeling his way forward, he said, "So, look, around the time I left the firm there was some . . . you might call it bad blood. And what I believe is—and I'm not accusing anyone of any wrongdoing. I believe a lawyer named Jack Pierce may know the intruder."

"Uh-huh."

"But I should make it clear, Officer," very formal now, "I cannot talk about certain aspects of my employment at Fanelli and Pierce."

"One of those nondisclose deals?"

"Like I just said. I cannot, and will not, discuss that."

"Right, you *cannot* and *will not* talk about it now? So I'm not writing it down."

"Right, Officer, you're smarter than they say."

Robert knew he needed to speak only to current facts. "Let me put it this way, Officer. Alison Maxwell and I were at the Santa Monica courthouse *today*. We were in Judge Rosen's courtroom *today*. Mr. Pierce's divorce was the only case on her docket *today*. I was there because Mr. Pierce invited me to come to court yesterday, and I saw him there *today*."

"He dared you to come to court?"

"Asked me," Robert said, but it had been a dare. "Based also on what I observed *today*, I believe that the intruder broke into our condo while we were at the courthouse or in transit."

Erik digested those words. "Meaning Pierce would be alibied-up for the break-in. And you know he's alibied-up because you saw him in court."

Exactly right, Robert was thinking. What he said was: "I'm only telling you where I saw Jack Pierce *today*, Officer. That's a matter of public record, and I was there along with several other witnesses. Feel free to draw your own conclusions about the break-in."

But they were on the same page now, same paragraph. Erik said, "You're gonna need hard evidence before you even think about accusing a big-time lawyer. You know that, right?"

"I haven't accused a big-time lawyer of anything," he said, because he hadn't.

"I'm crystal on that, bro. But we both know, going off half-cocked? That's what guys like . . . that's what big-time . . . that's what a certain type of person lives for. But what you just told me—*about today*—that might be helpful going forward."

"Glad to help you with today's break-in," Robert said.

"I'll write it up. Make sure you come by the station and sign it. It's no good till you do."

A severe woman in a white jacket came into the cubicle. About thirty-eight, slightly cross-eyed, her reading glasses hanging from a seashell-chain necklace.

"Will do, gotta go," Robert said.

Erik told him. "Your girl's lucky she lives with a maniac."

Robert clicked off, and the woman said, "Mr. Worth. I'm Dr. Zweig."

"Call me *Robert*," he offered.

She picked up his chart and read it. "Tetanus shot . . . bruised ribs. I think you'll live, Mr. Worth."

"Looks like it. Alison, how's she doing?"

"I'm not quite sure yet. Reading her chart, I noticed you were with her last time she was admitted to our care. Bruised wrists, that time. This time, a bruised neck."

She wasn't looking at him the way doctors look at patients. She looked at him like he was something else altogether.

"And it's me with her both times?"

She didn't answer, and he was blocked from explaining that Jack had assaulted Alison on the first visit.

"If these two sets of bruises, wrists and neck, are merely a coincidence, maybe you could explain it?" she asked, putting on those glasses now for emphasis.

"It is a coincidence," he said. "And because it is a coincidence, I can't explain it. Other than to say that it's a coincidence. You might want to cool it before you get in trouble, Doctor."

"I don't plan to cool it about anything. Matter of fact, I may or may not take the next official step."

That meant one thing: calling the cops about an abuser. Him. So he told her, "Tell you what, Doc. Let's get that nurse back in here."

"Why? Are you in pain?" She smiled for the first time.

"Not me," he said, handing her a business card. "I want you to repeat what you told me in front of her. When the time comes, that'll beef up my defamation damages against you and the hospital."

"I never said that you—"

"You implied it, so let's get her in here, get specific, and get this party started."

She stared at his card. When she looked up, she tried to look the same as before. But she didn't.

"Sad to say, I'm out of work. So I've got nothing but time on my hands to deal with situations like this. Like you," he added.

"Oh," she said.

Once she backed off, he explained about the break-in, what happened to Alison, and about the police report she would be welcome to read once it was available.

"Oh," she said again.

"Now," he said, "you gonna tell me how she's doing, or are we going down that other road?"

In the elevator up to Alison's room, he went over what Dr. Zweig had decided to tell him. Turned out, Alison was too doped up to tell her anything useful. That's why Dr. Zweig had built up such a head of steam with him. He didn't blame her. Abuse was what it looked like, and once they talked it out, Dr. Zweig was comfortable telling him this: Alison had an elevated heart rate from acute anxiety, leading to tachycardia, same as before.

Made perfect sense. After all, she'd had a knife to her throat. Her heart rate was probably elevated anyway, coming off their argument driving home in her car.

The elevator door opened onto the sixth floor. He followed the arrows to Room 665. He was already thinking about a room-number joke to lighten things up. *Satan's laid up next door in 666*, something like that, then he stopped walking.

What was Dr. Zweig's last question to him: "When these attacks come on, what were her initial symptoms?"

He explained what he had seen at Alison's apartment. Then Dr. Zweig asked him about the latest incident, and he told her he hadn't been there to observe it.

As they were winding up, Dr. Zweig shook his hand. Shook it twice, he recalled. Then she said, "After what she went through today, I'd be surprised if this didn't happen."

"Guess so," he told her. "Me, too."

That last exchange stuck with him. How her doctor would be surprised if Alison *didn't* have another attack. Come to think of it, he would have been surprised, too. That's what slowed him down three doors before reaching her room. What stopped him outside her door, where he was still thinking about it: *elevated heart rate.*

"Robert?" Alison's voice, dope-groggy inside her room.

Heart rate elevated, he was thinking, and pictured Alison doing Kundalini yoga on the roof deck.

"That you?" he heard her asking.

He started to push open her door, but his mind coiled around what Dr. Zweig said: "I'd be surprised if this *didn't* happen."

He'd been with her in the condo after the attack. Then he left. And then it *did* happen.

His hand fell from Alison's door, and as he walked back toward the elevator, he muttered, "Sonya . . ."

CHAPTER 42

Stanley thought the barren front yard of his one-bedroom stucco rental house reflected poorly on him. The first thing he'd do next week, he decided, was get some Mexicans over to plant some killer plants. No, he next decided, he'd pick out the plants, do the job himself. Learn everything there was to know about landscaping, save money, and get in a hard workout doing it.

Plants, not the water-using kind, he was thinking. The desert kind with fat leaves like movie stars planted to save water and be cool.

A cactus, he decided, unlocking his front door and going inside. A giant cactus.

"I'm all about the environment." That's what he'd tell dates now that he had a stash. He tossed Jack's white package onto his kitchen counter, unwrapped the paper, and there it was: big stacks of wrapped hundreds. He opened the refrigerator door and slung his stacks inside, digging the idea of having *cool cash.*

"Cool, baby," he said to no one in particular, picturing how he'd leave Tesla brochures scattered around so his dates could groove on his friend-of-the-planet persona.

Opening the cabinets, he pulled out the blender, Muscle Milk, whey powder, and a carton of blueberries. Shake time, baby.

Looking outside, he caught a glimpse of his Sikh mailman's turban strolling away from his box, so he stepped out to the street to grab his mail. Alongside flyers for another new fitness place and Go Go Wok lay a small white package. Six inches long, an inch wide. There were no stamps, but it vibed *Open me first*, so he unwrapped it by his mailbox.

Seeing its contents, his palms began sweating instantly and stayed wet because the box contained a ziplock baggie of heroin. That familiar quick pulse started, too, back of his throat. And both sensations settled in on him and stayed there.

From Jack. He knew it. *That fucker.*

As he ran inside to his bathroom, Jack's slurs in the parking lot surged at him. *Once a junkie, always a junkie.* Stanley recalled that truism in particular as he dropped the ziplock in the commode and flushed it.

"Junkie that, bitch!" he yelled.

But it wedged in the drain. Would not go down the chute. He grabbed it from the toilet bowl and unzipped it to dump the contents. Then the drug's smell hit him, that whiff of vinegar, and he felt himself getting hard.

Ninety seconds later, Jack's cruel, provocative behavior disappeared from Stanley's personal calculus. He was on his landline; it was ringing. If his guy didn't answer on this first try, he'd flush the stuff, but the guy did answer, and yes, he had an insulin rig. Quite a few insulin rigs, in fact.

When Stanley hurried out the door to stock up on rigs, his neighbor was kicked back in a lawn chair, slamming a beer.

"Shoulda saw her," his neighbor called out. When Stanley kept going, his neighbor asked, "How long's UPS been using porn stars to make deliveries?"

Stanley didn't stop to wonder about the inane comment about UPS porn stars. Only one thing in his world was clear. His old dealer answering the phone, having rigs to spare? That was God's hand at work.

And later, when he tied off in his kitchen to shoot up for the first time in twenty-four months and change, the last thing he remembered thinking was: *Got twenty G's, cash on hand, so I'm good to go for what, a year? Shit, I slow-track shooting this stuff, two years, easy.*

CHAPTER 43

No yogistas streamed out of Amoroso walk street today, but Robert found the gate to Sonya's easily enough. Her house was still and quiet, so he clanged her bell and waited. Nothing happened, so he gave it another try. Same deal. Maybe he'd walk down to Abbot Kinney, break down and grab a coffee at Intelligentsia and try again in an hour.

Then he heard a woman's scream. Houses here were close together, but he was sure it came from behind Sonya's bungalow. Another scream sent him rushing into her yard, tracking the pine-bark path toward her garage.

Midpoint of her house, another scream pelted him from behind a wood-louvered open window. Then another.

"Sonya?" he said. "Sonya?"

Through the slats, he made out a naked dude jumping off a woman's prone body. Then Sonya rose from her bed, strolled toward him, and slammed the wooden slats all the way open.

"The hell are you doing?" Sonya asked, naked and unabashed.

"I was at your gate and—"

"Ringing my bell, I know. Who are you?"

"I'm Bob. I . . . saw your flyers over at the bookstore and wondered if . . ."

"Sonya?" That same dude stood in her doorway. Another dude beside him had a towel around his waist.

"You cool, Sonya?" one of them asked. The one with a towel.

"I'm good," she told them. Lighting a smoke, she inhaled fiercely, swung open the louvers, and stared at him. "Kind of a bad time, Bob, don't you think?"

"So sorry, really," he said, looking at her, trying not to. "Just need a minute of your time."

"Go," she said, blowing a stream of cigarette smoke down at him.

"I heard you taught Kundalini yoga," he said.

"Studied it a little, but no. I don't know it so I don't teach it."

"Too bad. I have asthma, it sounded great."

"It would be. It can give you total control of your breathing dynamic."

He could swear she was checking him out and wondered if she planned to throw on a robe or something.

"I'm curious," she asked. "When did you see my flyer?"

"About a week ago?" he said, guessing at a right answer.

"Thought the bookstore took 'em down. Had to after some jackass reported me to the city about needing a license. I can't teach here anymore."

"Sorry to hear that. You said *the breathing dynamic*? Would that affect your heart rate, too?"

"If you're advanced enough, definitely. Total control. I'll start teaching at a studio next month. If you're interested, my system could be as beneficial for asthma as Kundalini." She leaned down, her back to the dudes. "Or a cup of coffee, Bob."

From somewhere, she came up with a business card. He didn't know how because she was perched now on the windowsill like a sleek, toned animal.

He said, "I read somewhere, with Kundalini there might be some risk of passing out."

"Not really." Then she smiled and added, "Well, not unless you wanted to. If you wanted to pass out, Bob, and you were skilled enough, it would be easy."

Easy to pass out . . . if you wanted to.

His face hardened with realization. His eyes closed, and his mouth went dry. He didn't say anything, he couldn't, but Sonya did.

"I had a student, not too long ago, she was advanced in Kundalini. Actually, she was good enough to teach. For some reason, she quit coming to class."

He looked up. "Was her last name *Maxwell?*"

"No," she said. "It was *Ellison. Maxine Ellison.* Do you know her?"

Robert thinking: *Alison Maxwell? Maxine Ellison?* Close enough.

"Thought so for a second," he told her, "but no."

"Well, Bob, don't be a stranger." Grinding out her smoke, she said, "And be well."

As Robert walked back to his car, recent memories gouged him.

"Alison Maxwell," he said.

Saying it because that was her real name. The name he'd seen on her birth certificate. The name she had to use for Brian Maxwell's lawsuit because she was, in fact, Brian Maxwell's sister, his only living blood relative and administrator of his estate by accident of birth.

Alison Maxwell. A Kundalini yoga pro.

Not a novice like she told him that day he showed up at Sonya's. The day he was supposed to pick up his blue Escort. The new car wasn't ready, so he'd surprised her. Same thing the day his bike tire popped. He'd surprised her on the roof doing yoga. No, *performing yoga.* That was no novice on the roof when he first saw her, deep into Kundalini breathing. But once she realized he was there, she lost her balance. More than once, he recalled. Messing up on purpose, he was sure of it, to bolster her novice status in his eyes.

That day on the roof, he didn't focus on yoga. It was the calf scar from her lasered-off tattoo and the Saddle Peak Lodge that had him going. In the wrong direction, it turned out.

Sonya must have troubled Alison. Her lawyer, soon to be her boyfriend, knew where Sonya lived. If he talked to Sonya again, he could stumble onto Alison's alias or her Kundalini skill set. Skills so advanced, he might learn, that Alison could manipulate her breathing and heart rate enough to pass out. And Robert knowing either of those pieces of her puzzle? That would call into doubt her whole story about Jack's sexual assault.

Lawsuit-ending doubt.

Did Sonya ever come on to Alison like she'd told him? He didn't think so anymore. Sonya had been eyeing him just now like he was the last tiramisu on a dessert cart. Besides, whether or not Sonya dug girls didn't matter to Alison. But *her story* about Sonya coming on to her? That mattered to her because Sonya's come-on explained Alison's dropping Sonya's yoga class—even after Alison told him the classes were *a lifesaver* and a source of spiritual well-being after Jack attacked her.

And Alison's story mattered, too, because her easygoing persona mattered. What was it she told him outside Sonya's that day he'd shown up? She had reservations about suing Jack. *I just want to have my life back.* And that afternoon on their roof deck when he'd pressed her about the scar? *Let's never talk about that lawsuit again.*

A simple woman with simple needs. That was Alison's mask, her pose, and it was a good one, too—as long as he stopped thinking about her past and about their past together.

Nice try, Tattoo Girl, he was thinking. *Jesus, is she slick, or what?*

He didn't remember driving home, but that's what he must've done because next thing he knew, he was in the condo kitchen. His back to the ocean, Alison's handgun on the kitchen counter beside his computer. This time, he knew the weapon was loaded because he made sure of it.

Tarzana, he was thinking. A town out in the Valley, west of Encino.

He remembered Alison's joke, early on, about a made-up TV show, *Storage Wars Tarzana.* The town where her belongings were still stored. Maybe she slipped up and told him the truth about living there before moving to Topanga. Made sense. It was the second day they'd met at the bookstore, still casual. If he'd never learned her alias, it would never matter if he knew she'd lived in Tarzana.

But now he did know her alias, so he gave it a shot. Placed his hands on the keyboard and typed *Maxine Ellison* into his *Plaintiffs and Defendants* program, searching Tarzana for lawsuits. This search came back robust: three cases involved *Maxine Ellison, Plaintiff.* Each one was for less than $10,000, and each was dismissed before an answer was ever filed by the defendant. Dismissed by agreement of the parties with prejudice, he noticed. That meant she couldn't sue that party again on the same set of facts.

Each defendant had something else in common: each was a professional corporation, a PC, but none of the defendants were MDs. That meant she had most likely sued three different lawyers.

Based on what he knew now, she'd been shaking down Tarzana lawyers. Who knows? Shaking down lawyers all over the San Fernando Valley. Maxine Ellison, a serial shakedown artist.

Staring at the screen, his anger built until he stood up. Thinking, *You scamming little tattooed bitch. All along, you were banging Jack Pierce's brains out. I can't believe I fell for—*

A human shadow moved across the kitchen wall. Robert grabbed the gun. A fist pounded on the slider, and he whirled to the sound.

Reyes peered in from the deck, his hands raised once he saw the piece in Robert's hand. *"Ay, pendejo. Soy yo, Roberto."*

Robert lowered the pistol. Together, they finally managed to muscle open the patio door, and Reyes came inside. Eyeing that firearm, Reyes said, "Good idea, you carrying. Hear there's a bad element down at the beach."

"Been having a few problems," Robert said.

"No shit?" Reyes said, noticing the fingerprint powder scattered everywhere. "Why I'm here." Reyes pulled out his iPhone, opened his photos file. *"Mira esto, chico,* his name's Stanley Tifton. *Señor* Lark Man."

What Robert saw: a fuzzed photo. A middle-aged man, tanned, about the size he remembered from tangling with him. Standing at a convenience-store checkout counter, a purple Larks carton in front of him. Looking closer at the grainy photo of a video, he didn't see any marks on the man's face, but it was *Stanley Tifton,* he knew now.

"Where was it taken?"

"Day and Night Liquor, Beer, Cigarettes, and Wine," Reyes said.

"That's a real name?"

"Sí. On Beethoven. Paid 'em a hundred; they let me take a shot of their tape. So that's the other five hundred plus the one makes six hundred more I got you down for."

"Stanley. When was he there?"

"Today, *jefe.* Three and a half, four hours ago."

Before the break-in, Robert thought. No marks yet appeared on Stanley's face.

"Sounds about right," he told Reyes, who grabbed a beer from the refrigerator.

Robert started to make a call. "Lemme see if Jacobson knows anything about—"

"Hang up, *chico,* got us some straight junkie-to-junkie dope."

Reyes swigged his beer, told him one of the Chinese clerks at Day and Night knew Stanley from *Narcóticos Anónimos*, a meeting over in Ocean Park. The Asian sayin' Stanley dropped by the store, bought cartons of those hard-to-find Larks, and usually stuck around to shoot the breeze, talk himself up.

"So, it's not *anonymous*?" Robert asked.

"Once I paid my boy that hundred, *todo es posible*."

Turned out, Stanley called himself a private eye for a long time, but all he was, was a smack-talking junkie. "Guy was in and out of the joint, but somewhere along the line he got popped for burglary plus some kinda aggro assault. Finally got clean this last go-round but still sells nickels and dimes of *marimba*, X, poppers. *Pero no narcóticos* is what homey tells me."

"No heroin. Just reefer and amyl nitrites?"

"*Sí.*"

Amyls. There it was again. Another unprovable link between the man who attacked him and Jack Pierce.

The Asian clerk, it turned out, didn't much like Stanley. "Stanley, he was always tellin' my boy, Wang Chung, without sayin' it out loud, 'I'm better'n you.' Made like he knew big people, people who kept him out of jail back when he was using regular."

Big people. Big-time-lawyer people. Jack Pierce again.

"Got Stanley's address right here," Reyes said, "if you want to check . . ."

Reyes looked around. That loaded handgun was jammed in Robert's waist, and he was already headed for the stairs.

Blueberries had spilled off the kitchen counter, rolled past the heroin ziplock onto a buckling, checkerboard floor. The refrigerator door was open. So was Stanley's mouth, his body lying in front of his fridge, his breathing shallow.

Robert and Reyes stood over him. The front door had been open, so they let themselves in after spotting his splayed bare feet through his torn-screen slammer.

"Day and Night dude thought he was clean, *chico*."

"Not clean enough," Robert said, peering closely at the ziplock. Kneeling, he caught those welts he put on Stanley's face and upper arms. No doubt about it. Stanley was his attacker, and Stanley was still alive.

Using a plastic picnic fork on the counter, Reyes pulled open the ziplock, took a closer look at the junk. "*Chiva, Roberto*, but not no Mexican brown shit."

"*¿No? ¿Es buena?*"

"*Sí, es prima.* Inside the refrigerator, *mira*," Reyes said, pointing.

Looking in at Stanley's wrapped hundreds, Robert counted them. Looked to him like twenty grand. Jack Pierce's blood money to Stanley.

Reyes reached for a stack of bills. Robert stopped him. "Don't touch it, *hermano*."

"C'mon, dude, *este pendejo* tried ending you."

"Can't do it, Reyes," he said, talking as he went over to Stanley's landline and called 911.

"Aw, man. Why not grab his stacks, let his spirit move on to a better place?"

"*No es posible.*"

"*¿Por qué?*"

Because I need bread crumbs, Robert was thinking.

Reyes's lowrider was parked a long city block away from Stanley's house. In the passenger seat, Robert was on his cell phone. On the other end, Erik was giving him his take on the situation from Stanley's kitchen.

"Talked to the Culver City narcotics," Erik was saying. "They didn't think Tifton was selling the real deal anymore. But they plan to hang out here, see who shows up to buy smack, who calls his landline."

"No cell phone?" Robert asked.

"If Stanley had one, we can't find it," Erik said.

Cops had seen Stanley's ziplock and cash and had drawn the natural conclusion: Stanley was a serious dealer who OD'd on his own product. Robert didn't quite buy it as he watched paramedics load Stanley into an ambulance with Erik not far behind.

"So, he's definitely still alive?" Robert asked.

Erik must have figured Robert was scoping him because he said, "Where you at, dickhead?"

"Up the road."

Erik spotted the lowrider. "With Reyes? You kidding, right?"

"From what I've seen, he'd make a fine police officer."

"Tell *Yacobson*, no, a *primo* detective," Reyes corrected.

"*Detective*? Fuck you both," Erik said, but Robert could see him laughing.

"What's next?" Robert asked.

"Docs'll jolt him with Narcan at the hospital. If he comes to, he'll be one miserable criminal, but he's our boy. You marked him good like you said, face and arms."

"And once he comes to, you'll what?"

"If he comes to and he feels like it, and if you two homeys don't feed me any more shit? He doesn't ask for a lawyer, I'll ask him who put him up to it. Any way you can help me with motive?"

Robert gave it some thought. "Safe to say, somebody out there hates my guts."

"Helpful," Erik said. "You sign that last report?"

"No, but I'll bring it by tomorrow."

"Family's splitting for SeaWorld, all of us, at twelve hundred hours, so don't slip up."

Not long after winding up that call, Reyes and Robert crossed Lincoln Boulevard, rumbling west from Culver City into Venice.

"*¿A dónde ahora, mi abogado?*"

"Brentwood," Robert said.

"Uh-uh, not in this ride, *chico*. You gonna be rollin' solo over in Brentwood . . ."

CHAPTER 44

A golf ball landed near Gia. It was a Titleist. She was cutting roses in her front yard's rose bed. Not far away, Jack was working on his short game. He walked over, leaned his gap wedge against one of her bushes.

"If I could secure you access to that alley, back of your house? We build a garage back there and your house value doubles overnight."

"How does that work?"

"Sue your neighbors on either side for access."

"For what?" she asked.

"Eating? Breathing?" he said.

He put his arms around her, held her from behind. "You all right? You haven't said much since the courthouse."

"Where did you go after that?" she asked.

"Had to see an old friend. He slipped up, started using again. I should dump him but we go back—so far back I can't pull the trigger."

"Oh," she said, kneeling to hand-spade the ground. When she made that move, he had to let her go.

Looking down at her: "Thought he was going to take a swing at me, didn't you?"

"Who?" she asked, making him work for it.

"In the courthouse. *Worth*. Beautiful, wasn't it?"

She said, "Guess that was pretty sweet."

"Hey, I get it. I can't expect you to get off on it like I do." He grabbed his wedge and went back to his practice balls.

"Just that I knew him day one," she said. "We were both in the trenches, working together."

"Hadn't looked at it that way," he said. "You two were kinda tight."

"Once you get to know him," she said, "he's an amazing guy. I'm not a lawyer or anything, but—"

"You could have been. You're a killer, baby."

She smiled but was spading the ground harder than was called for. "What I mean is, I thought he was the best lawyer in the firm." She waited till she saw his body stiffen. Saw him look up from his shot. "Besides you. But he's an interesting . . . no . . . what's the right word . . . an *amazing* guy once you get to know him."

"Heard you say that already. How so?" he asked.

"All I mean is, coming from up in the boonies, winding up in LA, killing it until everything got messed up. Well, you know."

"I *do* know," he laughed. "Don't take this the wrong way, but I'm beginning to think you two were more than friends." She didn't answer, so he asked, "What I mean is, did you have sex with the guy?"

She stood and approached him, fresh-cut roses gathered in her arms. He chipped a ball near his hat.

"Nice shot," she said. "You gonna win today?"

"C'mon, just tell me. You sleep with him or what?"

"We promised each other, didn't we? This time, no more games."

"That's our deal and that's why it's going to work."

"So, yes," she said, "I did. I slept with him one time at the Bel-Air. In Suite 207. I was so mad at you, knew how much you hated him. It was just to get back at you and I'm really sorry."

Jack didn't speak. Savoring her lie about Robert and moving closer to Jack, Gia asked, "We can get past it, though, can't we?"

He let his club fall to the ground, took her by the shoulders, and looked into her eyes. "After all my women you put up with? All those stupid, mindless times and you forgave me? I had that coming. Whatever you did, anything you did, I had it coming for a long time."

He started to hug her but her armful of roses let her say, "Ow. Don't."

She walked up the stairs onto her shaded front porch and set the roses in a bucket of water. In the shadows, he couldn't see the tears streaming down her cheeks. Tears from knowing one certain thing in this life: Jack Pierce would never forgive her for sleeping with Robert Worth—not if he cared one bit about her.

Sitting down on her stairs, she trimmed lower leaves from the stems and wiped her tears away. "We're a real good team, you and me," she told him.

"The best," he said, walking over. "We took them down, didn't we? All of them." He sat down and began to rub her feet.

"Sure did. Like with Leslie," she said.

"Leslie? How so?" he asked.

"Don't you remember?" she asked, pulling more roses from the bucket, trimming them.

"I remember everything. It's on me to remember everything, but I'm not sure what you mean saying, *Like with Leslie.*"

She said, "I was so sure she'd want a dollar share, but she went for keeping her job, keeping her benefits. Just like you said. She actually cried when I gave her my Healey."

"C'mon, I made a living reading juries. I met her that one time with you, but she was easy. Acts like a dim bulb but isn't, low self-esteem, she'd do anything in the world you asked her to do."

"And she did. *Just like you said.*" Repeating the phrase.

He stood up. "Tomorrow," he said, "once you get your share, promise me you'll pay off your mortgage."

"What about money? I mean, money for us to live on?"

"Look, my share of the settlement hurt, I'm not gonna lie, but I have a few irons in the fire, so don't worry about money. We're good. How about grilled lobster tonight? I'll stop by Santa Monica Seafood."

"Yum," she said.

"See you tonight, babe."

"Sure," she said. "Tonight."

She watched him walk down to the street, put his golf bag in the trunk of his rental car, and drive away. Once he did, she opened her left hand, squeezing a rose stem so tight that blood oozed through her fingers. She held that hand under her bucket's cold water, reached in her pocket with the other hand. She found her car key, chirped her Prius rental on the street. Then Gia stood up.

Everything about Leslie, she was thinking, *was just like Jack said.*

CHAPTER 45

Philip was wearing a kimono when Robert spotted him standing by his pool. Rocking heel to toe in Puma slaps, Philip was grooving to pool-speaker Sinatra, who was giving it up via "One for My Baby."

Robert had taken the side-yard walkway to the unlocked back gate. Philip didn't see him till Robert had already passed the pool house and was close by.

"Mr. Fanelli?"

"Robert," he said, "I'll be damned. I planned to call you next week but here you are."

Call me? "I need your help. I have no right to ask, I know that, but I'm asking anyway."

Robert hovered somewhere over angry and desperate. Philip pulled a remote from his kimono, pointed it at the pool house, and lowered Sinatra's voice.

"Had you called ahead, I might have invited you over. Since you didn't, go ahead and explain why you're trespassing."

"Because," Robert said, "I think Jack tried to have me killed."

"What? Are you sure?" Philip said, alarmed by the news.

"No, I'm not. But I know it. It doesn't make sense, though. Nothing makes sense to me."

"Have you talked to the police?"

"Yes and no," Robert said. "I can't talk to them about Jack's motives without—"

"Our nondisclose." Philip nodded. "Come to think of it, neither can I. Where do you stand?"

He didn't answer. Something caught his eye. He moved toward a large living room window looking over the backyard. Inside, over the fireplace, hung that California coastline landscape missing from the firm lobby.

"Looks good, doesn't it?" Philip asked, joining him.

"I thought you—"

"Sold it? You mean *had to sell it* to raise funds? Almost," Philip said. "Again, where do you stand?"

He told Philip about Stanley's assault, how he was hamstrung filing police reports, about Jack and Gia outside Judge Rosen's courtroom. "You weren't in court, so you must already know that Roxanne Paris reps the Brightwells. I'm sorry."

"Sorry that I lost the Brightwell business? After all my big talk about keeping it?"

Robert nodded.

"What's done is done, but I don't see how I can assist you."

"You told me Jack was destroyed. *Destroyed*, your exact word."

"I remember. I chose it carefully."

"He wasn't destroyed, not the least bit."

"I'm well aware of that. Then again, I let you down so dramatically."

"So, you lied about it?"

"It cost me nothing to tell you what you deserved to hear. To give you a free pound of Jack Pierce's flesh." Philip smiled. "Wine?"

"No," Robert said. He followed Philip to a wrought iron dining table. Philip poured a glass of merlot. "What happened? What really happened at the firm?" he asked.

"That's between me and the firm, isn't it?"

"I'm asking anyway," Robert said.

"Even though I'm free to discuss it with you, legally, I choose not to."

"I get it. I understand," he said, knowing he had that coming and more.

"Unless I secure proper clearance," Philip added.

Philip seemed to be talking in circles. "Clearance from . . ."

A splash in the pool. He turned. Someone was swimming an underwater lap.

"Need to talk to the boss about it," Philip said.

A woman stepped out of the shallow end. At first, Robert didn't recognize her in the gloom. Then Dorothy Brightwell smoothed back her hair, walked over to them in a sedate two-piece. Radiant, sober, trim, she looked happier than Robert could ever remember.

"What do you think, boss?" Philip asked her. "Should I talk to this impertinent gentleman?"

"Dorothy," Robert said.

"Robert," she replied.

He didn't know what to say next. Philip did. "He likes our painting, Dottie."

"I know, Philip. Robert once told me there's *something about it*. Looks more at home over here than at the firm, don't you think?" she asked Philip, holding his hand.

Philip told him that, years ago, he and Dorothy happened on the painting one weekend on a drive down the coast. Two friends taking a break. His wife dying a slow, painful death, and Oliver, her husband, working himself to death. That day, they stumbled on the landscape in a small Newport Beach gallery. Dorothy loved it. So did he and he bought it, hung it in his living room.

"That was the day I fell in love with her," he told Robert.

Day of Oliver's funeral, Robert recalled leaving Philip sitting in front of that very landscape. In his living room, where it was hanging now. A man lost in his cups that day, Philip saying the painting reminded him of *the most wonderful woman he'd ever met, the love of his life.* Because Philip's wife had died recently, Robert assumed he was carrying on about her. But he meant the woman beside him now.

And the two cypresses clinging to the bluff? In Philip's world—and later, hers—they represented Dorothy and him.

"After Jack swept me off my feet and married me," she said, "Philip moved our painting over to the firm. That way, I saw it whenever I dropped by. My Philip, letting me know, whenever I came to my senses, he would be there."

She took her sweetheart's other hand. Philip kissed hers, and they kept looking at each other, drinking each other in.

No, Robert was thinking. *They aren't lovers—they're in love. Good for them,* he thought, even as his own day caved in.

She told Philip, "Put your trunks on, dear. You're almost indecent in that skimpy thing."

"Pardon me, Robert, if you will. And tell him, Dottie, whatever you're comfortable telling him about your divorce. Not one syllable more."

As he walked toward the pool house, she swatted him on the ass. "Scoot along, Philip," she told him, and he did.

From out of the blue, she turned to him and said, "Ten million dollars, Robert."

"I'm sorry?" That was all he could think to say.

"I paid the firm's way out of your lawsuit."

He was thinking, *Why ten million, then? The firm only owed five million.*

Before he could ask, she said, "I felt responsible—I was responsible—for putting the firm in such a horrendous position. It wasn't Jack Pierce, attorney, who caused all the problems. It was Jack Pierce—*my husband*—who took the firm's reins, leveraged the Brightwell name, and poisoned the water for everyone."

He thought about it. She was right.

"On top of that, I paid Jack five million dollars to leave our so-called marriage."

His adrenaline ramped. "You paid *him* five million? But your pre-nup, he was . . . well, you know."

"What? Cheating? Serially? Such a gentleman. You remind me of Philip in that way."

"But you didn't have to pay him anything."

"Legally that's true, but he made it very clear—he would fight our prenup. Our trial would present a vivid, public spectacle of his affairs, of our marriage. And, I suppose, once he looked into it long enough, my own affair with Philip would come to light. I'm certain, as was Jack, that the public ordeal would've killed Father."

Now it all made more sense to Robert. Chase had not been called on to pay for Jack's mistake. That was why Chase was capable of sitting down to a civil lunch with Jack at the Sidewalk Cafe. And Dorothy's prenuptial agreement cutting Jack out? There are contracts people sign, and the people who have to live with them. The two didn't always match up.

"You had no idea I was here with Philip that night, did you?"

"The night . . . ," he started to ask.

Philip interrupted, rejoining them. "Our night at the Alibi Room."

The night in question. The night Alison called him. He recalled Philip telling him on the phone: *I have an out-of-town guest.* Then again, outside the Alibi: *I'm older, not dead.*

Dorothy told Robert, "That night, right in front of Father, Jack took a call in the limo and left for . . . for who knows where? And I did what I started doing when he hurt me."

"She came to me," Philip said, owning it.

Turned out, Philip didn't tell her about Alison Maxwell's allegations until Robert filed suit on her behalf. Then Philip asked Dorothy to lunch by the pool, handed her Robert's full-blown complaint, and left her alone to read it.

"And reading it, I could see my dear husband," she said, "captured in your vivid prose. It was as if . . . I hate clichés, but it's true . . . a fog lifted. And now? I'd pay twice that amount just to be rid of him."

Philip said, "Well, there it is, Robert. Patience rewarded. Are you clear?"

Very clear. His lawsuit freed Jack from his marriage. Jack didn't pay one dollar of the firm's liability. His wife did. And to any sane outsider, Robert Worth led Jack Pierce around his prenup, out of an unhappy marriage, and deposited $5 million into his personal account. Meaning that Jack had no objective motive to murder him. To the world, he was Jack Pierce's new best pal.

A few minutes later, Philip walked Robert to the back gate. Robert waved to Dorothy. She waved back, then dove into the pool again.

Philip asked him, "Tell me, why did I have no certified funds available at closing?"

"Well, the partners weren't actually paying, so they weren't giving you problems settling like you told me. That means you were waiting for Dorothy's funds to clear from somewhere else. Even wealthy as she is, she would never keep ten million wasting away in a bank account."

"Exactly right." Philip smiled, his opinion of his protégé vindicated again.

"Never get emotional about clients," Robert said. "That's what you always told me. What about you and Dorothy?"

"Good lawyers don't get emotional, but the best lawyers? Lawyers like us? We always get emotional about certain clients. And now, for some unknowable reason, she asked me to offer you a partnership in the firm. It would be very junior but a partnership nonetheless. I love her enough to yield, both to her and to my better angels."

"I sued you, sued your firm. Any way you ever trust me again?"

"Over time, perhaps, never like I did before. It's a onetime offer."

He thought about it. Thought about Alison, too, before he said, "What kind of partners can't trust each other?"

Philip nodded, understanding. "I believe you may have entered a dark forest. What must one always do, finding oneself in such a forbidding place?"

"Leave behind a trail of bread crumbs to find one's way out."

"A paper trail. And the case citation?"

"*Hansel and Gretel vs. The Evil Witch.*"

They started to shake hands. Philip hugged him instead. As Robert hugged him back, he felt their history sliding away, and it saddened him more than he thought possible. Philip's chest moved, and a choked sob escaped his mentor's mouth. Or maybe it was his own sob. He was never sure because the two men didn't look at each other after that.

CHAPTER 46

It was pushing four-thirty that afternoon by the time Robert made it back to the condo. On the way home, he called the same movers he'd used before, left a message to meet up with them tomorrow after he finished up at the bank.

He called Leslie from his car, too. His call went straight to voice mail, so he left her a message: "Leslie, it's Robert Worth. See you at 9:00 a.m. at the bank. Call me at this number to confirm right away. Thanks."

He grabbed a seat at the kitchen counter. Alison crossed his mind again. Hard for her not to with his phone vibrating every half hour or so. Her calling, her texting: Where are you? You OK? Groggy voice mails with the same message: *I miss you. Where are you?*

"Blah, blah, blah," he said and texted her back: Wouldn't let me visit your room. Tied up with police. Feel better! See you tomorrow.

That would hold her off. She'd come back here; he'd be gone. He'd get his old place back, or not, and she could stay here through the lease, or not. If he never saw her again, that would be fine.

Fuckin' Tattoo Girl, he was thinking.

Good thing he wasn't her lawyer anymore. The bank, her money, what to do with it—that was all up to her. Good thing, too, he'd been so clear at Shutters, getting her to sign off on his withdrawal from representing her. Even noting the time of day, getting cute with it, knowing he wouldn't have been so precise without sex on his mind.

Got lucky on that one, he thought. *Score one for the home team.*

Didn't matter now. Nothing either of them could say would make a difference. There was no real them and never had been. Not like Philip. That was the real deal, a man waiting years for the woman he loved. "Patience rewarded," Philip told him, and Robert knew why Philip missed out on Dorothy after Oliver died. Oliver was his friend and they'd started the firm together. Even though Philip was already in love with her, he felt obliged to wait a decent interval before making his feelings known.

One-of-a-kind gent, he was thinking. If he weren't careful, pretty soon he'd be blubbering over Cat Stevens's *"Father and Son."* Still, he wondered if he would ever wait it out for what he wanted most. He doubted it and guessed he took after his impulsive father that way.

The living room was trashed from Stanley and from the cops and their fingerprint dust. That prom photograph of Rosalind and him somehow wound up on the floor. He picked it up, set it on the kitchen counter, cracked a beer from the fridge. After sweeping print dust off the counter, he looked at the old photo.

"Well, Rosalind, what do you think? Lotsa crazy shit going on, huh?"

He kept looking at them standing on the front porch of the family home and remembered the live oak growing at an angle on the farm's steep hillside, angled so sharp into the hill that its lowest branch brushed the ground. They would walk out into it and sit there hidden for hours, eating Abba-Zaba candy bars, drinking Yoo-hoos, and shooting the breeze.

"I miss talking to you, Ros. Hope you're okay."

After that, he gave Erik a shout. Left him a message asking what Stanley had to say for himself, then decided to call the condo's owner about the break-in. That's what he was doing when he noticed fingerprint dust on top of his filing cabinet. Lots of dust. Even more of it around the lock cylinder on its top, right-hand side.

Moving closer, scratch marks were visible around the cylinder. *New scratch marks.* He started to reach behind the cabinet for its key, then remembered moving it the night before. Sliding his key ring from his pocket, he found the cabinet key. Then he noticed: the cabinet's key slot ran horizontal, not vertical. The cabinet was already unlocked. He'd relocked it, hadn't he? Definitely, he'd locked it.

He slid open the top drawer. Inside were his file folders of documents: Jack's prenup, Alison's original case file with the firm, her case file with him. Flipping through the folders, he saw that they all seemed to be in order. Why would Stanley go into his filing cabinet for Jack, anyway? He didn't get it—Jack was either Alison's lawyer or a defendant to her plaintiff. Every document here had already been at Jack's disposal.

The only other folder in the drawer was his bank folder. So he pulled it out, opened it on top of the cabinet. Once he did, he saw his bank receipt wasn't there. Neither was Alison's receipt.

The bank receipts' folder was empty.

He dumped all the top-drawer files on the floor. Looked inside the drawer bottom for their receipts—*nada*. Opened the drawer next below: pairs of his old sneakers, a couple of his dumbbells from the move. But no bank receipts. The bottom drawer. It was empty, too.

He had no concrete idea what this meant. Checking his watch, he had twenty-seven minutes till Leslie's bank closed. Ninety seconds later, he was speeding up Pacific Avenue toward Santa Monica, telling himself to obey all rules of the road. He needed to locate Leslie DeRider. Something was wrong again, and again, he didn't know what *something* was. He called Leslie's cell once more. Went straight to voice mail. He Siri-called 411, checking for her home-phone listing, and Siri came back with an unlisted number. That left the bank. So he called it and was put on hold. Not at all reassured by the recording, telling him how much his business was appreciated. Then: "Qualify for a new car loan. It's easy."

After jumping two four-way stops, blowing through three yellows, and averaging fifty-five in a thirty-five, he made the bank in under twenty-four minutes. He parked in a handicapped spot and was at the bank's front door in under thirty seconds.

But its front door was locked. Employees wandered around, doing whatever bankers do after hours. Planting his face against the window, he didn't see Leslie but spotted the manager on the floor. The one with the loud sports coat. Leslie had called him *Jerome*. He knuckled the plate glass till Jerome saw him. Kept knuckling till Jerome came over and mouthed, "Closed. We close at six."

"It's not six," he mouthed back. He showed him his iPhone. It read 6:01.

"It's 6:01," the manager said with a banker's helpless shrug.

"I was here two minutes ago," he yelled, banging the glass. "Before six o'clock. It's an emergency."

Employees were looking now. So were customers, still inside. Guess banks didn't like irate customers banging on their doors. Whatever the reason, Jerome keyed the door, peered through an open slice, and said, "We're closed, sir."

"Before you close the door, take this into account." Robert slipped him a business card and Jerome read it. "Jerome, right?'

"Jerome Hartung, yes?"

"My client and I deposited four and a half million dollars with your bank. I was here before 6:00 p.m. today. Maybe there's a problem, maybe not, but someone closed this door one minute early. Now, Jerome Hartung, are you gonna talk to me today about my problem or not?"

Jerome checked his watch, as if that somehow mattered, and swung open the door. "Let's talk in my office, Mr. Worth."

"Great idea," Robert said. "Thanks." They walked across the lobby toward Jerome's glass cubicle.

"Do you have your account number?" Jerome asked.

"No, I don't. I've been using counter checks."

Jerome nodded. "Debit card?" he asked.

"Not for another five, six days," Robert said.

"Driver's license?"

"Sure," he said, reaching for his wallet. It was there. So was his license. For some reason, being inside the bank took his headache down a notch.

"Think I might remember seeing you," Jerome said.

"Good," Robert told him, breathing easier. That didn't last long.

Jerome turned away from his computer screen a second time. Away from his array of family photographs and a row of carved Navajo fetishes.

"I'm sorry, Mr. Worth. Like I said, there's no—" Jerome started to say.

"That's not possible. Seriously. That is impossible."

"Believe me, it would show up in our system if you had such a large amount here. Any amount, for that matter. Other than your checking account, there's no . . . Would you like to see your checking-account balance?"

"No."

He stood, looked over at Leslie's desk for the fifth time. It was clean—her nameplate gone. His eyes closed. If he kept them open, he might throw his chair through this glass-walled office.

"Where is Leslie DeRider? She quit, get fired, what?"

"She took a sick day yesterday. Today was her last day, but . . ."

"She never showed," he said, keeping his eyes closed. "Did she?"

"Today was her last day and that's all I plan to say."

Leslie's repeated phone calls to Alison and him had been a nuisance, a running joke. But her calls stopped yesterday, and today his call went straight to her voice mail.

"I'm sorry," Jerome said. "There's nothing further I can do."

"I need to know where she lives."

"Are you serious?"

"Dead," Robert said, slamming the desk.

"I cannot possibly give out that information. To you or to anyone else, and that's that."

"Listen up, you're gonna give me her address before I leave here. Or you're going to drag her in here while I wait. Your call, take your pick."

"You expect me to believe *you* don't know her address?"

"I'm supposed to know her home address? What's wrong with you? I'm her customer."

"Oh, well," Jerome said.

"*Oh, well*, what?"

"I mean . . . that . . . I was under the impression you two were . . . you know."

"Me and . . ." He sprung to his feet, fists digging into the desk. "No, Jerome. I don't know. What are you trying to say?"

"Her boyfriend, her fiancé, whatever. She pointed you out to me—you and your sister."

"My sis—" Now he realized: Jerome was talking about Alison and him.

Jerome said, "Leslie asked if I wanted to meet her fiancé and his sister. But I was tied up right then."

Robert pictured Leslie standing inside Jerome's cubicle. Jerome waving at him. Leslie returning to her desk with their receipts: receipts initialed by her and supposedly initialed by Jerome.

"*Sorry that took so long,*" Leslie told Alison and him. "*Bank stuff.*"

Jerome told Robert, "We can clear all this up easily, if you'll come back tomorrow with your receipt."

Robert was thinking, *My receipt is gone. Stolen.* His stomach knotted. His nailed shoulder throbbed. His cell vibrated in his pocket—it had to be Alison again.

"You're telling me . . . you're saying when Leslie came into your office that day, that day I was sitting over there at her desk, that you did not initial two receipts for her?"

"Did I initial receipts for *four-plus million dollars*? Absolutely not. And I would never be too busy to meet customers making that size deposit. Ever."

He was telling the truth. Robert could see that. And he knew it because Jerome's words rang true.

Jerome asked, "Are you implying that a former bank officer may have engaged in some kind of impropriety?"

Impropriety? Robert took a seat, touched the floor with his fingertips, and exhaled. As he did, something dawned on him about Leslie and Jerome. Once he straightened up, he went with it.

"She knew, didn't she?"

"Knew that . . . ?" Jerome asked.

"She came in here to tell you about her fiancé and his sister. And she knew you wouldn't cross the lobby to meet us. Excuse me—to meet *her fiancé.* Leslie was sure of that, wasn't she?"

"What?" Jerome asked.

It's difficult to lie uttering a one-word question, but Jerome just pulled it off. Robert turned around a family photograph for Jerome to look at: Jerome with his wife, two kids, all of them trying to look casual.

"You two hooked up, didn't you? You and Leslie? But it was more than that for you, wasn't it?"

"Colleagues, nothing more." Jerome twisted his wedding band.

Robert knew he was right: they had hooked up and she was way out of his league. Odds were excellent they'd gone to her place—not to his wife's.

"Leslie," he said. "She live in a house or an apartment?"

Jerome pretended not to hear him. At the same time, he was looking over Robert's shoulder. In the glass facing him, Robert caught a security guard's reflected image.

"Let's hear it, man. House or apartment?"

Nodding to that guard now, Jerome asked Robert, "Will that be all, Mr. Worth?"

"Excuse me, Mr. Hartung?" Behind Robert, the security guard hand-grazed his weapon. "Everything all right in here, sir?"

"Mr. Worth." Jerome stood. "Glad to be of assistance."

Robert stood, too. Jerome knew Leslie's address but didn't have clue one about his money. Neither did Robert, who decided if he didn't move on right this second, he'd wind up Tased and hog-tied, back of a cop car.

When he got outside, a handicapped-parking ticket for $385 fluttered on his windshield. A new game plan was coming to him: follow Jerome to his home after he left work and make noise—real loud noise—about Leslie until Jerome coughed up her address.

He checked his vibrating phone. Six new texts showed up. None were from Alison.

All were from Gia, and all of them gave a Venice address on Garfield Avenue and said: Get over here.

Garfield. Over on the streets that real estate agents called President's Row. Maybe Gia had cooled down after their heated words at the courthouse. Maybe she would tell him how to find her banker friend.

CHAPTER 47

I ♥ Banking! That's how Leslie's T-shirt at Santa Anita Park read.

Didn't heart it that much, did you? Robert was thinking, fighting traffic back to Venice, his mind twitching.

Several things he was sure of now. Leslie played Jerome hard. She quit the bank and lied to Robert about it, never planning to show for tomorrow's meeting. Even so, $50,000 in real US dollars showed up in his and Alison's checking accounts. Another wrapped $20,000 had been in Stanley's refrigerator. A total of $70,000, hard cash. Robert's endorsed check was never deposited at Leslie's bank. Even so, Stanley Tifton had stolen Robert's receipt from the condo. That meant their receipts—the ones Leslie signed and forged Jerome's initials onto? Those receipts had to be forged, too: photoshopped at someone's house, office, wherever.

And what Robert *believed*: all this was engineered by Jack Pierce using Stanley Tifton and Leslie DeRider. Whatever scheme Jack was working, it went beyond Erik, beyond LAPD. This was federal. This would involve the FBI.

What exactly had happened and why, he still wondered as he pulled up to the Garfield address. Things he knew swirled around his mind, caroming off things he could only guess as he stepped through the open door of this run-down house into an empty living room. Nothing but trash bins and ready-for-kindling furniture.

Down a shotgun hall, he saw Gia on the patio and made his way out a rusted sliding door, into the backyard. Two stackable plastic chairs and a matching table overlooked the parched yard. A bottle of whiskey rested on the table alongside two filmy glasses. A handful of dead rose-bushes bristled in random, cracked clay pots.

"Not too big on answering texts, are you?" she said.

"Needed to see you anyway. I need to find Leslie."

"You did. This was her place. President Garfield. Assassinated, wasn't he?"

"Shot by a crazed gunman," he said, taking the other plastic chair. She poured herself a couple fingers of whiskey.

"You?" she asked. He was too messed up to answer. She poured him a jolt just in case. "Good light back here for roses, I told her," she said, looking at the cracked pots.

Still thinking, he didn't answer. Leslie never deposited his endorsed check at her bank. Their stolen receipts were forgeries—but their endorsed checks must have been deposited into a bank account. *Deposited into a bank account somewhere.*

"I need to find her, ASAP," he said.

"Tattoo Girl?" Gia asked.

"No, she's in the hospital," he answered.

"No, she isn't," Gia said.

"I need to find Leslie," he said. "Not Alison."

"Alison has one, too?"

"Hold up—Leslie has a tattoo?" he asked.

"*Tattoo Girl.* Leslie. At the courthouse, that's who you were talking about, right?"

"I saw Leslie at the Bel-Air pool," he said. "No way she had a tattoo."

Gia said, "She drove to the hotel from work. Bank policy: no visible tattoos. She used major cover-up whenever she wore a skirt. Like she did that day."

He pictured Leslie's bank attire, her skirt folded neatly on a pool chair. He downed that whiskey.

"Leslie's tattoo?" he asked. "Top of her calf?"

"Top of her right calf," Gia added.

He turned the whiskey bottle till its label faced him: O'Bannion Single Malt. Jack's brand.

"Found this bottle here?" he asked.

"In her kitchen cabinet," she said. "They split town together."

"Split town . . ."

He started wandering around the backyard. Jack, O'Bannion, Saddle Peak, and Tattoo Girl; Jack and Leslie and O'Bannion; Jack and Leslie and all his money. The pieces clicked into place.

"Which airline?" he asked Gia.

"They're not flying from LA."

"Burbank? Ontario? John Wayne?"

"No, they're driving. I followed him, watched him turn in his rental. Then she picked him up—even brought along a picnic basket—and they split in my Healey. I followed them till they took PCH north. That's all I needed to see."

"You don't understand. They hired someone to steal my receipt."

"So?"

He explained what he knew about his and Alison's endorsed checks. "I think Jack took the checks to the Caribbean, to South America or Asia. Somewhere offshore. After that, he deposited them into an account that he controls."

That made sense to Gia, too. Both of them knew Jack made his bones defending money launderers. To defend people accused of that crime, Jack understood how it worked and definitely came in contact with bankers who could make things happen.

"I don't get it. Why steal a fake receipt?"

He said, "If I have a fake receipt signed by a bank officer . . ."

"Like Leslie." She nodded.

"Even with a fake, her bank's obligated to pay up for its officer's fraud. A scam like that, for that kind of money, the Feds never stop looking for Leslie. *For Leslie and Jack.* Without my receipt as evidence and without Leslie, it's almost all on my say-so. I'll have real problems proving there was a crime. And the firm? Once its check clears, no way the firm pays twice."

"You and Alison, he hates. Me, he could take or leave."

He said, "You mean *Maxine Ellison*?"

"Who?"

"That's Alison's Tarzana alias. One of 'em, anyway. The little scammer's in Brotman overnight, faking another anxiety attack."

Gia said she was sorry about it. Then she took it back.

"A miracle I ever found out Alison's alias," he said. "Look, if I don't find Leslie and Jack, I could wind up doing time, losing my license."

"Oh," she said. "Taxes?"

"Yeah, federal and state income tax."

Taxes coming due for the million eight legal fee he earned on Alison's case.

"I told you," she said, "this was never about money for me."

"I know, but . . ."

She stood up. "Let's take mine to the IRS, fork it over, and see what they say?"

He couldn't believe what she was offering. "Ms. Marquez." He stood, too, and took her shoulders, looked in her eyes.

"Mr. Worth," she said, tearing up, "what Jack told me, he wanted out of his marriage, out of your lawsuit. To stick it on the firm, too, so it wasn't only him paying. That was the only way he could try for a few bucks from Dorothy on his prenup. I messed up everything, didn't I?"

"In love with the wrong guy," he said. Then he pulled her in and held her. "You're a sweetheart."

"So are you," she said, holding him, too.

He noticed blood on the tissue in her hand. Blood from her rose thorns.

"What's this?" he asked.

"A scratch. I can barely feel it now. But you?" she asked. "I still wonder who you are."

He didn't answer and he didn't want to let her go. But he did. "You know him better than anybody, and I gotta find him. If I don't . . ."

"You like seahorses?" she asked.

After that, she told him about the Seahorse Inn, that motel pictured in her framed postcard at home. Once she saw Jack and Leslie driving up PCH with a picnic basket, she knew exactly where they were headed.

"Name's cheesy, I know, but it was our place," she said. "Jack and Leslie, they'll stay north on PCH, have a picnic at Point Dume, same as we always did. My best guess, they finished eating an hour ago. After that, they'll stick to Highway 1 to Oxnard, then jump on the 101 all the way into Capitola."

He was already figuring his route: he'd take the I-5, cut the corner, take a chance speeding, and gain an hour on them.

She had more to tell him. "I'd always go in alone at the Seahorse. I'd pay cash, give fake license tags. Once we settled in, we'd act like we were normal. We weren't, but it's the closest to normal we ever were. Knotty-pine walls, no premium cable, busted remotes, no cell coverage or room phone. Ice machine working? That was sixty-forty. I mean, the best part of going was complaining how bad it was."

He knew places like it up and down the Central Coast. One day the ground lease runs out and developers tear it down. After that, everybody misses it.

She walked him to his car, watched him get inside. "Please don't go too radical up there. I know how you get sometimes."

"Like you told me before. 'In LA, you never know anybody.'"

She closed his door, leaned in, and asked, "Since when am I right about anything?"

※

After Robert burned away down Garfield, Gia went inside and found a sharp knife in the kitchen drawer. Her thoughts meandered until she saw herself stabbing the mattress in the bedroom where Jack and Leslie must have got it on.

Like radical therapy, she was thinking when the wall phone rang. She grabbed the receiver, held it to her ear, but she didn't speak.

"Babe?" Dougie said.

"Mmm-hmm," Gia said, pretending she was Leslie.

After *Babe,* Dougie said four more words and hung up.

※

"All aboard, Sunset Express," Dougie said, after powering off his cell phone at Union Station in downtown LA.

"It's another hour, sir, before we depart Los Angeles," the porter told him.

"Hey, man, I know, I ain't trippin'."

Dougie perched in the top level of the viewing car. He was early for the train's departure to New Orleans because Leslie warned him: "Don't screw anything up. If you do, I'll never speak to you again. Ever," she added.

"I won't. I swear," he told her.

Even so, she told him to wear a white T-shirt. Nothing memorable could appear on it. "No writing on it," she said. "Keep a low profile. I don't want anyone to remember you."

"Gimme a little credit, Les," he said.

"No, Dougie," she said. "Not any credit. Not until I see you again."

The viewing car's door opened. Two guys with cockney accents came in and sat across the aisle from him. Leaning over in his plain white T-shirt, he unzipped his travel bag on the floor. Bought on the boardwalk, his bag bore no words, only a logo he'd never seen before. Inside the bag, on top of his wetsuit, lay an iPhone and a roll of duct tape. He pulled both out and tore off two six-inch tape strips.

He powered on this phone. It had 99 percent of its battery life left. A few calls showed from that guy Robert Worth. He remembered Worth, the dude from Santa Anita. A few old calls from Gia showed up, too, and that was it.

"A babe," he said, meaning Gia.

Five minutes later, the porter left the car. Dougie stuck his tape strips to the iPhone and casually taped the phone under his seat.

"Red Devils, mate?"

One of the Brits across from him said it, pointing at Dougie's travel bag.

Seconals? Dougie wondered. *Red Devils* were their street name. Guy had to be a narc, but man, a couple red devils would take the edge off that long drive ahead of him.

"No, thanks, bro, I'm twelve years sober," Dougie told him, lying.

Between the two Brits, he heard: "Your logo, you bleedin' tosser. Football, ya knob. Talkin' about the Red Devils football team, ya daft cunt."

They were laughing and pointing at his bag like he had drugs inside instead of a wetsuit. So Dougie grabbed his knockoff Manchester Red Devils bag and booked on out of there like Leslie told him to do.

CHAPTER 48

Ninety miles north of LA, clouds scudded past a sullen moon as Robert hit the I-5 Grapevine downslope, rolling into the San Fernando Valley.

Headed for the Seahorse Inn, located a handful of miles south of Santa Cruz in Capitola. A sleepy mix of surfers and retirees when he was a kid, all bundled together on the cheap along the bluffs dominating town.

A bug splatted his windshield, jarred him back to I-5 reality. A gulp of Red Bull helped, and he wasn't surprised his mind revisited Alison. Returned to that scar on her calf. Must've been from an actual exhaust-pipe burn from her brother's bike, after all. So what if she told the truth about one thing? That she wasn't *the* Tattoo Girl? She was poison from the get-go.

Another slug of Bull. He could picture her, all alone in her small apartment. Brian's handcuffs around both her wrists, tugging against them. Sobbing into her phone so he would drive over.

She would have hung up, removed the cuffs, something like that. However she went about it, she knew her bruises were visible before she risked calling him. And there she was in his mind now: scattering her books, toppling her furniture, one finger closing a nostril, breathing deep, exhaling. Getting ready for her big show.

Kundalini yoga time, Robert remembered, draining that Bull.

Later, the San Fernando Valley haze obscured the stars over the state's stale breadbasket. Up ahead lay Corcoran Prison. The thought of being cellies with Charles Manson was too much, so he pictured the firm party instead: Jack in the Brightwell study after he'd backed Jack into an alibi corner: *Then where were you that night? Prove to me you weren't in Culver City and this whole thing goes away.*

Yeah, where were you, Jack? he thought. *If you weren't assaulting Yoga Girl, where were you?*

He switched on his wipers, pressed his cleaner button. It was out of fluid, and his worn blades smeared dead-insect film across his view. His thoughts jumped to Jack and his pal Stanley, breaking in his condo—was that only this morning?

What was it Jack told him at the courthouse while Stanley was doing his thing? *Remember this, Worth, as you count the endless hours of your new life dragging by.*

Endless hours . . . dragging by . . . new life? If Stanley had been waiting to kill him, Jack's words made no sense. He would be dead—not counting hours or anything else. Could be Stanley broke in for the receipts and nothing more. To steal them for Jack and to punish Alison and him for crossing Jack in the first place. That way, Jack takes a couple pounds of their flesh before he splits town with their money. And that way, Robert could spend the next slab of his *new life* fighting the IRS, losing his law license, going to prison, too, if Jack had his way.

He thought about Alison's revolver, loaded, in the tire well. About Jack messing with his life on a whim, and he hated what Jack had done to him.

A guy like him, he was thinking. *A girl like Gia, screwing up her life for him.*

Gia. That night in the firm's garage. Freshly fired by the man she loved, still she worried whether Robert would make partner. Even threw him a piece of advice: *Always let him win.* And after he drove her home from Santa Anita, she tried to help again: *Do yourself a favor. Try to put this behind you . . . Jack makes people crazy.*

"You think?" he said, crushing the empty Bull can.

She'd done bad things—he knew that—but in the end, she wound up with $500,000 that was actually paid by Dorothy, a billionaire's daughter. And she fascinated him, not only because she was so cool and funny and beautiful. There was something decent about her. Something he'd always liked and still did. Nobody but Gia would ask him to use her money to help him with the IRS.

Who says that in LA and means it? he wondered.

Up ahead on the I-5: the turnoff to CA 152. As he exited, Erik called him back and brought him up to speed: "Stanley came to, but he's not helping you out. Claims your marks on his face and arms is an allergy and says he gets it every year about this time."

"Jesus," was all Robert could think to say.

"Imagination like that, Stan should be writing movies," Erik said.

For the time being, Robert decided to keep quiet about Stanley's theft-only motive. Let Venice police keep murder pressure on him. That was magnitudes stronger than burglary-gone-bad-and-I-panicked pressure.

Screw Stanley, Robert decided. *Let him make his own case.*

And right then, something clicked inside his tired, Bull-ramped head, and Robert asked his friend to write up a new report: "There's a two-by-four, back of a construction site on Quarterdeck, north side of the street. Stanley tried taking my head off with it. Might be wrong, but I think there was wet paint on it."

"What color?"

"Green, I think."

"Like a Forest Green?" Erik said, messing with him.

Erik told him he would check the site for Stanley's fingerprints, and Robert decided to introduce Erik's new police report to his missing banker: "A woman named Leslie DeRider used to work for a bank in

Santa Monica. She quit her job today. I was told *today* by an eyewitness that she's on the road in an Austin-Healey with a man named Jack Pierce."

"Pierce," Erik said.

"Right, and it's possible they will try to leave the country. If they do that, I will be harmed financially. Harmed irreparably."

"Hold on. That one *p* or two?"

"One *p*, three *r*'s," he said. "So I'm going to try to talk to them, to stop them, before they can do that to me."

"Stop them how?"

"Stop them with any legal means at my disposal," he replied.

"Look, I'll write it up. I don't know what you're up to, but you gotta come by and sign these last two reports."

"Or they're no good," Robert finished for him. He didn't want to get blasted for taking his Capitola road trip. "Can't come in right now."

"Look, my kids gotta see Shamu before he's canceled or it's my ass. I'm leaving for SeaWorld tomorrow come hell or—"

"I'll try," was how Robert ended it. That left Erik to check for Stanley's paint prints and to give Robert's regards to the world's most famous killer whale.

CHAPTER 49

"You're her sister?" the Brotman's floor nurse asked, looking at Gia's features.

"Half sister," Gia said.

She stood at the nurses' station on the sixth floor, saying she was in town on business from Vancouver, heard Alison was in the hospital.

"Room 665," the nurse told her. "She's the sweetest girl, no trouble at all."

"Too sweet sometimes," Gia said.

"Don't upset her, all right?"

"Last thing anybody wants," Gia said.

When Gia reached Alison's door, she knocked. Waited till she heard, "*Robert? That you?*" She smiled and then walked in the room.

Alison lay in bed, her meds and a glucose IV marching into her arm.

Gia strolled over to the window and looked out. A good ten seconds passed before Alison said, "Who let you in, skank?" Dope slurry and anger cruised her voice.

"I don't mind women sticking together," Gia said, "but I've got to draw the line somewhere."

"Lost? STD unit? Check the directory," Alison said. She reached for her controls and rang the nurses' station. They both heard faint ringing down the hall.

Gia looked at her now. "Mr. Worth's not coming. Can you blame him?"

A nurse's voice said, "Yes, Alison?"

"Not using *Maxine Ellison* tonight?" Gia asked Alison.

Even doped up, hearing her alias caught Alison by surprise.

"Hello?" the nurse's voice said.

"Would it be too much trouble to get some cracked ice?" Alison asked, eyeing Gia now.

"Of course not," the nurse said. "It'll take a few minutes. How do you like your surprise?"

"You're the best, Lupe," she replied, clicking off the nurse.

"Like I said, he's not coming," Gia told her. "Hard to blame him, once he knew for sure you fucked Jack."

Her hard words hung there while Alison sized Gia up.

"Think you can play at my level?" Alison asked.

Gia didn't answer yet. She checked out this hard-core girl who'd revealed part of her real self. Gia took a chair by the bed. "Think so. You made tons of mistakes."

"Think I screwed Pierce? Tell me how that works?"

"Let's see. Oh, yeah. He was with me the night you claim he was assaulting you at your place. At the exact time you said, plus a few hours after that."

"Doesn't mean I fucked him," Alison said. "She said, she said, right?"

"To the rest of the world, sure, but between us? I always knew you were a liar. Day one, I never trusted you."

"I can live with your trust issues, but much as I'd like to, I can't talk about the case. That nondisclosure agreement, so sorry."

"You forget? I'm a party, too, so we can chat up a storm about the case."

A direct hit. Alison lowered her mask even more. "Couldn't help yourself, could you?" she asked. "You couldn't wait to tell Robert your theory about me and Jack."

"Guy that smart, he didn't need me to tell him. Mr. Worth has had you figured out for a long, long time." Lying for Robert seemed to Gia like the honest thing to do.

"Think he minded when he went down on me last night? Or was it this morning?" Alison asked.

Gia didn't take the bait. "Is he into amyl nitrites, too? Or is that just Jack?"

"With me, Robert never needed anything extra."

"Something I keep asking myself—something you knew about Jack—sure you don't mind?"

"Take a shot," Alison said.

Gia stood up. "How does a client know that Jack Pierce—her lawyer that she never had sex with—how does that client know Jack pops amyls during sex?"

Alison didn't answer. Because there was no plausible answer.

"See," Gia said, "you're right about the amyls. I know from personal experience, so I know you had sex with him at least once. Otherwise, a client doesn't ever guess that. Or risk being wrong about such a rare kink. One detail too many, hotshot."

She must've nailed it because Alison sat up on the other side of the bed and checked her phone for texts.

Gia said, "Knowing Jack, I'm guessing you two had a deal and he switched gears on you."

"One time, straight sex," Alison said, dropping her front. "So he'd try my brother's case. Then it was again and again, then complaining about his time on the case, and then he wanted a three-way, and I saw how it was really gonna go."

"Coulda saved you the trouble. It never ends with that guy."

"With either of them," Alison said.

"Who, Mr. Worth?"

Alison nodded. "He's obsessed with beating Pierce, has dead-sister issues, too. Kept lots of her pictures around his old place, and for a farm boy? God knows what that's all about."

"The girl in the prom dress? Rosalind?" Gia asked.

"Yeah. Got raped, OD'd, killed herself." Alison shrugged, yawning.

Gia went back to that north-facing window. Somewhere up there, Robert was racing toward Capitola. *Fuckin' guy,* she was thinking, missing him already. Then she asked Alison, "You ever wonder about your lawyer's angle?"

"Him, an angle? Straight shooters don't have angles, but I banked two-point-seven million that's saying I don't care."

Gia walked around the bed to face Alison. To take a long look into the other woman's eyes. Nothing good was lurking behind them, Gia decided.

"On your two-point-seven million, *Maxine?* When you show up at the bank, all scrubbed up and excited tomorrow, you better hope the bank never needs to look into your background. With your alias, *Maxine*, and God knows how many more, they might figure you for a con artist on that two-point-seven. They might not believe a word that comes out of your mouth, *Maxine*, about that money."

Alison shrugged off Gia's commentary. "Bank's not looking at me, skank. It's my money."

"You say so," Gia said.

Gia took a last look at the patient. "And you're all wrong about Mr. Worth. He's a sure thing. The only sure thing I ever met."

As Gia was leaving, that floor nurse carried in a glass of cracked ice on a tray. She heard the nurse saying, "You shouldn't be up, Alison."

And Alison telling her, "Fuck off, Lupe!"

CHAPTER 50

Oncoming headlights flashed across Leslie's tattooed calf.

"Always liked your tat. You didn't overdo it like most girls," Jack told her.

"Thanks, baby," she said.

The Healey rolled past a road sign in the dark: **Aptos, CA Pop. 25,708**. Top was up, Jack behind the wheel. In a short skirt, Leslie had her back against her door, her feet resting in his lap.

Since leaving Point Dume four hours ago, they made good time. After the picnic, they burned those stolen receipts in a champagne flute and watched them float away.

"We did it. We're free," she told him back on the beach.

"Finally," he said.

"It's unbelievable," she'd said. "Fuck the world, Jack. Nobody knows where we are, where we're going."

"You're right," he said. "We're amazing. We pulled it off."

Not far up the road from Point Dume, she'd suggested using her burner phone to call Stanley's landline.

"Just to see if Stanley answers," she told Jack.

"Bad idea," he'd said.

He explained that either Stanley was dead, dying, or hadn't taken the bait. That Stanley could be as pissed off as much as he wanted about the heroin in his mailbox but couldn't mention his suspicions without implicating himself.

"For Stanley, dropping a dime on me means him doing time, and believe me, he fears jail. Fears it more than dying."

"C'mon, baby, my phone's a throwaway," she said.

"What do we know about throwaways?" he asked. "The Feds ever start looking for you, who knows how deep they dig? So why risk it? I don't know what I'd do if you got in trouble."

Since day one, she had always taken his advice on risk. Sure, both of them had taken risks, but they'd been calculated ones: her keeping Jerome in his office, away from Robert—*her fiancé*—and Alison; Jack waiting for her at the airport to fly two endorsed checks out of the States, to deposit them with those Antigua bankers before rerouting the funds to Asia; and her delivering heroin to Stanley's house in that UPS getup.

But Stanley had lingered in her thoughts. Earlier, she'd asked Jack, "Best guess, you think Stanley's toast or what?"

"Dead. He's been clean so long, he'll OD. He's never run smack that pure in his life."

"Dougie scored for us big-time, huh?"

"For once," he said.

She laughed. "I know. He was born to fuck up."

Dougie had scored that junk in Stanley's mailbox from an addict he knew from beach volleyball: a walking-around addict who lived on one of the Venice canals. In Suite 207 one afternoon, she and Jack had boxed up the junk in a jewelry box with slick, white wrapping paper.

"Think Dougie finds a way to mess up?" he asked.

"Fifty-fifty," she said.

They'd already decided it was okay if Dougie dropped the ball leaving her cell phone on the train. So what? It was a last-minute touch, anyway: Leslie's phone pinging on the eastbound Sunset Express till its battery died. A bogus signal for anyone who might be looking for her. Or looking for them. They figured her phone would die somewhere in New Mexico.

Now the Healey rolled out of Aptos. Another road sign ahead: **CAPITOLA, CA.**

"Shit, Capitola," she said, looking at Google Maps.

"Almost there," he told her. "Grab my briefcase."

She leaned over and massaged his crotch. "This one?"

"No, the other one." He smiled.

She pulled his briefcase from the small storage space in back. "We could've burned Gia," she said. "Would've been easier for me than burning those other two."

"Too many ties to me, angel. I lived with the woman."

"For a week is all."

"One day is too long. Neighbors probably saw me, and you never know who Gia talked to about me."

"She never talked about you. Long as I knew her, not once. It was unbelievable."

"I'd still be the live-in guy," he said. "The dude."

"Worse, the live-in lawyer dude." She smiled. "I think you still dig her."

"You're the one, Les. Want me to prove it again?"

"Anytime you want, baby."

"Then open my briefcase, grab a pen, and write down the password."

"I memorized it already. It's in your wallet, too, right?"

"Not anymore. Now, it's only in my head."

"What if you fucked my brains out," she said, "and I couldn't remember anyway? Or we fucked each other to death?"

Both of them laughing.

"Humor me, would you? Write it down and show it to me," he said.

She tore off a sheet of legal paper from a pad. She wrote a long series of characters and numbers. She showed him the result.

"Bravo," he told her. "Again."

"Why? It's easy, *it's you*," she said, writing while she talked. "After I check us in, I want to do it like you did it with her. Only better. Everything better than her."

"Gia was never up for the ocean at night. Afraid of it. Think you can cut it? Water's three, four degrees colder up here. I mean, if you're not up for it?"

"Let's see who can cut it in the morning, *Ironman*."

She was talking about the plan they'd made, the other reason she'd packed their long-sleeve wetsuit vests. Tonight, they'd hit the ocean down below the motel, and at sunup, they'd walk into that break north of Santa Cruz, the one called Four Mile. After, they'd leave behind their wetsuits like they walked into the ocean together.

"There it is," he told her.

Ahead of them pulsed half the letters of a neon sign: SEAHORSE INN. Sixteen run-down, board-and-batten cabins. The cabin's back walls faced the road and fronted the ocean. A convenience store glowed across the street. A banner out front: SILVER BULLETS ON SALE!

Pulling to the shoulder, well away from the office, he cut the lights and engine.

"Down and dirty, I love it," she said, kneeling in her seat, staring back at the cabins.

"Thought you would," he said. "Everything I promised and less."

"No, seriously, I love it." She wadded up her scrap paper, tossed it back in his briefcase, and opened her door.

Undoing her scrap paper, Jack double-checked Leslie's password work, then closed his briefcase. Now he watched her moving into the parking lot. Her tattoo, he wasn't kidding about liking it. Three simple symbols starting with $. Next was the British pound sign: an *L* with a single hatch mark on the stem. Last, a *Y* with a double-hatch-marked base: symbol for the Chinese *yuan*.

"It's money, baby," she liked telling him, using that line from the old *Swingers* movie.

As Leslie neared the inn's office, Jack's thoughts drifted to Worth. To tomorrow morning when Worth showed up at the bank for his nine o'clock and found out his banker was MIA. Looking around for his receipts after that—*oh, no!* Worth might never know exactly how he got blindsided.

Checking the inn's office again, he saw a heavyset female guest walking out. Past her, Leslie was inside, talking to one of those Paki owners. He recalled that in all the times he'd stayed here with Gia, he'd never once spoken to them.

He rested his head on the steering wheel, mulling over one of the things Stanley had reported to him a week ago. Leslie had been hanging with Dougie outside the Brig on the sidewalk. Reporting on it, Stanley had joked around about Dougie: "The whole world loves a junkie, right, Jackie Boy?"

"Right you are, Stanley," he'd answered.

Dougie being Leslie's first love, Jack got it that they still hung out. Still, he wondered why she'd lied to him about still seeing the guy. Even told him a week ago she was *done with his skinny, loser ass forever*. Lying to him twice about that waste of breath, Dougie? Go figure.

She was coming back across the parking lot, holding their room key over her head, skipping as she came. He gave her a thumbs-up and smiled.

Right before she opened the passenger-side door, he whispered: "You little heartbreaker."

CHAPTER 51

Two hours later in Capitola, Robert parked on the shoulder past that convenience store running the Silver Bullet special. He got out of his car, opened the rear door, and pulled the revolver from his tire well. Slipping it in his waist, he crossed the road to the Seahorse Inn. With his head down, he strolled past the office. A low-watt hula-dancer lamp burned inside, the check-in counter deserted.

Farther along the driveway, he saw **NOTICE OF DEMOLITION** posted on a cabin wall. Made sense. Nobody wanted to drop any coin keeping the place up. Why bother at this point?

In the middle of the sixteen cabins, a wooden arch framed the drive-through. An ice machine sat inside the arch with a handwritten sign: **OUT OF ORDER. GO ACROSS STREET FOR ICE.** The soft-drink machine was unplugged and unlit, same as the snack machine.

Ahead of him, the driveway split left and right, eight cabins on each side, and it was easy to spot the Healey. Only one car was parked on the right-hand side. The Healey. In front of the last cabin.

He tried placing a call and picked up zero bars, like Gia'd said.

Moving toward the parked car, thirty or forty yards away, he came to the last cabin. Edged past its peeling paint and rotting wooden porch, keeping low to sneak a look inside the large front window. The only light inside, a bedside lamp. A second quick look, he didn't see them, and a longer look revealed an open bathroom door. The small cabin was unoccupied.

Heading back the way he came, he walked out to the cliff onto a ten-by-ten-foot deck at the top of the beach stairs. A white towel was draped over the wood railing. A rusted sign at the stair top: SHOWER GUEST ONLY. DANGEROUS WATER. NO SWIMMING. STRONG CURRENT.

As he looked down at the hundred rickety, switchback stairs, he caught movement beyond the surf line: two adults swimming. Wearing wetsuits it appeared from here, and not far beyond them loomed a heavy fog bank.

Reaching for his gun, he started down the stairs, then he stopped and decided the smart move was the cabin. Once he ran back over to its front porch, he tried the front door. It was locked. Around the right side of the cabin, he found an unlocked bathroom window. Unlocked because there was no lock in the rotting frame. He forced the warped wooden window up, grabbed hold of the sill, and squeezed his body through.

After he rolled onto the bathroom floor, he stood and looked around. A shaving kit lay on the edge of the sink. Inside it: a pair of handcuffs and four amyl-nitrite ampules. He headed into the bedroom.

As he did, he missed a light flickering on in the next-to-last cabin. The shadow of that cabin's occupant appeared at its window behind him.

Inside the main room of the cabin. Gia's description was on the money again: knotty pine, a cheap seahorse painting, an old-school TV set, and no landline. A small wooden table and two low-slung chairs over by the ocean-facing window. A double bed, rumpled, car keys on a bedside table. That was pretty much it.

After he snagged the Healey's keys, he hurried to the open closet. Patted Jack's jacket and trousers and found nothing of interest. Did the same with Leslie's hanging clothes and came up empty again. Then he spotted Jack's briefcase under the bed. He knelt, slid it out, and tried to open it. It was locked.

Craning his neck, he could make out the top of the beach stairs through that big front window. Still no sign of the swimmers. After banging and banging the butt of the handgun against the lock, he saw it finally giving way. With both hands, he muscled it open and laid it on the bed.

First thing he saw inside: their passports. He pocketed both. That would slow them down, no matter what.

Then a travel guide: *Fodor's Southeast Asia*, and slipped inside its pages, a Singapore Airlines ticket folder. In the folder, a boarding pass for tomorrow: 1:12 p.m. A nonstop flight out of San Francisco International to Hong Kong.

Last thing he found was another, thicker folder: *Bank of Hong Kong*. A custom, rectangular aluminum case was slotted inside the cover's sleeve. Sliding open the custom case, he found a flash drive. Seeing it, he felt a much-needed jolt of adrenaline and slipped the drive into his shirt pocket.

That was it. Except for two wads of paper in the briefcase's corner.

He glanced out the window. That fog bank had made its way onshore. Top of the beach stairs was barely visible and the lovebirds nowhere in sight.

Once he undid the wadded-up paper, he saw *L@L@9181 51413114L@L@*. Staring at the handwritten numbers, he remembered the pocketed flash drive. Knew that he had it made. For the next thirty seconds, the series of capital letters, symbols, and numbers had his full attention. So much so, he didn't notice that Jack had bounded to the top of those stairs, taking a breather on that wooden deck.

Robert glanced up from what he was doing. Happened to catch movement through the front window. Saw that Jack was looking back down the stairs.

Quickly, Robert slid the briefcase back under the bed and dropped to the floor. Slotted himself into a space between the bed and the wall farthest from the door. Face to the floor, he cocked the loaded gun. And he waited. His heart slammed against the frayed sea-foam-colored carpet, slammed blood hard into his neck, his bruised ribs, his punctured shoulder, all the way into his fingertips, and his head felt light.

Five . . . ten . . . fifteen seconds later, the cabin door opened. Once he heard it close, Robert sprang from his position without a word, his gun pointed at Jack's chest.

"Jesus Christ."

That's all Jack said as he fell back against the door. Robert stood twelve feet away from him, that revolver leveled.

"Sit down," Robert told him.

He didn't move. Robert knew that to Jack Pierce, Robert Worth finding him and standing in this small Capitola motel room was a physical impossibility. Robert headed toward him in the small area, knowing anything could happen in a tight space like this. Jack, still wet, probably cold and stiff, too, looked like he wasn't planning to comply. Robert knew he had to seize control.

"Where is she?"

Robert closed on him, gun outstretched, glancing out the window. The fog had rolled in fast. Was that her, outside in the gloom? No—it was that white beach towel on the rail.

"She's across the road, getting ice, drinks. Why don't you and me talk about—"

That's all he got out of his mouth. Robert tossed the gun on the bed. Moving fast, first thing he did was to strike Jack's chin with a hard-swung left-elbow shot. Before Jack went down, Robert dug a right uppercut into his solar plexus, hard as he could.

Like Luis always told him at the farm: "Guy doesn't fold after that, *Roberto*, better run."

But Jack did fold and gagged, too, and Robert shoved him down into the closest chair, grabbed that revolver off the bed. That's when his system decided to let his wounds hurt. His shoulder, his head, his ribs, and they hurt a lot.

"You saw me at the courthouse," Jack said. "Important friends, I got 'em all over town, Worth. Judges in my pocket. Whatever you got, I'll beat it."

"Can you beat Stanley's alive?

"Stanley's . . ."

"*Stanley Tifton.* Alive and talking to the police—and all he's talking about is *you.*"

He was lying, sure. Stanley hadn't broken, far as Robert knew, but he liked the expression that news put on Jack's face. Then he asked, "Wonder how long Leslie keeps quiet about you, once she's facing serious time back in LA?"

"Long as I say—we love each other. Your receipts are in the wind, Worth. Let's work something out now or we'll never tell you where the money is."

"Bank of Hong Kong sound right?" Robert asked.

Jack sagged farther into the chair, his face in his hands.

"Let her go. Let her come back, find me gone. I talked her into it, all of it. She doesn't deserve prison."

"Yeah," Robert said, "she does."

He didn't want to wind up in this room, not with these two. Not unless he wanted to start blazing, and he didn't want that. And Leslie? If she came back, saw them, and took off? So what? Better, even. Keys to the Healey were in his pocket, so let her run. Girl in a wetsuit who looked like that, local cops would find her sooner than later.

So he opened the front door. Grabbed the front of Jack's neoprene wetsuit, jerked him to his feet, and shoved him outside. Going over that bank-account password in his head till it was locked in. That and keeping an eye on Jack in the rolling fog as it slowly swallowed up both of them.

336

In the Seahorse Inn office, a corn-fed white woman in curlers pounded the counter bell, and that hula-dancer lamp shimmied from the vibration. "Hey. Back there. Yeah, you!" she was yelling.

The motel owner padded out, rubbing sleep from his eyes. Pakistani, he looked about sixty and wore an eye patch over his right eye.

"What is it? What is wrong?" he asked her.

"Somebody just broke into Cabin 8!" Curlers screamed.

The owner didn't need to check the register. "Mrs. Jones's cabin? You are sure of this?"

"They climbed in the bathroom window, got it?"

"Maybe lock self out, happen sometimes," he said.

Through the fog, a Santa Cruz County cruiser pulled into that convenience store.

"It was a man breaking in. Not a woman, a man!"

The owner came around the counter. "A man, okay, I hear, I hear."

But she wasn't done with him. "Know how many times my bus stopped getting here?"

"No care about you bus."

"Many times, Long John!" she screamed. "Coulda stayed in Modesto I wanted crap like this."

"I hear," he said again as he opened the door and hurried toward that cruiser.

Infused, misted air muffled the swelling surf below the cliff. Gun drawn, Robert followed Jack across the bluff, almost even with those wooden beach stairs.

"You don't know our password, Worth. Let's put our heads together and work it out."

Robert's eyes darted ahead, scanning for Leslie in case she showed up out of nowhere.

"How about I give up half?" Jack asked. "That's almost five million headed your way. We cut out your client and I guarantee you, Leslie goes along."

Five million? Jack was including Dorothy's payment to him.

Maybe it was hearing that big number or the fog or this being the longest day of his life. Whatever the reason, he never saw Jack's free hand work that knife from his right wetsuit sleeve.

He was about to tell Jack he was wrong—that he *did* know the account's password, *L@L@* and all the rest, when Jack ducked low and quick and whirled his knife arm around in an arc. The blade sunk deep into Robert's right thigh, and he screamed in pain. Almost dropped the gun as Jack sprung at him and hit him chest high, driving him back till they broke through the railing, top of the stairs. Together, they started rolling, tumbling down them as the revolver clattered ahead and randomly thumped onto a sandy ledge.

Jack recovered from their crash landing first and dove off the stairs for the gun. Robert leaped up and over the rail and landed on Jack's back, the two of them struggling for the revolver on that sandy two-man slot. As Robert tried to choke him out from behind, Jack's hand inched for the gun. Almost there. About to reach it when Robert gave up his hold, lunging for it, too. It skittered away from their hands, tumbling away into darkness.

Robert rolled him over, smashed his face once, enraged, then again. "Gonna kill you, motherfucker!" he screamed.

Jack reached down and ripped the knife out of Robert's leg. When he did, a flash of light creased the inside of Robert's head. He sagged, nearly passed out. Jack used that synapse to jump on top, the knife poised for a downward kill thrust.

Robert grabbed Jack's wrist with both hands. Jack bore down, the knifepoint inching toward Robert's throat. That knife, touching skin now, drawing blood.

"You took my life . . . everything I worked for . . ." Jack's voice was hoarse, whispered rage.

About to die, Robert found one last surge of strength. All at once, he kneed Jack in the groin, bucked his own body as hard as he could, and twisted Jack's wrist.

The upward force of his body bounced Jack off him. Losing his grip on Robert, he started sliding over that ledge. Desperate for a handhold, he grabbed Robert's shirtfront.

"You, too . . . ," he whispered.

Robert tried to pull away, his shirt ripping. Digging his knees into the sand, his palm heels, too, but there was little to no traction in the sand. Jack's weight pulled him over the side, and they slid over the edge. Falling and twisting together, thirty more feet through the air until they splashed into a shallow tidal pool.

At its deepest, the pool was two feet deep. Impossible to tell which man wound up on top. Not until Robert's body rolled off Jack's. He splashed onto his back, rolled over. Hacking saltwater on all fours, Robert made it onto the sandbar.

It was just then that he realized he didn't know his own name. That he'd been knocked out. For how long, he had no idea. A few seconds later, his name came to him . . . *Robert . . . Worth.* Then *Logan*, his middle name. Then his situation emerged, his problems in LA, and the ID of the man lying beside him.

Best he could, he cleared his head, rose to his knees, and studied Jack in the tidal pool. His face rested beneath one inch of saltwater. Enough light down here so Robert could see Jack's open eyes. Looked like they were pleading with him as air bubbles trickled from his mouth and cleared the saltwater's surface.

He stared at the helpless man, bitter. "Go ahead and die, you miserable prick."

No way in the world Robert would lift a finger to save him. He felt the two passports in his pocket. The flash drive, too. That wadded-up piece of password paper from the briefcase, though—it was gone. So was the memorized password to the Hong Kong account. He could not recall it.

Before he could grapple with recollecting that series of letters, symbols, and numbers, movement tickled the corner of his eye. Something moving down the beach stairs. He looked up in time to see a uniformed cop headed down them.

Jack's air bubbles slowed to single file. Robert had no choice. Reaching down, he lifted Jack's limp body from the water, lay him on the sand beside him.

"Hey," he shouted to the cop. "Help. Down here!"

Up on the stairs, the cop drew his pistol and shouted: "Hands in the air. Don't move."

"Down here!" Robert screamed. "I think he's still alive."

Rising, hands raised, he turned toward the cop. As he moved closer to Robert, his silver name tag ID'd him as SEDGWICK, J.

As he approached, Robert saw a faint black flicker at waterline. A wetsuit shimmered. Leslie DeRider was wearing it. The incoming tide rolled her dead body onto the sand, and even from here, Robert could see her throat gaping open from a deep-slicing knife wound.

CHAPTER 52

"Ready when you are, Worth?" Detective DeGrasso asked Robert.

He wasn't on the dark beach anymore. He was handcuffed to a metal chair on Water Street in downtown Santa Cruz. DeGrasso was the man who'd been outside Robert's cell five hours ago, the one who'd hard-eyed him from the freedom side of the bars.

He'd asked Robert that one question, and without waiting for a reply, DeGrasso got busy away from his desk, trying to sweat his prisoner.

When DeGrasso returned, Robert asked, "Where's Officer Sedgwick?"

"We don't need Sedgwick. All we need is what Sedgwick wrote up last night after he took you in. Let's see," DeGrasso said, reading: "Two men on the beach, one murdered girl floating nearby. But it turns out one of the men was totally incapacitated at the time—drowning, in fact."

Incapacitated? At the time? He had to wonder what DeGrasso meant by that. If Jack was conscious and talking, he would have his own fabricated version of last night, but so far, it looked like DeGrasso was taking all his cues from Sedgwick's report.

"And the other gentleman on the beach, the one not drowning?" DeGrasso asked. "Uh-oh, he broke into the dead girl's cabin fifteen minutes earlier—and I got an eyewitness on that."

An eyewitness. Robert could still hear that lady in curlers from the next cabin. She'd been screaming, "That's him! That's him!" once he and Sedgwick cleared the top of the stairs.

Robert asked, "No communication from Venice PD about any of this?"

"Not word one from Venice."

"Well," was all Robert decided to say.

He recalled his one allowed phone call before they locked him up. He had called Gia. Asked her to find Erik Jacobson and have him forward Robert's signed police reports to the arresting officer. *Sedgwick, J.,* he told her, was on the officer's nameplate. Looked like the faxes hadn't arrived. Worse yet, Robert had never signed the last two—the ones most likely to link Jack Pierce with the intruder who almost killed him.

The first two reports, wherever they were, would help him a little, but he wondered again: was he going to need a criminal lawyer?

"Oh, Worth. Your knife?" DeGrasso asked now. "The one with your prints on it and no one else's?"

Your knife? That item tightened Robert's chest. Only his prints on Jack's knife? Jack's prints must've smudged during their struggle for it.

Robert wanted to ask: "The knife I stabbed myself in the leg with? That knife?"

But he cooled it instead.

DeGrasso again, and he was asking, "What was it drove you to follow her all the way up here from LA? Then you trespass Seahorse, break in her room to pocket her car keys and their passports. Because of this other man, right, this Pierce? The gentleman your girl was shacked up with. The one you tried to kill, correct?"

Robert knew better than to answer. Look what happened to Jack when he committed to his version of the truth too soon.

"I got all day," DeGrasso said, "and tomorrow after that. The dead girl, she was afraid of you if that's any consolation. Checked in, paid cash, even used an alias. Must've had a feeling you were coming after her. A premonition, you think, or was she responding to an actual threat you made down in LA?"

It was hard for Robert to stay quiet, but the truth was incredible. As in, *not believable*. He had to admit, his explanation would sound contrived, even to him.

DeGrasso still hadn't asked him about a firearm. The revolver. Lying somewhere on the Pacific Ocean's bottom, Robert was hoping.

DeGrasso said, "Still not hearing what went down after you broke in her cabin. Where did you and Pierce start fighting over the girl? Was it before or after you pocketed her car keys and passport?"

When Robert didn't answer, DeGrasso did it for him. "I hear you. Musta been after, huh? After you took her keys and made sure she couldn't drive away."

Robert was fighting every accused's urge to defend himself—innocent or guilty—but knew it was a bad idea. Especially with residual codeine and fierce antibiotics raging in his bloodstream.

They were still staring at each other when DeGrasso's phone rang. DeGrasso picked it up and said, "DeGrasso, yeah?" He kept his eye on Robert and kept listening to his caller, too. Then he looked away from Robert and said, "Oh," to the caller.

Right then, his fax machine started up. He turned his back on Robert and grabbed the incoming faxes, reading them as they rolled in.

A couple minutes later, somebody dropped the Leslie DeRider preliminary autopsy in DeGrasso's basket. After DeGrasso finished reading that and the faxes, the room temperature cooled way down. Five minutes after that, DeGrasso uncuffed Robert.

DeGrasso even let Robert use his phone. So he called Erik's cell and caught him on the fourth ring. It didn't take Robert long to find out part of why the cuffs came off: Stanley started talking down in Venice.

Turned out, he'd left paint prints on a two-by-four at the Peninsula construction site. Those prints, that's what cooked Stanley. So much for his allergies. Given that Stanley repeatedly denied ever being on the Peninsula, he was done, so he rolled over on his high school pal.

"Rolled over on Pierce late last night," Erik said. "All about how Pierce hired him to break in to your place, steal a file, and how it went bad when you two showed up."

Turned out, Stanley said, the filing-cabinet key was supposed to be taped behind Robert's cabinet. From the cameras he'd planted inside Unit 1, Stanley knew the hiding place and figured the key would still be there.

Behind the cabinet—not on my key ring, Robert was thinking.

Erik said, "Sorry about the mix-up on where I sent the faxes." He explained that Sedgwick worked out of the Aptos substation, and Erik had faxed the police reports there, not to downtown Santa Cruz.

"Every one of your police reports," Erik added. "Faxed 'em at 4:07 a.m."

Good friend that he was, a half hour ago Erik also double-checked with Sedgwick, who was taking his sweet time sending the reports downtown. So Erik told him that Robert Worth was a one-man legal wrecking crew who'd never lost a case in court.

"Never lost one, did you?" Erik asked Robert.

"Perfect record," Robert said.

Looked to Robert like Sedgwick just phoned in Erik's wrecking-crew fiction to DeGrasso, who just became Robert's new best friend.

"So you'll know," Erik said, "I faxed Sedgwick all four reports. Every single one that you signed."

All four signed reports? "Uh-huh," Robert said.

That meant Erik had forged Robert's signature on the last two.

"That cop I told you about?" Erik said. "The one I heard about who Pierce ruined downtown? Maybe I knew that cop better than I let on. Maybe we graduated same year from the Academy."

Robert could hear Erik's kids crying in the background and Erik talking them off the ledge at SeaWorld. While Robert waited, he recalled Jack tossing around that cliché: what goes around comes around.

He decided there was comes-around justice buried somewhere among Erik's cop friend and the last two unsigned police reports, but he was too worn down to sort through it.

Erik came back on the line.

Robert said, "Know what all this means, don't you? Free legal services for life." Before Erik could turn down the offer, Robert hung up.

"Coffee?"

It was DeGrasso asking, making his face create a smile.

"Yeah, and I want copies of all those faxes."

"Get 'em from Venice, all right. Cream?" DeGrasso asked.

"And sugar." He handed DeGrasso his property voucher. "And all my possessions from when you took me into custody."

DeGrasso handed the voucher to another cop, told him to get Robert's property envelope.

Robert asked, "Jack Pierce, what's his status?"

"I'm not free to discuss that," DeGrasso said. Before Robert could suggest why he damn well better, DeGrasso tossed the autopsy report in front of Robert.

"Better check on that coffee," said DeGrasso, splitting as he said it.

"And a bear claw," Robert called out.

Then he eyed the autopsy report. Short and sweet, it filled more gaps in what he already knew. Like Leslie's scratch marks on Jack's neck and Leslie's bruised neck from Jack trying to strangle her in the ocean. She must've put up quite a fight because he wound up slicing open her throat instead. One of her fingernails even broke off in the struggle and turned up inside Jack's wetsuit. Doctors found it when they cut him out of the wetsuit at the hospital.

As far as Robert's evolving story went? His prints were on the knife, sure. But wasn't he actually holding a murderer for police—holding him *at gunpoint*, but who needed to know that?—when the murderer attacked him with the knife? Attacked Robert with the same knife Jack used on Leslie minutes earlier.

And now, according to Robert's just-faxed police reports, this murderer had hired a man who almost killed Robert down in LA. And Robert was pursuing that very murderer and his girlfriend to stop them from leaving the country—not because he was a jealous lover.

Putting all that together with Leslie's broken fingernail *inside* Pierce's wetsuit? There went DeGrasso's theory of the case, and Robert felt damn near bulletproof in Santa Cruz.

Across the room, DeGrasso huddled by a large Palladian window with a few other cops. All of them were looking outside. A red Ferrari California had parked in front, top down, and Robert could just make out Gia Marquez in oversize shades kicked back behind its wheel.

His pulse quickened. *Stay focused,* he told himself.

He sorted through Jack's game plan. Leslie, aka Ms. Jones, would be nothing more than a drowned Jane Doe if she'd ever been found. Jack would ditch her car in San Francisco, remove the plates, and leave the keys inside. In the Tenderloin, a car like that disappears fast. After that, it's a short cab ride to San Francisco International, and eighteen hours later, hello, Hong Kong. What Jack couldn't imagine: that Robert would learn enough to put his head together with Gia's and cut him off in Capitola.

DeGrasso set down Robert's coffee along with an envelope: keys, wallet, and his iPhone. Jack's flash drive was not in the mix. Neither was the bear claw.

He asked DeGrasso, "Pierce, is he dead?"

"In a coma, I hear. Paralyzed from the neck down."

Robert stood, pocketed his belongings. He was stiff and sore, tired and angry, and he started to gear up for taking back the flash drive he'd lifted from Jack's briefcase.

"Pierce ever comes out of it, he stands trial for murder," DeGrasso said. "Me? I'd rather be dead. Tell me, why'd he have it in for you? What was this *financial harm* you mentioned in that last police report?"

"He ever comes out of it, ask him."

As they started for the door, DeGrasso said, "Sorry about those cuffs, they may leave a bruise."

"Yeah, I know." Then Robert stopped. "Where's the flash drive?" he asked.

"Oh, right," DeGrasso said back. Over at his desk, he fished an evidence bag from the drawer. The flash drive was inside it.

"This one?" DeGrasso asked.

"So, what you'll want to do now, Detective, is return that to my possession, which is where it was when you brought me in." Careful not to say he owned it. Not wanting to lie to police during an investigation.

"Not till I have a chance to look at it," DeGrasso countered.

"You can't. We both know it's encrypted because you already tried to look. So I'm asking—are you gonna make me go to court again to take it back?"

"To court *again*?"

"*Again*. If you keep going like you're going, I'll already be in court suing you for false imprisonment."

"Good luck with—"

"At 4:07 a.m., Venice PD sent the faxes to Sedgwick at Aptos. That means they were received by Santa Cruz County hours ago."

"You saw what happened. I didn't get 'em till now."

"Not my problem. Santa Cruz County had constructive possession since 4:07. From the first time I entered my cell, I asked about Sedgwick. I continued to do so, but nobody knew anything about him until you picked up his report just now. I was held for hours after I first asked. Even though I had a painful, throbbing knife wound—it could be MRSA-infected—you cuffed me to a chair, grilled me like a murderer, and did it with all the answers available. I'll camp out here,

DeGrasso, me and my lovely assistant outside, and we'll stay here and turn your life inside out."

"She's your assistant?" That was all DeGrasso could muster, handing over the drive.

"One of them." It was a lie, but he couldn't help himself.

"That your Ferrari?"

"Hers. We're very good at what we do. One more thing, Detective. I was never arrested, right? If you want my help, and you *will* want it, keep my name out of the newspaper."

"Why would I—"

"Couple of things you don't know," Robert said.

He told DeGrasso how both passports were in Jack's briefcase, but the airline-ticket folder, also in Jack's possession, held only one ticket.

"Check with Singapore Air," Robert said. "You're going to learn Pierce never bought her a ticket, that he always planned to kill her."

DeGrasso liked it: two passports but no ticket for the girl. That went to Pierce's premeditation, and he said, "Once he ditched her passport and her ID, there's no nexus between him and *Ms. Jones*. Know this Pierce pretty well, huh?'

Robert thought about it. "Not really. Nobody knows him. But they say he used to be a decent lawyer."

CHAPTER 53

Gia watched Robert hobble out of the station onto Water Street. Saw his bum leg and started to get out of the Ferrari to give him a hand.

"Stay in the car," he said. "They're watching and you're my assistant."

"What's it pay?"

"Must pay pretty good, look what you're driving."

He opened his door, easing into the seat.

"A rental," she said. "Brought your laptop like you asked, and I made PB and Js."

"You were sure I'd get out?" he asked.

"You're a sure thing," she told him. Then she asked, "When you called me from the pay phone, you told me I'm the only one you trust. That right?"

As he was saying "Yes," that unmistakable, wailing Ferrari engine drowned out his voice. She booked down Water and turned the first corner, pulling tight to the curb right after. She reached over and hugged him. He slipped his arms around her, too, best he could with his banged-up body.

"Glad you're in one piece," she said.

He drank in the sweet smell of her. "Thanks for showing up."

She squeezed him a little harder. He heard her sniffle against his shoulder and pulled away, then slipped off her shades and looked into her dark eyes. They glistened with tears.

"What?" she asked.

"Just looking," he told her.

Something about her was missing, misplaced, or diminished. Now she seemed more like *a girl* to him, and he wondered for the first time: What was it like for her, being in love with Jack Pierce for all those years? Handsome, a powerful attorney, man about town, cruel and manipulative and all the rest. That cool attitude of hers must have helped keep the world at bay. Or maybe she used it to keep some distance from herself. Hard to know, but either way, a layer had peeled away from her, and he bet with time, more layers would dissolve. Not all of them, he hoped. If that happened, she wouldn't be Gia Marquez anymore.

"Who messed up worse?" she finally asked. "You or me?"

Jack or Alison, she meant. "Me worse," he said. "You longer."

A few minutes later, she parked in front of a drugstore to buy supplies. Before she went inside, she handed his laptop to him.

"I wasn't wrong about everything," she said. "Our old friend *was* hanging on."

She left him with a computer screen headline:

LIONEL BRIGHTWELL, DEAD AT 89

"Damn," he said, and clicked the link: Dorothy in the front passenger seat of the Maybach as it rolled out of the estate's front gate. The driver wasn't visible, but Robert's best guess: Philip Fanelli was behind the wheel. Lionel had lasted less than twenty-four hours after Dorothy's divorce, slipping away quietly in his sleep, they were saying in the report. Maybe Lionel knew she was with Philip now and decided his little girl was in good hands with the wolf gone from his door.

When Gia got back in the car with her buys, he was still staring at the screen.

"Amazing, huh?" she asked.

"I liked Lionel. He never made big mistakes." Then he held up the flash drive. "We need to get a room."

"Think I'm that easy?"

With that, they had their first good laugh of the day.

A blinking panel on Robert's laptop screen: *PASSWORD?* Behind the request: the logo of Bank of Hong Kong. That flash drive was jacked into his external port.

They'd been at Capitola's West Cliff Inn more than an hour now. Robert sat at a desk in a white motel robe. Reluctantly, he'd opened an online account at his own bank and chosen his first-ever banking password: *-M-a-y-o-Z-a-c-k-*

Outside, random gulls squawked and scavenged Monterey Bay, and Gia lazed in a deck chair, fully clothed. He'd asked her to think about the partial password he'd written down for her on hotel stationery.

He called to her, "C'mon, do you know his password or not?"

"Let me tell you about me," she said, getting up and easing inside. "Not now, please?"

"Here goes," she said, sitting in his lap. Her weight hurt him, but he manned up as she told him: "Dad was Hispanic, Mom was Chinese, and they met at Mann's Theater in LA. No, not Mann's Chinese, Mann's Westwood, and they fell in love, got married, and had one child. A girl, and they named me *Jia Temple*. *Jia* became *Gia* so I'd fit in better, and no, *Temple* wasn't because of Chinese

351

Buddhism. I was named after Shirley Temple. Mom met her once working the counter at the Beverly Hills Hotel coffee shop. Dad, he was a gardener—they'd call him a landscaper today—but he was a gardener. Together, they saved and scraped up enough money to buy a house on a substandard lot in Brentwood, hoping their daughter would attend UCLA on scholarship. Whoops, their daughter did not. When I was sixteen, they died on the first vacation they ever took. Mexican police called what their car hit was a pothole, but back here, we'd call it a washed-out road."

She showed him a photograph on her iPhone: two gravestones in a Spanish-style church graveyard.

He looked at her. "Miss them?"

"Sure, but it's been so long now. They were such good people. Solid, wonderful people, but me? Young, dumb, living in that house, pretty much on my own? I ran into Jack one night at the Viper Room when that was a big deal, kind of. Knew him from work but nothing more than that. So, anyway," she said, "Jack and I hit it off for a long time, until we didn't hit it off anymore. I tried getting back at him, but it didn't work out, then I tried pretending it wasn't over when it was. Oh, yeah. I like girls occasionally—but I love men. I think you could say I'm very loyal. *Jia*, it turns out, means "*loyal*" in Mandarin."

"Really?"

"No." She smiled. "But I'm loyal to a fault. Questions?"

"Hundreds," he said. "But look, do you know Pierce's password or not?"

She showed him what he'd already written down: *L@L@918------ -----L@L@.*

"How many blank spaces do you remember before you got knocked out?" she asked.

Twelve or thirteen, like I told you. So . . ."

"I don't know *it* exactly. But I know what it *is*."

He closed his eyes and exhaled.

"Look, Mr. Worth, I've known a few farm boys, guys from money, and way too many lawyers, but you? No Facebook, Twitter, LinkedIn, no direct deposit. I Googled your family, but the Worths are extremely private. We both know you're no Boy Scout, but I don't know who you are. So if I'm right about this password, we're driving over the mountain to Gilroy, and you're going to show me who you are. No kidding around, you feel me, *homey*?"

He couldn't help comparing Gia to Alison, trying to route their Winnebago through San Francisco: *Oh, and why not drop by the farm and meet your parents?* He'd bet even money that Alison's long play had been locking onto a chunk of Worth real estate.

"Why do you want to know more about me?" he asked her.

"Because I like you way too much." He kept looking at her till she said, "Seriously."

"If you're right, okay."

She made him shake on it. Then she started writing in the password blanks.

"Jack was always busy, so lots of times I'd run down to the machine and get cash for him. So, I had his password for that account."

His dry mouth made it hard to speak. He looked at what she wrote: *L@L@918151413114L@L@.*

"His account password in Los Angeles was only numbers," Gia said. "None of this *L@* stuff. But the letters of the alphabet represented by those numbers would have spelled *Ironman*."

He got it now. The number he remembered wasn't *918.* It was a *nine.* Then an *eighteen. I,* the ninth letter in the alphabet. Then *R,* the eighteenth letter, and so on.

"Ironman," he repeated.

"That's how I see it," she said.

And the *L@*? He had just now seen Bank of Hong Kong require that at least one symbol be used in an account's password. So *L@*

meant *LA* to Jack Pierce. He remembered Jack's finish-line photo, last leg of the Ironman. Jack telling Robert he couldn't *go the distance* the day Jack fired him.

"LA Ironman LA," he said.

"Ironman was a big deal to him," Gia said. "Competing with guys ten years younger."

Not anymore, he was thinking.

He wondered how many bites at the apple Bank of Hong Kong would allow him to nail the password. Usually it was three, but with Asian banks, who knew? If he burned up his last try, he'd be told to call the bank, and that would be that until he sued them to be made whole. That meant fighting Leslie's bank, fighting an Asian bank, fighting the IRS, broke, possible jail time. Not how he wanted to spend his life—as Jack put it to him—with *the hours dragging by.*

"Okay, then," he said.

Hands shaking, he typed the entire password into the box. Then he looked at Gia. "Good to go?" he asked.

"He's predictable when you know him," she said, squeezing his hand. "Very predictable."

He hit Enter and the hourglass tumbled.

"Jack was with you that night. You or Alison, it didn't matter. He was screwed with Dorothy either way. That's why he had no alibi, why you never liked Alison."

"Still care?"

He looked in her eyes. She looked in his. And he let it all go.

"No," he said, "I don't."

The screen showed: *Password Accepted/Transfer Instructions?* The account balance was slightly under $10 million.

"Genius!" he shouted, and hugged her harder than she hugged him.

Once he entered the account information for his own account, he typed: *$1,800,000.*

She asked, "Million eight, that's all you're taking?"

"That's all he owes me," he said. And he hit Enter again. The transfer went through and his eyes slowly closed.

"What about Yoga Girl's stash?" she asked.

He gave it some thought. Alison wasn't his client anymore. Was there some other legal duty he owed her? He wasn't even her boyfriend, whatever that meant to a sociopath, so he considered whether or not to be a saintly human being.

"If she ever finds hers," he told Gia, "she can have it."

CHAPTER 54

"Liar, liar, fucking liar!" Alison screamed from the back seat of the police cruiser.

The cruiser hugged the curb in front of Leslie's former employer. Jerome Hartung had the ear of a pair of Santa Monica cops out front of the bank.

"First time Ms. Maxwell came in, I told her to come back with her receipt. The second time she came in, well, no receipt, and she went off like you're seeing now, right in my office."

"How much did she say again?"

"Two million eight. *Give or take*, as she put it. Not exactly a rounding error for a sane person," Jerome added.

Alison was cuffed in the cruiser's backseat, lying on her back and screaming. When she started booting a rear window with both feet, the cops hurried over.

One of them said, "Miss, stop it."

The other one said, "I do not want to hog-tie you, Miss."

"Fuck you," was all they got back till they heard her sobbing. Then they heard her whimper something through a sliver of their open window.

One of them asked. "What did you say?"

"Robert . . . Robert . . . no . . ."

"*Robert?* Who is Robert?" he asked.

"I don't know!" she screamed. "Fuck if I know who he is!"

So the cops asked Jerome if he knew who Robert was. Jerome thought about it, chose self-interest over sound banking practice. "I probably know twenty Roberts. Can you be more specific?"

※

On her way to the Santa Monica slam, Alison cooled down enough to think straight. She still had about eighteen grand in the bank and wished she hadn't paid the hospital for her first ER visit. But that's how she wanted to come across to Robert: a simple girl paying her debt because she had the money. Just a girl trying to do what was right. Same pose she used when she told him she might drop her lawsuit against Jack Pierce.

"*I just want my life back,*" she'd told him outside Sonya's house, all the while thinking, *What life?*

Her thoughts turned to Brian. To what a loser her brother was. That was one thing Pierce had right. Brian's two work buddies had each scored a hundred grand from Consolidated—but they were employees. Not her brother, no, not Brian; he worked for an independent contractor.

Give me a break, she said to herself. He was a loser like Dad. Her slob father: wasted, stumbling home from a clambake, choked to death on a conch fritter.

Lawyers, she hated all of them. Starting with the lawyer who'd screwed up her mom's lawsuit after she picked up a fatal staph infection in the hospital. Took it on contingency, showed up drunk at a deposition, and later the case was thrown out of court. She didn't dare sue him—his sister was the local prosecutor—but she packed a suitcase full of lawyer venom when she split for California.

So easy getting over on those Valley lawyers. Made her smile even now, back of the squad car. She kept her lawsuits small, dealt only with married men who didn't like seeing photographs of themselves, fully erect, cuffed to a motel headboard. Lawyers realizing: "I'm fucked. How much does this bitch, Maxine Ellison, want to keep quiet?"

And leaving Tarzana, moving in with Brian? That was for the free rent. Brian, that guy. Gets cancer, still smokes Lucky Strike straights. He'd fire one up right there in his bed, the oxygen tube running up his nose.

"Loser!" she yelled.

"What?" a cop up front asked.

She didn't bother answering, went back to figuring out where she stood. Robert would clear out of the condo—his movers already showed up. That gave her a place to work out what came next. She didn't believe he'd stolen her receipt. If her money wasn't banked, neither was his, meaning Leslie split on both of them. Something terrible had happened at the bank that even Robert hadn't seen coming.

No way he would help her; that would never happen. *One detail too many.* That's what the Marquez skeze told her in the hospital. Had she overplayed her hand with Robert? She couldn't see it: good guy, good manners, real good-looking, all she ever wanted was for him to come over to her apartment. See her bruises, watch her pass out, and call the hospital. He'd go back to the firm, right? Tell them what Pierce did, right? Cause a big stink and after that, she would have been happy to keep quiet about it for a hundred grand. A tip to a waiter for the power couple, the ones who got off showing off their modern-art crap in the firm lobby.

Till the day she died, she'd never forget calling Robert that night. Earlier, she'd parked outside the Bel-Air Hotel and got lucky. With Brian's handcuffs already snapped around one wrist, watching from her car, Pierce showed up. Making it with someone in Suite 207 that night—someone besides her. One thing she then knew for sure: Pierce couldn't account for his time.

That's what cooked Pierce, and that was her doing, not Robert's.

But she had to admit, Robert took the ball and ran with it harder than she believed possible. Ran with it till he banked her $2.8 million. And each day she waited for her money, it took every ounce of willpower not to bring it up every second of every day. To play it off, like having that kind of money was no big deal.

Screw Robert. Somehow she'd find that banker chick, prove her check had been banked. But with her background, all her aliases? She had to give it to that Marquez bitch—she saw this problem coming. Problems where her own honesty was the issue. Not like Brian's case, where she'd simply been a conduit for him. Only *his* character mattered there, but the next case would involve *her* character.

Had it really been so easy for Robert to see through her? Gia Marquez said he was onto her for a long time. And he *was* gone, never even called her back at the hospital. So, yeah, he must've dug up *Maxine Ellison* somehow.

But how could that be? Sonya? After she'd ratted out Sonya's yoga classes to zoning? He'd never think to check with Sonya—she just couldn't see it.

With Robert gone, what she needed now was serious legal firepower to get back what was hers, but with no real coin for lawyers, investigators—her mind started to spin out on her new problems. Until a calming thought came to her as the cruiser rolled up to Santa Monica jail.

Lionel Brightwell's live-in nurse.

He'd definitely want to help her, right? Pay for a serious firm to get on top of her bank. Who knows? At Lionel's age, maybe she'd wind up with that big house on the hill. It was nothing compared with all that Gilroy farmland a half hour from San Jose, but waiting for that payday would have taken years. That Tudor up on Stone Canyon? That's $20 million on a lit fuse.

As the cops opened the back door, she didn't give them any trouble. Didn't bother with a slip-and-fall with these two pretty boys, wearing bulletproof vests in case a latte spilled on them.

Better start acting sweet with this pair—that would be part of her record, too—because she was already thinking about her premier score.

My man, Lionel, she was thinking. *Hey, LB, let's get this party started!*

CHAPTER 55

"Long as Big Worth was alive, everything was golden," Robert told Gia.

Highway 1 slipped away, and Gia let him drive the Ferrari inland, winding up and over the Santa Cruz Mountains.

"Big Worth?" Gia asked.

"My grandfather, the original stakeholder, settled north of Gilroy. Now, Grandmother Tav, she wanted to be an actress. Blonde, like Marilyn Monroe and Grace Kelly in her day, she was headed from Seattle to LA when her car broke down on Highway 1, same station where Big Worth was gassing up. Once he fell for her, that was that. They came over the hill to Gilroy and moved into the big house."

"The one in your pictures?"

"Right, a modest ten bedrooms. They had two sons, Robert and Garrett. Each one had a kid, and we all lived in the big house. Grandma Tav died early on, I didn't know her, and Big Worth never remarried, but he believed in two things. The family farm, that was first, and second, that was the family farm, too. He assumed both sons felt the same way he did about farming, but they didn't, and his lawyer finally talked him into spelling out who got what. Then, on his way to the guy's office, he stroked out and crashed into a eucalyptus, end of our driveway."

"Your driveway? Worth Avenue?"

He nodded. "Family called it Big Worth Avenue after that, but things changed. The younger son, Garrett, wanted to leave for Texas, and the older, Robert, wanted to farm. Common family-farm situation, but without the new will, things got ugly. Finally, the older brother bit the bullet, took out a huge loan on the farm, and paid his brother to leave."

He asked her to open a file on his laptop called *RLW STUFF*. "Password is *Z-A-C-K-M-A-Y-O*."

She started typing in the password. "Where have I heard that name?"

"*Officer and a Gentleman*. Richard Gere's movie name," he said.

"And at the end, he picks up the girl in his white uniform and carries her out of the factory. Girls love that ending."

"Still?" he asked.

"We can't help it," she said. The desktop file opened. First thing she saw: an array of photos, many of them of young Robert and Rosalind.

"You're looking at prom night, right?"

"Maybe," she said. "How'd you know?"

"Women always go to that one. It speaks to them. The flush of young love, hopes and dreams for the future."

"Lost virginity?" she asked.

"You tell me," he asked. "Alison did the same thing you're doing."

He recalled for her that day in his apartment after Alison wavered on suing Jack. How he left that prom photo on the mantel so she would face it from his couch. From the kitchen, he watched her pick up *that picture* in his living room mirror. That put Rosalind's story in play: his sister, sexually assaulted by a stranger on prom night. After hearing that story, Alison signed the power of attorney.

Gia remembered what Alison told her about Rosalind in the hospital.

"Rosalind? The one who overdosed and died?"

"She's alive," was all he said. "See that old newspaper article?"

On his computer screen: a Gilroy newspaper article. The headline:

GOODBYE, GILROY! HELLO, TEXAS!

Ten people gathered in a bon-voyage party photo. Robert is there, Rosalind, too, both midteens. So are the Worth brothers.

Robert pointed out his stunning mother to Gia: standing between the brothers.

"I was getting ready to start boarding school over in San Jose."

After the bon-voyage party, he explained, Garrett, the younger brother, left for Houston with a few million, his birthright payday. It took him twenty-three months to lose every nickel of it in that big market meltdown. Twenty-three months to turn tail and come back home.

"He was always a little squirrelly," Robert said, "a dreamer, but after that? Garrett's never been right since."

"Right?"

"Late-onset schizophrenia. And while he was losing his shirt, big brother Robert went long on the right crops, got every weather break, and made a killing. Took him ten years and three divorces to pay off the loan, and now he owns that three thousand acres plus, free and clear."

"Your father, which one is he?"

"The younger brother's full name is *Garrett Logan Worth*. His older brother's name is *Robert Kendall Worth*."

"You're . . . let's see . . . *Robert Logan Worth*?"

Not an exact match to either brother's name. Before she could point that out, he asked, "What I like most about *Officer and a Gentleman* is Sergeant Foley trying to make Zack Mayo quit OCS. Mayo's been running with his rifle, no sleep, Foley's hosing him down in the cold, trying to break him, till Mayo screams at Foley: '*I got nowhere to go . . . I got nothing else . . .*'"

His voice was soft, saying it. She knew he was talking about himself.

"Tenth grade, that's when the prom picture with Rosalind was taken. That year the market crashed on my father, and my life wasn't laid out for me anymore."

"You're Garrett's son?"

"Yeah. Named after Uncle Robert when the brothers were still tight. Now they live on the same farm, but . . ." His voice trailed off.

"So, your mom divorced Garrett after he flamed out in Texas?"

He looked at her. "I wish. She lives in the big house now. Dad lives over the garage in the old servant's quarters. I never know when he's going to be delusional or when he's going to act normal. Depends on his meds, his dosage. Sometimes, when the others aren't at home, he wanders around the house, goes into the study, acts like he's paying bills, and feels like he's the big dog."

"And Mom is . . ."

"Shacked up with Uncle Robert. I can't blame her, but . . ."

"But you do anyway," she said. "*To be or not to be.* The mom hooks up with the uncle. *Hamlet,* right?"

"*Hamlet,*" he said. "And *East of Eden,* that old movie *Giant,* and *Dallas* on TV. You name it, we got it all at *Rancho Rosalinda.* Uncle Robert gets off having Dad under his thumb, same as he did me. Lending me money for law school, letting me pay him off but making me work the farm weekends and summers. Nowhere else—had to be at the farm."

"And Rosalind is his daughter?"

"Yeah, my first cousin. Alive, taking the reins at the farm. We were never the same after Dad split for Texas—*turned his back on the farm* is how their side looked at it. Rosalind was my best friend in the world for fifteen years, and then she was gone in an instant."

They cruised through Gilroy, headed toward the Diablo Range. He told her that manipulating his family history at the firm started off small. Misleading Philip with farm-fresh garlic to separate himself from the pack of law students. But Philip bought into his whole Worth Avenue, landed-gentry bio.

"It got out of hand over the years, so I'd say my parents were visiting LA when I knew Philip was going to be out of town."

She nodded, imitating Robert: "Damn, Philip, you just missed 'em."

"Like that," he said. "I couldn't risk telling him the truth. He might've felt obligated to tell his partners."

"I doubt it," she said. "I could tell he loved you."

Another five minutes and he wheeled the Ferrari onto Worth Avenue, pulled onto the gravel shoulder. He called the farm manager, Luis, on his cell, speaking Spanish, laughing now and then, and finally asking him where he could find Rosalind.

Once he hung up, he walked Gia to a tarred-over eucalyptus stump. The remains of the tree Big Worth hit on his last drive, ever. They stepped up onto a white wooden fence. Several hundred yards away, a truck rolled along, and workers tossed irrigation pipes off the back of it. A stocky woman his age followed behind on foot.

When she looked his way, Robert waved both arms overhead. Shielding her eyes from the sun, she recognized him and waved back. One-handed, quick, and to the point. After that, Rosalind went back to what she was doing.

"Civil, that's all," he said. "That's me and Rosalind. Tears me up, still."

"Her, too, I bet," Gia said.

"I talk to her pictures sometimes. Alison thought I had a sister thing. Hard to blame her after that story I told her."

Gazing out at Rosalind, he put his arm around Gia's shoulder. "Seeing her now, even her pictures, reminds me of when we were kids, how simple it was. You wake up, do your work, grow things, eat fresh vegetables, and hope for the right weather. Then all the rest of it happened and I had to get away."

It didn't dawn on him fully till now how much Jack reminded him of his uncle. And Philip of a mythic father, kind and wise, the father he wanted and never had.

"Thanks for telling me," Gia said.

"Good to get it off my chest."

"You told me that you trusted me, Robert."

"Funny thing, Gia. I do trust you."

That was the first time they'd ever addressed each other by their given names. He liked the way it sounded, how it felt saying it, and hoped she felt the same way. Beside him, she smelled like roses and cinnamon, and he slipped his hand inside her shirt, cupping one of her firm breasts. She laid her hand top of his, outside her shirt, both gestures more intimate than sexual, then slipped her hand inside his shirt, too, and stroked his back.

She said, "No matter what, we wait a month before sleeping together. Deal?"

"With our track records?"

"All this farm mess? Nowhere else to go—you're like Zack Mayo, aren't you? That's why you're such a hard charger?"

"That's me," he said.

As they headed over to the car, he thought about what she'd said. *A hard charger?* She was right about that, but he wasn't alone like Mayo had been. Not like Spartacus, either. Not *the last fish in the tank* that Philip warned him against becoming. Gia was standing right here with him.

"I promised you," he said. "Do you want to go through the gate, meet the family?" he asked.

"Not unless you want to. Down that driveway, that's who you used to be. Not who you are now."

She smiled at him, so they left right then.

CHAPTER 56

"He killed that poor girl," the black nurse observed at the hospital room door.

The Asian nurse looked up from checking Jack's IV. "Down in Capitola, below the Seahorse, he slit her throat."

"Who does that?" the black nurse said.

"I know, right?"

The black nurse came in the room for a closer look: Jack lying in bed, his blank eyes facing the wall-mounted TV where CNN Headline News looped every half hour on the hour.

"How old was she?"

"Young, thirty?" the Asian nurse said. "Hot, too, I heard."

"Wow," she said, leaning closer. "With him?"

"Some hot-shit lawyer down in LA. *Was,* anyway."

"Why'd he kill her?" the black nurse asked.

"They don't know yet, the *Sentinel* said. It's even on the news-news," nodding at the CNN loop. "After what he did to that poor girl? I'm not gonna bathe him."

"You've been a very bad boy, Jack, so you will not get a sponge bath today. Maybe all week," the black nurse said.

Both laughed.

"Anybody show up to visit?" the black nurse asked.

"That detective last night. He showed me his gun."

"Was he wearing a uniform?"

The Asian nurse said, "A jacket, but he said he liked mine."

"Your uniform? Did you tell him about us?"

"Didn't come up."

"You better have told him or I'll kill you," she said, smiling at her Asian lover, kidding around.

The pair finished up with Jack's IV and started to leave.

"The TV? Leave it on?" the Asian nurse asked.

"Stimulus is supposed to do him good."

"That news hardly ever changes. Maybe he'll get so tired of it, he'll kill himself."

It was ten minutes later when a California segment of Headline News LA came back around. The same story Robert had watched in the Ferrari. Lionel Brightwell's death now played out in front of Jack's blank stare: Dorothy in the Maybach, driving out of the estate; the announcer saying Lionel's daughter, Dorothy, was now the sole heir to the Brightwell fortune.

Impossible to say whether Jack could hear or see what was going on down in Bel-Air. Or if he was aware how close he came to running out the clock on Lionel's grind-down. But on his haggard, unshaven face, maybe it was just a coincidence. His left eyelid twitched twice.

CHAPTER 57

On the last leg back to LA, Robert woke up in the Ferrari's passenger seat, sweating from the antibiotics, the pain meds, and from his dream. Disoriented at first, he stirred, saw Gia driving and stared ahead into the xenon headlamp's focused path.

The last thing he recalled before tapping out: Gia asking him what his plans were, mumbling back to her something about not having a clue.

"You awake?" she asked, reaching for his hand.

"Getting there," he said.

Still coming to his senses, he didn't mention his dream about the Venice Boardwalk. But it was still vivid, and he wondered if he should let go of it or not.

"Forgot to tell you," Gia said. "Dougie called Leslie's landline after you split for Capitola."

"What'd he want?" he asked, stretching.

"Not much. All he said was, '*Tomorrow, sunrise, Four Mile.*' No wait. First, he said, '*Babe,*' meaning Leslie. Then he said his *tomorrow, sunrise, Four-Mile* bit and hung up."

He came straight up in his seat and looked at her. "What a minute. Sunrise today would be *tomorrow, sunrise.*"

"Doesn't make sense, right?"

"Four Mile, sunrise, *today*? That makes perfect sense."

Then he told her about Four Mile, the surf destination north of Santa Cruz and the Seahorse Inn. "Leslie asked me about surfing Four Mile at the Bel-Air pool."

"Four Mile, oh," Gia said. "Think they were going to what? Kill Jack?"

"Kill Jack, I know they were. Dougie was waiting there—he's probably still there waiting for Leslie to show. They planned to get Jack down to that beach at sunrise today. Kill him and take the money."

They quickly decided Leslie would have known the password. Agreed, too, that Jack would have gotten off on giving it to her, knowing she would never use it.

"Would what Dougie did still be a crime?" she asked. "I mean, Jack's a vegetable and Leslie's dead? Dougie can't pull it off now, no matter what."

Gia had just covered a week's worth of first-year criminal law with her single question. "I think it's still conspiracy to commit murder," he said.

He debated whether to tell DeGrasso about Dougie, let him pull Dougie in for questioning. Surely, Dougie would screw up somehow, might even wind up doing time. But Robert decided to leave well enough alone. If he started rattling DeGrasso's cage, no telling what kind of beast might slip loose up in Santa Cruz and come after him. Gia, too, for all he knew.

More than that, it wasn't his place to sit in judgment of Dougie. In his own heart last night, if only for a moment, he was going to let Jack Pierce drown in that tidal pool. Only the grace of God saved him—in the form of Officer Sedgwick coming down the beach stairs. Letting Jack die and doing nothing wouldn't have been murder—Robert had no legal duty to save him. Far as he knew, that was a duty the law didn't impose. But in his heart, Robert knew it was wrong and was familiar now with where his darkest heart resided.

Better let the Dougie situation lie, he was thinking as Santa Clarita's lights ahead turned into LA.

"The beach lawyer," he heard Gia say to him.

"What?" he asked.

"That's who you are—beach lawyer."

"Beach lawyer," he repeated.

Sliding down the smooth-sloped interstate, the Ferrari purred in fourth, coiled beside the majestic, three-abreast power lines juicing the inevitable city ahead. Locus, he knew, of everything you could possibly want and every possible problem.

And he wondered, did he already tell her about his lawyer dream? Had it somehow slipped his mind? His dream of the Venice Boardwalk where he was out of place in a jacket and tie, sitting underneath a beach umbrella? A long oak table rested in front of him. Looked like a conference table at the firm. Fresh flowers in a clear vase were on the table, too: birds-of-paradise, if he remembered right. And sitting there on the boardwalk, he recalled, he'd been interviewing people. All sorts of people he didn't know. Gia was there. Seemed like Erik showed up at some point, and wasn't Reyes in the picture, too?

Had he forgotten telling Gia, or did she really read him that true? Maybe he was still asleep and about to come to his senses.

"Beach lawyer," he said again, liking the sound of it more.

New ideas began to come at him fast and clear. Pieces of a puzzle. Ideas on how to make use of his legal skills and create momentum. His pulse quickened, the Ferrari whispering, and then he knew for sure: he wasn't dreaming.

ACKNOWLEDGMENTS

For their early reads, research, and encouragement: Lawrie and Ben Smylie, Ana Shorr and Dr. Bobby, Ryan Gustafson, John Paoletti, Blackwell Smith, Wendy Gerrish, Happy Baker, Randall Batinkoff, Sensei Rooney, Avery Woods, Andrea Mattoon, Bret Carter, Christian Corado, T.J. Hall, John F. Henry, K.P. Fischer, and the staff of the Somerset, Thonglor.

And certainly: Darren Trattner.

For their patience and skill, copy editor Valerie Kalfrin and proofreader Jill Kramer.

Also, special thanks to my stoic, "brutal" manager, Chris George; and to my tireless, intrepid agent, Beth Davey. And finally to Liz Pearsons at Thomas & Mercer. I have two heartfelt words to send your way, Liz, for your instant and adamant belief in *Beach Lawyer*. *Thank you.*

ABOUT THE AUTHOR

Avery Duff was born in Chattanooga, Tennessee, where he attended Baylor School and graduated summa cum laude. After graduating Phi Beta Kappa from the University of North Carolina at Chapel Hill, he earned a JD from Georgetown University Law Center. He then joined a prestigious Tennessee law firm, becoming a partner in five years before moving to Los Angeles. His screenwriting credits include the 2010 heist drama *Takers*, starring Matt Dillon, Idris Elba, Paul Walker, T.I., Jay Hernandez, Zoe Saldana, and Hayden Christensen. Duff lives at the beach in Los Angeles and spends his time writing fiction. *Beach Lawyer* is his first published novel.